ACKNOWLEDGMENT

The author wishes to extend his sincerest appreciation to his friend, Harold N. Moody, for the assistance, encouragement, and ideas Harold so freely contributed in bringing this project to fruition.

1

Outside a gun exploded. An instant later, a second shot roared out. The plate glass window shattered and crashed down on the workbench where Matt Ritter had been working.

Hell was in session in Abilene—again.

Moments before, a sudden unnatural silence had descended on the world. Even the birds seemed to hold their breath. Matt'd laid down the pistol he'd been working on and glanced out the plate glass window.

Out front, two raggedy cowboys, fresh off the trail, had squared off in the middle of the narrow, dusty street. Now, what, Matt wondered, are those two galoots up to? Crouched, tense as coiled steel springs, weight slightly forward on the balls of their feet, they glared at each other. Each man's right hand, fingers extended and slightly flexed, hovered near the six-shooter holstered on his hip.

Suddenly it hit Matt.

"Oh, my God!" he yelled. "Get down, Paw, get down!"

John Ritter half-turned from the roll-top desk where he sat gossiping with a gun salesman about old times in Cincinnati. Burke Harte, the salesman, started to rise. Instantly Matt flung himself at the two older men. The three sprawled on the floor in a tangle of arms and legs. His father tried to struggle to his feet, but Matt, at five eleven and 180 pounds, ten pounds lighter but two inches taller than his sire, hauled the older man down again.

"Great jumpin' Jehoshaphat," Paw roared, "have you gone crazy, boy?"

An eerie silence replaced the roar of gunfire.

Now, lying on the floor, Matt surveyed the damage and shook his head. Paw'd been mighty proud of that window. Many's the time he'd told Matt that havin' a plate glass window brought some distinction to the gunsmith shop.

John Ritter clambered to his feet. Normally a quiet, gentle man, his agonized bellow shocked his son.

"Oh, no! Look what those two bastards done to my window. Jesus Christ! Burke, I had that beauty hauled all the way out from Kansas City. Even had my name lettered on it. In gold. Now look at it." Ritter pounded a fist into his calloused palm. "My God, Matt and I've been here three years, and the shootin' and killin' just keeps goin' on and on. Don't matter who the marshal is. Won't we *ever* have any peace in this godforsaken town?"

Absentmindedly he smoothed his blonde handlebar mustache and sank back down into his chair. Meanwhile the rotund, bug-eyed drummer had struggled to his feet. Laying a consoling hand on John Ritter's shoulder, he gazed around, all the while muttering, "Oh my, oh my."

Matt slowly climbed to his feet and then rushed to the front door and jerked it open. He peered out. The street was still empty.

Except for one of the cowboys.

The man lay flat on his back, one leg extended, the other doubled under him. His gun lay in the dust. One hand still jerked convulsively. He tried to rise up on his elbows. Blood soaked through his shirt. Short grunts emerged from his lips. Then the cowboy lapsed into silence and fell back.

Matt froze. The cowboy was dead. Matt was sure of it. And, God Almighty, he'd never seen a man die before.

Heads began to peek out of doors along the street. From around the corner on Texas Street, Wild Bill Hickok, the town marshal, came running, long hair streaming behind him, a drawn Navy Colt in each hand. At the sight of the dead cowboy, he came to an abrupt halt. Slowly he peered around.

"Where'd he go, god damn it? Where'd that other son of a bitch go?"

Nauseated, bile welling up in his throat, Matt turned and stumbled back inside the shop, gently closing the door behind him. Slowly he made for a chair and slumped into it. Taking deep breaths, he leaned forward and put his head between his hands.

John Ritter glanced over at his son, then got up and came over to where he huddled. He bent down and patted Matt on the back. "What is it, son? What happened out there?"

Matt looked up, tears forming in his eyes. "Aw, Paw, there's a dead man out there. That other feller shot him."

John straightened up and, one hand still on his son's shoulder, turned to the drummer. "You see, Burke? You see what I mean? Matt and me should've stayed in Cincinnati 'stead of comin' to this hellhole. I just don't know why I ever listened to Frank."

Burke Harte, the drummer, knit his brow. "Frank who?"

"Frank Brinkman, my brother-in-law. He worked for me for a while in Cincinnati. Back when you used to call on me there. You met him a couple of times, didn't you?"

Harte nodded. "Oh, sure, that Frank. He out here, too?"

"Yep. Been farmin' out here for quite a spell. Does some preachin', too. Guess he got tired of working for someone else, so 'bout ten years ago, he and Elly—she was my wife's sister—came out here to homestead. Got their 160 acres and built themselves a sod hut. I gotta hand it to him. Hell, come to that, I gotta hand it to both of 'em. They worked like dogs, and now they got over 300 acres. In fact, Matt and I live with 'em."

The drummer's eyebrows went up. "All four of you in a sod hut?"

John snorted. "Not on your life. They got a proper house now. One of those ready-mades shipped out from Chicago. Matt and me helped Frank and some of his congregation put it up. It's got two stories and two big bedrooms. He and Elly have one, and they let me and Matt move in and share the other one."

"Mighty nice of 'em."

John Ritter nodded. "Sure is, ain't it?"

"But, John, how'd you and Matt end up out here? Last time I saw you, Matt was just a little shaver. Back in Cincy, in '67—or was it '68?"

"Most likely early '68. Matt and I came out here in the summer of '68. Frank wrote me in late '67. Bragged what a roarin' success Abilene was goin' to be. A real rip-snortin' boom town, he claimed. Said this fellow McCoy had built cattle pens, and the railroad was ready to haul steers back East. Said Texans'd be drivin' hundreds of thousands of head up here every year. Claimed there'd be plenty of business for a good gunsmith. Told me to pack up and come on out. Said for old times sake, he'd help me get started." Ritter shook his head ruefully. "And like a damn fool, I took 'im up on it."

"Far's I can see, you're doing pretty well, John. Got your own shop and plenty of business."

"I just rent the place, Burke. I don't own it."

"So why'd you put in that expensive plate glass window?"

"Gave better light at the work bench. At thirty-eight, my eyes ain't what they used to be, you know."

The drummer looked skeptical.

"And I figgered it'd be good for business," Ritter added. "I'm off here on this narrow little side street, you see, and I needed somethin' to bring in the customers. Figgered puttin' in a big plate glass window with my name on it would help 'em find me. Thought it'd be safe enough seein' as how I'm not on the main thoroughfare. Last count I heard this town's got eleven saloons, but none of 'em on this street. And my landlord sure didn't object, long's I spent my own money to improve the place."

Harte still looked skeptical.

"Besides," Ritter admitted sheepishly, "I like it. Havin' my name on that window made me feel like I'd done somethin' in the world. Like I amounted to somethin'."

The drummer looked around the snug little gunsmith shop. The front door stood to the left of the place. A twenty-foot counter ran toward the rear of the building. The main workbench—where Matt had been working when he spotted the two duelists—ran the width of that portion of the shop enclosed by the counter. At the rear of the shop, a door with a small window on each side allowed light into a storage area.

"Well, I can see why you're upset about your window, but it still looks to me like you're doin' pretty well."

"I'm gettin' by, Burke, I'm gettin' by, but this is a dangerous place to live. It's quiet enough here in the winter, but once the drovers start arrivin' with their herds in the spring, this town's a real hellhole until late fall. I worry every time Matt steps out on the street."

The drummer smiled and looked over at Matt. "You remember me, Matt?"

Matt looked up. "Yes, sir. From back in Cincinnati."

"That's right, son. I used to sell your daddy guns and supplies for his shop back there, and now by golly, here I am trying to sell him supplies way out here in Kansas. Truly a small world, isn't it?"

Matt nodded. "Yes, sir, sure is."

The drummer nodded toward the beaming John Ritter. "You know, Matt, your daddy's about the best gunsmith I ever knew. The most honest one, too. And travelin' like I do, I've knowed a lot of 'em."

Matt nodded again. "Yes, sir. I'm sure he is."

The drummer clapped him on the back. "But you sure have grown since I last saw you. You were just a skinny little kid then. How old are you now, anyway?"

"Be eighteen next month."

Burke Harte peered closely at Matt and whistled. "Well, boy, for seventeen, you're a big one. How'd you manage to put all those muscles on your arms and chest? Choppin' wood?"

Matt grinned. "Sometimes. When I'm not workin' here in the shop with Paw, learnin' the gunsmithin' trade, I help Uncle Frank with all kinds of chores on the farm."

John Ritter, grinning proudly, came over and draped his arm around his son's shoulder. "Not only does he help Frank and me with our chores, but he helps out Les Duggin, the blacksmith. I figger that puts some of that muscle on 'im. Makes some extry money at it, too."

"So, with all that work, what do you do for fun?"

Matt shrugged. "Well, I play the piano—"

John Ritter broke in, face somber. "Just before Alice died back in '58—Matt was only four then—she made me promise the boy'd learn to play the piano." His expression lightened. "And he plays right well now. Don't you, Matt?"

Matt nodded.

Burke grinned. "How about girls? With that blonde hair and blue eyes and that nice smile, you sure are a handsome young fellow."

Matt blushed and looked down at the floor. "Aw, gee, I don't know Mr. Harte. I don't know any girls." He brightened. "But I sure like to play baseball."

John grinned. "Don't let him josh you, Burke. He's a pretty popular young man. I see the way the girls look at him."

Embarrassed, Matt shoved his hands into his pockets.

"Aw, Paw."

The drummer winked. "The town got a baseball team?"

Matt brightened again. "Sure does. They say I'm the fastest man on it. I pitch for it, too."

"You do, huh. That gives me an idea. Let me just step out

to my rig for a minute. I got somethin' might interest you both."

When he came back in carrying a satchel, Harte motioned them over to a table. He reached into the satchel and took out three round metal balls each about the size of a small grapefruit. "Ever see anything like these before, John?"

Ritter picked up one of the round objects and peered closely at it. "Can't say's I have. What are they?"

"Grenades. Hand grenades. These were manufactured during the Civil War. You don't see 'em much anymore. In fact, I just have a few I picked up somewhere. Brought 'em along as a curiosity. Thought they might interest you."

Ritter studied more closely the grenade he was holding. A seam ran around it at the mid-line. "I've heard of these things but never saw one before." He gently set it back on the table. "Kinda dangerous, ain't they?"

Burke Harte grinned. "They can be. They can really do damage if you're not careful with 'em. But don't worry. These aren't armed. Let me show you."

Harte picked up a grenade and cupped it in the palms of his hands. Then he gently twisted it. The grenade separated at the mid-line into two pieces. "Now, look. You see, there's an inner core and an outer shell. That inner core's loaded with explosive and pieces of metal. When it's armed, this little beauty explodes on impact, and the metal fragments whizzing around are real killers."

Ritter pursed his lips. "So, how do you arm them?"

"Well, feel the outer shell." He held it out for Matt and John to feel. "See how flexible it is? Now," he reached into the satchel, "you just screw these percussion caps into these little holes in the inner core, so they stick out a bit, and then put the outer shell back on." He gingerly suited action to words. "Now it's armed. If you dropped it, the outer shell'd compress on the percussion caps, and she'd explode."

He tossed it up an inch or two and caught it.

John Ritter's eyes widened. "For God's sake, Burke, don't do that!"

The drummer laughed. "You're right, John. Pretty stupid of me. But, hell, let me just disarm it, and there's no danger." Cautiously he separated the outer shell and unscrewed the percussion caps. "There. Perfectly safe now."

Ritter let out a breath. "What do you figger to do with those things?"

Burke laughed. "I got no use for 'em, so I thought I'd give 'em to you. Matt's a baseball pitcher, so maybe he can think of somethin' to do with 'em."

John Ritter shook his head. "I don't know's I want the blamed things around."

"Aw, let's keep 'em, Paw. They're kinda interestin'."

"Well..."

"John, without the percussion caps, they're perfectly safe. Just not very handy for civilian life is all."

"You're sure, Burke?"

The drummer nodded.

"Well, all right. I don't suppose it'll do any harm."

Burke Harte grinned. "Good. You can keep the satchel and all three grenades. Gotta mosey along now. Gotta turn my rig into the livery stable and catch the train to Junction City." He shook hands with John and then Matt. "See you on my next trip, Matt. Be interested to hear what you do with those little beauties."

2

"Have some more mashed potatoes, Matt?"

Matt looked up at his aunt. She'd been a mother to him, and he often wondered whether his real mother had been as nice as Aunt Elly. Elly Brinkman was a pretty woman, and Matt knew from pictures of his mother that she and his aunt had looked a lot alike. His aunt's hair was dark, though, and his Paw always said his Maw was blonde and fair complexioned. Matt just didn't remember her too well.

"Yes, ma'am, I will. Thank you kindly."

Frank Brinkman grinned at his wife. "Elly, you're goin' to have the boy so stuffed he can't move."

She smiled. "Never you mind, Frank Brinkman. Does my heart good to see a young fellow eat after I've gone to the trouble to fix a meal."

That was another thing Matt liked about her. Aunt Elly was always so good-natured, always ready with a smile. "Can I have another biscuit?"

"You sure can," she said, passing him the plate of biscuits and ignoring the two grinning older men.

The four of them were seated at the large, round table in the Brinkman's dining room. Supper was just winding up.

Frank turned his attention to Matt. "It's still light out. Think you'll be able to go out and have a little tussle? Or have you had too much to eat?"

"Now, Frank, I want you to be careful with the boy. You gotta promise you won't hurt him."

Her husband guffawed, his white teeth flashing against his swarthy complexion. He was a big man, just turned forty-five and just starting to run a bit to fat but still strong and muscular. His bushy shock of black hair and his full beard had only in the last year or two begun to show sprinkles of gray.

"Promise I won't hurt him? Why it's all I can do to hold my own anymore. Last week he knocked me down twice, and once when we were rasslin', he pinned me. Now, what do you think of that?"

John Ritter put down his fork. "You joshin', Frank?"

Ritter's brother-in-law turned serious. "No, I'm not. When you two first moved here, what was it? Three years ago?"

John Ritter nodded.

"Well, three years ago, when I said I'd teach the boy a thing or two 'bout fightin' and rasslin', I had no idea what a bearcat he'd turn into." Frank grinned. "When he knocked me down last week, I begun to think I'd taught him too derned good."

Ritter, a slow smile spreading over his ruddy, slightly sunburned face, looked across at his son. "Humph. Good for you, Matt." He turned back to Frank. "How about his shootin'? How's that comin'?"

"He's gettin' to be a purty fair to middlin' marksman. With both rifle and pistol. Purty fair to middlin', I'd say. If he's willin' to practice a little more, I believe he'll develop into a crack shot." Brinkman grinned. "Maybe give ol' Wild Bill a run for his money."

John Ritter's face darkened. "I wish you wouldn't say things like that, Frank. I want the boy to stay outta trouble. I don't want him gettin' mixed up with any of those murderin' gunslingers."

Frank turned apologetic. "You're right, John. I'm sorry I said that. Sure don't want to give the boy any foolish ideas."

"Well, I should hope not, Frank Brinkman!" said his outraged wife. "You just keep a tight rein on that mouth of yours."

John Ritter turned to his son. "Matt, I want you to promise you won't carry a gun on you. Any shootin' you do has to be outside of town. There's a law, you know, against even carryin' a weapon in Abilene."

Matt nodded. "I know, Paw."

"Most other towns, too."

"Besides, boy," chimed in his uncle, "no matter how good a shot you are, those gunslingers know tricks you never even thought of. Sooner or later you'd get yourself killed."

"I know, Uncle Frank."

His father stared intently at him. "You promise, Matt?"

Matt made a cross with his right index finger over his heart. "I promise. Cross my heart."

His father smiled. "Good, son." He glanced at his brother-in-law and then turned back to Matt. "Your Uncle Frank ever tell you how he learned to fight?"

Matt furrowed his brow. "Can't say's he did, Paw."

"Well, when he was a young feller, your Uncle Frank was a real harum-scarum." John Ritter grinned. "Pretty handy with the ladies, too, so I've heard tell."

"Why, John Ritter, what sort of talk is that? In front of your young son, too!" Elly turned to her husband. "Frank, I don't want a word out of you about your romancin'. Bad enough all this talk about fightin' and shootin', let alone goin' on about women! And you a man of the cloth!"

Uncle Frank winked at Matt. "All right, Matt. It's gettin'

kinda late to go out and tussle, so sit back and fill up your coffee cup. Here's the story."

Each of them poured another cup and settled back. Clearly, despite her outrage, Aunt Elly wanted to hear the story again, too.

"Well, let's see, it was back in Ohio when I was just a couple of years older than you are now, Matt. At that time I stood six two and weighed 'bout 225 and was always on the lookout for a good time. I admit I liked to drink and had an eye for a good-lookin'—"

"Frank," warned Aunt Elly.

Uncle Frank winked at Matt. "Yes, Elly?"

"Behave yourself."

Uncle Frank nodded. "As I was sayin', it was back in Ohio when one Saturday I went to a carnival. I was with some other fellers, and we played a few games of chance. Saw the Bearded Lady," he grinned at his wife, "and what not. And then we noticed this big crowd. We went up to it, and here was this feller shoutin', 'Me name's Biff O'Malley, boys, and I'll give any man a hundred dollars who can stay three rounds with me.'"

"He must've been big, huh, Uncle Frank?"

Uncle Frank smiled. "Well, that's the funny thing. He wasn't. Not really. Oh, he wasn't little. Stood 'bout five ten and weighed mebbe 165, soakin' wet. But I was a lot bigger and figured I could take the bully boy easy. Besides, a hundred dollars is a lot of money, specially back then. So I yelled out that I'd fight 'im.

"Well, I took off my shirt—it was in the month of June and kinda warm—and got into the ring with him. A coupla my pals yelled, 'Go get him, Frankie!' O'Malley didn't seem too impressed, though. Well, anyway, we met in the center of the ring. I figgered it was kinda warm, and so I'd just as soon get it over with."

"Weren't you a little nervous, Uncle Frank?"

"Naw. Not then, anyway. So I told myself, no time like the present and took a roundhouse swing with my right hand.

Well, do you know, all I hit was air. That foxy lad just ducked under my swing and jabbed me a good one in the nose. And it started to bleed. That made me mad but a little cautious, too. So I tried a left hook and followed it with a right cross. Same result. Nothin' but air."

Perplexed, Matt asked, "How come?"

"Well, do you know, that Fancy Dan just jerked his head back away from my left and blocked my right with his arm. Next thing I knew, he caught me square on the jaw with a good solid right. I never even saw it comin'. I found myself sittin' on the seat of my britches with my ears ringin', tryin' to figger out what hit me."

"But you got up and licked him, didn't you?"

Uncle Frank grinned. "No, Matt, but I learned a little lesson, and I want you to remember it."

"What's that, Uncle Frank?"

"He who runs away, lives to fight another day."

"Aw, Uncle Frank. You're joshin' me."

"No, I'm not, boy. That's one of the most important lessons you'll ever learn, whether you're a boxer, a general, or a gunslinger. No, sir. I knew I was overmatched that day. I tried to get up, but my legs were weak and wobblin'. I waved that crusher away and crawled out of that ring."

"And that was that?" Matt's voice betrayed his disappointment.

Uncle Frank grinned. "No, no, it wasn't. I didn't much care for the results of that fight, but I wasn't ready to give up. Seems the carnival needed a couple of men, so I hired on and traveled around with it for several years."

"What did you do?"

"Well, for quite a while I was just a general handyman, what they call a roustabout. They gave me any job to do that required a man to be short on brains but long on muscle. Biff, though, he took a likin' to me for some reason. I became his sparring partner, and he taught me a few things about fightin'.

"'Frank,' he said, 'here's a few choice spots to plug a man.' And he tapped me on the jaw, just in front of the ear, on the temple, on the Adam's apple, on the solar plexus, and on the kidneys. 'And Frank,' he went on, 'ya gotta plant your feet, bend your knees, and get all your body weight into your swing. You do that and land your punch on one of those spots, and I guarantee your man's goin' down. And out.'"

Matt's face lit up. "And did it work?"

"Sure did, Matt. Long's I was quick. It's what I been teachin' you, ain't it?"

"Yes, sir."

"That and how to put up a good defense. Duck, dodge, weave, and roll with the punches. If you can do that, size don't mean too much. At least not most of the time. But, when you're overmatched, don't forget that first rule. He who runs away, lives to fight another day."

Matt, face solemn, nodded. If Uncle Frank said it, it must be true.

"Well, anyway, after a few months and a lotta practice, Biff began to let me fill in for him now and then. Then one day, he up and quit. I don't know why. Mebbe he was just tired of fightin'. Or mebbe he was tired of carnival life. Whatever. One day he was there, and the next he was gone. So the boss asked me to take over, and I did."

"And that's the end of the story?"

Uncle Frank closed his eyes for a moment and then opened them. "The end of the story? No, not quite." He turned to his wife. "Elly, before I go on, why don't you serve each of us a piece of that pie I know you got out in the kitchen."

Aunt Elly nodded and without a word got up and headed for the kitchen. She came back and set a piece of pie in front of each of them. Quickly Frank Brinkman gobbled down his piece. Then he looked around at the other three.

"Well, now. While you three finish your pie, I'll go on with my story. First, though, anybody want more coffee?"

Uncle Frank looked around. Matt, eager for the story to resume shook his head, but his Paw indicated he'd like some more. Aunt Elly got the coffee pot and filled his cup.

"Anyway," Uncle Frank resumed, "like I said, I took over

when Biff O'Malley left the carnival. And that carnival traveled all over the United States, from the Atlantic to the Mississippi. I fought in more small towns than I can ever remember. In the beginning, I used the London Prize Ring rules as much as possible. Kickin', gougin', buttin, bitin', and low blows were out. We drew a 24-foot square in the dirt, and a round lasted until somebody went down. The downed man was helped to his corner, and he got a thirty-second rest. If he couldn't get back to the center of the square before another eight seconds went by, he was the loser."

"How long did those fights last, Frank?"

"Well, that was the trouble, John. Time's money, and with those rules, I was losin' money. The challengers had to put up two dollars, but to make much money, I'd have to fight a bunch of 'em, and with those London Prize Ring rules, there wasn't time to do that. Some of the men I fought were tough. It took too long, not to mention it was rough on me. Besides, a lot of those boys I fought didn't believe in rules. So, in the end, I went back to O'Malley's system, except I made the rounds three minutes."

"Did you ever lose, Uncle Frank?"

Uncle Frank laughed. "You mean did I ever have to pay off the hundred dollars? Oh, mebbe half-a-dozen times in the six years I fought."

"No, I mean did you ever get beat?"

"Well, there was one time, no, two times, I still remember. Did'cha ever hear of a feller named John Heenan? John C. Heenan."

"Well, Frank, I believe I did. Wasn't he the United States champion? Went over to England in 1860 and lost a real tough fight to the English champion. Fight lasted somethin' like 42 rounds."

Uncle Frank slapped the table with the palm of his hand. "That's him, John," he roared. "That's the feller. Anyhow, one day in '57—or was it '56—well, doesn't matter, a feller stepped up and said he wanted to fight me. He looked to be 'bout 200 hundred pounds and stood 'bout six feet. Pretty good size, but still smaller'n me. Anyway, I never asked names, and at that time, it wouldn't've meant anything to me in any case. I should've been suspicious, though, when his friends started laying bets."

"But, Uncle Frank, the man was a professional."

Uncle Frank grinned. "So he was. But then, so was I, you know. We were both makin' a livin' fightin', weren't we?"

"I guess so."

"Trouble was, even though it was early in his career, this feller was trained and, in another couple of years, was goin' to be the U.S. of A. champion. He was damn near the world champion. But I didn't know that then.

"Worst of all, not only was he pretty big, he was quick. Real quick. After 'bout one minute in the ring with him, I knew I was overmatched. Right then I'd like to've called on rule number one and run away to live and fight another day, but of course, I couldn't. So I tried to just hang on. I used every bit of know-how I had to keep out of his way."

"Oh, Frank," moaned Elly, "you never told me about that."

"Didn't I? Well, probably just as well. I fought a real defensive gem, if I do say so myself. I lasted until late in the third round, but with 'bout thirty seconds to go, I ducked smack into his right fist. That did it, although he did hit me two or three more times as I was on my way down. By the time I woke up, the man had collected his hundred dollars and his bets and had long since left."

"Did he take your job, Uncle Frank?"

Uncle Frank laughed until tears ran down his cheeks.

"No, Matt, he didn't. First of all, he had his sights set on bigger game. That bout with me was just a lark for him. Luckily, even though I'd never heard of the man, my boss, Sam Nelson, had. In fact he'd seen him fight once. Trouble was there was nothing Sam could do about it. He didn't blame me for losing. But every cloud has a silver lining. Sam started billing me as a man who'd fought John C. Heenan."

"I knew you were tough, Frank, but I never knew you

fought John C. Heenan. You got any other stories you haven't told me or Elly?"

Uncle Frank grinned. "Well, I fought a Frenchman once."

"Frank, I warned you," said Elly, glaring. "Is this some disgusting story about...you know, sex?"

Uncle Frank chuckled. "No, Elly, it isn't. It's about savate."

"Frank," her voice dripped with suspicion, "what's this savate?"

Uncle Frank grinned some more. "It's boxing French style. The Frenchies use their fists and their feet. It's amazin' how they can jump up and kick a man in the head or the belly."

"But, Uncle Frank, I thought you said kickin' was against the rules."

"It was against the London Prize Ring rules, but when I went back to Biff O'Malley's style, anything went."

"Oh."

"The first time I ever fought one of those kickfighters, I'd never seen anything like it. That frog leaped up and caught me square in the mouth with both feet. I still have trouble believin' he did that. Almost did me in, I tell you. From then on I was mighty careful. Finally, though, in the second round, I caught him a good one, and it was good night Mr. Frog."

"Is that why you quit fightin'? Because of losing to Heenan and what that Frenchy did?"

Uncle Frank's expression grew serious. "No, Matt, it was because of a fight I won."

Matt's voice showed his skepticism. "How could that be?"

"Well, it was in the summer '58. The carnival was in a little town in Wisconsin. I was givin' my spiel to the crowd, waitin' for a challenger. The townspeople were joshin' a big blonde fellow, encouragin' him to get in the ring with me. He wasn't just big, he was a giant. 'Bout six six or better and at least 250 pound. None of if fat.

"'Go on, Swede,' they shouted. 'Get in there and fight the man. We'll put up the money. You can pay us back out of the hundred dollars you're goin' to win.'

"Well, finally, the fellow jumped into the ring and immediately charged me. I dodged, but he still hit me a glancin' shot. Good thing it was glancin', because if he'd hit me square, he'd've killed me, I swear he would."

"Oh, no, Frank!"

"Oh, yes, Elly, he would've. As it was, it staggered me. My God, I thought, this feller's strong—and fast. I tried three quick jabs. I hit him, but he brushed 'em away like they was mosquitoes. Then I caught him with a good, solid right. That was progress, but not much. Because that right that would've floored many a good man, just caused him to shake his head a bit. Then the giant swung with a quick left and right combination. Thank God I caught them on my arms, but my arms went numb." Frank took a sip of coffee. "Well, I tell you I was worried, mighty worried. Wasn't just the idea of payin' out the hundred dollars. No, sir! This feller's blood was up. He was a real killer, and I was his target. I was goin' to have to box this giant just to stay alive. At least that's what I thought right then."

"Oh, Frank." Elly's face mirrored her concern.

"Yep, Elly, that's the way it was. I jabbed some, but I bobbed and ducked and weaved a whole lot more. The three minutes of the first round came and went, but this man wasn't about to quit. He was out for blood."

Matt was almost breathless. "What happened then?"

"Well, he took a great roundhouse swing at me which I just barely ducked. In doin' so, though, he turned so's his back was partly toward me, exposin' his right kidney area. Figgering it was now or never, I stepped forward and hit him with a left with everything I had. He let out a kinda muffled scream and wobbled, and then—I couldn't believe it—he straightened up and came forward, glaring and a'yellin' like I'd never heard."

Ever the consummate story-teller, Uncle Frank paused and took a sip of coffee.

"Well, come on, Frank. What happened?"

"John, I figgered I had mebbe one more good shot left in me. As this human oak tree bore down on me, I could see he was set to finish me off. That shot to the kidney had really annoyed him. Teeth bared, he drew back that huge right arm of his and started to swing. Quick's I could, I stepped forward and buried a left upper cut into his privates. Well, that shot must've been a little off, although I don't see how, because he kept comin', kinda hunched over like, though, if you know what I mean. Like I say, it didn't stop him, but it did distract him, because he missed me.

"Well, sir, at that point I planted my feet square on the ground, bent my knees, and, steppin' inside of him, hit him harder than I ever hit anyone else before or since. His head snapped back, and he started to topple. I probably should've yelled 'tiiim-ber.' It was just like watching a giant oak come crashin' down. I stepped back to get out of the way, and when he hit, a cloud of dust flew."

"Was he out, Uncle Frank?"

"Was he out, Matt? He didn't move a muscle. Not a twitch. Well, after 'bout four or five minutes, it was clear he wasn't goin' to get up. Four of his friends got a hold of him and carried him into one of the tents. A doctor finally showed up, and the Swede was moved to what passed for a hospital in that little town. Didn't do a bit of good, though. The poor feller died a day and a half later. Without ever comin' conscious again."

"Aw, gee, Uncle Frank."

Uncle Frank seemed lost in his own thoughts. "I went to his funeral. Found out he was only twenty-two and supposed to get married in two months."

"Oh, no, Frank."

Frank nodded his head. "Oh, yes, Elly, he was. I got drunk, but it didn't do any good. At the funeral, I realized I'd had enough. No more fightin' for me. I looked up Sam Nelson and told him I quit. He didn't try to talk me out of it and paid me off."

"What'd you do then?"

"Came back to Cincinnati, quit drinkin', and married Elly. Then I worked for you a spell before Elly and I decided we'd like to come out here and farm."

"When'd you begin preachin', Uncle Frank?"

"Not long after we got out here. I'd been doin' some studyin' on it for two, three years. When we come out here in '61, there wasn't much to Abilene. A few log huts, a general store, and a church. Preacher was one of them there hell-fire-and-brimstone fellers, though. I didn't cotton to it, so I started my own church."

"There was lots of folks liked Frank's style of religion a whole lot better'n Preacher Merton's, but," said Elly, shaking her head wonderingly, "some still seem to prefer the brimstone."

"Well, live and let live. But John, I want you to know I'm mighty proud that you and Matt come to my services every Sunday."

"Well, Frank, you know I'm a believer in a gentle Jesus and Lord God, don't you?"

"I know you are." Frank cleared his throat. "And, John,...I just want to say I think you're one of the kindest men I've ever known. A real fine, Christian gentleman."

"And, what's more," added Elly, "I know Matt is proud of you. Many's the time he's told me so. Not only since you came out here, but even when he was a little feller and I took care of him after Alice died."

John Ritter looked at his son. "That so, son?"

Matt nodded. "Sure is, Paw."

His father blinked a couple of times, then brushed the back of his hand across his eyes. "You know, I believe Frank's pipe smoke's makin' my eyes water."

"I ain't been smokin', John."

"Oh." Ritter took a gulp of coffee. "Well, anyway, Matt, remember. I don't want you carryin' a gun in town or havin' anything to do with them gunslingers."

Matt nodded once more. "Sure, Paw. I'll remember."

"Howdy, John." Frank Brinkman took off his hat and swabbed his forehead with a large bandanna. "Mighty warm for the first of June."

John Ritter looked up. His brother-in-law stood in the open doorway of the shop. "Well, howdy, Frank. Come on in out of the sun and set a spell. Not often you're in town in the middle of the day."

"Like to, John," said uncle Frank, leaning his elbows on the counter and fanning himself with his hat, "but I haven't got much time. I'm tryin' to get this here association goin', and we're having a meetin' today."

Oh?" John Ritter laid the gun in his hand down on the workbench. "What association you talkin' about?"

"Just a bunch of farmers like me. I think we're goin' to call it the Farmers' Protective Association. I'm on the board, and we're meetin' with ol' T.C. and some of the likeminded town folk."

"How come you're not meetin' at one of the farms?"

"Oh, it's handiest for everybody just to meet in town. We're gettin' together over at the *Chronicle* office in a little while. Just thought I'd stop by and see how you're doin'." Uncle Frank gestured. "I see you got your window fixed."

"Yep. Just an ordinary one, though. Can't afford another plate glass window. Some damn fool'd probably shoot it out again, anyway."

"Well, now. I hear ol' Wild Bill's got a grip on the town. No more totin' guns, and no more shootin'."

"Seems that way, Frank, but how long's it goin' to last? Some crazy fool'll come along and plug him, and then hell'll be in session all over again. Just like with poor ol' Bear River Tom last year. Things were fine for a few months till that crazy farmer and his friend shot ol' Bear River and chopped his head off."

Uncle Frank nodded. "You may be right. That's why I'm in town." He looked at the work bench where Matt was working. "What're you up to, Matt?"

Matt put down the tools he'd been working with and looked up. "Paw's got a great idea, Uncle Frank. He's fixin' to make an eight-shot revolver."

Skeptical, Uncle Frank looked at Ritter. "You really think you can do that?"

"Don't see why not. Back durin' the War somebody, I don't remember who, made a .31 caliber nine-shot for the Navy. So it ain't exactly a new idea, but there ain't no such gun around these days as I know of. Although I don't see why there shouldn't be."

"You goin' to sell 'em?"

"Don't think so. I'm figgerin' to make just one for Matt here, and that'll be it, I guess. I'm only doin' it so's to give Matt some protection. Like I told you, Wild Bill or no Wild Bill, I worry every time the boy sets foot outside in this town."

Uncle Frank nodded. "I see. Well, John, if things go as the Protective Association plans, you won't have to worry too much longer. We figger if we can get rid of these Texas cattle drives, Abilene'll be a peaceful place to live in."

Ritter said nothing, but his raised eyebrows conveyed his doubts.

Uncle Frank sensed Ritter's skepticism. "John, farmers like me are real tired of those cowboys and their rampagin' steers tearin' up our land. Real tired. And more 'n more of the town folks are gettin' tired of all the trouble those drovers bring here. If the cattle drives stop, there won't be no more cowboys coming to Abilene, and if there ain't no more cowboys coming here, the scum'll leave. Only reason all the whores and card sharps and saloons are around's to take money off the cowboys. With no cowboy pay 'round for the taking, they'll go somewhere else."

"The business men in town aren't goin' to like it, are they, Frank?"

"Mebbe and mebbe not. I don't know for sure. But me and the rest of the farmers think they'll come around. The law's on our side, you know. Or maybe I forgot to tell you. There's a state law, a quarantine it's called, against bringin' those Texas steers into Kansas. Those longhorns carry splenic fever and infect our livestock. Abilene's already in the quarantine zone. We just ain't been enforcin' the law. But we will."

John Ritter chewed on his lower lip for a moment. "You know, Frank, if the drovers stop comin' here, it'll sure put a dent in my business."

"I know, John, and I'm sorry 'bout that, but it's got to be done."

"Oh, I agree with you, Frank. It's got to be done." John Ritter sighed. "I just wish you'd told me all this when you convinced me to sell out in Cincy and come here to Abilene."

Frank shrugged. "Didn't know it then, John. We none of us dreamed things'd turn out like they have."

"When's all this goin' to take place?"

"Well, we don't figger we can do much 'bout this year, but

we hope to get a notice out in the *Chronicle* and maybe eventually in some Texas newspapers telling the drovers to take their business elsewhere next year."

"You really think it'll work, Frank?"

Uncle Frank, jaw set, nodded. "I'm sure of it. As it is, it looks like Newton down south of here's goin' to take a lot of the business. Mebbe all of it. The Atchinson, Topeka, and Santa Fe's runnin' a branch line in there, and by next year, the Texans won't have to come all the way up here. After all, Newton's 65 miles south of here. That'd save those drovers a lot of saddle polishin'. As a matter of fact, I hear McCoy's already down there building cattle pens and a hotel."

Ritter's face lit up. "Is he now? Best news I've heard in quite a spell. Anyway, I wish you and your friends good luck with your plans. But, for right now, I'm goin' to go ahead with makin' Matt an eight-shot revolver."

"You do that, John, but I promise you 1872 in Abilene'll be a lot different." Uncle Frank shook hands with both of them. "Gotta get along now. Don't want to keep folks waitin'. I'll tell you 'bout the meetin' at supper tonight."

Uncle Frank started out the door, then hesitated and turned back. "By the way, Matt, when's your birthday?"

"A week from this Wednesday, Uncle Frank. June 10."

Uncle Frank nodded and smiled. "I'm sure Elly knows exactly when it is, but I'll be thinkin' about it, too."

Uncle Frank waved a hand and set off down the street. John Ritter watched him out of sight and then turned back to Matt. "All right, son, best get down to business. Now, what I plan to do is convert this here six-shot Colt Army .44 into an eight-shot .32 revolver. Probably put an extra charge into some hollow nose .32 ammo for it, too, long's I'm at it."

"Can you really do it, Paw?"

"You'll see. You're goin' to help me do it, so you'll see."

Matt looked admiringly at his father and grinned. "The gun'll have two extra shots in it, won't it? That'll sure surprise 'em."

John Ritter winked. "Three extra shots."

Matt's brow furrowed. "Three? How d'ya figger, Paw?"

"Well, now, son, remember 'most everybody carries his gun with an empty chamber under the hammer. For safety, so it won't go off accidental-like."

"Yes, but so do I."

"True, but with this new weapon, that won't be necessary. I'm fixin' to put a little steel pin right in here." He pointed to a position in front of the hammer. "That'll keep the gun from accidentally firin', but that pin'll draw back when the weapon's cocked so's to let the gun fire. Now, what do you think of that?"

Matt was awestruck. "Gee! Paw. Sounds great." His brow furrowed again. "Wonder why nobody else ever thought of that?"

"Oh, I reckon they probably did, but that's goin' to take some real fine gunsmithin'. And remember what Burke Harte said. Not every gunsmith's as clever as your ol' Paw." He winked at his son. "And besides, it's slow work and would make a gun pretty danged expensive. I imagine that's the real reason. Never forget, son, money talks. He who holds the purse strings calls the tune."

"Oh." Matt still looked doubtful. "But, Paw, do you think a .32 will be powerful enough?"

"Son, I reckon with that extra charge in the ammo and hollow nose balls, it'll have all the stoppin' power of a .44 and then some."

The older Ritter picked up the Colt Army revolver.

"First thing to do is take out this six-chamber cylinder. We'll have to replace it with a brand new eight-chamber cylinder."

He fastened the gun into a vise on the bench. Then he took a small pick, shaped like a fine pointed nail set, and placed it against one of the pins that locked the gun's cylinder in place. A couple of taps with a small hammer on the pin and the pin emerged into his hand. He repeated the operation on a second pin. After the second pin fell into his hand, he loosened the vise and picked up the gun. Finally, he twisted the rod running through the center of the cylinder, and the cylinder dropped into his hand.

"There." He peered closely at the revolver "Pretty fair piece of work, but," he said, laying it down on the bench, "we won't be needin' it."

"What'll we use, Paw? I mean, where we goin' to get an eight-chamber cylinder?"

John Ritter grinned. "Already got one. You didn't think Burke Harte came all the way to Abilene just to jaw about the old days in Cincinnati, did you?"

Matt looked dubious. "No, I guess not."

"Well, you guess right. He was here on business. I didn't know it'd be him that'd deliver it, but some time ago I wrote to his company and asked 'em to have a new eight-chamber .32 caliber cylinder cast for me in a basic .44 caliber mold." John Ritter grinned again. "You know, it took three letters and a good deal of money to convince that company your old Paw wasn't crazy, but, they finally came around."

Ritter walked over to his desk and opened a drawer. He reached in and took out an object wrapped in flannel, then peeled back the flannel. "Here it is, all shiny and new. Course, I'll have to do the final machinin' on it, and then she'll fit slick as a whistle."

Mouth open, Matt could only grin at his father.

"Course, that's not all there is to it."

"Oh? What else is there?"

"Well, we gotta change a spring in here," said Matt's father, pointing to the cocking mechanism, "so instead of turning one sixth of the way around, the cylinder'll only go one eighth."

"That all, then?"

"Well, no, we gotta change the barrel, too. See that .32 you were playing with when your Uncle Frank came in?"

Matt nodded.

"Well, we'll just pull the barrel offa that weapon and put it on the .44. A good polishin' to get any burrs off, and that should do it."

Over the next several days, father and son worked on the new gun. John Ritter couldn't devote his full time to the project; he still had a business to run and a living to earn. Matt, although eager to assist, could, for the most part, work only under the supervision of his father.

Nevertheless, little by little, the work progressed. Matt observed and learned all the procedures his father had described. His dexterity impressed his father.

"Son, you use your fingers well. You're mighty skillful with fine work. And I'm surprised at how patient you are with tedious things."

"Thank you. I do believe mebbe piano playin's payin' off. All that practicin' makes a person's fingers mighty agile. Makes for patience too."

Late in the afternoon of the day preceding Matt's birthday, they gave the new Ritter eight-shot Special its final polish. Then they assembled the weapon. John Ritter dry fired it a couple of times.

He nodded. "Seems to work just fine. What do you say we give it a test firin'?" He looked around and shook his head. "That ordinance barrin' the firin' of guns inside Abilene's a damned nuisance. Afraid the best we can do is to test fire it into this barrel of sand I've got back here." He looked at Matt. "Here. It's yours. You do the honors."

Matt grinned and took the gun. "Thanks, Paw."

He walked back to the barrel, cautiously aimed it into the sand, placed a pillow over his gun hand, and pulled the trigger. The pillow muffled the explosion, but confined in the small shop as it was, it still rattled the windows.

John Ritter let out a yell. "By golly, she really works."

Matt cocked the gun and pulled the trigger again. Once more the weapon functioned flawlessly. He stood speechless for a moment, then broke into a grin. "Oh, what a beauty! I can hardly wait to get home and try her out."

"Seein's how it's your birthday, Matt, I fixed your favorite meal. Fried chicken and dumplings. With mashed potatoes and gravy. And then there's some chocolate cake waitin' for you."

Matt smiled at his raven-haired aunt. "Thank you. I surely do love your fried chicken."

Uncle Frank grinned. "Never met a man yet that didn't love Elly's fried chicken. How 'bout you, John?"

John Ritter winked at his sister-in-law. "Kinda partial to it myself, Elly."

Matt's aunt took her place at the dining room table.

"It's won me a few ribbons at county fairs," she said, looking a bit smug.

"Speakin' of winnin' things, John, I think that new gun of

yours is a real winner," said Uncle Frank. "Matt was showin' it to me just before we sat down to dinner. We're goin' to try it out tomorrow afternoon. But where'd you find a .32 barrel for it?"

"Took it off'n an ol' 1861 Smith and Wesson .32 I had in the shop. A six-shot Smith and Wesson. As a matter of fact, that gun gave me the idea for an eight-shot revolver."

Uncle Frank looked puzzled. "How so?"

John Ritter put down the drumstick he was chewing on.

"Well, you see the Smith and Wessons when they first come out back in '57 were seven-shot .22s. Weren't till 1861 they added the six-shot to the line in either a .22 or .32 caliber. Anyhow, that ol' Smith and Wesson jogged my memory and got me thinkin' about an eight-shot gun."

They chewed in silence for a few minutes. Then Uncle Frank laid down his knife and fork. "That gun's a mighty nice birthday present—"

"Oh," John Ritter interrupted, "that's not his birthday present."

"It's not?"

"No, it was just a coincidence that we finished it yesterday. Took me longer'n I expected is all."

"I see. Well, Matt, I've got a present for you. Now just you sit right there while I go fetch it."

Uncle Frank got up from the table and went into the next room. When he returned, he carried a long slender package wrapped in paper. "Here you are."

Matt took the proffered package and looked at his father. John Ritter nodded to him. Matt began to tear the paper loose. Gradually, from the wrappings, a large-caliber rifle emerged.

Mouth open, Matt held the weapon up. "Why look, Paw. I believe this is Uncle Frank's buffalo gun."

John Ritter held out his hand. Matt passed him the rifle. Ritter examined the gun closely and then looked up at his brother-in-law. "This *is* your .50 caliber Sharps, isn't it, Frank?"

Uncle Frank nodded. "Yep, sure is."

"It's a beauty, Uncle Frank, but I can't take it."

"Sure, you can." Uncle Frank turned to Matt's father. "The boy's been usin' this for a couple of months now, and John, he does better with it now than I ever did. Besides," he said, picking up his fork and attacking his chicken, "I don't figger to be shootin' me any more buffalo." He smiled at his wife. "I'll just stick to Elly's chicken and roast beef."

"Gosh, Uncle Frank, I don't know what to say."

"How 'bout a plain, old thank you?"

"Well, sure, Uncle Frank. Thank you, thanks a lot."

"Well, now," said Aunt Elly, "is it present time? I thought I'd wait till after the cake, but if we're goin' to hand out presents, I'll get mine."

Matt's aunt bustled out, and the three men went on eating. When she came back, she had two packages in her arms. She laid them on the table beside Matt.

"There you are, Matt. Got 'em when I was in Topeka last month. Liked 'em both and couldn't decide which to get you, so I bought 'em both." She smiled at him. "Go on now, open 'em."

"Gosh, Aunt Elly, you shouldn't've. What are they?"

"Well, open 'em and see. Don't just sit there like a silly goose."

He picked up a large, oblong parcel and began ripping the wrappings off. Suddenly he broke into a grin. "Well, I'll be! Will you look at that?"

"What is it, Matt?"

"A pair of moccasins, Paw. Real Indian moccasins. My gosh, but they're soft."

"I figgered you'd like 'em," said his aunt. "You can relax in 'em. I'm sure they'll be more comfortable than those clodhoppers you usually wear. So, go ahead, try 'em on."

Matt pushed back from the table and kicked his heavy shoes off. Then he slipped into the moccasins and stood up. He rocked back and forth tentatively and then took a few steps. "Oh, say, but these feel good. Thank you, Aunt Elly. I've never felt anything so comfortable."

"That's a mighty nice present, Elly," said John Ritter.

She shrugged. "Well, he's a mighty nice boy. I don't know anybody I'd rather get a present for. Now, open the other one." She winked. "It's somethin' we'll all like."

Matt came back to the table and sat down. Quickly he picked up the second package and ripped the coverings off.

"Well, look at that! It's music, all kinds of sheet music. There must be twenty, thirty pieces here."

"Well, actually there's eighteen. One for each year of your life." She winked at the two men and then grinned at Matt. "I'm as religious as the next person, and I do enjoy hearing Matt play the songs in that hymn book of yours, Frank, but I do declare, at thirty-five, I'm not so old but what it'll be nice to hear some other tunes for a change."

"Well, sure, Aunt Elly. I'll play one right now. What would you like to hear?"

"Well, I *am* kinda partial to 'Beautiful Dreamer' or maybe 'Take Me Home Where the Sweet Magnolia Bloom.' But let's finish dinner first. We can do some singin' later."

"Oh, sure." Matt sat down and resumed eating. The others followed his lead. Nothing more was said. When the chicken and dumplings and mashed potatoes were gone, Aunt Elly brought in a chocolate cake. She cut a piece for each of them and then filled the coffee cups.

At this point, John Ritter cleared his throat and spoke.

"Like I said, that gun ain't Matt's birthday present." He reached into his pocket and took out a fat envelope and turned to Matt. "Here, son. I think you'll like this."

Puzzled, Matt took the envelope and slowly opened it. From it, he extracted a long piece of paper. He knit his brows. "What is it, Paw?"

"That's a round trip ticket to Kansas City. In one week, you're leavin' to visit your Uncle Claude and Aunt Martha. He works for the *Kansas City Times*, and he's got a special treat in mind for you."

Uncle Frank winked. "Well, tell the boy what it is. Don't keep him in suspense."

John Ritter smiled. "Matt, Uncle Claude knows you love baseball. That's right, ain't it?"

Matt grinned. "You know I do."

His father grinned back. "And you know who the Cincinnati Redlegs are, don't you?"

"You bet I do. They're the first professional baseball team in the world. Nobody can beat 'em."

"Well, now," said Uncle Frank, "I don't know about that. They *were* the first professional team, back in 1869, but this year, back East, there's a whole new league of professionals."

"Well," said John Ritter, "that's true as far's it goes, but the Redlegs have been on a tour of the country clear out to San Francisco and now back. And so far, nobody's beat 'em." He turned to Matt. "Anyway, son, the Redlegs are playing in Kansas City in ten days, and your Uncle Claude's arranged to take you. To all three games."

Matt sat back in his chair, speechless. His aunt and smiled at him. Finally he got to his feet and went where his father sat; he put his arms around his father and hugged him. "Paw, nobody ever had a father like you. I swear I'm the luckiest feller in the world. I mean it. The luckiest in the whole world."

A hot June afternoon. Bees buzzed lazily. The only cloud in the sky, a thunderhead, far off in the distance. Matt and Uncle Frank headed out into the fields. Two hundred yards from the house, they halted.

"Well, sir, that was a pretty nice birthday party last night, wasn't it?"

"Sure was. I just can't get over the great presents you all gave me."

"Well, boy, I don't know anybody who deserves nice presents more'n you. And, Matt, that's what all the folks in the congregation say, too. You're a pretty nice young feller, and I'm proud to have you for a nephew. That's all there is to it."

Matt shrugged. He could feel himself blushing. "Aw, Uncle Frank, you don't have to say that."

"I know I don't, but I said it anyway. Now, let's get down

to business. You're accurate with a gun, Matt, but I want to see how fast you are."

Uncle Frank paced off about twenty yards from where Matt stood and arranged eight large pieces of firewood in a row. Then he came back to where Matt waited.

"Now," said Uncle Frank, "you got your holster down low on your right thigh, I see." Matt's uncle reached down and tugged at the holster. "That's fine. Nice and snug."

Matt, his right hand hanging near his holster, nodded.

"That firewood there's your target. Now raise your right arm straight out in front of you, palm down."

Matt did as he was told.

"Fine. Now I'm goin' to lay this silver dollar on the back of your hand." He did so. "There, like that. When I say to go, you turn your hand until the coin slides off. Soon's that coin falls off, go for your gun. Draw and get off a shot before the dollar hits the ground. Ready?"

Matt, coin flat on his hand, nodded.

"Go."

Matt slowly turned his hand. The coin began to slide, gained speed, and fell free. Matt's hand blurred as he whipped it back to the holster. His gun appeared to leap into his hand. A shot roared; simultaneously, the coin hit the ground.

"That was pretty quick, all right," said Uncle Frank. "But all you hit was the ground. Wouldn't do you much good in a gun fight, now would it?"

"Matt, you know the best way to win a gun fight?"

Matt shrugged. "Be the fastest on the draw, I reckon."

Uncle Frank smiled. "No, the best way is don't get into a gun fight at all. Remember that first rule of fightin' I mentioned a while ago? Well, this is the second rule. Don't get into a fight, especially a gun fight, because sooner or later you're goin' to lose one. There's always somebody comin' along somewhere that's goin' to beat you. And with gun fightin', that could really spoil your day."

"You mean you don't want me to be a gun fighter, is that it?"

"That's it exactly. I don't want you to be a gun fighter, and your Paw surely doesn't, either."

Puzzled, Matt said, "Well, then, why're you showin' me all this?"

"Well, now, that's a question that deserves an answer. And the answer is that, even though you do your best, you can't always avoid one, so it's a good idea to be prepared. So, now, what's the second best way to win?"

Matt grinned. "Be the fastest on the draw?"

Uncle Frank shook his head. "No, the best thing to do is to hit your man before he hits you. And that ain't necessarily the same as being quickest on the draw. You don't want to dawdle, but you want to take enough time to make sure your shot hits home. You don't want to miss. You could make 'I missed' the epitaph on the tombstone of many a fast-draw artist."

"Oh."

"I don't usually hang out with gun fighters, but in my life, I've heard more'n one of 'em say that very thing, includin' ol' Wild Bill. So you see, bein' too fast may do you in as well as bein' too slow."

Matt shrugged. "So, what am I supposed to do?"

"Stay outta fights, 'specially at close quarters, but practice your draw and your aim in case you can't."

Matt nodded. "I see."

Uncle Frank grinned. "And, Matt, if you're goin' to pick a fight, do what any sensible gun fighter'd do. Use a rifle. Fight at long range. That way the best shot wins. Gets rid of a lot of the luck element."

Matt nodded again. "I'll remember that, but what's the best rifle?"

"Well, it depends. That buffalo gun I gave you will shoot a long way and still be accurate, you can reload it fast, and when it hits something even as big's a buffalo, the beast stays down." Matt's uncle looked thoughtful for a moment. "Course, there's a lot to be said for the Yellow Boy. That's what they call a Winchester '66. There's times it'd be nice to have a good, accurate, lever action, repeatin' rifle." He pursed his lips. "I don't know. I'd have to think 'bout that one."

Matt shrugged and raised his eyebrows but said nothing.

"Well, now let's get back to work. This time I want you to get off a shot before the coin hits the ground—if you can—but even more important, I want you to hit your targets. All eight of 'em. Oh! And a couple of other things. Don't ever fan your gun, and don't get too finicky with your aimin'. Just hit your man in the chest. That'll do the job 'most every time."

5

The waiting train had two passenger coaches; a baggage car preceded the passenger accommodations and a freight car followed them. Six cattle cars, filled with Texas longhorns headed for the Kansas City stockyards, trailed behind.

The air was heavy; thunderheads off to the east spelled rain in the offing for the first time in weeks.

Matt's fellow passengers began boarding the train.

"Gosh, Paw, I wish I could take my new gun with me. I'd like to show it to Uncle Claude."

John Ritter smiled. He and Uncle Frank and Aunt Elly had all come down to the station to see Matt off to Kansas City. "I suppose you would, son, but you can't carry a gun in Kansas City any more'n you can here in Abilene."

Matt nodded toward two men about to board the train.

"Looks to me like those two fellers are carryin' guns."

Uncle Frank turned and looked where Matt had indicated. Two men stood talking. One looked to be in his late twenties. Slender, about five ten, sandy-haired and square-jawed, he moved slowly, almost languorously.

His companion looked two or three years younger. He was the shorter and sturdier of the two with an upturned nose and thin lips. Unlike the slow moving first man, this fellow gave an impression of pent-up energy.

"You know," said Uncle Frank, "I think I've seen those fellers somewhere around town, but I don't recall just where. Anyway, you're right, Matt. They are carryin' guns, but they're probably not goin' all the way to Kansas City."

The engineer let go with a blast on the whistle.

"Well, son," said John Ritter, "time to get aboard." He clapped Matt on the back and shook his hand. "Have a good time and be careful. Your Paw wants you home safe 'n sound."

"Oh, I'll be all right, Paw." Actually, thought Matt, I got more reason to worry about Paw than he does about me. He turned and shook hands with his uncle.

Uncle Frank patted Matt on the back. "Enjoy yourself, boy. When you get back, we'll do some more practicin'." He turned to Matt's father. "You should've seen Matt drawin' and knockin' off those targets. Quicker'n you could spit and say howdy. I swear, he gets better all the time."

Aunt Elly stepped forward and put her arms around Matt. Matt almost towered over her petite, rounded figure. She drew his head down and planted a kiss on his cheek.

"Take care, Matt, and look out for those girls in Kansas City."

Matt felt himself blushing. Feeling her soft body pressed even fleetingly against him, aroused a mixture of exciting, but disconcerting feelings in him. The rumble of distant thunder fit in with his perturbation. He tried to pull away. "Aw, Aunt Elly."

His aunt dropped her arms and stepped back. She smiled, showing her dimples. Matt picked up his carpet bag and climbed aboard the end passenger coach. His father waved to him and called out, "Have a good time, son. Don't be gone too long."

Matt waved one last time and, feeling a little reluctant, now that the time was here, turned and entered the coach. He looked down the aisle. He hoped to get a seat by the window but was disappointed. The coach was full, only one seat remained, and it was on the aisle about the middle of the coach.

The train slowly got under way as Matt slid into his seat. He stuffed his carpetbag under the seat and then looked around. A tight-lipped, grim-visaged, bewhiskered old man occupied the seat next to the window. His mien did not invite conversation.

Matt glanced to his right. The two gun-toting strangers he'd noted on the station platform sat in the seat directly across the aisle from him. They had their heads together, deeply engrossed in a private conversation. The train, by this time, had left the station and was beginning to move at a pretty fair clip.

Matt shrugged and looked past his seatmate at the prairie slipping by. Not much in the way of scenery, he thought. He'd lived in Abilene for three years now, and the flat, monotonous landscape of Kansas came as no surprise. The day grew darker as the train rushed eastward. Thunder rumbled ever louder; lightning lit up the sky with great jagged bolts.

In another five minutes, the first huge raindrops spattered on the coach's windows. Those windows that had been open were lowered. The interior of the coach grew warm and muggy. Fortunately, the main storm struck within a matter of minutes. Sheets of water poured down, blotting out what landscape there was. The temperature dropped precipitously, bringing cooling relief to the coach's interior.

Matt settled back in his seat. He hadn't been on a train since he and his Paw made the trip from Cincy to Abilene, more than three years earlier. They'd taken the train from Cincinnati to Kansas City and then traveled the rest of the way by stagecoach. But this was his first trip alone by train or any other way, for that matter.

A touch of homesickness assailed him. His thoughts turned to Paw back in Abilene, getting farther and farther away. He hoped he was all right. He doubted his father had ever been really well. Not with that shortness of breath and that swelling of his legs. They'd never been able to wrestle or go hunting as Matt had with his Uncle Frank. And whatever it was had worsened in the past year. He wished his father would see Doc Wiggins.

Matt wondered whether it was a touch of whatever had killed his mother. He wished he remembered more about her. He'd been only four when she died. He sighed. Lucky Aunt Elly had been there to take care of him. Was Maw as pretty as Aunt Elly? Hard to tell from that picture Paw had of her. Paw says she was pretty. In fact, she says she was downright beautiful.

Says she had talent, too. Played the piano really well. If she hadn't married Paw and had Matt, she could've played in concert halls. She and Aunt Elly grew up somewhere in the South, and piano playing was important in the South. Why'd they ever come to Cincinnati, though, he wondered? Paw says they were still just young girls in their teens. He'd have to ask Aunt Elly one of these days.

Maybe that's why he liked to play the piano. He wondered what it'd be like to be a professional piano player? Better than being a gunsmith probably. But he'd never tell Paw that. It'd hurt his feelings for sure. Matt'd been lucky to have a gentle, kind man like Paw for a father. And he'd always looked out for Matt. No, he just couldn't tell him. He'd settle for gunsmithing. That way they could work together.

Or maybe now there was a professional league, he could be a baseball player. A pitcher, maybe. Everybody said he had a strong arm and could knock a jaybird out of a tree at twenty paces. That might be just the thing. Make a living doing what he loved, by gosh. Maybe Paw'd like that.

Rain continued to fall. The train rocked along. Matt grew sleepy. He snapped awake again, though, when they halted in Junction City. A few people got off; others climbed aboard.

One a blue-coated army officer, with a woman. Must be a soldier from Fort Riley and his wife, thought Matt.

Glancing across the aisle, Matt saw that the two guntoters had also taken notice of the army officer. Matt wondered why the one on the aisle, the one with a face like a schoolgirl, kept batting his eyes. He hoped the feller wasn't one of those queer sort he'd heard about.

The train chugged along. The rain slackened but didn't stop. Matt slumped in his seat, still thinking about his father. He recalled the day Miss Gregory, his school teacher, came to call. He was fifteen at the time, and Paw was terribly worried. Aunt Elly had left them in the parlor so's they could have some privacy.

"Well, do come in, Miss Gregory," Paw had said. "Can I get you somethin'?"

Miss Gregory smiled. "Why, thank you, Mr. Ritter, but I don't believe so."

"There's nothin' wrong, is there? You haven't had any trouble with Matt, have you?"

"Oh, no. Quite the contrary. Matt's been one of my better students. In fact, when it comes to deportment, perhaps the best I've ever had."

Paw had smiled. "Well, I surely am pleased to hear that." Then he looked worried. "Is it his grades?"

"No, oh, no! Like I said, Matt is a good student and obviously very intelligent. He catches on to things quickly. No, he reads and writes well, and he has an excellent grasp of history and geography. Does extremely well with numbers, too."

Paw scratched his head. "Well, please, then, Miss Gregory, tell me what it is."

She smiled again. "It's just that I wanted the pleasure of being the bearer of good tidings for a change. I wanted to give a parent some good news. You see, it's just that I think Matt has gotten all he can from me. Intellectually he's outgrown our little school, and I think he's ready to make his way in the world."

Thinking about the episode, Matt smiled. Paw sure had

been pleased. And it had pleased him to be able to make Paw happy.

The train rolled on; the wheels clacked their monotonous refrain. Stations and miles slipped by. Matt grew sleepier. In a few minutes, he drowsed. He had no idea how long he slept. When he awoke, he did so with a start. The rain had ceased; the sun was shining. The air was warm and humid.

Matt unbuttoned his shirt collar. He glanced to his right, just in time to see the guntoter on the aisle, still batting his eyes, jump to his feet as though to follow his companion who was already several feet up the aisle. As he jumped up, the girlish-faced one's pistol fell from his belt. Matt's hand shot out; he caught the gun before it could hit the floor of the coach.

"Hey, mister!"

The guntoter whirled.

"Here. You dropped this. I caught it before it hit the floor. I was afraid it might go off." Matt offered the gun, butt first, to the stranger.

The stranger, coiled tense as a rattler ready to strike, dropped his hand from the butt of the second pistol he had reached for. He relaxed; his thin lips broke into a smile.

"Well, that's mighty nice of you, stranger."

He came back to his seat and took the pistol from Matt. Then he motioned for Matt to join him. "Why don't you take this place by the window where my brother was sittin'? He can take your seat when he comes back."

"Well, thank you. That's mighty nice of you." Matt slid into the seat by the window. The window was open and a breeze coming in. "Can't say's the scenery's much on this side, either, though."

The stranger sat down in the aisle seat. "Well, maybe we can pass the time talking. My name's Dingus Woodson." He offered his hand.

Matt took it. "I'm Matt Ritter. My Paw's the gunsmith in Abilene. He even did some work for Wild Bill Hickok."

"Did he now? My brother'n me just passed a few days in Abilene ourselves. Sent ol' Wild Bill a note, but he didn't bother to look us up. Probably just as well. So, tell me, where you headed?"

Matt tried to ignore Dingus's blinking eyes. "I'm goin' to visit my uncle in Kansas City. He works on the newspaper. He's going to take me to see the Cincinnati Redlegs play. My Paw and I are from Cincinnati. We've only been in Abilene 'bout three years."

Dingus's blue eyes narrowed. "Is that right? So you're a Yankee, huh?"

"Well, I guess so, but my mother and my Aunt Elly were from South Carolina."

"Good southern girls and they married Yankees?" Dingus sounded incredulous.

"My mother's dead."

"Sorry to hear it."

Matt nodded. He decided it'd be best not to dwell on North-South matters. "Those are fine lookin' guns you have there. Navy Colts, aren't they? They a matched pair?"

Dingus grinned. "That's right, they are. My brother likes Remingtons, but I favor Colt weapons. You like to see 'em?" He handed both pistols to Matt.

Matt peered at the guns closely. "Nice, very nice. Don't see a thing wrong with 'em. You'll never have any trouble with these, not if you keep 'em like this."

Matt handed the guns back to Dingus.

Just then Dingus's companion came back. He stood glaring down at Dingus and Matt.

Dingus grinned. "Matt, this is my brother Frank, my older brother Frank." Dingus smiled up at his brother. "Frank, this here's Matt Ritter. He's an expert on guns, even if he is part Yankee. Why don't you just sit down in his place there?"

Brother Frank chewed on his lip for a moment. "Dingus, you talk too much. Someday it's goin' to get you in a heap of trouble." Frank shook his head and slowly sank down into the seat Matt had vacated. "You gotta be more careful who you associate with."

Dingus's face darkened for a moment, then he smiled.

"All right, Frank. No more lectures." He turned to Matt. "Frank reads books, so he thinks he has to lecture me."

Dingus turned back to his brother. "Cole all ready in the front car? The deal all set?"

Frank nodded.

"Good." Dingus turned back to Matt. "We got some business to take care of later today. What business you in?"

"Well, like I said my Paw's a gunsmith and I'm learning the trade."

"Like it?"

Matt shrugged. "I guess, but I'm afraid after this year there may not be much gun business in Abilene. Or any other business, for that matter."

Dingus nodded. "That's what I hear, too. Shame, isn't it? But I tell you what. Mebbe I can offer you a job. I can use a good gunsmith. Course we don't work much. Only two or three times a year at the most. But the pay's good, real good. And you're outdoors a lot. Not just settin' around in towns. And you get to ride some mighty fine horses."

Frank leaned over the aisle. "Dingus, will you shut up?"

Dingus glowered at his brother and then turned back to Matt. "How about it, Matt? You interested?"

"Well, that's real nice of you, Dingus, but I can't leave my Paw. He's not in real good health, and I wouldn't want to hurt his feelings by leavin' him to work for someone else."

"All right, Matt. I know how you feel. And I respect you for it. Family loyalty's important. I feel the same way about my Maw and my brother here."

Just then the conductor, a short, bald, rotund man walked by. Matt called to him. "Oh, Mr. Conductor, we got much longer to go?"

"Not much, son. About another hour, maybe. There's no more stops till we hit Kansas City." The conductor adjusted his glasses, smiled, and walked on.

Dingus grinned at Matt. "He's wrong, you know."

Matt furrowed his brow. "He can't be wrong. He's the conductor."

Dingus grinned. "You want to bet? How much money you got?"

Matt didn't want to appear small. He just wouldn't mention the ten dollars in his shoe. He took out the money in his pocket and counted it. "Thirty dollars."

"All right," said Dingus, "I'll tell you what. You put up two dollars, and I'll put ten dollars. If the train doesn't stop before Kansas City, the ten dollars is yours. How's that for a deal?"

Matt thought about it. He couldn't see any flaws. "It's a bet. Who's going to hold the money?"

Dingus grinned. "You can hold it. That all right with you, Frank?"

His older brother shook his head. "Dingus, you talk too much."

"Do I, Frank? Why don't you just get set to take care of business?" Dingus turned to Matt. "Look up ahead there. See that little town on the curve? About half mile ahead. That's where this train's goin' to stop."

The train's progress continued unabated another moment or two. Then the train whistle let go a sudden, shrill blast. Brake shoes began to shriek and grind. The train slowed to a snail's pace, then jolted to a halt.

Dingus bounced to his feet, a gun in each hand. Frank stood beside him, guns trained on the passengers in the rear of the coach.

"All right," Dingus shouted, waving his guns toward the front of the coach, "everybody sit still, and you all just might live longer."

Suddenly, another man, gun in hand, appeared at the front of the coach. He pointed his sawed-off shotgun at the passengers, thoroughly cowing them.

"All right, Jesse," the man shouted through the bandanna covering the lower half of his face, "Cole's got everything in hand up front."

6

"Now, folks," said the man known to Matt as Dingus Woodson, "let's not have no misunderstanding." He grinned. "You're about to participate in a little business venture with the James brothers and associates." Still grinning, he surveyed the coach from front to back. "If you all cooperate, nobody'll get hurt." His face turned grim. "If you don't, man or woman, I promise you'll be shot dead. That clear?"

The bewildered passengers nodded their heads. A fourth bandit appeared at the rear entrance of the coach; he carried a large sack.

"My associate there at the rear of the car will pass along the aisle, and you'll each contribute anything of value you have. Cash, watches, jewelry. Wedding rings excepted. First, though, before he makes a contribution, I want to see each man's hands. Those with calluses are excused. They work for their money. We only want money from those with soft hands, capitalists and professors and suchlike."

Silence, except for scattered gasps. Jesse jerked his head toward his confederate at the end of the coach; the man advanced slowly, holding the sack open. Jesse, as promised, examined the hands of each man. Passengers quickly complied with his demands.

Then, two rows ahead of where Jesse stood, the blue-coated army officer sprang to his feet and turned to face the James brothers. He appeared to be in his late thirties. The woman who sat beside him reached up and laid a tentative hand on his sleeve as though to restrain him. He shook her off.

"You can't get away with this," he bellowed. "I don't care who you are."

Jesse looked at Frank. Frank gave a slight nod. Jesse turned back to the officer. "And just who might you be?"

"I'm Major Thomas Wilson of the U.S. cavalry."

"Where're you from? What's your home state?

"I don't see what difference that makes, but I'm proud to claim Vermont as my place of birth."

"I see." Jesse grinned. "I always heard you Vermont Yankees were stubborn fools." The grin disappeared. "Did you take part in the recent war, Major?"

The major straightened and drew back his shoulders. "I did, indeed, sir."

"Where'd you fight, Major?"

"I'm proud to say I rode with General Phil Sheridan from Winchester to Cedar Creek."

Jesse glanced back at his brother. "Did you hear that, Frank?" He turned back to the officer confronting him. "My cousin was killed at Cedar Creek."

He spat at the feet of the major. Suddenly Jesse thrust one of the Navy Colts at the cavalryman. A shot roared out; the soldier staggered back, blood spouting from a wound in his chest. Before his body could slide to the floor, a second shot hit him just below the nose.

"Vengeance is mine, saith the Lord," intoned Jesse in the stunned silence, "but sometimes the Lord needs a little help."

"Dingus always was a religious sort," said Frank, tongue in cheek. "Regular churchgoer, too."

The new widow, moaning, collapsed on the body of her husband. "Oh, Tom! Tom! Oh, no!"

She raised a stricken face toward Jesse. Suddenly, face contorted, she leaped to her feet and lunged at the murderer, nails like talons thrust forward. Jesse calmly stepped back. Savagely he brought the barrel of his pistol down across her head. Semi-conscious, she dropped to the floor. Blood oozed from her scalp and trickled down her face.

"All right," snarled Jesse, "I warned you people. Now, let's not have any more heroics." Jesse stood back; the sack man slipped past his leader. "Get on with your collectin', Jake. When you're done, take it out to where Mike's holding the horses."

Matt had sat open-mouthed, disbelieving, throughout the entire episode. He felt nauseated. He tried to stagger to his feet. "Dingus," he screamed, "what are you doing?"

Jesse whirled and stuck one of the Navy Colts in Matt's face. Matt sank back into his seat.

"All right, Matt, just stay down there. I like you, boy, even if you are half Yankee. But I don't stand for any nonsense. That clear?"

Terrified, staring down the barrel of Jesse's gun, Matt nodded.

Jesse grinned. "I notice you didn't contribute when Jake went by, so pass over that thirty dollars of yours and the ten I gave you. That was a foolish bet, boy."

Matt did as he was told. "How'd you know the train would stop, Dingus?"

Jesse laughed. "Nothin' to it. I planned the whole thing. I arranged for Cole and the boys to take over this little two-bit station. I wrote and told 'em to arrest the agent, so to speak, and tear out the telegraph line. Then all they had to do was throw the switch and flag the train onto this siding. Right now, Clell and Charlie are getting contributions from the folks in the car up front."

Matt looked around. "Seems like a lot of trouble to go to, Dingus, for the little bit you can get from these folks."

Jesse smiled. "You're right about that, but you see, in the safe up in that baggage car there's $100,000. Cole's arrangin' with the conductor right now for its transfer."

Matt's eyes widened. "That really true?"

Jesse's eyes narrowed. "You doubtin' my word?"

"No, no! Of course not."

"Good, because I don't tell lies. And I go to church whenever I get the chance, just like my Maw taught me."

Matt nodded. "You really Jesse James?"

Jesse guffawed. "You hear that, Frank? He wants to know if I'm really me."

"I heard, Dingus. But stop your jawin'. We're wastin' too much time."

"In a minute, Frank." He turned back to Matt. "I'm Jesse Woodson James, all right. But my family, like Frank here, call me Dingus. So, you see, I didn't lie to you, now did I?"

Matt shook his head.

Jesse smirked. "You see how easy this business is? Too bad you didn't join us when I offered you the chance. You'd be rich in no time at all. Then you could really help your Paw."

Just then a heavyset six-footer burst through the front entrance of the coach. "Jesse, we got a problem."

The smirk left Jesse's face. "What's the trouble, Cole? The money's there, ain't it?"

"It's there all right, but I don't see how we can handle it. It's $100,000, but it's all in silver bullion!"

"Bullion!"

"That's right. Bullion. That fat conductor says it's bein' shipped from Denver back East."

"Well, what of it?"

"Dingus," snapped his brother, "use your head. What are we goin' to do with silver bullion? We can't spend the stuff. It'd have to be melted down and cast into coins."

"Besides," added Cole, "it must weigh over a ton. More like two or three tons, in fact. Even with ten of us, we'd each have to lug away five hundred pounds. Mebbe more. Don't see how the horses can manage."

"Well, hell, get some more horses and a wagon or two," fumed Jesse.

"Dingus, for God's sake, we can't take wagons or pack horses. They'd be too slow. We gotta get outta here."

"Frank, I'm not leavin' without the money."

"Dingus, you got no choice."

Jesse was adamant. "I want the money, Frank. It'll be the biggest haul anybody ever made."

"Ain't goin' to do any good, Dingus, if we get caught haulin' it away."

Jesse chewed on his lip and scratched behind his ear with his front gunsight. "Well, hell, Frank."

Frank's brow furrowed. "Dingus, how'd you know about the money, anyway?"

Jesse looked sheepish. "Well, it was Wild Bill."

Frank looked incredulous. "Wild Bill? Wild Bill Hickok?"

"That's right, Frank. After we sent Wild Bill that note when we was in Abilene, he sent one back tellin' me there'd be $100,000 in the baggage car of this train. I figgered him bein' the marshal and all he should know."

"But he didn't tell you it'd be in bullion, I suppose."

Jesse looked even more sheepish. "Well, no, he didn't. I just figgered it'd be cash, greenbacks." Jesse shrugged. "Come on, Frank, didn't you ever make a mistake?"

Frank looked pained. "We gotta get goin', Dingus. You've wasted too much time now with all your braggin'."

"All right, all right, Frank. I see your point, but you read books, so if you're so smart, how much's silver worth a pound?"

"About seventeen dollars."

"Well, then, let's have each man carry what he can. Hell," he hesitated, counting to himself on his fingers, "forty pounds'd be almost seven hundred dollars each. That'd be all right, wouldn't it?"

"Fine." Frank James nodded toward Matt. "You gonna shoot this Yankee whelp?"

Jesse looked at Matt. "Forgot all about you there for a minute, Matt. You see the problems I have to deal with. Not always fun being a leader." He pointed a pistol at Matt and cocked it. Matt shrank back. Jesse pursed his lips. He seemed to be debating with himself. The he lowered the weapon. "Well, no, Frank. He's half Yankee, but his Maw's from the South, so let's leave him be."

Matt slumped in his seat and let out his breath. He was shaking all over. He looked up. "Dingus, what're you goin' to do about that poor woman layin' there bleedin'?"

"Nothin'. If you're so tenderhearted, you take care of her."

The gunmen moved toward the front entrance of the coach. As Jesse passed Major Wilson, he put the toe of his boot under the lifeless body and thrust it aside.

At the coach door, Jesse turned to the passengers. "I'm leavin' Archie and his shotgun right here until we're ready to leave. Don't nobody do nothin' foolish."

He turned and waved one of his Navy Colts toward Matt.

"See you in church next time I'm in Abilene, Matt. Or mebbe in hell." He muttered the last. Then he jumped down and headed toward the baggage car.

Matt got to his feet.

Archie advanced two steps, waving his shotgun. "Sit down, boy!"

"I'm just goin' to take care of this poor lady here. Jesse said I should. You heard him."

Archie looked uncertain. "Well...all right...but don't make any wrong moves, or you and a few others in here are dead pigeons."

Matt pulled his carpet bag from under the seat. Then he began rooting around in it. Finally, he found what he wanted. He pulled out his only white shirt and tore it into strips. He moved to the seat the Wilsons had occupied together. The injured woman still huddled against the side of the coach, blood oozing down her face.

Matt moved in beside her; she gave a little scream and shrank from him. "There, now, ma'am, I ain't goin' to harm you." Gently he put her hands to her side; carefully he bandaged her head in the shirt fragments, staunching the flow of blood. Even more gently he wiped the blood from her face. Then he sat down beside her and took her hand in his.

A deathly silence held sway, broken only by the occasional whimper of a woman near the rear of the coach. As he held the widow's hand, Matt tried to keep track of the minutes. Time dragged.

Suddenly a blast from the train whistle rent the air; the passengers started involuntarily. Archie, their jailer, wheeled and disappeared. Matt patted the woman's hand and then struggled to his feet. Quickly he made his way to the seat he had so recently shared with Jesse James; he stuck his head outside and surveyed the landscape. Then he brought his head back in.

"All right, folks, they're gone."

7

Ten minutes later, the conductor, accompanied by a man wearing a plug hat, boarded the coach. The two men advanced down the aisle; the widow, still weeping, sat slumped in her seat. By this time, two women had taken over from Matt and were attempting to comfort her.

"Ladies," said the conductor, "this is Doctor Morton. He's going to examine Mrs. Wilson for us." Then he turned to the rest of the passengers. "Folks, I've talked to the people from this here village, and they tell me there's no law officer here. Those cussed bandits cut the telegraph wires, so there's no way we can communicate with the outside world. We've been here about forty minutes now, and it seems to me the best thing to do is to continue on to Kansas City where I can report this outrage."

A general nodding of heads by the subdued passengers indicated their agreement. The conductor lowered his voice and turned to Matt and three nearby male passengers. "I'd appreciate it if you fellows could help me get Major Wilson to the baggage coach up ahead. Can't leave the poor fellow just lie here."

The four quickly got together and lifted the Major's body. His wife, seeing them about to depart, screamed. "Oh, no! God, no! Don't take my Tom!"

At a nod from the doctor, the two ladies moved in to help him control the now hysterically weeping woman.

The conductor motioned for the four men to move out of the coach as quickly as possible. Sweating profusely, fearful of dropping the corpse, they clambered down from the coach. Stolidly they bore the deadweight forward along the dusty right-of-way. When they reached the baggage coach, they hoisted the body into it. Inside, surrounded by low piles of silver ingots, sat a new coffin, a simple pine box.

"Mr. Laidlaw, the village carpenter, just built this a couple of days ago," the conductor informed the four men. "On speculation he said. When he heard what'd happened to the poor Major, he kindly donated it, free of charge."

They placed the corpse in the coffin and laid the lid on it. The conductor anchored the lid by laying a silver ingot on top of it. Then they all returned to the passenger coach.

When they climbed aboard, the doctor approached the conductor. He spoke in a low voice. "Mr. Moncrief, how long will it take you to reach Kansas City?"

"Less than an hour, I figger."

"Good. The lady's had a nasty blow to the head, but I believe she'll do better to go on to Kansas City where she can be observed in a hospital. I understand she's got relatives there, too. Fortunately, the bandage has stopped the bleeding, so that's no longer a problem. Good thing somebody was quick about it, though." He nodded toward the two women standing by. "These two ladies have kindly agreed to look after her until she gets there."

"What's your fee, Doctor?" asked the conductor.

"None, sir. There's no charge. I just hope somebody takes it out of the hide of those miserable, murdering curs, that's all."

He put on his hat and nodded to the conductor. Then he proceeded to the coach entrance, waved once, and climbed down.

The crew backed the train until it was once again on the main line. The whistle blew, and the train set off on its belated journey to Kansas City.

Matt sank back into the seat he'd so recently shared with the outlaw, Jesse James. The interior of the coach was warm and growing warmer. He slid across the seat to the open window. Then leaned his elbow on the window sill and cupped his head in his hand. Now that the excitement was over, he felt exhausted, drained.

Despite the rush of wind in his face, the rhythmic clickety-clack of the train passing over the rail joints and the sun beating on the flat prairie made him drowsy. Lulled by the ever monotonous landscape slipping by, his thoughts turned to the events of the last hour or so.

In his head, he again heard the roar of Jesse James's pistol. In his mind's eye, he saw Major Wilson stagger and fall from the shot. He still found it hard to believe that anyone could be as calloused and savage as the younger James had shown himself to be. How could a human being do such a thing?

Wonder what Paw or Uncle Frank would've done if they'd been here? Uncle Frank surely would've done somethin'. He wouldn't've just set there and let it happen. Even Paw, much as he hates violence, would've done somethin'. But like a great, stupid lump, he, Matt Ritter, who liked to think he was gettin' to be a man, had just set there.

Great God a'mighty, at one point, Dingus had even handed him his guns. If he'd had any sense, he could've put a stop to the whole thing right then and there. But no, he just set and listened to Dingus brag. It galled to think the outlaw was all the time laughin' at him. And why'd he keep callin' that son of a bitch Dingus? Was it supposed to ease his conscience for not havin' done somethin'? Call him by his right name, Jesse Murderin' James. He cringed as he recalled how terrified he'd felt, starin' into the muzzle of Jesse's Navy Colt.

That poor Mrs. Wilson. Wonder if they had any kids? He knew how terrible it felt to have a parent die. But he'd been lucky. Aunt Elly'd taken over and helped Paw out. Jesus! What would he ever do if Paw died. He shuddered. It didn't bear even thinkin' about. When he got home he was goin' to see to it that Paw went to see ol' Doc Wiggins whether he wanted to or not, by gosh.

He thought he heard someone say his name behind him. He looked over his shoulder. What are those fellers back there talkin' about? he wondered. Why're they lookin' at me like that? Do they think I should've done somethin', too?

Depressed, disappointed in himself, Matt slumped back in his seat. The train rolled on. He yawned. His head nodded, drooped closer to his chest. Sounds grew jumbled, indistinct. He slept.

Matt opened his eyes. Things were bleary. The train had stopped. He glanced out the window. It looked like a pretty big town. Big crowd on the platform, too. Must be Kansas City. He wondered if Uncle Claude and Aunt Milly were waiting out there for him. He yawned and stretched.

"Don't move, boy. Just you hold it, right there."

Matt turned his head toward the sound of the voice. He froze. Two determined looking men stood in the aisle beside his seat. Each man wore a silver badge pinned to his vest. One badge said U.S. Marshal; the other Deputy U.S. Marshal.

The man with the marshal's badge, a big, well-muscled fellow, was pointing a long-barreled revolver at Matt. Looked like a .44 caliber Colt Army pistol to Matt. It'd surely blow a man—or boy—to kingdom come mighty quick. The shorter feller, the deputy marshal, held a Yellow Boy, a Winchester '66, at the ready; he looked like he knew how to use it, too. And neither man was smiling. This was no joke.

Matt tried to hold still, not move a muscle. But he couldn't help shaking a bit. The man holding the revolver looked meaner than a centipede with shin splints.

"Why're you doin' this, Marshal? I ain't done nothin'."

"Don't give me any sass, boy. Just do like I tell ya. Now, real slow like, slide outta that seat and into the aisle."

Matt started to comply. He lowered his hands.

"Keep your hands up."

Worried, confused, Matt did as the marshal directed. When he was standing in the aisle, the marshal told him to lower his arms and put them behind his back. He did so. The marshal quickly anchored Matt's hands with a set of shackles.

"All right, now, young feller, I don't want any nonsense from you. I want to get this over as quick as I can."

"Get what over, Marshal? I don't know what's goin' on here."

"What's goin' on? A U.S. Army officer's been murdered right here in this car, and you ask what's goin' on. Don't get me any more riled than I already am. This is a *federal* crime, and naturally the governors of Kansas and Missouri have turned the whole mess over to federal officers."

"But I didn't have anythin' to do with that. Not a thing."

The marshal's eyes narrowed. "These folks say otherwise. Mebbe you didn't do the shootin', but they swear you're a friend of that murderin' bastard, Jesse James. One of his gang like as not."

Horrified, Matt couldn't believe what he heard. He looked around. Several of his fellow passengers, the ones he thought he'd heard talking about him, glared at him.

One of them, an older man who looked as though he might be a prosperous businessman, spat at Matt. "He's a friend of James all right. The two of them sat in that very seat, laughing and talking for the best part of an hour. Oh, he's a crony of that murdering James bully, no doubt about that. Anyway, I say string him up!"

Several other passengers muttered agreement with this inflammatory speech. Matt looked wildly about, hoping to secure support from the woman he'd befriended.

"Where's Mrs. Wilson? She'll tell you."

"Not that it's any of your business, but she's been taken to the hospital."

"Where's the other two ladies, the ones who were lookin' after her?"

"They went with her. Now stop tryin' to confuse things. I don't relish protectin' people like you from necktie parties, but it's my duty so I will—if I can."

"Necktie parties!"

"That's right. Some of those folks out on the platform are relatives of Major Wilson, and they're gettin' in a mighty ugly mood. Not only that, but some of the men out there are from Lawrence, Kansas, and they remember that Frank James was with Quantrill. They haven't forgotten what Quantrill did there durin' the war. There's been some talk of a lynchin', boy."

Matt shuddered. "My Uncle Claude must be out there on the platform, waitin' for me. He works for the *Kansas City Times*. He'll tell you."

"Don't matter who he works for. When a mob starts to howl, they want blood. Right now, those people got no more conscience than a skunk in a perfume factory. So we better get you out of here and safe into jail. It'll get sorted out later." He turned to the other passengers. "Now, I don't want to take a chance on any of you people bein' hurt, so please go to the rear of the coach and stay there. If any of you had friends in the front coach, those folks've already gotten off."

The remaining passengers did as the marshal asked but slowly, almost reluctantly. As though they were afraid they might miss something of the unfolding drama. The marshal took Matt by the arm. He shoved Matt along in front of him toward the forward entrance of the coach. The deputy marshal trailed behind.

"Now, boy," said the marshal in a low voice, "if you want to for sure get out of this with a whole skin, do exactly what I tell you and don't waste any time. Hear?"

Matt nodded. The angry muttering of those outside chilled

his blood.

"All right, now. We're not gettin' down into that mob out there. When I say go, you quick get through the door into the forward passenger car. Understand?"

Again Matt nodded.

"All right, go!"

Quickly, Matt and the marshal ducked through into the lead coach, followed immediately by the deputy marshal. As soon as all three were through the door, the conductor, Mr. Moncrief, who had been waiting in the empty forward coach, locked the door behind them, effectively closing them off from the passengers in the rear coach and the milling mob on the platform.

Instantly Mr. Moncrief tugged on his signal cord; the train whistle sounded, and the locomotive began hauling them east. The passenger coach they'd just vacated and the rest of the train stayed where it was. Before the surprised rabble on the platform realized what was happening, the locomotive, unencumbered by the second passenger coach and the freight car and six cattle cars behind it, rapidly picked up speed. The roar of the angry mob faded in the distance.

The marshal grinned and shook Mr. Moncrief's hand.

"Well, sir, worked slicker 'n a greased pig at a county fair. Glad you thought to have the train disconnected. Much obliged to you." He turned to Matt. "Let me get those shackles off you, then you sit down over there." He pointed to a seat in the middle of the coach. "Our business ain't finished yet."

The marshal unlocked the shackles, and Matt gratefully subsided into the seat indicated. He wondered what Uncle Claude and Aunt Milly were thinking. As the train had pulled out, he'd spotted them, standing on the platform, bewildered, unaware of what was happening to Matt.

The marshal and Mr. Moncrief sat down in the seat directly behind Matt. "Well, what do you think we should do now?" the marshal asked the conductor.

"Well, Mr. Felton, I for sure don't think we should stop right now."

Marshal Felton rubbed his nose. "What do you suggest?"

"I think we should keep right on going to Jefferson City or at least Sedalia. That was a mighty ugly scene developing back there, and I wouldn't put it past them to try and follow us, especially those Lawrence folks. I sympathize with their feelings, but the whole thing was getting out of hand. I don't think they'd come as far's Jefferson City or even Sedalia, though."

The marshal chewed on his lip a minute. "How do you figger to do it? This railroad don't go all the way, does it?"

Mr. Moncrief smiled. "Well, yes and no. At the moment, we're on the Kansas Pacific, but shortly we can be on the Missouri Pacific tracks. You see, there's been a lot of talk about building a union station and connecting the two lines. It'd make a lot of sense for all concerned."

The marshal nodded. "Sure would, but how's that goin' to help us? Right now, there ain't no union station."

"That's right, there isn't," conceded the conductor, "but the presidents of the two lines, knowing how long it takes to get something done like building a union station, put their heads together and had a spur built connecting the two lines. They figured it's bound to happen sooner or later so why not sooner."

The marshal grinned and nodded. "Well, sure, why not? I always did like train rides." He gestured at Matt. "We can put this young feller in the hoosegow in either place. Don't really matter much which."

Mr. Moncrief nodded. "Of course not. But, Marshal, maybe you should see what the young man has to say. I'm not at all sure he knew who Jesse was. It may've been another case of Jesse playing games."

The marshal's eyebrows went up. "You think so?" He pursed his lips, then leaned forward on the back of Matt's seat. "All right, let's hear it, young feller. What's your story?"

Matt breathed a sigh of relief. Somebody was finally goin' to listen to him. He recited his tale with as much earnestness as he could muster. Recollections of the frightening mob lent eloquence to his recitation. As he talked, he watched the faces of his listeners. At first the marshal seemed skeptical. As the tale went on, though, his face lightened; by the time Matt finished, he was grinning.

"Well, if that don't beat all. Did you ever hear such a tale, Harvey?"

The deputy marshal grinned and shook his head. "Nope, never did."

"Well...what's your name again?"

Matt repeated it.

"Well, Matt, I'm sure glad we got you away from that mob back there. Would've been a downright shame if you'd gotten hung, now wouldn't it?"

Matt gulped. "Yes, sir."

The marshal turned serious. "But I don't want to take the responsibility of turning you loose myself. I think we'll just go on through to Jefferson City. Bein' the state capital and all, there's bound to be a judge there who can make the decision. Won't hurt you to spend a night or two in jail. Mebbe the judge can get this uncle of yours to come speak up for you."

Matt was stricken. He pounded his fist into his palm.

"But, Marshal, I'll miss the ball games. There's a single game tomorrow and a doubleheader the next day. I came all the way from Abilene to see the Redlegs play, but if I'm in jail I won't get to."

The marshal sat back in his seat and frowned. Harvey snickered.

Mr. Moncrief shook his head. "Son, the last thing for you to worry about is a baseball game. Just hope the judge decides to turn you loose. In the meantime, be grateful to Marshal Felton for saving your bacon back there. Believe me, you'll be better off in jail in Jefferson City tonight than you would be in Kansas City. Think about it." He turned to the marshal. "Mr. Felton, I'm going up forward to tell the engineer."

8

"You one of the James gang, like they say?"

Matt glanced up. The sole occupant of a ten-by-twelve cell in the Cole County jail, he sat huddled on the floor, wondering what his future held. His inquisitor was one of two scruffy individuals occupying the cell on his left.

The two of them had turned up during the preceding night. Both looked to be in their forties. They wore filthy, ragged clothes that easily accounted for the fetid odor faintly permeating the cell block.

"No, I ain't."

"You ain't, huh." The fellow beckoned Matt to come closer. Matt got to his feet and approached the man. The ruffianly-looking prisoner lowered his voice. "I'm not sure Big Jack over there believes you."

Matt turned his head and looked over his shoulder. In the cell on his right, another newcomer, an unshaven giant of a man, glowered at him out of bloodshot eyes. Long, matted red hair added to his appearance of ferocity. He spat toward Matt.

"Who's he?" Matt whispered.

"That's Big Jack McCall. They say he killed three men. With his bare hands." The man grinned. "Better stay out of his way when they take us out for exercise. And don't get too near his cell. He might get his hands on you. He thinks Jesse James had a hand in killin' his daddy. Claims he'll strangle anybody who's had anything to do with Jesse."

"But I never had a thing to do with Jesse James. I was just comin' from Abilene to visit my aunt and uncle and go to the ballgame."

Matt's new companion closed one eye and slowly nodded his head. "Why, sure. You stick to that story. Best thing you can do in the circumstances." He turned to the other raggedy fellow sharing his cell. "You hear that, Jake? You hear what this young feller said?"

His equally disreputable companion nodded. "Yep. I heard. You gave him good advice, Jim. Not that it'll do him much good." He laughed. "Hell, if they don't hang him, sooner or later, Big Jack'll get him."

Good God, what've I gotten myself into? wondered Matt. He turned and made his way back to his bunk. Thank God, it's too far from Big Jack's side of my cell for him to get his hands on me. He lay down and contemplated the ceiling.

Wonder if Uncle Claude even knows where I'm at? Sure do hope so. Two days and not a word from him. No tellin' if that Marshal Felton or Mr. Moncrief ever sent a telegram like they said they would. God a'mighty, I can't sleep in this place. And the food's awful. Just atrocious.

He glanced over at Big Jack. The big man stared at him with an intensity that made Matt shudder. He turned away and resumed his contemplation of the ceiling. Maybe, he speculated, I can pretend I'm sick and not have to go out in the exercise yard. Wouldn't be far from the truth, either. How do they expect a person to eat swill like they served for breakfast?

Just then, the cell block door opened. A deputy came through. In his arm he cradled a double-barreled shotgun.

"All right, you beauties, shake a leg. Time to get out and get your morning exercise."

In his cell, Big Jack lumbered to his feet and looked over at Matt. His face creased in a grin. He looked eager to be up and out in the exercise yard. Matt sat up but stayed where he was on his bunk. The deputy herded Jake and Jim out of their cell toward the door to the exercise yard. Big Jack already waited there. The deputy unlocked the door to the outside and waved them through.

Big Jack gestured at Matt. "What about him?"

"Never you mind. I'll take care of him soon's you get yourselves out the door."

Big Jack muttered something under his breath but turned and grudgingly followed Jake and Jim out. The deputy closed and locked the door. Then he returned to where Matt, trying his best to appear ill, sprawled on his bunk.

"All right, now, young feller—"

"I don't think I can go out there," interrupted Matt. "I'm not feelin' too good this mornin'."

"Well, now. That's too bad, isn't it? 'Cause someone's here to see you. Name's Claude Ritter. Says he's your uncle. But if you're too sick..."

"Uncle Claude!" Matt sprang to his feet. "Oh, no. I'm not that sick. I gotta see him."

The deputy grinned. "I thought so. He's with Judge McIntyre right now, but I'll tell him you want to see him."

Two hours later, Matt and Uncle Claude boarded the Missouri and Pacific afternoon train for Kansas City. Matt heaved a sigh of relief as the train pulled out of Jefferson City.

Matt couldn't remember when he'd ever been so happy as when the deputy had marched him into Judge McIntyre's office, and there sat Uncle Claude. Uncle Claude was older than Paw by three years. He was bigger than Paw, too, but in the face, he sure did look like Paw. He dressed and spoke like the educated man he was. Matt remembered his Paw telling him how Uncle Claude had moved to Saint Louis after graduating from college and then later on to Kansas City. Now, according to what his Paw said, Uncle Claude was a man of some importance in Missouri.

Matt still wore the clothes he'd left Abilene in. Now, after three days, they were pretty smelly and dirty.

"I'm sure glad Judge McIntyre didn't mind the way I was dressed. I was afraid he wouldn't believe a word I said, lookin' the way I do. Mebbe when we get to Kansas City, I can wash my clothes at your place, Uncle Claude."

"I think, Matt, when we get back to Kansas City, we better get you some new clothes. Didn't you bring anything else?"

"Oh, yes sir, but my carpetbag got left on the train. I'm just glad I was wearin' the moccasins Aunt Elly gave me. Everything else is gone, though. Even my shoes."

"I'm sorry I wasn't able to do something sooner, Matt. Your Aunt Milly and I were down at the station to meet—"

"I know, sir. I saw you in the crowd."

"You did, did you? Well, we simply had no idea you were the center of all that commotion. We just thought you weren't on the train. I had to leave on business early next morning for St. Joe, and it wasn't till I got back that night that Marshal Felton's telegram caught up with me."

"I'm sure glad he sent a telegram. He promised he would."

Uncle Claude smiled. "Well, he did, and I sent a wire to Judge McIntyre asking him to hold on to you and telling him I'd be there as soon as I could."

"I sure was glad to see you, Uncle Claude. But how'd you convince the judge to let me go?"

"Judge McIntyre and I are old friends. You see he's originally from Cincinnati, too. On top of that, we went to Harvard together. That's where he went to law school." Claude Ritter grinned. "Many's the time he and I played cards and had a few drinks together."

"You mean he let me go just because you and him were friends?"

"Not entirely. It helped, of course, but it was plain to him the whole thing was a big mistake. Even Marshal Felton was skeptical, you know. And when conductor Moncrief told his story, Judge McIntyre was convinced. As William Shakespeare said, 'All's well that ends well.'"

"Except I didn't get to see the Redlegs play."

Uncle Claude laughed. "Don't worry, Matt, there'll be other days and other games. There's a regular professional baseball league now. I wouldn't be surprised but what the Redlegs'll be in it before long. Maybe we can go up to Chicago someday and watch the Redlegs play the White Stockings."

They rode in silence for a while. Matt reviewed in his mind the events of the past few days. Thoughts of the murder of Major Wilson kept coming back to him. Finally, he broke the silence.

"Uncle Claude, you know somethin' that bothers me?"

His uncle turned to look at him. "What's that?"

"The way Jesse James said 'Vengeance is mine saith the Lord.' Like somehow that made it all right for him to murder the Major."

Uncle Claude nodded. "I know what you mean. Some people seem to think they can justify anything by quoting the Bible. And terrible things are done in the name of vengeance." He turned to look at Matt again. "Do you know who Sir Francis Bacon was?"

Matt shook his head. "No, sir."

"Well, Sir Francis Bacon was a very wise man who lived about the same time as William Shakespeare. He wrote many things, and one of his essays was called 'Of Revenge.' In it he said, 'Revenge is a kind of wild justice, which the more man's nature runs to, the more ought law to weed it out.' That's something to think about, Matt. I hope you never have cause to think about revenge, but if you do, I hope you remember what Bacon said and pay heed to it."

Matt nodded. "Yes, sir, I will. But I admit I'm still pretty angry over what that James feller's jokin' almost did to me. And what kind of a man is he, anyway, to kill a man like he did over nothin' at all?"

"That wasn't the first time he's done that. Only a couple of years ago he murdered a bank cashier at a little place called Gallatin, just because he thought the poor fellow looked like a Yankee officer whose troops killed Bloody Bill Anderson during the war."

Matt thought for a while. "Uncle Claude, it just don't make sense. How can a man act like that?"

Uncle Claude shook his head. "I don't know, Matt. I don't think anyone knows. Just bad seed, I guess. But Jesse James isn't the only one. There's been a bunch of them. Especially out West. They start out young, and for the most part, they're loners. They don't care a thing about anyone but themselves. And they haven't got an ounce of conscience among the lot of them."

The train rumbled on. Matt settled back in the seat. The warm June afternoon and the swaying of the coach lulled him. He hadn't slept well the night before. By the time they reached Sedalia, his head was nodding. The stop there was brief. Within a short time of leaving Sedalia, he succumbed to the monotony of the clacking rails and slumbered.

When he awoke, it was late afternoon. They were just pulling into Kansas City. Uncle Claude was shaking him by the shoulder. "We're here. Time to wake up."

Matt sat up and looked out the window. Everything looked strange. "Where are we, Uncle Claude?"

"This is the Missouri Pacific station. You came into the Kansas Pacific station before. We won't be needing either one here much longer. Another couple of years and we'll have a brand new union station for all the trains to come into."

"By the way, what was all that about the men from Lawrence? Why were they so angry with me?"

"You don't know about that?"

"No, sir."

"They were a bunch from Lawrence, Kansas, mostly from the university there, I think, here for some kind of meeting.

When they heard a member of the James gang had been taken, they could hardly wait to lay hands on him to make up for what happened at Lawrence during the war. You see, Quantrill and his bully boys raided the town and killed more than 200 of the citizens. Frank James was one of those murderers, and that's why people from Lawrence are so anxious to do him and any of his cronies in."

"I guess I was pretty lucky they didn't get me, wasn't I?"

Uncle Claude nodded. "You were indeed, Matt. But you can forget all that now. Aunt Milly'll have a nice supper waiting for us, and you'll have a comfortable bed to get a good night's sleep in. Tomorrow we'll get you some new clothes."

They were in luck. Two coaches stood waiting for business across from the station. They climbed into the first one, and Uncle Claude gave the driver instructions.

Fifteen minutes later they were rolling down a broad, tree-lined avenue. The homes on each side of the thoroughfare were, for the most part, white, two story wooden buildings. Large, green lawns surrounded each home.

The cab slowed, and Uncle Claude called out. "There it is, driver. The second house on the right."

While his uncle paid the driver, Matt looked up at the house. It was the largest on the block. He had never before seen a house like it. Everything about it impressed him. The front door opened, and there was Aunt Milly beckoning to them.

"Come along, Matt. Let's see what your aunt wants. She doesn't usually come to the door like this until somebody knocks."

Matt felt the smile fading from his face. Was something wrong? Uncle Claude sounded worried. He followed his uncle up the walk to where Aunt Milly waited. Her face held no welcoming smile. In her hand she held a piece of paper.

"I'm so worried. This came about an hour ago. It's for Matt."

"Well, give it to the boy, Milly."

She handed the telegram to Matt. He stared at it as though mesmerized. He'd never received one of these bearers of bad news before. He turned to Uncle Claude. "What should I do with it?"

Uncle Claude's voice was gentle. "Let's go in the house. You can open it and read it inside."

They stepped into the foyer. Matt ripped open the envelope. His hand trembling, he had trouble focusing on the message: FATHER SHOT. COME HOME IMMEDIATELY. SORRY. WILL MEET TRAIN. LOVE, UNCLE FRANK.

9

When the train rounded the final curve into Abilene, Matt, leaning out a window, spotted Uncle Frank and Aunt Elly waiting for him in front of the station. Before the coach even ceased rolling, unburdened by luggage, he hit the station platform running, dodging among passengers waiting to board for the train's continued run to its eventual destination, Denver.

He waved. "Uncle Frank, Uncle Frank!"

At the sound of his voice, his aunt and uncle turned and hurried toward him. As they approached, he could see they weren't smiling. Instead, they looked somber. When they met, he seized a hand of each and squeezed. "Take me to him. Right away. I've got to see him."

His aunt and uncle, faces distorted with anguish, said nothing.

"Well, come on. Where is he? At the ranch or Doc

Wiggins's place?"

His uncle laid a hand on his shoulder. "Matt—"

He grabbed his uncle by the elbow and shook him. "Don't just stand there. Say somethin', for God's sake! How is he? Is he hurt bad?"

Uncle Frank put his hand up and released his elbow from, Matt's grip. "Matt, he's—"

"No! Oh no! Don't say it. You're wrong. You gotta be. This is no time for jokin', Uncle Frank. He can't be..." He turned to Aunt Elly. "Aunt Elly, make him stop. Why's he sayin' this?"

Aunt Elly laid her hand on his arm. Her voice was gentle. "Matt, he's gone. He died last night."

Perplexed, brow furrowed, Matt squinted. Aunt Elly wouldn't lie. He was sure of it. But what did she just say? A swelling rose in his chest. He felt weak. His vision blurred. He couldn't see clearly. Suddenly a tremendous sob broke from his throat. "Oh, Jesus, Jesus. No! Noooo."

People stared. He shook off Aunt Elly's hand and wrenched himself free from Uncle Frank's grip. He turned and stumbled away. Three steps, then blundered into the side of the station. Unseeing, he leaned his head against the sooty wood. For a few moments, he stood there quietly, then twisted and slowly slid down the side of the building. He came to rest sitting on the platform.

His aunt and uncle hovered over him, faces contorted with grief, uncertain what to do. One more shuddering sob tore from his chest. He looked up at them. "Where is he?"

Uncle Frank reached down and helped him to his feet.

"He's at Mr. Langley's place. The funeral's tomorrow afternoon. I already sent a telegram to Claude and Milly. I reckon they'll be here on the morning train. 'Fraid there won't be time for anybody to make it from Cincy."

Aunt Elly brushed her soft, cool palm across Matt's forehead. "We plan to bury him out at our place if that's all right with you, Matt."

He looked into her face, puzzled, trying to grasp her

meaning. Then he shrugged and nodded. "All right. Now, take me to him, please."

The world seemed distant. Like an automaton, he followed them to the buckboard Uncle Frank had waiting out front. He climbed in the back seat; Aunt Elly sat beside him. Uncle Frank set off for the undertaker's establishment. He allowed the horse to proceed at a slow walk.

Aunt Elly took Matt's hand in her own. "Matt, Frank and I'll do anything we can to help you. We want you to know that. And you'll always have a home with us."

He nodded. "Sure, fine." What was she nattering on about? He couldn't take it in. He stared straight ahead. After a few moments, he made himself ask, "What happened?"

"We're not sure. Your father left for work yesterday as usual. Far's we know, he went straight to the shop."

He turned and looked at her. "Didn't anybody see anything?"

"Mrs. Lafferty did. She runs the laundry just across the street and about three doors down."

"I know. I think she and Paw were kinda…friends."

Aunt Elly looked surprised. "Well, anyway, she says she heard a commotion in the shop about ten o'clock. She says a hammer came flyin' right through the front window, and then she heard two shots. Couple of minutes later, a feller came bustin' out and jumped on his horse and went tearin' away around the corner onto Texas Street."

"What'd he look like?"

"We don't know. She says she never really got a good look at him."

"How'd you hear about it?"

"Mrs. Lafferty roused the whole neighborhood, and when the marshal finally got there, he sent his deputy out to tell us. Frank hurried right on in."

"Was Paw still alive when Uncle Frank got there?"

"He was still alive but unconscious. One shot took him in the chest and one got him in the head." She sighed. "He never did regain consciousness, so he wasn't able to tell us a thing.

He died about four o'clock this mornin'."

"The marshal do anything?"

"Not really. Wasn't anything he could do. Course, he didn't get there till half an hour after Mrs. Lafferty found your Paw lyin' behind the counter in the shop. They say he was off playin' cards somewheres, and it took a good while to find him. By that time, the feller that'd done it had probably hightailed it outta town."

Matt nodded. "More'n likely."

Matt's aunt studied him closely. He seemed to be taking the whole thing remarkably calmly. "The shop was all tore up. Looked like there'd been a tremendous scrap. All the money was gone, although I don't think John had much in the shop. John's own gun was missing, too. We think the bandit got it."

Matt nodded again but stared straight ahead. His aunt peered closely at him once more. "You all right?"

He shrugged but said nothing.

"You sure? You've hardly said a word. We thought you'd be all tore up over this."

He turned and looked at her. "Aunt Elly, I just don't know what to say. It just don't seem real. I feel…empty. I just can't believe what you're sayin'."

She pursed her lips.

"Oh, I know you ain't lyin'," he hastened to assure her. "I don't mean that. But I just don't see how God could let somethin' like this happen. My brain tells me it must be so, but I just can't accept it."

The buckboard drew up in front of the undertaking parlor.

Frank Brinkman turned to his nephew. "Ready, Matt?"

Matt took a deep breath and nodded. He climbed down from the carriage and then turned back to offer his hand to his aunt. She followed him down, and the three of them proceeded into the funeral home.

John Ritter'd been well known and well liked by his neighbors. Several people stood about the room where the body was on view, conversing in hushed tones. When Matt entered, the people drew back to make way for him. With his aunt on one side and his uncle on the other, he approached the coffin. He forced himself to look down at the body.

"Oh, my God!" he cried out. "It's Paw. It's really Paw."

He reached into the coffin and ran his fingers across his father's forehead. The flesh was cold, doughy. Paw's face remained empty, unmoved. The hands folded across the chest lay still.

"Paw, Paw," he whispered, "it's me, Matt. Say somethin'."

A small, round hole was visible just behind his father's left ear. Unbelieving, Matt turned and looked at his uncle. His uncle slowly shook his head. Matt turned to his aunt. Tears trickled down her cheeks. She threw her arms around him and hugged him. Gently he brought his arms up and disengaged her embrace.

He turned back to his father's corpse. How could God let this happen? Paw never harmed a soul in his whole life. He again slowly ran his fingers along his father's brow, straightening a lock of hair that had been disturbed. What am I goin' to do without him? Eyes blurring with tears, he turned and shuffled to a chair near the head of the coffin. Slowly he slumped into it. He stared straight ahead; tears began to flow more copiously.

Uncle Frank placed a hand on his shoulder. "Matt, let's go home for a while."

He shook his head. "I don't want to. You go. I want to stay here with Paw."

Aunt Elly pulled his head against her waist and leaned over him. "I know, Matt, but you need something to eat and some fresh clothes. Let's go home for a little while. We'll come back later, I promise you."

Expressionless, he looked up at her. She took his hand and drew him gently to his feet. Without protest, looking neither right nor left, he followed her from the funeral parlor.

On the ride home he said nothing, merely staring into space. Again Aunt Elly held his hand, but he didn't respond. Seeing Paw's body had brought him face to face with reality. He couldn't deny it.

When Uncle Frank brought the buckboard to a halt in front of the house, Matt climbed down and, without a backward glance, rushed into the house. Weary, sick at heart, he climbed the stairs to the room he'd shared with Paw.

Closing the door, he looked around at the myriad of things reminding him of his father. The eight-shot revolver Paw had so lovingly crafted for him sat on top of the dresser. He picked it up and idly spun the empty cylinder.

Suddenly tears flooded down his face. Ugly sobs racked his body. He flung himself face down on the bed. He lay there, unwilling and unable to stem the flow. The tears, unchecked, soaked the coverlet. He felt lost; the world was empty.

He had no idea how long he lay there. At some point, exhausted by the emotional wringer he'd been through in the last few days, he fell asleep. When he awoke, dusk had fallen. Aunt Elly stood by his bed. He rolled on his back and looked up at her. In her hand, she held a damp washcloth.

She sank down beside him on the bed. Her cool hand brushed the hair back from his eyes. Then she bathed his face with the cool, moist cloth.

The events of the previous forty-eight hours came rushing back. A shuddering sob escaped his lips. Tears once again welled up. He rolled toward his aunt and buried his face in her lap. She ran her fingers through his hair and massaged the back of his neck.

"Matt, I've got a nice, warm bath drawn for you. I know you feel terrible, but you'll feel better if you come down and take a bath and put on some clean clothes. I've got some food ready, too."

He rolled on his back again and looked up at her. He brushed his sleeve across his eyes to mop up the tears.

"I'm not hungry."

"Well, maybe not, but you've got to eat somethin' if you're goin' back to the funeral parlor."

He heaved a sigh and stared up at the ceiling. After a moment he struggled to a standing position. "All right. I guess you're right."

They buried John Ritter under a giant oak tree about fifty yards from the house. He'd loved sitting under that tree of a spring or summer evening, whittling or just talking with the three of them.

They'd moved the coffin to Uncle Frank's church, so the funeral officially began there. Black clouds gathered overhead, threatening a thunder storm, as though God Himself were displeased at the turn events had taken. Despite flickering lightning and distant thunder, though, the Almighty granted the mourners a reprieve, and the rain held off until John Ritter was laid to rest.

Uncle Frank conducted the service. Uncle Claude and Aunt Milly arrived from Kansas City in time to share a front pew with Matt and Aunt Elly. A crowd filled the small church to overflowing. A good many mourners stood outside.

As the service drew to a close, Uncle Frank gave the eulogy. Then Matt surprised himself by getting to his feet. He addressed himself to his uncle. "Uncle Frank, I'd like to say a few words."

Uncle Frank looked equally surprised but nodded and said, "Why, sure, Matt. Go right ahead."

Matt turned and faced the assemblage. "John Ritter was my Paw, and I'll always consider myself one of the luckiest people on earth, because he was my Paw. He was the kindest, gentlest man I ever knew or will know, but he was an honest, hardworkin' man, too. And a brave man. My Maw died when I was only four, and Paw worked hard to see to it I had a good bringin' up. I loved my Paw, and I don't know what I'll do without him."

He paused for a moment and then turned and looked at Uncle Frank. "Uncle Frank, I've heard you say many times right here in this church that the Lord has a plan and that nothing happens that the Lord hasn't planned for. Well, I sure don't understand that now. I don't see how the Lord could let some useless, dirty son of a bitch kill my Paw. I know we all gotta die, but Paw was took long before his time. Maybe I'll come to understand it someday, but I sure don't right now, I can tell you that."

Matt's eyes narrowed, and he turned again to face the front pew. "Uncle Claude, I know what you said about revenge just a couple of days ago. About how that Sir Francis Bacon feller said revenge is a kind of wild justice that the law oughtta weed out. But, damn it, it *is* justice, and I think my poor Paw needs justice done. I know I sure do.

"Maybe you and that Bacon feller are right, but I can tell you I'm not at all sure about that. I don't know what I'm goin' to do, but I can guarantee I'm goin' to do some serious thinkin' on the subject."

Matt stopped talking and looked around. He suddenly felt embarrassed. The crowd, clearly surprised by his outburst, stared at him. He felt his face burn and shrugged.

"Well, that's all I guess." He nodded to Uncle Frank and sat down.

Matt spent the next three days wandering around the farm. He didn't set foot in town; the gunsmith shop remained closed. He had little to say to his aunt and uncle. Aunt Elly tried to tempt him with his favorite dishes, but he merely picked at her best efforts. Uncle Frank tried to engage him in conversation, but he only replied with mere grunts or monosyllables. At night, he slept fitfully, often getting up to wander around the house or sit in the moonlight beside his father's grave.

"Frank, I swear my heart goes out to that poor boy," said Aunt Elly as, on the third night, she and her husband prepared for bed. "I wish I could do something to ease his pain."

"I do, too, Elly. I do, too. Seems like the bastard who killed John has just about done in poor Matt as well. The boy was such a happy-go-lucky sort till this happened. I could always get through to him, but now it's as though he's a different person."

His wife slipped into her nightgown and nodded. "I know just what you mean. He used to be so polite and always had a smile for me. But now it's almost like he doesn't even know I'm there. Like my talkin' to him is just a bother. Not that I'd expect him to be happy and lighthearted after what happened to his Paw, but I don't know what to make of this. I feel so…so…helpless. Far's I know he hasn't shed a tear since that first day. He just goes around with that grim look on his face. He kinda scares me."

The next morning, the fourth day after the funeral, Matt came down to breakfast and took his usual place at the table.

"Mornin', Aunt Elly. Mornin', Uncle Frank."

They looked at each other. Matt wasn't smiling, but he didn't seem so distracted and distant as he had the previous three days, either.

"Mornin', Matt," said his uncle.

"Mornin', Matt," echoed his aunt. "What can I get you for breakfast?"

"The usual. Same as Uncle Frank's havin'. I'm kinda hungry this mornin'."

Aunt Elly smiled. "Glad to hear it." She placed a cup of coffee in front of him, then bustled over to the stove and added five more slices of bacon to those already frying in the large, black skillet. She turned back to Matt. "Two eggs?"

He nodded. "Fine, Aunt Elly."

Uncle Frank, eyebrows raised, looked at his wife. Then he turned back to Matt. "What're you fixin' to do today?"

Matt took a sip of coffee. He didn't seem to notice he hadn't ladled the usual teaspoon of sugar into it. "Well, sir, if you can spare the time, I'd like to do some target shootin'. If you can't, though, I reckon I can do some practicin' on my own."

His uncle smiled. "No, no, that's all right. I can spare the time. We can go out right after breakfast."

"Much obliged, sir. I figger I better practice my quick draws, too. I'm liable to need that one of these days."

Uncle Frank looked surprised. "Oh? Why's that?"

Aunt Elly set a plate of bacon and eggs in front of each of them and then took her own seat at the table. "I thought only gunfighters had to practice quick draws. You thinkin' of doin' some gunfightin'? Your Paw wouldn't've approved of you mixin' with that gunfightin' riff-raff, you know. For that matter, neither do your Uncle Frank and I."

Matt took a bite of bacon and some egg and chewed for a

few moments. His aunt and uncle eyed him expectantly. Finally, he looked up and sat back. He glanced from one to the other. "I know he didn't, but I been doin' some thinkin' these last few days." He paused, appearing to organize his thoughts, all the while chewing on his lower lip. Then he spoke. "Times are different now, ain't they, Aunt Elly?"

She glanced at her husband, as though inviting him to respond for her.

Uncle Frank scratched his head. "Well, yes, Matt, I guess they are. But I'm not sure they're that different. What do you have in mind, boy?"

Matt took a deep breath. "That's what I want to talk to you and Aunt Elly about. First of all, though, I want you to know I love both of you. But I wish you wouldn't call me boy anymore. Now that Paw's gone, I hafta to be a man, and it'll help if you treat me like one."

Frank and Elly looked at each other. Again he answered for both of them. "Fair enough, Matt. Now, what do you want to talk about?"

"Well, I been doin' some serious thinkin' about what Uncle Claude said about revenge and what the Bible says about turnin' the other cheek."

His aunt, sounding relieved, interrupted. "I'm glad to hear you say that, Matt."

"You are? Well, there's another way to look at things, you know. The Golden Rule says do unto others as you'd have 'em do unto you, doesn't it, Uncle Frank?"

His uncle nodded.

Matt's voice took on a hard edge. "Well, then, when that rascal killed my Paw, accordin' to the Golden Rule, he was askin' to be killed himself, wasn't he? And I aim to oblige him."

His uncle's eyebrows went up. His aunt drew back, then said, "You sure of that, Matt?"

He nodded. "I'm sure. The only problem is I gotta find him first."

His uncle took a swallow of coffee, then said. "You don't

want to get the wrong man, you know."

Again Matt nodded. "I know I don't, but the sooner I start lookin', the sooner I'll find him."

"He could be most anywhere by now," his uncle reminded him. "How do you plan to start lookin'?"

"Well, first, I gotta get as good an idea as to what he looks like as I can."

"Nobody saw him, you know, exceptin' Mrs. Lafferty."

"All right, then, that's where I'll start. I'm goin' into town later this mornin' to straighten up the shop and show people John Ritter and Son's still in business. Then I'll see what more Mrs. Lafferty can tell me about that owlhoot."

10

From outside, the shop looked in good shape. Uncle Frank or someone—maybe Mr. Long, the landlord—had patched the broken window through which Mrs. Lafferty had said a hammer came flying. Even inside, the damage was less than he'd feared. Tools were strewn about on the floor, the back workbench lay on its side, and two of the three chairs in the place were overturned. The third had been reduced to kindling, as had the high stool Matt perched on when working at the front workbench.

Every drawer of Paw's roll-top stood open, but the desk appeared undamaged. The cash drawer under the counter hung open, too, a few coins scattered about the floor under it. In the back of the shop, the forge stood cold but unscathed.

Matt picked up one of the two undamaged chairs and

placed it on its feet. Then he sank into it and gazed around. Clearly Paw'd put up a tremendous battle before the intruder had ended the struggle with gunshots.

Paw's own gun belt and holster still hung on the peg on the wall where he customarily put it each day before starting work. But where was Paw's gun? The holster yawned empty. Paw had prized that gun. A small, engraved silver plate on the bottom of the handle identified it as the first prize in a shooting contest he'd won years ago in Cincy.

Why hadn't Paw just given the bastard what he wanted? Maybe he'd still be alive today. But Matt knew why. Paw might've favored nonviolence, but if pushed too far, his temper'd get the best of him, and he'd be a holy terror.

Matt'd never forgotten when he was about ten seeing his father just about kill a bigger man who'd been beating a dog. Matt shared his father's love of animals and admired his courage in attacking the larger man. Things like that didn't happen often, but when they did, Paw was really a sight to behold. For days after, though, he'd be remorseful.

Shaking his head regretfully, Matt got to his feet and set to work putting things to rights. It didn't take him long to straighten up the furniture, and the tools were quickly restored to their proper places. He pushed drawers back in; the papers scattered about the shop, he gathered up and shoved into the desk for later study. The remains of the smashed chair and stool went into a corner in the back of the shop to be used later for kindling. He'd have to order a new stool from Mr. Jasper, he reminded himself.

All that done, he stopped and surveyed the shop. It didn't look too bad. At least it was fit to resume business in. Still no sign of Paw's gun, though. The murderer probably took it with him. Maybe even shot Paw with his own gun. Matt grimaced angrily at the thought.

Satisfied he'd done as much as he could for the present, he hung a sign on the door to inform visitors he'd be back later and headed across the street, three doors down to Mrs. Lafferty's laundry.

Paw'd often talked about the widow Lafferty. Sometimes Matt thought she might be more than just a friend to Paw. He suspected that when Paw went out of an evening it was often to visit the laundress. And not just to have his clothes laundered.

Paw'd said she was about his own age, thirty-eight, and he'd considered her a fine looking woman. At five eight, she was only an inch shorter than Paw and weighed maybe about 140. Surprisingly, her reddish-blond hair and fair complexion had somehow managed to withstand the assaults of the pitiless hot Kansas sun.

Her first husband had been a corporal at Fort Riley. They'd lived in their own log shanty on Soapsuds Row, and like all other laundresses on army posts, she had official standing and drew regular rations, fuel, and medical care from the army. Her laundress services were paid for by the soldiers at an official rate prescribed by the army. Some months she made as much as forty dollars.

When her husband met his death while on a foray against the Comanches, she decided to open her own business in the then newly booming Abilene. She was industrious and had quickly built up a loyal clientele. Matt suspected she had reciprocated his father's admiration, and she always seemed friendly toward Matt.

When he opened the door to her establishment, a bell clanged above his head. "I'm out back," he heard her shout.

He found her in the shade of a small tree, up to her elbows in suds in a wooden washtub.

"Mornin', Mrs. Lafferty."

She looked up and ceased scrubbing the shirt spread on her washboard. "Mornin', Matt."

She straightened up and began drying her hands and arms on a towel. Her face somber, she said, "Awful sorry about your Paw. Never knew a finer man in my life."

He nodded. "Thank you. Can I ask you a few questions? I understand you saw the dirty son of a bitch—beggin' your pardon—that killed him."

She waved her hand. "No need to ask my pardon. I've already called the bastard names I wouldn't want to repeat to a nice young feller like you."

"You really did see him then?"

She shrugged. "Oh, yes. That I did. 'Fraid I can't be of much help, though. I didn't really get much of a look at him. It all happened too fast."

"Well, I don't know. Maybe you can. Maybe you saw more'n you realize."

"Don't know's I follow you, but if you want to ask some questions, just you go right ahead."

"Thank you. You see, I been doin' a lot of thinkin' about this, and I believe maybe you can help. First of all, if you're willin', I'd like to try somethin'."

She nodded.

"Good. Now, just close your eyes and try to go back and see what happened that day."

"I see. Kinda relive it, you mean?"

"That's the ticket."

"Might help if I stood in the door of my shop like I did that day."

Her willingness to cooperate encouraged him, helped fuel his optimism.

"Good idea. It might at that."

They went through the shop, and she took her position in the doorway, looking out toward the gunsmith shop.

"All right, my eyes are closed."

"Fine. Now, try to go back in your mind. It's that day. What time is it?"

"Just about what it is now, ten o'clock."

"Remember how the air felt? Was it warm?"

"Oh yes. Warmer'n today. Downright hot, in fact."

"Good. Now, your eyes still closed?"

She nodded.

"What do you hear?"

She screwed up her face, eyes shut tightly. "A yell from your Paw's shop. And breakin' glass. Now a shot. Then another. Now silence, except for the sounds of folks goin' about their business over on Texas Street."

"That's fine, just fine. Now, eyes still closed, what do you see?"

"Just the street. A horse's tied to the hitchin' post in front of your Paw's place. It's a big horse…it's…it's brown, I think. Yes, that's right, it's brown. Now, a hammer's sailin' right through your Paw's front window. That was the breakin' glass I heard. The horse rears up. Shots scared him, I think. Nothin' happenin' right now. Oh, here comes a feller bustin' outta your Paw's shop."

Matt had trouble containing himself. The experiment was working better than he could've hoped. "All right, now, keep your eyes closed. Concentrate real hard. Reeeal hard."

She nodded again.

"Now, what's he look like?"

"A man. Just a man. Kinda dirty, though. Like he'd been on the trail for a good while. Clothes sure need a good launderin'." She turned to Matt and, grinning, opened her eyes. "Course I'd be sure to notice a thing like that, wouldn't I?"

He tried to hide his frustration. "I know, but close your eyes. What else do you see?"

She screwed her eyes shut again. "Clothes are ragged, too, now that I think of it."

"How big's he? How tall

"Oh…about six feet."

"How heavy?"

"He's big. Must weigh all of two hundred pounds, maybe more."

"We're gettin' there. Now, what color's his shirt? And has he got a beard?"

"No. No beard. He needs a shave but no real beard. And his shirt…his shirt…is…now I see it! His shirt's red, bright red…and it's torn in back. The left sleeve's ripped, too. And his pants are green, I think. Hard to tell, though, they're so dirty."

"You're doin' great, Mrs. Lafferty, just great. Now, he's out the door. What's he do?"

She clasped her hands together and hunched her shoulders.

"He stops and looks toward Texas Street. He don't see nothin', leastwise there ain't nothin' to see. He's got a gun in his hand. Kind of a long barrel. I'm afraid he'll see me, so I duck back in my own door, into the shadow, but I can still see him."

"Then what?"

She faded back into her own doorway as presumably she'd done that day. "He's glancin' this way, but he don't see me. Leastwise, I don't think he did." She turned toward Matt and opened her eyes. "I was scared to death, I tell you, that he'd come after me."

"I understand, ma'am, but now please close your eyes and go back to that day. Now, what's happening?"

She did as he asked, squeezing her eyes shut and facing toward the Ritters' door. "He's climbin' on the horse…"

He interrupted. "What kinda saddle's on the horse?"

She shrugged. "I don't know. I don't know one saddle from another. Sorry."

"That's all right, but what's he doin' now?"

"He's climbin' on the horse, but," she sounded excited, "but, now he's gettin' off again. A gust of wind just blew his hat off. He's mad, hoppin' mad. He has to chase it a couple of steps, still holdin' on to the horse's reins." She laughed. "Such language! Now he's got it, but you know what? His hair is black, but he's got a gray streak about three, four inches wide runnin, all the way back from his forehead. Like the streak on a skunk's back."

"That's interestin'. Now, tell me about his hat."

"His hat?"

"Yep. His hat. Uncle Frank says a cowboy's hat's his proudest personal possession, kinda his identity. So what's his hat like? Can you see it? Has it got a tall crown or is it flat? Is it a sombrero, what they call a sugar-loaf or is it Texas style? Or maybe it's plainsman style. Or does it have a Montana peak on it?

She shook her head and smiled. "None of those. It was a bowler."

"A bowler?"

"Yep. That's what they call it in England. Over here you call it a derby, I guess."

Matt grinned. "Well, what do you know? What color is it?"

"It's...brown. Yep, that's it. Brown. He's wearin' a brown bowler."

"He's a white man, I suppose? Not black or Mexican?"

"Oh, he's white. Dirty as he is, I can see he's a white man."

"Good. We're beginnin' to get a picture, ain't we?"

She smiled and nodded.

"Now, you're still concentratin', what about his face? He needed a shave you said, but did you see any scars on him?"

She shook her head.

He thought for a moment. "How about his nose? Is it small? Maybe a pug nose? Or crooked?"

She remained silent, concentrating, her tongue peeking out of the corner of her mouth. "Nooo," she said slowly, "now that you mention it, it's not small. No siree, it's big. In fact, the biggest nose I ever saw on a man."

"Now we're makin' progress. What's his voice like?"

She shrugged. "Nothin' special."

"Well, did he sound like a southerner or a Britisher or an Irisher?"

"Well...now that you mention it, he might've been from the South. I can't say for sure. I only heard him cussin' when his hat blew off."

She frowned. "You know, I almost forgot, but now I recall thinkin' at the time that he sounded hoarse, like he'd been doin' a lot of yellin', if you know what I mean."

She went on to tell Matt how the killer had galloped off and disappeared around the corner of Texas Street. She said she'd never seen him before that day nor since. She described running over to the gun shop and finding Paw lying on the floor unconscious. She'd run screaming from the shop, alerting others to the shooting. Matt asked a few more questions, but she had nothing more to add to her description of the culprit.

"Well, Mrs. Lafferty, I surely do want to thank you for all your help. It's a good beginnin'."

"Think nothin' of it, Matt. If I can do anything else, don't hesitate to ask. I sure liked your Paw, and I'd give a lot to catch the dirty, murderin' spalpeen that shot him."

"Glad to see you got your appetite back, Matt," said Aunt Elly, passing him the potatoes that night at dinner.

He smiled. "It's your cookin' that does it."

"How're things at the shop?" asked his uncle.

"Well, I got it pretty well straightened up, and I'm hopin' to get started doin' business pretty soon. Probably not as much as I'd like, though."

His uncle looked surprised. "Why do you say that?"

"Well, I was Paw's apprentice, you know. I'm not sure folks'll think I can handle things like he did. Comes to that, I'm not sure either. Then, too, I'm only plannin' to keep the shop open about four hours a day."

"Oh, why's that?"

"Well, sir, I still aim to find the rascal that killed Paw, so I gotta wander around lookin' people over."

"Did you talk to Mrs. Lafferty?"

"Yes sir. This mornin'. She was a big help. I got a much better idea what the killer looks like now."

"Too bad you don't have a picture to show folks," said Aunt Elly. "Why don't you see if you could draw a picture?"

He shrugged. "Aw, I can't draw."

"Well, maybe you could get some help."

"Some help? What do you mean?"

"You know the Maxwells, don't you?"

Matt nodded.

"Well, Jenny Maxwell can draw real well. You've seen some of her work. In fact, she drew that likeness of me your uncle has hangin' on our bedroom wall."

"But she was lookin' at you when she drew that."

Aunt Elly laughed. "I know, but she's pretty clever with her pencils and crayons. It occurs to me if you had her talk to Mrs. Lafferty, she might be able to come up with a likeness of the feller from Mrs. Lafferty's description of him. She could draw somethin', and Mrs. Lafferty could say whether it was close to what she saw. If it wasn't, she could change it a little and then keep on changin' it till it fit what Mrs. Lafferty saw."

Uncle Frank chuckled. "By golly, Elly, that's a pretty smart idea."

"Well, don't sound so surprised, Frank Brinkman. I have smart ideas every now and then."

Uncle Frank grinned. "I know you do, Elly. After all, you married me." He turned to Matt. "Why don't you give it a try, Matt?"

Matt thought for a moment. It might just work. It'd sure help to have something to show people when he asked them about the rascal. He grinned. "You're right. Why not give it a try? Sure couldn't hurt. I'll get right over to see Jenny in the mornin'." He got up and went around to his aunt; he leaned down and kissed her on the cheek.

"Thanks for the great idea."

The following morning, before going into town, Matt saddled a horse and rode the three miles to the Maxwell farm.

A slender, dark haired woman, Jenny Maxwell greeted him warmly. "Well, Matt, it's good to see you again. I hear you haven't been out much since you got back to town."

"That's so, Mrs. Maxwell, but I've got a mission in life now, and I'm hopin' you can help me."

She looked surprised. "Well, certainly, Matt."

She invited him in, and they sat at the kitchen table. She insisted that Matt have a doughnut and a cup of coffee. He explained about his vow to find his father's killer and the idea Aunt Elly'd come up with to get a likeness of the killer.

"Well, of course, Matt. We can give it a try if it's all right with Mrs. Lafferty, although," her face took on a skeptical look, "I'm not at all sure I can do anything really useful."

"Well, ma'am, I think it's worth a shot, and like I told Aunt Elly, it sure can't hurt anything."

She explained she couldn't do anything that day, but she'd be willing to go with him the following morning. He promised to make arrangements with Mrs. Lafferty and told Mrs. Maxwell he'd call for her to take her into town.

Next morning, with Uncle Frank's permission, Matt hitched a team to the buckboard and drove to the Maxwell farm. George Maxwell took time off to wish them luck, and Matt and Jenny Maxwell set out for town. An hour later, they were in Mrs. Lafferty's laundry.

"Matt explained yesterday what you hope to do, Mrs. Maxwell, so I'm just goin' to close the place till we're done." She locked the front door and hung a sign in it advising customers she wouldn't be available the rest of the morning. Then she led them to the back room where she poured them each a cup of coffee. "Now, how do we start?"

"Well," said Jenny Maxwell, "let's all sit down and make ourselves comfortable. I've brought a supply of pencils and paper along with some charcoal." She laid the items on the table. The morning was cool, but she rolled up her sleeves. "Now, first, let's start with a description of the man as a whole. Later I'll try to work with details of his face."

"Well," said Mrs. Lafferty, "since I talked with Matt, I've been doin' some thinkin' and maybe I've got a little clearer picture in my mind of the rascal."

She described once again a black haired man about six feet in height and weighing around 200 pounds. She again described his clothes and hat but this time added that his pant legs had been stuffed into his boot tops. She also brought to mind that he'd walked with a slight limp, as though, she said, his right leg was a tiny bit shorter than his left.

"Like a trooper I once knew when I was still workin' on Soapsuds Row at Fort Riley."

Patiently Jenny listened and then attempted to reproduce on paper what Mrs. Lafferty had described. When she'd completed her pencil strokes, she'd present the likeness for Mrs. Lafferty's comments. "That looks a bit like him, but now that I think of it, his sleeves were rolled up, and I could see he had hairy, muscular forearms. Kinda like a blacksmith."

Jenny rubbed out a few lines and then sketched a few more. She showed it to the laundress again who smiled and nodded. "That's better, but he was wearin' wide, black braces, what you call suspenders."

Jenny made the corrections. Again Judy Lafferty nodded, then wrinkled her brow. "And, you know, I think I recall a pipe stickin' out of his shirt pocket—or no, wait a minute. It was a vest! He was wearin' a dirty, red vest. It was open but almost blended with his red shirt. That's why I didn't remember it at first."

Again Jenny revised the sketch. Eventually, the laundress declared herself satisfied. "All right," said the artist, "now let's see what we can do with the face." She turned to Matt who had been watching the whole process with fascination. "You know, this is kind of fun." She turned back to Mrs. Lafferty. "Now describe his face as best you can, and we'll go from there."

Mrs. Lafferty thought for a moment and then began to talk, eyes closed. Jenny listened carefully and then made a few strokes with charcoal. She showed the portrait to the witness. "How's that?"

Mrs. Lafferty knit her brow. "His nose was a little bigger, I think. And kinda squashed, as though someone had mashed it." She turned to Matt. "I hope somebody did smash the filthy spalpeen, you know." She turned back to the drawing. "I think...his...jaw was just a bit wider. But you're gettin' there. I really think you're gettin' there."

Slowly, patiently the process continued. "His eyebrows were a bit bushier, too. There was a big mole on his left cheek." One revision followed another; bit by bit, Judy Lafferty grew more satisfied with what Jenny Maxwell produced. Finally, after almost two hours effort, she gasped and covered her mouth with her hand. Her eyes widened. "That's him! That's the dirty limb of Satan. As far's I can recall, that's him."

Jenny drew a deep breath and wiggled her shoulders.

"Well, now, isn't that something? Who'd of guessed I could fashion a likeness of a man I've never seen."

Matt looked at her with awe. "It's miracle, that's what it is. I don't know how to thank you. This'll be a tremendous help."

Jenny smiled, obviously pleased, both with the results of her efforts and with Matt's gratitude. "I'll make another clean copy for you at home. I just hope it helps catch the ruffian."

Matt's face lit up. "Oh, I'm sure it will. I can show this to people, and they'll know just what I'm talkin' about." He stopped for a moment, embarrassed. Then he took a deep breath. "I know it's askin' a lot, Mrs. Maxwell, but would it be too much to ask you to make several copies of this?"

Her eyes widened. Then she laughed. "Be glad to, Matt. It'll take a while, but if you think it'll help catch him, I'll be glad to. As a matter of fact, though, maybe the people who make wanted posters could make some from this drawing. See what they say at the *Chronicle*. They ought to know what can be done by a printer."

He nodded. "That's a fine idea. I'll do it for sure." He turned to Mrs. Lafferty. "And Mrs. Lafferty, I surely do want to thank you for all your help. Without you, I wouldn't've had the slightest idea who I was lookin' for."

The laundress smiled at him. "I'm happy to help, Matt. Like I told you the other day, I thought a lot of your Paw."

He nodded once more. "I wish I could repay you somehow."

"You can." Her voice grew fierce. "When you catch the miserable reprobate, cut off a piece of his hide and send it to me."

11

The sound of someone coming in the front door caught Matt's attention. He glanced up. "Well, howdy, Mr. Harte." He laid down the pistol he was working on.

The drummer carried his coat slung over one arm. He fanned himself with his hat and mopped his brow and neck with his handkerchief. "My God, but it's hot!"

Matt grinned. "'Fraid that's the way it gets in Kansas in July. Just wait'll August gets here."

"I can wait. Why, I swear, it's so hot out there if a fellow died and went to hell, he'd wire back for blankets."

Matt chuckled. "That's about right, ain't it? It's why I got the front and back door open. Don't do a whole lotta good, though, does it?"

"Maybe not, but at least you're out of the sun in here. That sun's downright murderous out there. Don't see how you folks stand it, but I suppose you get used to it after a year or two."

"Can't say's we get used to it, but we manage to bear with it." Matt walked over to the rolltop and sank into his chair. He pointed to another chair. "Have a seat, sir."

With a sigh, Burke Harte sat down. "Would you happen to have some water around, Matt?"

Matt sprang to his feet, embarrassed at failing to offer his guest a drink without his having to ask. "Why, surely, Mr. Harte." He hurried to pour a drink for the drummer. "Here you go."

Harte gratefully took the tall glass and quickly drained it. "Whooee, that's better!"

Matt resumed his seat. "Quite a while since you been her, sir."

"Two months, give or take a few days. Didn't plan to be here for another month," his face grew somber, "but I just heard about your daddy a week or so ago. Felt I ought to come by and give you my sympathies. How'd it happen, anyway?"

Matt winced. "He was murdered, but I'd rather not talk about it."

"Murdered! Oh. Well...I...ah...like I said, I'm sorry, really sorry. John Ritter was more than just a customer to me. I always thought of him as a friend. I know how you must feel."

"Do you?"

Harte drew back, obviously startled by Matt's fierce tone.

Matt threw up his hands. "I'm sorry. I shouldn't snarl at you. I appreciate your coming to see me. Thank you."

The drummer nodded. "How's the business going?"

Matt sighed. "Not too good, I'm afraid. There's another gunsmith in town who does work for the Frontier Store, that's the general store that's been here a good many years."

Harte nodded. "I sell 'em supplies, now and then."

"Paw worked for 'em when we first came to Abilene. Then, when Paw opened this place, the store owner hired another feller to handle his business. Actually, Paw had more business than they did, but I guess folks figger I'm not the gunsmith my Paw was. They're right, too, but I do a good job."

"If you're John Ritter's son, I'm sure you do. But there

weren't many around like your daddy."

Matt shrugged. "What worries me is what happens next year. Uncle Frank says there won't be any herds comin' to Abilene. He and his group of farmers are goin' to warn the drovers to stay away. Besides, they'll probably only go as far's Newton, anyway."

Burke Harte nodded. "Yep. I'm afraid that's right. But tell me. You still playing baseball?"

Matt sighed. "Yep. Didn't much feel like it, but Fourth of July we played a team from Junction City. Beat 'em, too. Six to nothin'. I struck out ten of their batters. Didn't walk none of 'em, neither." He shrugged. "Folks say I got quite a fast ball. And it's gettin' better all the time."

Harte grinned. "Just like tossing a grenade, I betcha."

Puzzled, Matt squinted. "I don't follow you."

"You mean you've forgotten about those grenades I left with you last time I was here?"

Light dawned. "Jumpin' Jehoshaphat! I did, I surely did. What with everything that's been happenin', I clean forgot about 'em. They're probably here somewhere." He began rummaging in drawers and shelves. Abruptly he stopped. "No, they're not. I remember now. They're out at the farm. I tucked 'em away in my closet."

"Unarmed I hope."

Matt frowned. "Oh, sure...or at least I think they are," he added a little uncertainly. "Tell you what, Mr. Harte. Why don't you come out to the farm for dinner? I'm sure Aunt Elly wouldn't mind a guest, and we can give one a try before we eat."

Harte thought for a moment. Then he nodded. "Sure. I've been wanting to see what one of those beauties would do. If you're sure your aunt won't mind, it'll be my pleasure."

Matt gave him instructions, and they agreed to meet at five o'clock. They shook hands, and Burke Harte headed for the Drovers' Cottage and a cold beer.

Matt guessed right. Aunt Elly was happy to have company

for dinner, especially someone like Burke Harte. He came from the outside world and could furnish fairly up-to-date news about all kinds of things. Not only that, Frank had known the man slightly back in Cincinnati.

The men shook hands, and Aunt Elly passed out cool glasses of lemonade to everyone. They chatted for a few minutes, and then Matt invited Uncle Frank and their guest to come out to the field where he practiced his shooting.

"There's somethin' I'd like to show you."

He winked at their guest. He felt it better not to mention in his aunt's presence that grenades were present in the house. Earlier that afternoon, when he'd come back from town, he'd smuggled a grenade out back and hidden it.

Uncle Frank sensed something was going on but only nodded and said nothing to his wife.

"Don't be too long," she called. "Dinner'll be ready very soon."

"We won't, Aunt Elly," promised Matt.

On the way to the distant field, Uncle Frank directed a quizzical look at Matt. "You up to something?"

Matt grinned. "You'll see."

At their destination, Matt produced the grenade from its hiding place. From his pocket, he took the necessary percussion caps to arm the bomb. He handed the grenade to Burke Harte. "It's been a while since you showed this thing to Paw and me, so maybe it'd be best if you armed it."

Harte nodded and took the grenade from Matt. He explained what it was to Matt's uncle. Brow furrowed, Uncle Frank glanced at Matt. Then Harte took the percussion caps from Matt and, working carefully, armed the grenade. "There you are."

"How far had we best be from this thing when it goes off?" asked Uncle Frank.

"Well, that's a bit of a problem," Harte admitted. "I don't really know. I've never actually seen one work. But," he turned to Matt, "Matt here tells me he's a fine baseball pitcher, so I figure he can toss it far enough so's we'll be safe."

"Oh," said Uncle Frank, skepticism written on his face. "What do you think, Matt? Can you do it?"

"Why sure." He drew back his arm.

"Wait a minute!" said the gun salesman. "That thing's heavy, so don't try to throw it like a baseball. You lob it like this."

Harte stretched his arm out full length, hand cupped as though holding an imaginary grenade. Then he took a couple of quick, hopping steps sideways and brought his extended arm up high, straight over his head, and released the imaginary grenade. "There. Get the idea?"

Matt nodded. "I think so. Here," he said, "you hold it while I try a couple of practice tosses."

The drummer gingerly took the armed grenade. Matt went through a couple of practice throws. Then he turned to the salesman. "There. How'd that look?"

Burke Harte nodded. "Fine. I think you've got it."

"I sure hope he has," interjected Uncle Frank.

Matt took the grenade back, leaned to his side, arm extended like a javelin thrower, took one quick step, and abruptly halted. The grenade jiggled in his hand.

"Look out," yelled Uncle Frank.

"What in the world are you doing, Matt?" said Harte, voice shaky.

Matt, abashed, said, "I'm sorry. It just occurred to me it'd be best if you two laid flat on the ground, and after I throw it, I'll drop down, too."

The drummer nodded. "Good idea."

The two men lay down flat on the ground. When they were settled, Matt yelled, "All right, here we go."

Once again he assumed the javelin-throwing position, took two rapid sideways strides, and launched the grenade. Quickly he dropped to the ground and covered his head with his hands.

Peering out between his fingers, he saw the grenade arc through the air and plunge to the ground about thirty yards distant. On impact, a loud explosion rent the air. Dirt erupted, and bits of metal flew in all directions, a few whistling just a few feet overhead.

For a few moments they lay quiet, staring at each other. Finally Uncle Frank found his voice. He looked at Burke Harte. "Satisfied?"

The drummer nodded. "Yep. No more grenades for me. Must be why the army quit using them. If they weren't alert, you could kill as many of your own men as you did the enemy."

Matt said nothing but winked at the drummer. Just as well, he told himself, not to mention the other two grenades to Uncle Frank, let alone Aunt Elly.

"Well," said Uncle Frank, "might's well go on in to supper. Elly'll have it ready about now I expect. But let's not mention the grenade to her."

The summer dragged on. As long as gunsmithing work was available, Matt worked in the shop. In addition, whenever he could, he helped Uncle Frank around the farm. He also made a little money as the blacksmith's assistant and occasionally filled in at the livery stable. Despite all this, he wasn't making a whole lot of money. What was worse, he didn't have much time to carry on his search for the killer.

Every chance he got, he showed people the picture Jenny Maxwell'd drawn for him, and he pinned copies up around town asking anybody that recognized the rascal to get in touch with him at the gun shop. At the *Chronicle*, they managed to run off a few posters, but they weren't real clear. Altogether he had about a dozen likenesses on hand. He just wasn't sure what to do with them. Uncle Frank suggested he put a few up around the madams' establishments down in the Devil's Addition.

"A lot of cowboys and others hang out there, and while they're waitin' their turn, they might notice it. Besides, there's a good chance one of the girls might recognize the bastard. They deal a lot with hard cases, and a lot of those soiled doves've been all over the West."

Matt thought it over. It was a good idea, he had to admit, but he just didn't like the idea of going in those places and mixing with those women. Uncle Frank might speak of them with sympathy in his voice as soiled doves, but when Aunt Elly referred to them—which wasn't often and not if she thought Matt was in hearing distance—her voice had an edge to it. And she called them "whores." Aunt Elly was a kindly person and, if she spoke so harshly about people, it seemed to Matt best not to mix with them.

Not only that, he had mixed feelings about it for other reasons. More and more when he thought about women—or girls—he got nervous. He'd find himself wondering what they looked like under their skirts. He knew they were different than men, but he didn't know in exactly what way.

He knew that, generally speaking, they smelled different and a whole lot better than men—although he'd smelled a few who'd been working and sweating who smelled a lot like men. But smelling the nice ones set off a peculiar feeling in him. Usually in his privates. But at the same time, for some reason, he'd get a nervous feeling in the pit of his stomach.

Females felt different, too. He'd never thought much about it, though, till just the last few years. He'd first noticed it in school. When he was about fifteen. Miss Gregory'd lean over him to look at his paper or book, and her bosom'd push against his shoulder or sometimes his cheek. The round softness he felt and her pleasant smell gave him that funny, excited feeling in his stomach. At such times, he felt like he wanted to do something. He just didn't know exactly what. Now, when Aunt Elly hugged him and kissed him, he'd get that same feeling. Except her kissing him made it a whole lot stronger.

He wasn't totally ignorant. He knew it had something to do with sex, but he just didn't know much about sex. At times he'd wanted to ask Paw about it but somehow just couldn't bring himself to do it. In the last couple of years, Paw'd sometimes joshed him about girls, and that'd made him leery that he'd make a fool of himself if he asked about things like men and women. Or sex.

He knew a man's thing would get big and hard if they were around women or even thought about them—it'd happened to him more than once—but damned if he knew why it happened or just what he was supposed to do about it. Of course, what he usually ended up doing, out in a field or in the barn, was exciting, but for some reason he always ended up thinking he'd done something he shouldn't.

Sometimes he thought he should ask Uncle Frank to explain it all to him. Uncle Frank seemed to know a lot about women, even if he was a preacher. In fact, it was Matt's impression that Aunt Elly thought Uncle Frank knew too much about women, although why she'd object to that was more than Matt could figure out. Well, one of these days, he'd ask Uncle Frank. After all, he was a man now, or almost anyway. Time he learned about women.

And yet, in a way, he did know about women. He knew how calves and foals were born. He knew how they came into being, knew what bulls and stallions did. He just couldn't connect all that up with men and women. Or didn't want to.

Anyhow, much as he wanted to find Paw's killer, he hadn't dared go down to the Devil's Addition with his posters. Then, one night at dinner, Uncle Frank had another suggestion.

"You know, Matt, I think there's a way you could kill two birds with one stone, so to speak."

Matt looked up from his plate. "How's that, Uncle Frank?"

"Well, you've been playin' the piano for our church services and our church meetin's, so you should be used to playin' in public by now."

Aunt Elly looked at her husband with suspicion. "What've you got in mind, Frank Brinkman? Nothin' to do with that Devil's Addition you're always goin' on about, I hope."

He snorted. "Of course not. How could you think I'd suggest such a thing to the boy—I mean Matt—even if he is practically grown up?"

She pursed her lips but held her peace. Matt thought he noticed a twinkle in Uncle Frank's eye, though.

"What do you have in mind, Uncle Frank?"

"Well, I hear the night piano player down at Jake Morton's saloon up and quit yesterday. Went chasin' off to Denver after one of the dance hall girls, so I'm told. The afternoon man's goin' to take over the nighttime slot—better tips when everybody's for sure drunk—so Jake needs somebody for afternoons. How about it? Think you can handle it?"

The idea startled Matt. He'd never entertained such a notion. He chewed reflectively on a piece of pork chop for a few moments. "I don't know. What's he pay?"

"I'm not sure, but it'll be better'n anybody else. And there's another thing."

Matt stopped chewing and looked expectantly at his uncle.

"Between the girls he hires to wait on tables—none of 'em are soiled doves, not as far's I know, anyway, though you never know what they do on their own time—and—"

"Frank, you tryin' to lead the boy—pardon me, Matt—your nephew astray?" Aunt Elly sounded indignant.

"Of course not, Elly, but you got to face facts." For a change, Uncle Frank sounded a bit nettled. "Matt's not a boy any longer, and he feels he's got a job to do." He turned to Matt. "Don't you?"

"Yes, sir. But how's your idea goin' to help me find Paw's killer?"

"Well, like I was sayin', between the girls workin' there and that billiard table in the place, practically every cowboy who comes to Abilene sooner or later turns up in Jake's place."

Matt nodded. Excitement colored his voice. "I see what you mean. It'd give me a chance to look 'em over and show 'em the picture."

Uncle Frank grinned. "Right! And I was so sure you'd see it my way, I spoke to Jake today, and he says for you to come in tomorrow and give him a sample of your playin'. If he likes it, you can start right away." He turned to his wife. "So what do you think of that? Any complaints?"

She sniffed. "No, but I don't see why Jake Morton's so anxious to oblige you, Frank Brinkman. Not when you and your association's tryin' to put him and others like him out of business."

Uncle Frank winked. "Maybe he figgers if Matt's workin' in his place, he'll have some influence with me and the association."

"Will he, Uncle Frank?"

"No, he won't. No need to tell him that, though."

12

After Uncle Frank proposed the idea, Matt, the very next morning, about ten o'clock, applied for the job. The place was already busy. He gazed around the room. Mirrors on the walls made it look larger than it actually was. He glanced at the paintings hanging on the walls. They were all of nude women. He blushed and quickly looked away.

He'd never been in a saloon before, but even to him, the Palace was something special. Uncle Frank'd assured him Jake Morton's Palace was one of the two fancier saloons in town, maybe the fanciest.

"The only real competition's the Alamo, two blocks down the street. By comparison, the rest of the saloons in town are crude. Jake took over two adjoining buildings and connected 'em by havin' the intervenin' wall knocked out. The single large room that formed is double the width of anything else in town."

Jake Morton, bald head gleaming, the usual stogie Matt came to associate with him projecting from his mouth, interviewed him.

"You're Preacher Brinkman's kid, are you?"

"No sir, I'm his nephew. John Ritter was my Paw. He got killed."

Jake nodded. "I heard about that. Nice man, your daddy. It was a damned shame." He squinted at Matt. "I understand you're lookin' for a job. What kinda job?"

"I'm a piano player."

"You are, huh? Well, let's hear what you can do."

He pointed to the piano, standing in the middle of the room. Matt went over, twirled the stool a couple of times, and thought for a moment. Then he played a dreamy "Come Where My Love Lies Dreaming." Morton looked thoughtful and scratched his nose. Then he requested something more spirited. Matt gave him a lively rendition of "A Life on the Ocean Wave." When Matt saw Morton tapping his foot in time to the music, he figured he had the job.

"That's good, kid. I'll give you a couple of day's trial, and we'll see how it goes. If you do all right, you got the job. You'll work the afternoon shift—this is the only place in town with two piano players—but on Streeter's night off, you fill in for him."

Morton noticed the questioning look on Matt's face.

"I'll start you at two dollars a day, and you get to keep all your tips. When you fill in on the night shift, you'll get an extra $1.50. You get fifteen minutes off every two hours. Stop in tonight, and Streeter'll show you the ropes." He started to turn away and then stopped. "Oh, and, kid, be nice to the customers. That's how you'll make your tips."

After a week on the job, Matt felt almost at home. The piano, a solid upright, was a good one. The boss even paid Darcy Streeter, the night pianist, a little extra to keep it tuned.

A mirror covered the front panel of the piano, so the piano player had a good view of the room behind him and could tell what was happening.

Things had gone well. The regular patrons of the place seemed to have accepted him, and the rest of the staff were friendly. Darcy, a tall, thin, sardonic man, had explained how it was the piano man's responsibility to help create a congenial atmosphere in the place.

"You gotta kinda sense the mood of the room and play something suitable. If there were a lotta Yankees in here, you'd want to be careful about playing 'Dixie.' And lf the place were full of southerners, you wouldn't want to give 'em 'Marchin' Through Georgia,' now, would you? See what I mean?"

Matt nodded.

"Course, if the place's getting too raucous, you might slow it down with something like 'Beautiful Dreamer' or maybe that old chestnut 'The Hazel Dell.' On the other hand, if things are on the dull side, you might want to give 'em something like 'Oh, Susanna.' Get the idea?"

Again Matt nodded.

"Naturally if a customer asks you for a specific tune, you try to oblige him. That's where your tips'll most likely come from, obliging the customer." He stopped and squinted at Matt. "You can play by ear, can't you? So you can fake it if need be."

Fortunately Matt had a good ear and often picked out tunes he'd never seen nor heard before. Once more he nodded.

Streeter, in turn, nodded approvingly. "Good. Piano man's not much good if he can't pretty well play what the people want." He frowned. "You can transpose, can't you? Case somebody's of a mind to sing."

Matt grinned. "Oh, sure. Learned that early, when I was just a kid playin' at church socials and such."

The older man smiled. "Fine. You'll do. Now, you notice these billiard balls sitting up here atop the piano?"

Matt nodded again.

"Well, the piano player's in charge of 'em. If some fellow wants to shoot a game on that billiard table over there," he ducked his head toward the opposite corner of the room, "you get five dollars from him as a deposit. When he brings the balls back, he gets his money back." He paused for a moment. "Well, I guess that's about it."

"Thanks Mr. Streeter."

"Call me Darcy."

"Yes sir, Darcy."

Matt studied the men playing cards at some of the numerous green baize-covered tables scattered around the saloon. "I thought gamblin' was against the law in Abilene."

Darcy Streeter winked. "Young fellow, I can see you really are kinda green. But you're right. It is against the law. Technically. But nobody pays any attention to the law, least of all Marshal Hickok. He loves a good game of cards. Spends most of his time playing cards—when he ain't busy with one of his whores. As for carrying guns, he don't raise a fuss unless you fire the blamed thing. Then he's apt to come down hard on you."

Now, a week later, after playing the afternoon shift, Matt was having his first go at filling in for Darcy. The place was packed. Usually he spent his fifteen minute break showing his picture of the killer around to the patrons of the saloon. So far, no one had recognized the owlhoot. Matt always made it a point to explain to the customers why he was showing the picture—he didn't want to get Jake mad at him for bothering the customers—and, so far, everybody'd been sympathetic. If anyone showed any signs of annoyance, he quickly left them alone.

This night, though, he'd been too tired to bother. Playing piano from two in the afternoon till late at night wasn't easy. It was only eleven o'clock, and he still had another three hours to go. Fortunately, crowded as it was, it'd been peaceful. Except for one little ruckus. About an hour earlier, a dispute'd broken out at a table where five customers were playing poker. One of the players, a skinny, ugly-looking rascal, pushed his chair back and sprang to his feet, yelling at the feller across the table from him.

"You yellow-bellied, Texas son of a bitch! You been

cheatin' all night. Gimme my money back, or I got a notion to blow you to kingdom come." His hand hovered near the gun on his hip.

The other feller, broad shouldered and blonde, just looked at him, cool as a skunk in the moonlight. "Mister," he drawled, "I reckon fingerin' at that gun in your holster is riskier than tryin' to braid a mule's tail." Suddenly, before his opponent could react, he was on his feet, a Colt Army .44 in his hand. The ugly one gaped at the pistol pointing at his belly and dropped his hand to his side.

"Now," drawled the Texan, "that's better. Why don't you just go outside and cool off, before I'm obliged to ventilate you right here and now?"

Mr. Ugly bared his teeth and looked around. All he saw were grim, unsympathetic faces. He sidled from the table and headed for the door. A volley of laughter followed him. When he disappeared through the door, the others went back to their cards. Since then, the atmosphere in the place had been congenial.

Matt heaved a tired sigh and resumed playing. So far, he'd been able to oblige a few music lovers, and they'd gratified him by tipping generously. One feller'd wanted to sing "Carry Me Back to The Sweet Sunny South," and when Matt'd been able to accompany the nostalgic singer, the feller'd been so grateful, he'd given Matt a five dollar gold piece. Matt was still in a state of euphoria when, glancing in the mirror in front of him, he spotted Mr. Ugly slinking in through the front door. Now what's that rascal up to? he wondered. The man headed for the bar where, in a loud voice, he ordered a whisky.

Matt continued playing, but all the while, glancing in the mirror, he kept his eye on the owlhoot. After a second whisky, the feller lurched away from the bar and began slithering around behind where the Texan, apparently unaware of his approaching nemesis, was still playing poker. Suddenly, when only about two feet behind the Texan, Ugly reached for his gun.

"Look out!" yelled Matt. At the same time he leaped to his

feet and with one swift, continuous motion snatched a billiard ball from on top of the piano, pivoted, and let fly with the sizzler that'd struck out ten Junction City batters.

The hard ivory ball caught the gunman in the side of the head. The ruffian dropped to his knees and pitched forward on his face. His gun clattered to the floor without discharging a shot. Chairs toppled to the floor as the card players, bewildered and confused, sprang to their feet.

Matt rushed over to the Texan. "You all right, sir?"

The Texan stared down at his would-be assassin, then turned to Matt and grinned. "Reckon I am, thanks to you." He extended his hand. "My name's Tom Adams. I just brought a herd up from Lampasas. Down in Texas."

Matt took the extended hand. "I'm Matt Ritter. I play the piano here. I usually work afternoons and do some gunsmithin' of a mornin'."

"Well, I'm sure glad you were here tonight. And I want to thank you. Now, what can I do for you? Maybe to start with, buy you a drink?"

"Thank you, but no sir. I don't drink."

"Well, in that case, I insist you let me at least buy you a meal at the Drovers' Cottage. I'm stayin' there, and I've found they set a pretty fair table."

Matt hesitated only a moment. He liked this feller from Texas, and what's more, he'd often wondered what it'd be like to dine at a place as fancy as the Drovers' Cottage. He'd heard they'd had a fine banquet there last April for the Odd Fellows.

"Thank you, sir. I'd surely like that. So happens tomorrow's my day off, so I could join you for dinner. And if any of your outfit needs any gunsmithin', just send 'em to John Ritter and Son."

Tom Adams grinned. "Fair enough. I'll plan to see you tomorrow evenin' at six o'clock. That agreeable?"

Matt nodded. "Sure is, thank you. I'll be there. Now I got to get back to the piano. I see the boss headin' this way."

Jake Morton shouldered through the crowd gathered around the combatants. "What's goin' on, Matt? Why ain't you at the piano? I'm payin' you good money, you know."

"Hold on, now, pardner," interrupted Tom Adams. "Your piano player just saved you a heap of trouble and saved me a lot more'n trouble. If it hadn't been for him and his quick thinkin' and fast throwin', you'd likely had a killin' on your hands."

Adams went on to explain what had taken place. "So, you see, friend, if it hadn't been for Matt here, you'd probably had lots of trouble. Instead, he settled the whole thing without a shot bein' fired or even so much as a single glass broken."

Jake turned to Matt. "That so, Matt?"

Matt nodded.

Tom Adams voice was soft, but his eyes narrowed. "I hope you're not doubtin' what I said, are you?"

Jake studied the large Texan for a moment. "Why, no sir, I'm not. Just thought Matt might like to say something." Jake turned to Matt. "Anything you want to say?"

Matt shrugged. "No sir. Mr. Adams pretty well said it all. I'll just be gettin' on back to the piano."

"Good," said his boss, "but from what I hear, you deserve a bonus for tonight's work." He broke into a grin and handed Matt a ten dollar gold piece. "Not every day I get a pretty fair piano player and a first-class fast ball pitcher."

"Seems to me, Morton," said Tom Adams, at the same time prodding his would-be assassin with the toe of his boot, "the only question is what to do with this bag of garbage. He's out cold, but I don't think Matt killed him."

"Don't worry about it, Mr. Adams. I'll have a couple of my boys haul the carcass off to the pokey. Marshal Hickok can put the fear of God into him in the mornin' so's he don't never want to set foot in Abilene again." Jake looked around. At the moment maybe fifty people occupied the place.

"All right," he roared, "a round of drinks on the house." He waved to the bartenders. "Take care of the folks, boys. In honor of Matt, here."

Promptly at six o'clock, Matt arrived at the Drovers' Cottage. He'd gotten himself as slicked up as he could and explained to his aunt and uncle why he was dining out.

Uncle Frank had grinned. "Good for you, Matt. I always figured somethin' good would come of your baseball playin'."

Aunt Elly had washed his best shirt and mended a small tear in his pants. "Pay attention to what you have for dinner and what they've got on the menu. I want to hear all about it when you come home. I've never been taken to the Drovers' Cottage," she added, casting a sharp glance at her husband.

A copy of the picture Jenny Maxwell had provided him in hand, he entered the Drovers' Cottage. Impressed by the splendor of the place, he looked around for a moment and then headed for the front desk. Before he was halfway across the lobby, a grinning Tom Adams came down the stairs, hand outstretched.

"Good to see you, Matt. Hope you got a good appetite."

They shook hands, and a smiling Matt nodded. "Sure have, Mr. Adams. I've never eaten here, and I'm looking forward to it."

"Well, come on, then. I got a nice table reserved for us. And call me Tom. I don't much cotton to that Mr. Adams hoorah."

As soon as they were seated at their table, Matt's host asked, "Sure you won't have somethin'? Maybe a cold beer?"

Matt paused. Well, why not? Paw sure liked his beer. Out loud he replied, "Well, sure…ah,…Tom. If you say so, I'll have one."

Adams gave the waiter an order for two beers and then turned back to Matt. "What do you say? Want to wait to order till we finish the beer?"

Again Matt hesitated. He had the appetite of a starving coyote and had been looking forward to eating. On the other hand, he didn't want to appear over anxious or impolite. He chewed on his lip for a moment.

Fortunately his host seemed to read his mind. "No, I can see you're hungry." He turned to the waiter. "Just leave us the menu. As soon as you bring us the beer, we'll order."

The waiter bowed and headed for the bar, leaving each of them a menu. They studied it in silence for a few minutes.

"So, Matt, what'll you have?"

Stumped, Matt scratched his head. With so many things on the bill of fare, he didn't know what to say. Besides, he didn't want to appear greedy. "Oh, I don't know. I guess I'll just have whatever you have."

Tom chuckled. "All right. Whatever you say."

The waiter returned and placed a huge mug of beer in front of each of them. Tom ordered a roast beef dinner for each of them with oyster soup, salad, mashed potatoes, cranberry sauce, tomatoes and corn, and hot bread. As the waiter hurried off, Tom turned to his guest and said, "We can decide on pastry later, I guess. Anything else you'd like?"

"No sir, that's plenty."

They each took some beer, Tom a large swallow and Matt a small sip. The beer was ice cold; Matt discovered he liked it. He took a large swallow. Tom, grinning, watched him.

"Good stuff, ain't it?"

Matt grinned and nodded.

"But," Tom cautioned, "if you're not used to it, it might be a good idea to go a little slow at first. Till you see how you get along with it. Specially if your stomach's empty."

"Yes sir."

"Now, if you don't mind my askin'," continued Tom, "what's that you got in your hand there?"

Matt unrolled the picture and showed it to Tom. "That's the miserable owlhoot who killed my Paw."

Tom examined the picture and then looked up at Matt.

"Oh. You want to tell me about it?"

Matt did. He explained how he was off in Kansas City when his Paw was killed and how it happened. He explained how Jenny Maxwell drew the picture, and he told Tom of his vow to find the murderer and avenge his father's death. He went on to describe his so far fruitless efforts to identify the rascal. He told about showing the picture to everyone he could and about his belief the ruffian had been a trail hand. He emphasized his conviction that, sooner or later, the killer himself or someone who knew him would turn up in Abilene.

Tom Adams listened quietly. When Matt ceased speaking, Tom pursed his lips and then shook his head. "I don't know, Matt. If I was that scoundrel, I sure wouldn't come anywhere near Abilene. And the trouble is, it's a mighty big country out there. Why, just Texas alone's so big you can't imagine it. Not to mention the Indian Territory and Arizona and New Mexico. Then there's California and all that northern country. I'm afraid the son of a bitch'll be harder to find than a fly in a currant pie."

Face grim, Matt shrugged. "Maybe so, but I'm goin' to try. I won't be happy till I find the murderin' bastard."

Tom looked thoughtful. "Well, I tell you what. I don't know as it'll help, but if you got a copy of that picture, I can show it to the boys in my outfit, and on the way home, I'll show it to everyone I run into. Not only the lawmen but anyone else I meet. And, when I get home, I'll see to it the word gets around Lampasas."

Just then the waiter showed up with their soup. While he spooned his soup, Matt studied his host. The man wore a short beard that reminded Matt of pictures he'd seen of President Grant. Over dinner, Tom told him a bit about himself.

"I'm originally from down San Antone way. My daddy had a spread not too far from Uvalde. I learned my ranchin' from him. And he was a mighty fine teacher. Met my wife, Patty, when I was only twenty-five. When a Comanche killed her daddy, we took over his spread near Lampasas, and we've lived there ever since. Done right well, too."

"What happened to your Paw's place?"

Tom looked pained. "Daddy lost it in a poker game."

"Were you in the war?"

Tom shook his head. "Nope. I managed to stay out of it. Figured I could be of more use supplyin' beef than chasin' Yankees all over the South."

Matt ate industriously for a while, then looked up.

"Got any kids?"

Tom sighed. "No, that's the one big regret of my life. Patty's, too. I'm goin' on forty-six, and she's thirty-eight, and try as we might for twenty years, we've never had a child."

The dinner was excellent. Matt kept his eating utensils busy. When dessert time came, he ordered raspberry pie and topped it off with vanilla ice cream. When he finished, Tom offered him a cigar. The offer tempted him, but never having smoked, he decided he didn't want to chance making a fool of himself.

"Thank you, but I think I'll pass if you don't mind. It's been a great dinner, though. I sure do want to thank you. "

"Well, son, I'm glad you enjoyed it, but after all, you did save my life. I'm the one to do the thankin', I reckon. I figger I'll be in your debt for a long time, a real long time. And I reckon Patty'll feel the same, although," he added with a lopsided grin, "you never can tell about women, can you?"

Matt wasn't sure how to answer Tom's implied man-to-man, worldly observation on the opposite sex. He felt sure if the same situation arose with Uncle Frank and Aunt Elly, his aunt would be just as grateful as his uncle. Maybe more so. Not knowing what to say, he merely shrugged.

Tom Adams regarded him for a moment but didn't press the issue. "Matt, I got a little idea how you feel about your daddy's killer, and I'll do all I can to help you out."

"I'll appreciate that."

Meal finished, they rose from the table. "And if you're ever of a mind to come down to Texas, I sure do want you to look us up. Our spread's not real big, only 300,000 acres or so, but we're only about ten miles west of Lampasas and most anybody in town can point you in the right direction."

"I'd like that, sir. I've never been to Texas or seen a cattle ranch, so I appreciate the invite, but I still think that sooner or later, I'll find a clue to that owlhoot right here in Abilene. So, if it's all the same to you, for now, I'll just keep on doin' what I been doin'."

Tom smiled and offered his hand. "Well, it's surely not my place to tell a man how to run his business, least of all the man who saved my life. But," he went on, as Matt was about to depart the Drovers' Cottage, "don't forget my invite. We'll look forward to seein' you someday."

13

"Well, now, young feller, how far you fixin' to go?"

"I can't rightly say, Mr Madigan. I'm just goin' to keep goin' till I find the owlhoot I'm lookin' for."

Uncle Frank had recommended Oops Madigan as the man to see about horses and some advice on heading south into Texas. His uncle had told Matt Oops wasn't the man's real name. His real name was Josh Madigan. According to Uncle Frank, Josh Madigan was a top hand when it came to handling horses and driving cows to market. But he'd never had much of a reputation when it came to handling guns, axes, and tools in general.

"He got the name Oops while on a drunk one night in Fort Worth," said Uncle Frank. "Got a permanent limp that night, too. Seems he tried to execute a fast draw for some reason—

maybe showing off for some dance hall dollies—and shot himself in the foot. After his own ball smashed into his left foot, all he could think to do was stand there and say, 'Oops!'"

After years of herding longhorns up the Shawnee Trail, Oops, in 1867, had come north with one of the first herds to hit Abilene. Nobody knew exactly where Oops had gotten the funds to acquire the horse trading business he operated from a place about ten miles south of Abilene, and nobody was inclined to inquire. A prudent man didn't ask too many questions.

Suffice to say, Oops had somehow acquired enough money to buy some horses from a trail boss who'd wanted to sell his remuda before heading back to Texas. Since then, in the intervening five years, Oops had prospered. Folks around Abilene regarded Oops as the local expert on matters pertaining to the cowboy end of the cattle business.

Although Oops looked ten years older, Uncle Frank thought he was somewhere in his forties. "He probably just got tired of the rough life a cowboy leads and decided to settle down."

"Well," said Oops, squirting a stream of tobacco juice into the dust, "if you decide to follow the Chisholm all the way down, you'll have about 600 miles to go. That's a far piece, and it ain't an easy ride for man nor hoss. You oughtta have more'n one hoss, so you can trade off and give the animal a rest. The one you ain't actually ridin' can serve as your pack hoss."

Matt nodded. "You got a couple of good horses you could sell me?"

Oops looked insulted. "Why sure I have. All my hosses are good hosses. They might do a little pitchin' of a chilly mornin', just kickin' the frost out, you know, but they're good ponies. All of 'em. I only buy the best."

Curious, Matt asked, "If you don't mind sayin', where do you get 'em?"

Oops grinned. "Don't mind at all. When a trail boss or owner—sometimes they're one and the same feller—sells his herd and pays off his hands, he usually wants to sell off his remuda. The waddies get to keep their personal hoss if they own one, but the rest of the remuda belongs to the outfit."

Matt's brow furrowed. "Why get rid of good horses?"

"Usually, the boss don't figger it's worth his trouble nor expense to drive 'em back home. That's where I come in. I look 'em over, pick out the best ones, and offer the man a fair price. Then I bring the hosses out here where I rest 'em and fatten 'em and then sell 'em to fellers like you, fellers that need a good hoss or two. Do a lot of business with the army, too."

"Well, all right, you got a couple for me?"

Oops paused for a moment before answering. "You fixin' to look for a job as a cowboy down in Texas? Because, frankly, son, if you don't mind my sayin' so, you don't look like a feller who's had much experience as a cowhand."

Matt shrugged. "I'm not a cowboy. I'm a gunsmith and a piano player."

Oops looked surprised. "Well, then, if I'm not bein' too nosy, why're you figgerin' to head down into Texas?"

"I'm plannin to hunt down my Paw's killer."

"On the prod, are you? And just who might this feller be you're lookin' for?"

"Well, that's just the problem. I don't know."

Oops chewed for a moment, then spit a stream of tobacco juice. "How do you expect to find him then?"

Matt went over to the buggy he'd driven out to Oops's ranch. "I've got his picture right here. I've showed it to just about everybody who's come through Abilene in the last year, but so far, nobody's recognized him."

"When'd all this happen?"

Once again Matt told his story. Oops listened patiently, occasionally punctuating the tale with a squirt of tobacco juice. "I'm goin' to hunt the rascal down and see to it he's hung," said Matt, winding up his tale.

"I guess I must've been over in Denver about then," volunteered Oops.

"It's been almost a year now since it happened, and I still don't know who he is. Between workin' at the Palace and in my own place, I swear I must've shown this picture to a couple thousand people, but nobody knows him. I've just about decided I'm goin' to have to go lookin' for him."

"What're you goin' to do with your gunsmith shop?"

"Don't have it no more. There ain't been no herds comin' to Abilene this year. Not since the Farmers' Association put that notice in the *Chronicle* last February invitin' the Texans to take their business elsewhere."

"Yep. I hear that polite warnin' even got printed in some Texas newspapers."

"Well, there's sure no business in Abilene. Even Jake Morton's goin' to close up the Palace and move on to Ellsworth or maybe Wichita. Anyway, I'm out of a job."

Oops nodded and spat again. "I know what you mean. Matter of fact, this year I'm fixin' to head down to Newton myself to buy horses. That's where most of the herds are endin' up. It's a long way for me, but I got no other choice." He stuck out his hand. "But let me have a look at that picture. I just don't go into town very often is why I haven't seen it before, I guess. Never can tell, though. I might know the scoundrel."

Matt unrolled the picture and handed it to Oops. The horse trader studied it a moment. "Why, sure. I know this rascal. Used to see him around San Antone. Real mean cuss. I always figgered he'd end up at the end of a rope."

Matt's face lit up. "Who is he? When'd you last see him?"

"Name's Bowler Bob Bixby. Must be five, six years ago I last saw him. He didn't work regular as a cowhand. Fancied himself as a gambler and gunman. More'n likely your daddy's not the first man he's killed. I don't think you're liable to see him up here in Abilene again, though. He's a cagey cuss. Might even be in Mexico. They say he liked the señoritas...that's why he always wore a bowler. Thought the ladies liked it."

Matt grunted. "Well, I'm really anxious to head south, Mr. Madigan, 'specially now I know who I'm lookin' for. So, can you fix me up with a couple of real good horses?"

Oops scratched his head. "Well, now, let's see. I don't

figger you'll be doin' night guard on a bunch of cows, so you won't need a night hoss. On the trail, every cowboy wants a good night hoss, and there's not too many of them, so they're expensive."

Matt frowned.

Oops grinned. "But like I said, you won't likely be needin' a night hoss. You'll have a lot of rivers to cross, though. Six or seven big ones and a bunch of smaller ones. So, you'll want a pair of good river hosses. Hosses that can swim and that'll get you across any river, no matter how high the water's runnin'."

Oops took Matt out to the pasture where about fifty horses were grazing. "See those two out there? That big bay and the chestnut?"

Matt nodded.

"Well, I figger they'll be just the ticket. How do they look to you?"

Matt knew he was no judge of horseflesh, but he believed that, working in the Palace and running his own business, he'd become a pretty fair judge of men. Besides, Uncle Frank'd said Oops Madigan was about as honest and fair a man as Matt was likely to find among horse traders. He pursed his lips and thought for a moment. "How much?"

"Well," said Oops, "since they're good river hosses, in good condition and well-behaved, I was plannin' to get $75.00 for each."

Matt's face must've shown what a steep price he thought the horse trader was asking. "I don't know's I could afford to buy two at that price."

"Well," said Oops, quickly seizing his cue, "considerin' your situation and all, I'll give you the pair of 'em for $120.00. Fair 'nough?"

Matt wondered where, considering how things were in Abilene, Oops could find another buyer, but decided it was an acceptable price. They shook on the deal.

"Now," said Oops, "what kind of saddle you got?"

Matt hesitated. "Well, to tell the truth, I ain't got none."

Oops grinned. "You ain't? You plannin' to ride to San Antone bareback? Like an Indian."

"Well, no..."

Oops shook his head. "Son, I like your spirit. Tell you what I'll do. I got a Texas-style saddle I ain't usin', and since you're not likely to do much ropin', I'll throw it into the deal for another $15.00. How's that?"

Matt nodded. "Sounds good."

Oops squirted more tobacco juice. "What about chaps? You got chaps?"

Matt's brow furrowed. "Chaps?"

Oops shook his head and grinned. "Yep. Chaps. Protects you from horse bites—not that you'll need protection from Horace and Queenie here—and also snake bites, thorns, and God only knows what else. You'll hit some mighty rough brush south of here."

Matt sighed. "How much?"

"Well...for you, I can throw in a pair of batwings for only another $5.00. Fair 'nough?"

Again Matt nodded. "I guess."

They shook again.

"But we got a problem," said Matt. "I don't have but $65.00 with me. I guess I'll have to come back tomorrow."

"Well, now, hold on." Oops appeared to think for a moment. "Matt, I've heard a bit about you from folks. They all say you're an honest young feller and wouldn't dream of cheatin' a man, so I tell you what. You just hitch Horace and Queenie to the back of your buckboard and toss the chaps and saddle into it. You just give me what you got, and I'll trust you to get the rest to me."

Matt broke into a grin. "Well, say now, that's mighty nice of you, Mr. Madigan. I have to come this way when I head south, so I'll stop by on my way to Newton."

Matt was as good as his word. The following morning about ten o'clock, he turned up at Oops's place. He was riding Queenie and had Horace trailing behind on a lead. When Oops greeted him, he grinned and climbed down to the ground.

"Brought both of the horses. Not leavin' today, but I never handled two horses at one time before, so I thought I best start practicin'. Anyhow, here's your money."

Oops grinned and shook hands. "I figgered I could count on you."

"Well, sir, I ain't lived out here all my life, but in the three or four years I have been here, I've learned a man's got to stand behind his word."

Oops nodded. "That's right, son. You never spoke a truer word. Now, when you fixin' to leave?"

Matt shrugged. "Maybe three or four days."

"Well, travelin' alone's not the best of ideas if you can avoid it. If you can afford to wait a week, I'll be headin' down to Newton to see what I can find in the way of horseflesh. If I find some likely lookin' critters, I can hire a couple of hands to help me drive 'em back up here, but if you're of a mind to, I'd be happy to share the ride down with you."

Oops's offer pleased Matt. Despite his determination, the proposed trip slightly daunted him. "I'll be happy to wait and go with you." This time he climbed on Horace and put Queenie on the lead. "I'll see you a week from today."

That night at dinner, he reported his good fortune to his aunt and uncle. "Havin' Mr. Madigan to ride with me as far's Newton'll sure be a great piece of luck for me. I reckon ridin' five, six hundred miles is a lot different than just ridin' around Abilene, and I figger spendin' a couple of days with him I can learn a lot about ridin' trail."

Uncle Frank frowned and rubbed his chin. "You're really plannin' to go then, are you?"

"Yes sir, sure am. Now that I know who the scoundrel is, I'm sure I'll find him somewhere down there."

"What do you plan to do if you do find him?" asked Aunt Elly.

"Haul him back to Abilene for a trial, so's he can be hung all legal like."

"And if he don't want to come?"

Matt sighed. "I reckon I'll just have to shoot him."

Aunt Elly looked at Uncle Frank, then turned back to Matt. "You know, we sure hate to see you go. I tend to think of you as my own son. Never entered my head you'd be leavin' us like this."

"And," added Uncle Frank, "I always figgered you'd be around to help with the farm. You're real knowledgeable when it comes to growin' things."

Matt wasn't sure what to say. He chewed on a piece of chicken and then took a sip of coffee. Finally he set the coffee mug down. "I want you to know it ain't easy for me leavin' you. I love you both, you know. After all, you're the only real family I have now. But," he pounded his fist on the table, "I gotta see that Paw gets justice. I can't just let that scoundrel get away with Paw's murder."

Aunt Elly shook her head. "I know, Matt, but it's been almost a year, and I was hopin' you would've come to terms with that. I was hopin' you wouldn't let it keep on tearing up your life. Like your Uncle Claude said, revenge is a terrible thing. It eats at your soul. Like acid. Can't you just put it aside and get on with your life?"

"No, Aunt Elly, I can't."

"You know, Matt," said Uncle Frank, "I was kinda lookin' forward to havin' you take over the farm someday."

Matt drew a deep breath and let it out in a long sigh.

"That's mighty generous of you, Uncle Frank, but the truth be known, I don't much cotton to farmin'. I realize it's important, but it's not what I want to do."

"No?" Uncle Frank sounded surprised. "What do you want to do? Be a cowboy?"

"Well, no, I don't think so. Bein' a cowboy don't really appeal to me, although you remember that feller Tom Adams? From down in Lampasas? The feller who bought me dinner at the Drovers' Cottage?"

They both nodded.

"Well, I've had a couple of letters from him, and he still wants me to visit him and his wife. So, I figger that's where I'll head for." He grinned. "I figger I'll get a firsthand look at bein' a cowboy. Come to that, though, I believe I'd rather be just what I am, a gunsmith and a piano player."

"And that's it?"

"Well, no." He frowned. "Now don't laugh, but sometimes I think it might be nice to be somethin' like a lawyer or a judge."

Aunt Elly's eyebrows went up. "Well, now, that's just fine, and I'm proud of you, but that'd take a lot of education."

"If that's what you'd like to do," interjected Uncle Frank, "don't you think it'd be better if you settled down to it instead of ridin' off on a wild goose chase, lookin' for a needle in a haystack?"

Matt shrugged. "Well, I'm not sure if I want to do it or not. But, anyway, I've got time. After all, I only just turned nineteen. And, besides, I still gotta find that owlhoot that killed Paw. Then I can think about other things."

Once again his aunt and uncle looked at each other. Then his aunt asked, "How much money you got?"

Matt scratched his head and shrugged again. "Enough. I managed to sell most of the equipment from the shop and all of the stock to Mr. Moon at the Frontier Store. Gave him a good price on everything, and he knows a bargain when he sees one."

"Glad to hear that," said Uncle Frank, "but if you don't mind, me 'n your aunt would like you to take $200 from us to help with expenses. After all, we were pretty close to your Paw, too, you know."

"Thank you. I know."

"And, Matt," said his aunt, wiping a tear from her eye, "You know you'll always be welcome here. And one thing more. I can see you're changin', growin' up, I mean, but whatever happens down there, don't let it turn you into a hard case."

He nodded. "No, ma'am, I won't. Now I reckon I better go take care of some chores."

14

The ride to Newton with Oops Madigan was an education. In more ways than one. Oops was waiting, ready to ride, when Matt showed up at Oops's place. Oops surveyed Horace and Queenie—Matt was riding Horace—and shook his head.

"Young feller, it looks like you surely are loaded for bear, if you don't mind my sayin' so. And that's all right. I don't begrudge you your armament. But I think, for openers, you'd do better to carry that Yellow Boy on the hoss you're ridin' where you can reach it quick if need be and let the pack hoss carry that Sharps."

Uncle Frank and Matt had discussed the question of whether he'd be better off to take the .50 caliber Sharps buffalo rifle or Paw's Yellow Boy Winchester.

"There's somethin' to be said for each of them," Uncle

Frank had said. "That .44 caliber Winchester of your Paw's is a mighty nice weapon. It's accurate to two or three hundred yards, and with that rifle's seventeen-shot magazine and lever-action, you can get off a whole lot of shots in a hurry if you have to."

Matt nodded his head. "Sounds good."

"But," Uncle Frank raised his hand, "the Sharps, on the other hand, has a much longer range and, with its .50 caliber ball, can knock a big animal down at a great distance. And it's pretty accurate even at extreme long range, specially with a tripod supportin' the barrel. But it's a single shot, and you gotta reload each time, although they do reload remarkably quick."

"But you gave it to me, and I appreciate it. I wouldn't want to leave it here."

Uncle Frank, brow furrowed, arms folded across his chest, nodded. "It's a real dilemma."

"Well, why don't I just take both? After all I got two horses, and from what I hear, this is real dangerous country I'll be travelin' through. Won't hurt to be well armed."

Again his uncle nodded. "You're right. It surely won't."

In the long run, Matt had decided to take both rifles along with a plentiful supply of ammunition for each of them and for his eight-shot special. In addition he decided to take the Remington derringer he'd gotten in the habit of carrying while working his piano jobs. He also realized he couldn't leave the grenades for Aunt Elly to come across, so he packed those, too—unarmed. But he slipped in a supply of percussion caps just in case he might someday need to arm the grenades.

The remaining pictures of his quarry he rolled in waterproofing and stuck them in a separate scabbard on the pack horse. He also carried a bedroll, two good size canteens, a slicker, and food. Coffee, beans, bacon, the makin's for biscuits, and the necessary cooking utensils.

For himself, he bought a new Texas-style hat—he figured he'd be spending a lot of time in Texas—and a good pair of boots. His moccasins—he'd found the pair Aunt Elly'd given him so comfortable that, when they'd worn out, he'd managed to scare up a new pair—he carried in his bedroll. He didn't like to wear boots when he didn't have to.

"When you're on your hoss and need a rifle," Oops cautioned, "you want one that'll snap off a lot of shots real quick. So leave the Sharps in the scabbard on the pack horse and keep the Yellow Boy handy. Now, come on down here and let me show you somethin'."

Matt dismounted, and Oops led him over to Queenie where he showed Matt how to properly load and secure the pack on the animal. That done, they each climbed aboard their horses and headed south. Oops, too, led a pack horse. Which surprised Matt, but he figured it wasn't his place to comment.

Early in the day, the horses waded the Solomon—the river was running low—without any trouble. Most of the day, they traveled over undulating prairie, the grass starting to turn brown and sere under the warm June skies.

"This is pretty much what you're goin' to see all the way down. This and dust. It'll get hotter, too, the farther south you go. Now and then you may see a hill or a rise but not often. Gets pretty monotonous."

They stopped for a rest and lunch at noontime. "No use pushin' hard. If you make five miles an hour, that's about as much as you can hope for. Maybe only four with a pack hoss. And you got a long way to go, so you want to take good care of Horace and Queenie. Don't wear 'em out. You don't want to have to buy new hosses if you can avoid it. By the way, glad to see you're usin' a curb bit."

Matt nodded. "Yes sir."

"Want to give the hosses plenty of rest, you know. Take the saddle and pack off and let 'em graze. But be sure to hobble 'em." Oops paused and looked quizzically at Matt. "You do have hobbles, don't you?"

Embarrassed Matt shrugged. "Well, no sir, I don't. I figger'd with Horace and Queenie, I wouldn't need none."

Oops shook his head. "Son, even the best of ponies could

get spooked, and you sure wouldn't want to be left afoot out here. That's why horse thieves get hung. No worse crime than leavin' a man afoot out on the prairie."

Oops dug into his saddle bags. "I figgered this might happen," he said. "Here. You can have 'em for two dollars."

He handed Matt two sets of hobbles. Each set of hobbles consisted of two rawhide loops connected by a metal ring.

"You don't absolutely need the metal rings. You can twist a piece of rawhide to form the loops. Now, just slip 'em over the hosses' forelegs. They can graze but won't run away from you."

"Thank you."

"By the way, you got a map of where you're goin'?"

"No sir."

Oops nodded. "I figgered that might be the case, too." He reached into a saddle bag. "Here. This is one of those maps the Kansas Pacific puts out. It'll help you get to Red River Station down in Texas. After that you're on your own. The railroad prints these up for the Texans comin' north through the Indian Territory and Kansas. They don't figger the Texans'll need a map travelin' through Texas."

"Well, thank you."

"Actually, you probably won't need it south of Newton. With all the cattle comin' north up the trail, the Chisholm's pretty well marked. Some places the cattle've trampled it as much as a quarter mile wide. Not only that, this time of year, you'll probably meet up with a lot of herds headin' north." He grinned. "Probably be able to get free meals all the way down. It's considered just good etiquette to offer a man a meal when he meets up with your outfit. Then, too, maybe some of the hand'll have news of ol' Bowler Bob for you."

Matt's face lit up. "I never thought of that."

Oops grinned. "Another thing, with all the herds headin' north through the Indian Territory these days, it makes it a lot safer. Almost like moseyin' down Texas Street in Abilene."

Oops was as good as his word and didn't push the pace too much. They rode for eight hours that first day and, late that afternoon, made camp about thirty miles south of Abilene on the north bank of the Cottonwood River.

"We're about halfway to Newton here, and we can get an early start tomorrow," Oops said. "If it's all tight with you, I'll handle the cookin' tonight."

Matt was grateful. He didn't know when he had been so tired and sore. Riding in and around Abilene was one thing. Riding thirty miles of trail was quite another. Not only that, although the morning had been cool, as the day had worn on, the sun got hotter and hotter. And there wasn't any shade to retreat to.

Next morning, they were well on their way before the sun grew really warm. The horses took to the water and swam the Cottonwood without a hitch, justifying Oops contention that they were "good river hosses."

Oops had a few more gems of trail wisdom for Matt. As another rider approached them from the direction of Newton, Oops said, "It's considered polite to keep on comin' when you see another rider headin' toward you. Don't veer off. Might make the other feller wonder if you're bein' furtive for a reason, make him wonder about your intentions. Just keep on acomin'."

"I see," said Matt. "Maybe just wave, huh?"

Oops looked aghast. "Oh, no. Don't wave. It ain't polite. Might spook his horse. When you get close to each other, just pass a friendly word or two. If he dismounts, then you dismount, too. Friendly like."

Matt, chastened, nodded. "All right."

"And," Oops went on, "while we're talkin' etiquette, always take your spurs off when you enter a man's house. Although," he glanced down, "I see you don't wear none, so that won't be a problem for you."

By that time, the approaching rider was on them. Polite nods and howdys were exchanged, and the man rode on.

Again at noontime they stopped for lunch and to rest the horses. Then, about the middle of the afternoon, Oops stopped again and dismounted. "Give the hosses a short breather while we do a little augurin'. Don't unsaddle or use hobbles. Just be sure to hold onto the reins."

Matt nodded and dismounted, clutching the reins tightly.

"Now, we're pretty close to Newton. Frankly, it ain't much of a town. They call it Bloody Newton. There ain't no law there, and they say a lot of people are gettin' killed. I will say one thing for Newton, though. This time, ol' Joe McCoy used a little sense and built his cattle pens about a mile and a half west of the town. Not like in Abilene where the cattle pens are right smack on the edge of town."

"Is there a hotel?"

"There is, but it don't amount to much. And it's hard to keep your belongings safe. Anyway, I suggest you camp outside of town and ride in if you think you have to. That's what I plan to do."

Matt thought for a moment. "I guess you're right. If you don't mind, I think I'll camp with you."

Oops nodded. "Fine. Besides, the bosses hold the herds outside of town, so most of the waddies'll spend most of their time out with the herds. If you want to show your pictures, it'll be easier."

Again Matt paused to think over Oops's words, then asked, "How far's it to the next town?"

"Wichita's about 25 miles down the trail."

"Well, maybe this afternoon, after we make camp, I'll just take a little ride into Newton and see if anyone's got any news of this owlhoot. Then tomorrow, I'll get an early start but stop and check with any herds I see."

"All right, son. You go in early, and I'll watch the camp. When you get back, I'll go on in and see if any trail bosses got any horses for sale."

They mounted their horses and rode on toward Newton. About a mile northeast of Newton, Oops found a place on the banks of a small moving stream. "This should do. Clean running water and we're not likely to get run over by a herd of cattle here."

They established camp and set the horses to grazing, all except for Horace. As soon as Horace had water and a little rest, Matt saddled him—Matt'd been riding Queenie—and headed for town. As Oops had prophesied, Newton wasn't much, consisting mostly of bare weatherboard buildings with false fronts. Scattered among these were crude shacks and tents.

It seemed to Matt that saloons were everywhere, so many that he lost count. Most of them south of the railroad tracks. Every now and then he heard the sound of a gunshot. Sometimes several at once. Drunken cowboys lurched through saloon doors out into the streets. And this, marveled Matt, was late afternoon. The sun was still fairly high in the sky. He wondered what it was like here after sundown.

He tried to interest some of the cowboys in looking at his picture of Bowler Bob but without much luck. Some just shook him off; some thought the whole idea was hilarious; a few were downright surly, because he'd interrupted their pursuit of pleasure.

Going by one saloon he heard someone pounding out "Old Dan Tucker" on a piano. He went in. There, on a raised platform, about two feet high, was an upright piano with a mirror on the front like the one he'd played at the Palace.

The piano player wore a battered, black stove pipe hat and was chewing on an unlit cigarillo. Except for the two frantically busy bartenders, he appeared to be soberest fellow in the place. Matt went up to him.

"Howdy."

The piano player glanced at him and nodded. "Howdy."

"Can I talk with you a minute?"

Finishing off the tune with a flourish, the pianist turned to Matt. "Now, young fellow, what can I do for you?"

Matt decided to be diplomatic. "Can I buy you a drink?"

The fellow shook his head. "No need for that. I'm always willing to talk. Besides, I've had enough to drink for a while." He smiled. "I'll be smearing my arpeggios if I don't look out."

Matt grinned. "I know just what you mean. I used to play at the Palace in Abilene."

The pianist peered closely at Matt. "Did you now? Are you

the young fellow that shows pictures and throws billiard balls? I've heard of you."

Matt's grin grew broader. "Sure am. Name's Matt Ritter." He stuck out his hand.

The piano man took it. "Bert Lisle. Pleased to meet you." He winked. "Bet you want me to look at your pictures. Am I right?"

"Right." Matt unrolled the drawing. "Ever see this rascal?"

Lisle glanced at the picture. "Nope. Never have. Why? Who is he?"

Matt once again told his story. Lisle's face grew somber as he listened to the tale. When Matt finished, Lisle shook his head. "I'm sure sorry to hear that, and I hope you manage to catch up with the scoundrel. Although," he took the cheroot out of his mouth, "are you sure you want to catch up to him? Fellow like that, I'm afraid you'll have about as much chance as a one-legged man in a kicking contest."

Matt's eyes narrowed. "Maybe, but I plan to hunt him down, anyhow."

"Hey! Piano man! Let's have some music. Play 'Lou'siana Belle.'" The order came from a bearded, hulking individual lounging at the bar.

Bert looked up and waved a hand. "Sure will. In just a minute or two."

The slovenly hulk straightened up and slammed his whisky glass down on the bar. "I said NOW!" He started to advance toward the piano platform.

Bert held up both hands in a placating manner. "I'm sorry. Just give me a minute. Can't you see I'm talking with a friend here?"

By this time the ruffian had reached the platform. He glared at Bert. Then he turned and grabbed Matt by the shoulder and shoved him—hard. Surprised, Matt staggered across the room and, off balance, tripped and crashed to the floor. His assailant ignored him and turned to Bert.

"Now, your friend's not talking to you anymore. So, you goin' to get back to that piano and play while you still can or do I have to break every finger you got?"

To punctuate his threat, he drew his pistol and slammed the barrel down on the edge of the piano. Then he leaned forward and spit at the mesmerized pianist's feet.

Suddenly a hand whipped the bully's hat off. He started to turn. "Wha—" He never got to finish his exclamation. A gun barrel smashed down on the crown of his head. His eyes rolled up, he lurched sidewise, tottered a step or two, and fell prostrate to the floor. When he hit the floor, his gun fired, sending a random bullet into the mirror behind the bar, shattering it.

In the barroom, action and sound came to a momentary halt.

Then a burly bartender, beer bung in hand, vaulted the bar and charged toward where Matt stood wiping hair oil and blood from the barrel of his eight-shot special. Matt, gun hand extended, turned toward the charging bartender. "Can I help you?"

The bartender's charge came to a sudden halt. "Why'd you have to do that?"

Matt's eyes narrowed. "What'd you want me to do? Shoot the son of a bitch." Suddenly he swiveled a quarter turn and raised the barrel of his gun. "Hold it right there," he snarled, his gun pointing at two unsavory looking characters just to the right of the bartender. "Get your hands up, you two, and don't move a muscle, or you'll have sawdust in your beard."

An eye still on the two now motionless would-be assailants, he addressed the bartender, "These two friends of yours?"

The bartender, hands at his side, shook his head. "No, they just spend a lot of time and money in here."

"Who are they?"

The bartender nodded toward the prone figure on the floor. "That's Catlow Moran." Just then the ruffian stirred and groaned.

Matt grunted. "Guess he's not dead. What about these two?"

"The skinny one calls himself John Maxon. The shorter one's Max Eagle."

"What outfit do they work for?"

The bartender grinned. "They don't work for any outfit. You might say they're in business for themselves." A couple of guffaws exploded from the crowd.

Behind Matt, Bert spoke up. "They do a little rustling, a little robbery, maybe a little killing."

"Specially when they think they've got easy pickin', like just now," a voice shouted from somewhere back in the crowd.

"Guess Catlow made a mistake this time," yelled another voice.

"Well," said Matt, "somebody get the marshal to haul these owlhoots off to the jail."

"Ain't no marshal," said the bartender.

"Ain't no jail, neither," somebody yelled.

"You want to get rid of 'em, son, you better shoot 'em right now."

"Won't nobody take no notice if you rid the world of these three skunks," someone else chimed in. "Why last week over in Tuttle's, nine men were gunned down. These three snakes won't make no difference."

Matt stared at Bert. "Good God, Bert, I can't do that. Not in cold blood."

The two gang members started to move.

"Get your hands up!" He waved his gun. "Maybe I won't shoot in cold blood, but you give me an excuse and see what happens. Now, you two bastards, get over here." Matt indicated the table next to him. "Put your guns on the table. Slow, now."

Cautiously the two did as they were told.

"Now, turn around." The two complied. Suddenly Matt brought his gun barrel down on the tall owlhoot's head. Before his other adversary could move, Matt quickly pivoted and disposed of the short rascal. Both slumped across the table and then rolled off to join their leader on the floor.

Matt holstered his gun and picked up the outlaws' guns from the table. Then from his pocket he took a punch and tapped the pin holding the cylinders. They each dropped free. He stowed them in his pocket and then repeated the operation with Catlow Moran's pistol.

By this time, the crowd was with Matt. They hadn't had so much entertainment in quite a while. "Now," he said, spreading his well-thumbed picture on the table, "I'd appreciate it if each one of you'd take a look at this picture and tell me if you ever seen this feller before, and if so, where."

In a holiday mood the bar patrons, one by one, stepped up and studied the picture. They all shook their heads.

"Well," said Matt, in a loud voice, "this owlhoot's name is Bowler Bob Bixby. Any of you heard anything about him?"

Again nothing but headshaking.

He glanced through the saloon door. "Well," he said, turning to Bert Lisle, "looks like dusk's comin' on, so I guess I'll be headin' back to camp. Much obliged for your help."

"Matt, the way you buffaloed those three was a sight to see, but when and if they come around, they're all three of 'em going to be meaner than centipedes with shin splints. And they're going to blame me for what happened to 'em, so if you don't mind, I think I'd like to go with you."

"Jumpin' Jehoshaphat! I never thought about that. You got a horse?"

"Indeed I do."

"Well, good. Let's go."

The piano man draped his swallowtail coat over his arm, tapped his stovepipe to settle it firmly on his head, and asked the bartender for the money owed him.

The bartender stared at him. "You ain't got no money comin', not when you're walking out like this. What're we goin' to do for entertainment tonight?"

Matt put his hand on his gun and smiled at the bartender.

"Why don't you just have Catlow and his boys do your entertainin'? If they don't play the piano too well, maybe they can do a recitation." He started to ease his gun out. "Now, how about it? You goin' to pay my friend his money?"

The bartender's eyes widened. "Why, sure. That sounds like a fine idea. How much do we owe you, Bert?"

"I ought to take a bonus for this, but just give me what I rightfully got coming."

The bartender nodded and counted out the money.

"And," said Matt, "if your boss's got any problem with that just tell him to send a bill to Matt Ritter, care of the Palace in Abilene."

Night had fallen by the time Matt and Bert rode into camp. Oops sounded a bit irritated. "Didn't think you'd be so late. Who's this with you?"

Matt introduced Bert. "Sorry, Mr. Madigan. I got involved in a little ruckus."

"Did you now? Well, tell me about it."

"Well,—"

Bert interrupted. "Let me tell about it, Matt. They say I got a knack for storytelling."

Matt shrugged and told him to go ahead. Bert related the whole episode without embellishment but with a talent that brought the whole thing to life. When Bert finished, Oops laughed out loud. "Son, I knew you had sand, but who'd believe you could carry off a thing like that."

"Well, gosh, Mr. Madigan, that owlhoot made me mad. Threatenin' Bert here and pushin' me around."

"But why'd you buffalo 'em? Why didn't you just shoot 'em? And where'd you learn that, anyway?"

"I didn't want to kill a man. And I saw Marshal Hickok do that one night last year at the Palace, buffalo a couple of fellers, that is. I didn't have time to do much thinkin', so I just thought I'd try it."

"Why'd you tell Jack, the barkeep, to send a bill to Abilene?" asked Bert.

"Because I don't expect to be there again for a long time, and I didn't want any of those fellers tellin' Catlow Moran and his bunch where I'm headin', to Wichita."

Oops laughed again and put his hand on Matt's shoulder.

"By God, Matt, you'll do. You'll surely do to ride the river with."

15

After an early breakfast, Matt said good-bye to Oops Madigan. "I do appreciate all you've done for me, Mr. Madigan. I surely have learned a lot in a short piece of time."

"That's quite all right, son. I've enjoyed ridin' with you. Hope you find your man and finish your business real quick. And when I get back to Abilene, I'll try to look up your aunt and uncle and give 'em your regards. Adios."

Matt spent most of the morning riding around to all the herds he could find in the Newton area, showing his drawing to any cowboys he encountered, but without any luck.

Nobody had seen nor heard of Bowler Bob Bixby. Bert Lisle rode with Matt but spent a good bit of time looking back over his shoulder.

"What're you lookin' for, Bert?"

"Nothing really. I just wouldn't want to run into Catlow Moran and his cronies is all."

Matt looked at his older companion, still wearing his stovepipe hat, the swallowtail coat draped across his saddle.

"Don't you have any other clothes?"

"I do, but I don't intend to go back into Newton to get 'em. If it's all the same to you, I'll wear what I've got on."

Matt shrugged. "All right. Whatever you say." He squinted at the sun. "I'd guess it's mighty close to noon now. Want to stop for lunch?"

"How far do you think we are from Newton?"

"Oh, I'd guess we've worked our way about five, six miles south. Probably got about twenty miles to go to Wichita."

Bert nodded. "I see." He turned and looked over his shoulder again. "If you don't mind, Matt, I'd like to put a few more miles between us and Newton."

Matt scratched his head and then shrugged. "All right. Let's ride another hour and then give the horses a rest. We can fix somethin' to eat, too. Accordin' to what Oops told me, though, if we come across another herd, they'll probably offer us a meal. That suit you?"

"Well," said the piano man with a sigh, "it's better than staying here. Which way?"

"The railroad track's just over there about a half mile. We can follow it straight into Wichita."

Matt was content to allow the horses to amble along at a leisurely pace. He kept his hat tilted over his eyes to keep out the glaring sun. Fortunately, a gentle breeze cooled them. From time to time, he glanced at his pocket watch.

The watch had formerly belonged to Catlow Moran, but Matt, when he'd relieved Catlow of the cylinder in his revolver, had also appropriated the watch. He had no qualms about it, figuring the outlaw owed him something for his trouble. Besides, going by the initials on the watch, the owlhoot'd probably stolen it from some other poor soul. The cylinders to the three guns Matt'd simply dropped on the prairie while riding back to camp the night before.

They met no other herds, so, when after an hour's riding, they came across a lonely, giant oak tree, Matt finally stopped. They hobbled the horses—Matt was surprised to discover Bert carried a set of hobbles—and set them out to graze.

Matt built a small fire and, squatting on his heels, brewed a pot of coffee and warmed some beans. Bert lounged in the shade. "You know, Matt, you should've shot those three bandits when you had the chance. Nobody would've complained ."

Matt looked back over his shoulder. "I told you I didn't want to kill a man."

The piano man snorted. "I thought that was the whole purpose of your trip. To kill a man. I thought you wanted to find the scoundrel who killed your father and get revenge."

Looking thoughtful, Matt handed a plate of beans to his companion and then took a plate for himself. He poured two cups of coffee and handed one to Bert. Then he settled down in the shade. Finally he broke his silence. "Not exactly. I plan to hunt him down and haul him back to Abilene to be hung."

Bert grunted. "You think if you find him way down in Texas somewhere, you can haul him four, five hundred miles back to Abilene?"

Matt shrugged. "I'm goin' to sure try."

Bert shook his head. "You know that's not going to work. Sooner or later you'll have to shoot the son of a bitch or he'll shoot you. For a fact, you've got to kill him. That's all there is to it."

"Maybe."

"There's another reason you should've shot those three bastards."

Matt took a forkful of beans and washed them down with a swig of coffee. The he looked up. "What's that?"

"You'd probably've saved a lot of other people's lives, including maybe ours. Those three are killers, and the only thing that'll stop them is if somebody kills them first."

Matt frowned. "Hadn't thought of that." He took another swig of coffee. "Maybe you're right. I'll have to think about it."

All the way to Wichita, Matt thought about what Bert'd said. It made sense. Maybe when he did run up against a real killer, he should take more direct action.

About two hours north of their destination, a train chugged by heading south. Bert grinned, as Matt whooped and waved his hat. When they rode into Wichita, the place was bustling. It seemed to Matt the streets swarmed with cowboys. He noticed quite a few Indians, too. He turned to Bert, riding beside him. "Looks like business is boomin' in Wichita. 'Cept for the Indians, kinda reminds me of Abilene a year or two ago."

"I never been to Abilene, so I wouldn't know about that, but now that the railroad's here, Wichita's probably going to take the cattle business away from Newton. I hear there's good farming around here, too. Already been trouble between the cattle people and the nesters."

"Just like Abilene, by golly."

"If the farmers had their way, the herds wouldn't come here at all. They claim the cows trample their crops and give tick fever to their livestock."

Bert's dissertation on Wichita's politics aroused Matt's curiosity. "You sure seem to know a lot about Wichita, Bert. How come?"

"Well, I worked here for a while. Played piano over at Rowdy Joe's." He nodded toward a dance hall. "That's it right there."

"How'd you end up in Newton?"

"Had a little trouble over a woman here in Wichita. Other fellow was downright testy about it. Anyway, it seemed like a good idea to leave town for a while."

"How's the hotel here?"

"A damn sight better than Newton's."

"You gonna stay there?"

Bert grinned. "Well, no, I think I'll look up an old friend. She owns a place just down the road a ways. Begged me to look her up if I ever hit town again." He winked. "She's a forty-five-year-old widow with a taste for music."

Bert's sly wink made Matt uneasy. He felt himself blushing. "Oh."

Matt's discomfiture seemed to amuse Bert. "She could probably fix you up, too, you know. She's got four or five girls living there with her. They're nicer than any of the girls in the joy houses around Wichita."

"Joy houses? What's a joy house."

Bert laughed. "That's a polite term for whorehouse. Sounds nicer, more genteel, don't you think?"

Matt reined in and looked at Bert. Was Bert joshin' him? "Are the girls...soiled doves?"

Bert snickered. "That's one way to put it, I guess. But, if you mean are they whores? Yes, they are. Wichita's full of them. Between Rowdy Joe's and the joy houses, not to mention the free lancers, there's probably more than 300 of those women you call soiled doves here in Wichita. And, what's more, I doubt there's more than 2,000 citizens in the whole town."

Matt stared at Bert. "You joshin' me?"

"No sir, I'm not. This town is growing, and it takes all kinds, but in a place like this, you're sure to have bartenders, gamblers, and whores. Now, how about it? Should I fix you up with Madam Bam?"

"Madam Bam?"

"Her full name's Beatrice Anne Mulligan. Bam for short. But don't call her Bam to her face. She doesn't think it's funny. She likes Madam Bea. And she carries a nasty little derringer. Rumor has it she's been known to use it." Bert laughed again. "Some people refer to her place as Mulligan's Stew."

Matt wrinkled his brow. Despite his timidity when it came to women, Bert's offer tempted him. Maybe this'd be a chance to learn about women. But, on the other hand....

"I hear you're liable to get diseases from women like that."

Bert shrugged. "It's been known to happen, I guess." Bert leaned closer. "Matt, you ever had a woman?"

Matt looked around. Here they were, horses reined in in the middle of the busiest street in Wichita, and he could feel himself getting excited. What kind of conversation was this?

"Well...ah...to tell the truth, no."

Bert slowly shook his head. "Matt, Matt. It's time."

"You really think so."

"I do, I certainly do. Why, you wouldn't want some owlhoot or some Indian to shoot you, and you go to your grave never having known the delight of having a woman, would you?"

"Well, no, but I don't plan to get shot any time soon."

"You never know, Matt, you never know." Bert leaned across and put his hand on Matt's shoulder. "I tell you what. Let's go to Lanigan's Livery Stable and leave the horses. It's just down the block there. I know old Jess Lanigan, and he'll look after our stuff for us. Then we can get spruced up. Go to the barber shop and get a shave and a bath. After that, I'll go on out to Madam Bam's and get things all set up. Just think. It'll save you the cost of a hotel room."

"What do you mean? I heard you only get to spend a few minutes with a whore."

Bert smiled. "Ordinarily that's true. But I told you. Madam Bam's got a taste for music, and she's partial to piano players. She says she likes the way I play, and," Bert winked, "she especially admires my fingering."

Matt's brow furrowed. Why the wink? Was Bert makin' some kind of joke? "Well...all right. If it'll save the price of a hotel room."

Bert clapped him on the back. "That's the spirit."

Just as Bert had predicted, Jess Lanigan agreed to keep their belongings for them and to take good care of their horses. With a sigh of relief, Matt slipped into his moccasins and left his boots with his other things. "Bert, you really ought to get a pair of these things. They surely do ease a man's feet."

"You really like them, huh? Maybe I will, even though I don't wear boots myself."

When they came out of the barber shop, bathed and cleanly shaved, Matt felt like a new man. His renewed cleanliness and the aura of bay rum about him gave him confidence—for the moment, anyway. Maybe he would be able to carry off the task that lay ahead.

Bert had rented a horse and buggy from Jess. "Now, I'll meet you at the First and Last Chance in about an hour."

"The what?"

"I forgot. You're a stranger here, aren't you? It's a saloon. Take's its name from the fact it claims to be the first chance for a drink for drovers heading north and the last chance for those heading south into the Indian Territory."

After Bert left, Matt decided to stop at the marshal's office and see whether there was any news of Bowler Bob. A passerby gave him directions. Might be some wanted posters that'd give an idea as to the owlhoot's whereabouts, he mused, strolling along, taking in the sights. As usual, he had his drawing tucked under his arm to show to whomever would look at it.

The marshal was in. When Matt entered and looked around, the marshal got up and stuck out his hand. "Howdy. Name's Charlie Lawton."

Matt shook the marshal's hand. "Howdy. I'm Matt Ritter. From up Abilene way, but I just got in from Newton a little while ago."

Marshal Lawton grinned. "Did you, now? You that young feller that caused all the commotion yesterday up there in Newton?"

Matt was taken aback. How'd the marshal hear about that?

"Well, now, there was a bit of a ruckus, but it wasn't really my fault, sir."

The marshal's grin grew broader. "Oh, I know it wasn't, leastwise not from what I hear."

Still puzzled, Matt asked, "If you don't mind my askin', Mr. Lawton, how did you hear about it?"

"Friend of mine came in on the train from Newton a couple of hours ago. He told me about it. Said you buffaloed that rascal Catlow Moran and those other two scalawags that ride with him."

"Well, yes sir, I guess I did. Hope I'm not in trouble over that."

The marshal roared with laughter. When he finally got a grip on himself and wiped the tears from his eyes, he said, "No, son, you're not in trouble. My only complaint is that you didn't shoot those three bastards and save us all a lot of trouble in the future. Unfortunately, accordin' to what my friend told me, those three skunks are still alive and kickin'."

"Oh." Matt thought for a moment. "Mr. Lawton, how come there's no marshal in Newton?"

"There was until just a few days ago. And he was doin' a fine job. Feller name of Buffalo Bill Brooks. He got offered a better deal by the folks over in Dodge City. So he left, although, I'm inclined to think maybe the fact that Sweet Alice Long left for Dodge City had more to do with Bill's leavin' than anything else."

"So there's no lawman there now?"

"Nope. Nobody seems to want the job. But speakin' of jobs, I could use a feller like you. How'd you like to be a deputy marshal right here in Wichita?"

Surprised at the offer, Matt's eyes widened. "Well, that's mighty nice of you to ask, and it probably would be an interesting job, but I'm afraid I can't accept. You see I got somethin' I got to do first." He then went on to explain about his father's death and about his own vow to get revenge.

Marshal Lawton listened to Matt's recital, every now and then nodding his head sympathetically. When Matt finished his story, the marshal said, "Well, I sure am sorry to hear about your Paw's death, but what can I do for you?"

Matt unrolled the dog-eared drawing. "This is a picture of the killer. Name's Bowler Bob Bixby. I was wonderin' if you ever heard of him or had any wanted posters on him from anywhere else."

Marshal Lawton studied the drawing for a few moments, then shook his head. "Nope. Can't say's I've ever seen him. I know most everybody who stays any length of time in Wichita, so I doubt he's ever been here. Might've passed through, but that's about it."

"What about wanted posters?"

The marshal pointed to a pile of papers on a table.

"There's a bunch of 'em you're welcome to look through, but I don't think his picture's there."

Matt thanked the marshal and began sorting through the posters. The marshal was right; there was nothing on Bowler Bob. There were posters on Jesse and Frank James, but Matt thought it'd be best not mention his ill-starred acquaintance with those two ruffians. Disappointed, he again thanked the marshal for his cooperation.

"That's quite all right, son. All I ask is if you ever meet Catlow Moran again, kill the son of a bitch. Now, you sure I can't persuade you to take a job as a deputy?"

"No sir, not right now. Maybe some other time if I'm ever in Wichita again."

"Well, all right, but if you meet up with any other owlhoots here in Wichita that need exterminatin', don't hesitate to shoot. You'll be doin' me and the law-abidin' citizens a genuine favor."

They shook hands and the marshal gave Matt directions to the First and Last Chance Saloon. "Although," said the marshal as they were parting, "if you want to steer clear of trouble, that and Rowdy Joe's are fine places to keep away from."

Just as Matt reached the saloon, Bert and his horse and buggy drew up in front. Matt climbed into the buggy, and they set off.

"Well," said a grinning Bert, "I told Madam Bea about you, and she's delighted to have another piano player. And when I told her about your run-in with Catlow Moran, she was beside herself. She had some trouble with Catlow a while back, and she's been itching to have somebody get the son of a bitch for her, but nobody had the guts."

For a moment Matt debated whether to tell Bert what the marshal had told him about Catlow Moran still being alive, but then decided to keep the news to himself. No use spoilin' Bert's evenin', he told himself.

"How many people are apt to be there tonight?"

"She's closing the place to outsiders for tonight and giving her piano player the night off, so there'll just be you and me. It'll be like old home week. And you get your pick of the girls, you lucky dog, not to mention the best room in the place, best next to hers, that is."

"You mean I got to choose one of the girls?"

"Sure, why not?"

Matt could foresee difficulties. "But I've never even met them."

Bert laughed. "Don't worry about it. This isn't your ordinary joy house, and these aren't your usual whores."

"They're not?"

"No, they're not. Neither's Bea's clientele your run-of-the-mill cowboy. All her customers have money, lots of it. And they're all men of power and influence, too. That's why she has just a few choice, refined girls. And why she doesn't have any trouble with the powers that be, if you get my drift."

Matt wasn't sure that he did, but he nodded his head as though he understood perfectly.

"Anyway," Bert went on, "we'll have dinner there, and it'll be a good one. Bea has a good cook. After dinner, you and I'll play a few tunes on the piano to entertain the ladies."

"When do I do this choosin'?"

Bert smiled. "You'll have plenty of time to choose. You just look them over and chat with them throughout the evening. When you finally decide which one you want, just let me know. Discreetly, of course. I'll pass the word to Madam Bea. That way, when it's time to go to bed, there won't be any strain nor fuss. You just go to your room, and whichever girl you choose will join you. How's that?"

Speechless, Matt simply nodded his head. He looked around. They had left the town limits a couple of minutes before, and the buggy was rolling down a narrow path off the beaten track. In a matter of perhaps five minutes, from behind a copse of trees, a large house came in view. It looked even bigger than Uncle Frank's place.

Bert drove around behind the house to where a small barn stood and halted. They got down, and an old black man came out of the barn and took over the horse and buggy.

"Take good care of her, Abraham. We might need her in the morning."

The black bobbed his head. "Yas suh, I surely will."

Bert noticed Matt staring at the house. "Quite a mansion, isn't it?"

Matt nodded. "Yep. It sure is."

"Bea had it shipped all the way from Chicago. It's got four bedrooms upstairs. Told me she paid $3,500 for it plus, of course, what it cost to get it assembled."

"I thought my uncle's place was something, but this sure beats all."

"Wait'll you see it inside. Come on."

Matt took a deep breath and followed his mentor around to the front door. A lantern lit the entrance. Bert turned to Matt and grinned. "Ready?"

Then he turned back to the door and knocked.

16

Madam Bea herself opened the door.

An imposing woman, Matt judged she stood about five seven. Her long, midnight blue velvet gown displayed a stunning figure. Coal-black hair contrasted with her milk-white complexion. Matt found it hard to believe she was, as Bert had claimed, in her early forties. She looked much younger, especially in the soft, diffused light provided by the oil lamps with their frosted glass globes that illuminated the house.

She smiled. "Come in, come in."

Bert stood back and indicated Matt should precede him into the house. A little hesitantly Matt stepped into the foyer. Madam Bea took his hand in both of her soft, white ones. She turned to Bert. "Is this the young man who so bravely dealt with that scoundrel, Catlow Moran?"

Bert grinned. "In the flesh."

She turned back to Matt. "Ordinarily Luna Belle—she's my maid and my cook—shows visitors in, but I couldn't wait to meet you. You, sir, are our honored guest tonight. Luna Belle is laying the table now, but first," she drew Matt toward a door to his right, "you must come into the parlor and meet my girls."

Matt turned toward the grinning Bert, but the older man, with a nod of his head, merely urged him on. Matt gulped and followed Madam Bea into the parlor.

He'd never seen anything like the room he now entered. Tasseled, brocaded draperies covered the windows. A thick, dark red carpet covered the floor. A marble fireplace stood in the middle of the outside wall; a painting of a nude female occupied a place of honor above it. A large mirror on the wall opposite the fireplace gave an illusion of greater spaciousness than even this room possessed. Paintings of lush country scenes adorned the remaining wall space.

On a pedestal just inside the door stood a marble statue of a nude winged male, a bow in hand and quiver of arrows at his side. Matt hurriedly averted his gaze. The figure's lifelike genitalia embarrassed him. Bert noticed his discomfiture.

"That's a statue of Eros, the Greek god of passion. Madam Bea thinks that, all things considered, it's appropriate for her parlor."

Madam gave Bert a vexed glance, and then smiled sweetly at Matt. "Matt, I want you to meet my young ladies."

Scattered about the room were plush chairs and a settee. Four young women, one a redhead, one a blonde, and two brunettes lolled in relaxed postures, one each on overstuffed chairs and two on the settee.

"Girls, this is Matt Ritter. I know you'll all want to be as nice to him as only my girls know how."

The four young women rose to their feet and smiled.

Matt grinned and nodded.

Madam Bea indicated the redhead. The young woman wore a snug-fitting green gown. "Matt, this is Erin O'Brien.

She's been with me for two years."

The redhead winked at Matt.

"The blonde young lady next to Erin is Nell Waters. Nell's been with me not quite as long."

The blonde woman seemed younger than the others, perhaps because her clothing resembled that of a schoolgirl, and she wore her hair braided. She gave Matt a shy smile.

Madam Bea nodded toward the two brunettes who had been lolling on the settee. "The young lady on the left is Sally Wilson. She's been with me the longest and is very versatile."

Sally's blue gown, while not as snug as Erin's, still did not hang loosely on her. She bowed and curtsied.

"Next to Sally is Peggy Stevens. Peggy's a former school mistress from England and is somewhat of a specialist. She's very serious about rules and discipline."

Peggy stared at Matt, the tip of her tongue gliding slowly back and forth along her upper lip. A challenging smile hovered on her lips. Matt felt intimidated but fascinated by her. He gave a brief, curt nod; at the same time a quick, little involuntary shiver ran through him.

At that moment, a black woman appeared in the doorway leading to the dining room. She looked older than the four young women, but not quite as old as Madam Bea.

"Yes, Luna? What is it?"

"Dinner's ready, Ma'am."

Everyone filed into the dining room. There the wall decorations and furniture were on a par with those in the parlor. When it came to furnishing her establishment, the madam had obviously spared no expense. "If you want a high class clientele," she explained, "you must maintain a high class establishment. It doesn't pay to cut corners."

Madam Bea sat at the head of the table, and Bert occupied the chair facing her at the foot of the table. Madam Bea insisted that Matt occupy the chair on her right hand. Peggy sat across from him; the other three young women took seats along either side of the table.

Dinner was excellent. Matt had never before tasted such

food. "Luna Belle's been with me quite a while now," said Madam Bea. "Ever since I opened my own establishment in New Orleans. She can not only prepare food in your usual southern style but also in the special style of New Orleans."

Surprised, Matt glanced at Bert.

Bert grinned. "That's right, New Orleans. I first met Madam Bea there and played piano in her place for a while. Peggy and Sally were there, too. When Madam Bea had a little trouble with some of the bigwigs in New Orleans—"

"I refused to be intimidated and taken undue advantage of," Madam Bea interjected.

Bert shrugged. "Well, anyway, the three of us decided to follow her out here to Wichita."

"I thought you said you played at Rowdy Joe's?"

Bert nodded. "I did play at Rowdy Joe's. For a while. You see, if Bea and I are together too long, things don't always go smoothly, so I go somewhere else." He sighed. "Sooner or later, though, it seems like Bea and I always end up together, don't we, Bea?"

A faint smile played across her features. "That's right, my dear. I hope this time you're here to stay for a while."

The evening progressed pretty much as Bert had predicted. Matt described his search for his father's killer, and the ladies offered their sympathies. Madam Bea wished him luck in finding the villain. After dinner they all repaired to a second front parlor. The madam had furnished this room too with a lavish hand. A grand piano occupied one corner of the room. Congeniality reigned.

Bert and Matt took turns playing the piano; the girls—and even madam—joined in singing some of the tunes. Bert astonished Matt with some of the music he'd learned in New Orleans. "They're developing a new style of music down there. The rhythm's catchier, but sometimes the mood's kind of sad. Only place I've ever heard it."

Even Matt shed his usual caution and had a couple of glasses of wine. All the while, in the back of his mind, he wrestled with the problem of which girl to choose. Finally, when he and Bert went outside to the privy, he made his choice known. By ten o'clock, he was ready to retire. Madam Bea decided to show him to his room herself.

"You're right across the hall from me, and Bert'll be with me. Those tapestries there on the wall absorb sound," she said, lighting the lamp on the bedside table, "so it should be nice and quiet for you. The bed's soft, too, and a little wider than most beds, so you should get a good night's sleep. Your young lady'll be in shortly."

She smiled and winked. "Good night."

It'd been a long day, and he was tired. The wine hadn't helped matters, either. But, despite his fatigue, he found himself shivering with anticipation. He managed to haul his boots off but didn't know what else he should do.

Should he keep his clothes on? Or strip and get into bed? He hadn't been naked in front of any woman except his mother and Aunt Elly, and then not since he was a little fellow. The idea of being naked in front of a strange woman unnerved him. And, he wondered, what do you say to a woman, anyway, when you're fixing to…Oh! Jesus…fuck her?

Good God, why had he let Bert talk him into this? But he knew he wanted to. He had to know what it was like. Excitement growing, he elected to sit shivering on the edge of the bed and stare at the door.

What seemed an eternity went by. Then a tap sounded on the door. Now that the moment was at hand, his anxiety level shot up. He gulped. "Yep," he managed to get out.

"It's me, Matt."

He took a deep breath. "Oh. Well…come on in."

The door slowly opened. Fragrance from her perfume invaded the room. She entered and glided toward him, her bare feet not making a sound. She stood before him, arms at her side. She'd let her hair down and was wrapped in a thin white garment of a sort he'd never seen before.

He sat there, too frightened to move or speak. Then she took his hands in hers and drew him to his feet. "Do you want to do it, or do you want me to?"

His chest felt full. His shivering increased. Unable to speak, he first shook his head and then nodded. She smiled and reached up to her throat. She untied the ribbons holding her garment together and then shrugged. Slowly the wrap slid from her shoulders and dropped to the floor. She stood naked before him, her body revealed in the soft lamplight.

"Oooh, my God," he whispered. Arms at his side, barely able to breathe, he stood rooted to the spot.

Once again she took his hands in hers. She brought them up to her breasts and gently guided his palms across her nipples. The nipples grew erect under his touch. He felt himself growing hard. He closed his eyes and tried to speak. His throat dry, nothing came.

She began unbuttoning his shirt. He didn't know what to do. Her hands brushed against his chest. He grew harder. Now she was unfastening his pants. They dropped to the floor. She stooped down and worked them free from his ankles. The two of them faced each other naked. All he could think of was how fortunate it was he'd gotten a bath and a shave.

Next she turned down the bed and climbed into it. Then once again she took his hand and this time drew him into the bed. He lay back, not sure what was expected of him.

She tried to draw him on top of her. Clumsily he scrambled to comply. His rod, now fully engorged, brushed against her soft, smooth belly. His shivering increased. Now what? Then he realized she'd taken it into her hand, was trying to work it between her legs. The touch of that soft hand sent tremors coursing through his body.

"Oh, no! Wait! Don't do that," he moaned. "I can't… can't…oooh…."

He exploded! All over her!

Oh, my God, he thought, what've I done? He collapsed on top of her, humiliated. "I'm sorry, I'm sorry."

He felt her relax beneath him. Her free hand reached up and stroked his hair. He lay inert. Finally he summoned enough energy to roll off her and lie back. Arms stiff at his sides, fists clenched, he stared at the ceiling. "I'm sorry," he whispered, "really I am."

She propped herself on one elbow and stared down at him. "Your first time? I mean, you've never been with a woman before?"

Miserable, he could only shake his head.

She sat up beside him. "Don't worry about it. It's not your fault. And, believe me, your not the first man it's ever happened to. Happens to a lot of 'em."

It was nice of her to try to cheer him up, but he felt like such a fool. He rolled on his side and looked away from her. She reached over and stroked his hair. "Look I should've known better and handled it differently." She suddenly seemed to realize what she'd said and couldn't suppress a giggle. "What I mean is I would've approached it differently if I'd known. We can try it again in a few minutes. Slower."

"I don't know's I want to. Same thing'll probably happen all over again," he said in a low voice. "Besides, I'm tired."

"Now, Matt," she sounded exasperated, "don't talk like that. I don't usually care what happens to a John, but this is a little different. I kind of like you. Besides," now she sounded worried, "Madam Bea's liable to skin me alive for this. She thinks a lot of you, and she'll hold me responsible."

"Don't worry. I won't tell her. I won't tell anyone."

She lay back and said nothing. After a few minutes, she reached over and began trailing her fingertips across his chest. It stirred him but made him want to squirm, too. He gave a slight moan. She rolled him on his back. Her fingers trailed down across his belly. He felt himself begin to respond ever so slightly. She focused all her efforts on his rod. After a minute or two, a little more progress—but not much.

He shook his head. "It's not goin' to work."

She stopped for a moment, propped herself up, and gazed down at him. "Matt, are you really trying?"

"I'm tryin', but I just don't know what's the matter. I guess I'm just too tired, and that wine made me sleepy. I'm not used to wine. Hell, I'm not used to any of this."

"Well," she snapped, "you're going to fuck me tonight or

my name's not—what are you doing?"

"I'm goin' to get up and take a walk."

"By God, you're not. I've got my professional pride to think of. You just lay yourself back down here." She caught him by the shoulder and pulled him down. "Now, just lie there and don't move. There's one more thing I can try and, mister, it *never* fails."

She slid down and leaned over him, putting her remedy into action. Outraged, he gasped and pushed her away. "What are you *doin'*?" He bounded to his feet. Hands across his crotch, he stared down at her. "That's...that's rotten! What kinda woman are you, anyway?"

Defeated, Sally heaved a sigh and lay back on the bed.

"Matt, for God's sake, get back into bed. I'll leave you alone, and we can both get a good night's sleep."

17

Matt slid into a chair at the dining room table. Bert was already there, his plate heaped with bacon and eggs and fried potatoes. He grinned at Matt. "You're up early."

"It's not early. It's almost eight o'clock."

"Around here that's early. Probably be ten o'clock before the ladies come down. They generally sleep in. Of course, they didn't have to stay up late last night." Bert winked. "I'm surprised to see you, though. I didn't think you'd want to leave Sally."

Matt shrugged. He'd left the young woman sleeping soundly. Cautiously he'd rolled out of bed and slipped into his pants. Then, shirt and moccasins in hand, he'd tiptoed quietly out of the room to finish dressing in the hall. He was just as well satisfied she'd slept through his getting up. Sometime during the night, she'd awakened him, and they'd had another go at it but with no more success than the first time. He still felt like a fool and didn't really want to have to face her again.

Bert poured a cup of coffee from the pot sitting at his elbow and handed it to Matt. "So, how was it?"

Matt took a drink of coffee. Luna Belle saved him from the need for an immediate answer when she appeared from the kitchen and set a plate of bacon and eggs and fried potatoes in front of him. He shoved a forkful of potatoes into his mouth and began chewing. He didn't want to discuss his romantic fiasco with Bert any more than he wanted to see Sally again. He decided to change the subject. Mouth still full, he said, "I wouldn't be surprised if Catlow Moran turns up again."

Bert immediately turned serious. "Why do you say that?"

"I had a talk with Marshal Lawton yesterday. He said somebody told him Catlow and his two friends were still alive and kickin'. Seemed to think Catlow might head back to Wichita." Matt didn't recall whether Charlie Lawton had actually said that or not. Ordinarily he believed in tellin' the God's truth, but he was beginnin' to think it didn't always pay to be so honest. Besides, Bert wouldn't know the difference.

Bert looked worried. "Damn! I knew you should've shot those three when you had the chance."

Matt nodded. "Maybe you're right. The marshal more or less said the same thing yesterday. Seemed to think I'd have done everybody a favor. Said if the same situation came up again, he wouldn't object if I shot the owlhoots. I'll just have to keep my eyes open. In case they come lookin' for us."

"You think they will?"

"They might. They just might, but I don't have to worry. I don't plan to be around Wichita much longer. I'm headin' south for Indian Territory today or tomorrow. What about you?"

"Well, now that you mention it, maybe I'll move along, too. Can't stay here. Madam Bea's got to open up for business again, and I'd just be underfoot."

"Want to come along with me?"

"Through the Indian Territory? No, I don't think so.

Thanks just the same, but I kind of like this head of hair I've got and would just as soon keep it. No, I think I'll head east to Saint Louis or maybe New Orleans. I always liked New Orleans. Anyway, someplace where good piano playing's appreciated. And Catlow Moran's not liable to turn up."

"When do you figger to leave?"

"Today. Soon's we finish breakfast."

"Won't we have to say good-bye to Madam Bea and thank her?"

"Luna Belle can explain to the ladies we got important business elsewhere."

Bert's cavalier approach to Madam Bea troubled Matt.

"Don't you think that's kinda rude?"

"Be simpler that way than trying to explain the whole thing to Bea."

Matt's doubts must've shown on his face. Bert attempted to smooth matters over. "You can come along and pick up your horses and gear from Lanigan, or I'll drop you off at the First and Last. Whichever you want. With Catlow Moran on the loose and looking for us, I'd just as soon be gone as quick as possible."

Matt felt a little guilty for not reminding Bert that more than likely, if Catlow and his cronies were looking for them, the owlhoots would head north to Abilene. Oh well, Bert probably wouldn't want to take the chance, so why confuse the man. At least he seemed to have lost interest in what'd transpired between Matt and Sally.

On the way into town, Matt turned over his options in his mind. He asked Bert to drop him off at the First and Last Chance. "I might's well show the picture around and see what I can find out. You never know. Somebody might know somethin'."

When they reached the saloon, Matt got out of the buggy and the two of them shook hands. "Well, Matt, it's been nice knowing you, and if you're ever in New Orleans, look me up. And," he said, grinning, "when you come back through Wichita, be sure and look up the Madam and her girls. She took a shine to you, and I suspect if I hadn't been there, she'd've taken you on herself."

Matt nodded. "Maybe I'll do that, but first I expect I got business down in Texas."

"I know you have, and I want to wish you the best of luck. So long."

Matt watched the buggy until Bert turned the corner two blocks down, heading for the livery stable. When the buggy disappeared from sight, Matt turned and headed for the saloon. Picture rolled up and tucked under his arm, he pushed through the swinging doors. Although only ten o'clock in the morning, the place was nonetheless doing a good business.

He surveyed the barroom, searching for a likely prospect to show his picture to. Suddenly he froze. "By God," he breathed. Sitting alone, hunched over a table in the corner, back to Matt, sat a scruffy-looking individual wearing a brown bowler. A large hulk with black hair, the man seemed intent on something on the table in front of him.

Slowly Matt laid his rolled-up picture down on an empty table, eased his Ritter Special out of its holster, and, on moccasined feet, silently slipped up behind the fellow. The man didn't move, apparently unaware of Matt's approach. When he was a foot away from his quarry, Matt cocked his pistol and thrust the end of the barrel against the man's backbone. The fellow stiffened and started to turn.

"Hold it!" Matt grated. "Don't move a muscle, or you're a dead man."

The stranger froze.

"Now, real slowlike, raise your hands." The fellow obeyed. "All right, now stand up. Slow!" Again the man complied. Matt took two steps back. By this time, everybody in the place had focused on Matt and his target. The only sounds were those that drifted in from the street.

"All right now, don't try anything, but real slow, turn around so I can get a look at you."

Once more, hands still high in the air, the stranger did as Matt had instructed. Slowly he pivoted, until he faced the tense, vigilant Matt.

"Well, damn!" said Matt. The feller didn't look a thing like Bowler Bob's picture. For one thing, his nose was small, and overall, he might even be called handsome. "I'm sorry, mister. You're not the feller I thought you were. You can put your hands down."

The stranger nodded and let out his breath. "That's mighty white of you, neighbor, but would you mind putting that hawgleg back in its holster?"

Matt, embarrassed by his mistake, glanced down. "Oh, sure." He holstered the gun.

"You should'a shot him, mister," a voice from the crowd said. "He's just a no-good nester."

"Besides," piped up another voice, "we ain't had no entertainment in several days now. Not since Catlow left town."

The implication he was in the same class with Catlow Moran upset Matt. The stranger, however, simply ignored the comments. He indicated a chair at the table. "Mind sitting down and telling me what this is all about?"

"Glad to, but let me get somethin' first." Matt retrieved the rolled up picture from where he'd laid it when he began stalking the stranger and then joined the man at his table. He felt he should make some kind of goodwill gesture. He held out his hand. "I'm Matt Ritter. Can I get you a beer?"

His newfound friend took his hand. "I'm Jack Matlock. Sounds good. Almost getting shot can raise a man's thirst."

Matt went over to the bar and placed an order for two beers. While he waiter, he glared at the ne'er-do-well who'd made the allusion to Catlow Moran. The scalawag took the hint and slunk out of the saloon. For the first time in his life, it occurred to Matt that maybe he was developing an impressive look. The thought pleased him.

He set a mug of beer in front of Matlock who looked at him quizzically. Matt unrolled his picture and proceeded to explain about his quest for his father's killer.

Matlock nodded. "I see. Well, I can understand why you feel as you do. I'm just glad you're not too trigger-happy.

Might've made quite a mess, lf you were."

Again Matt apologized. "But, tell me," he went on, "why'd those rascals want me to shoot you? Can't be just because you're a nester."

Matlock grinned wryly. "Well, no, but I guess the cattle people around here kind of see me as the head nester. There aren't a lot of us yet, at least not as many as the cattlemen, but what there are of us are getting mighty tired of having our fences destroyed and our fields trampled by longhorns. Not to mention the threat those Texas cows with their tick fever pose to our cattle."

Matt nodded. "I know just what you mean. I'm from Abilene and my Uncle Frank's a farmer up there. He had a lot to do with old T.C. Henry puttin' out that notice for the drovers to stay away from Abilene."

Matlock regarded Matt with increased interest. "You a farmer, too?"

"Not exactly. I did help my uncle on the farm, so I know somethin' about farmin', but I'm a gunsmith and a piano player."

Matlock grinned. "Why, say, you must be that young fellow everybody's talking about. The one that buffaloed that bastard Catlow Moran and his two bully-boys up in Newton."

Matt shrugged. "Well, yes, I guess I am. But you still haven't told me why those two wanted me to shoot you."

"Oh, those two are just a couple of no-accounts. Pay no attention to them. They just want to get in good with Jim Thompson."

"Who's this feller Thompson?"

"Thompson's the one to watch out for. He's a real murdering son of a bitch. It's a wonder he hasn't been hung. Some people think he's worse than your friend, Catlow. Anyway, he's leading the effort to keep us nesters in our place, and as far's he's concerned our place is six feet long and six feet down. He's even hired a bunch of gunslingers to help him get us. Especially me."

"But why you?"

"Well, I guess because I am sort of the leader. I got a little more education—spent a year at the University of Michigan—and I'm drawing up a petition, legal-like, to the governor to have the quarantine enforced down here. In fact, that's it right there on the table." He grinned. "I was working on it when I was so rudely interrupted."

Matt squirmed. "I said I was sorry."

Matlock laughed. "I know. I'm just joshing you. But you know what's really funny about all this?"

Matt shrugged. "What?"

"You ever hear of 'The Furrow'?"

"Can't say's I have."

"Well, sometime ago, down south of here, the towns of Wellington and Sumner City were competing something fierce for the business coming up the Chisholm. Well, some fellow got the bright idea to plow a furrow starting at the border of Kansas and the Indian Territory and running it right by Wellington but nowhere near Sumner City."

Puzzled, Matt could only say, "And so?"

Matlock grinned. "Well, the good folks of Wellington keep a couple of fellows stationed down there on the border, and when the Texans come along with their cattle and ask the way to Wichita, those fellows tell 'em, 'Just follow The Furrow, friends, just follow The Furrow. It'll take you right into Wellington and straight on to Wichita.'"

"Did it work?"

"You betcha it worked. Why Sumner City's dying on the vine, and Wellington's prospering. In fact, I hear it's going to be the county seat."

Matt sat back in his chair. "Doesn't sound too fair to me."

Matlock shrugged. "Maybe not, but all's fair in love and war, and believe me, this was war."

"So what'd it have to do with you? Was it your idea?"

"Nope, it wasn't. But it takes a farmer to plow a furrow like that, and I was one of the ones who helped plow it."

"And this Jim Thompson's from Summer City and wants to get even, huh?"

Matlock shook his head. "Nope, he's from Wellington,

but him and some more like him here in Wichita don't want to see the cattle drives diverted. The business they get from the drives is too important to 'em. They don't care what happens to the farmers. That's why they're out to get anybody who's a threat to the cattle business."

Matt chuckled. "So when you helped plow that furrow, you kinda outsmarted yourself."

Matlock nodded. "Yep. I'm afraid I did. But at the time, I had no idea how big the whole thing'd get to be or the effect it'd have on farming. Anyway, we gotta fight or our farms'll be destroyed."

"I see. And those cattle people and the business men behind 'em are willin' to kill to protect their interests. That about it?"

"Right. That's about it."

Matt glanced down at Matlock's waist. "With all these threats, how come you don't wear a gun?"

"I'm just not a gunslinger. In the long run, I figure more's to be gained by doing things legal. Winning by shooting's not going to be long lasting. And for growing crops and making a farm a success, a man needs some stability. Besides, if I packed a gun, I'd more than likely shoot myself."

Matt hauled out his watch and glanced at it. "My stomach and this watch tell me it's about time to eat. Got any suggestions?"

"Sure have. Place called Maude's Kitchen. Just a couple of blocks from here. Mind if I join you?"

Matt smiled. "My pleasure."

As they got up from the table, Matlock sighed and jammed the petition into his pocket. "I was going to see if Marshal Lawton would countersign my petition, but damn, wouldn't you know, he's not here today."

"He's not?"

"Nope," said Matlock, as they pushed through the swinging doors, "he took three of his four deputies with him to some kind of meeting over in the next county, and Zeke Fry, the one he left here's got no use for us nesters. In fact, Zeke might's well be on Thompson's payroll."

"Bad as that, huh? Don't hardly seem fair." Matt stepped down from the wooden sidewalk into the street and stumbled.

Matlock grabbed his arm and kept him from falling.

"Look out! Man's got to watch his step around here."

Matt looked down. He'd stepped off the sidewalk into a scattering of loose stones, each about the size of a hen's egg.

"Man could turn his ankle pretty bad on those stones," warned Matlock. "I tell you rocks are the bane of a farmer's life. Don't know why they're so many around here, though."

They set off up the street. They'd no sooner taken half-a-dozen steps then, about two blocks ahead of them, Matt spotted six or seven armed men coming their way. One carried a rifle and one carried a shotgun. The man with the shotgun had a rope looped over one shoulder. The rest of them had pistols in their hands. "What's that up ahead there, a posse?"

Matlock came to an abrupt halt. The color drained from his face. "Might as well be. That's Thompson and his gunslingers."

Just then, a man up on the sidewalk hollered, "They're comin' to get you, Matlock, you dirty grayback of a nester. Marshal ain't around to protect you today."

Matt turned to his companion. "You think they're really after you?"

Matlock nodded. "I'm sure of it. So you'd better get the hell away from me. You don't want to get involved. This isn't your fight."

Matt glanced at the man doing the taunting. It was the same scalawag he'd glared out of the saloon. Ordinarily he followed Uncle Frank's advice and kept out of affairs like this. After all, he could kinda sympathize with the viewpoint of both the farmers and cattlemen, but the unfairness of the whole situation made up his mind for him. Besides, he'd taken a liking to Matlock.

"Maybe not, but I'm dealin' myself in." He glanced again at the gang of bully-boys swaggering up the street and then turned again to Matlock. "Except for that feller with the rifle, they're still too far away to have much chance of hittin' anything, but I want them to fire first."

"Why, for God's sake?"

"'Cause then if some of them rascals get shot, nobody can say we started it."

"Started what?"

Matt grinned. "They probably don't know it, but they got a battle on their hands."

Matlock laid a hand on Matt's arm. "Don't be a damn fool, Ritter. Get away while you still can."

"Now, Jack, I got the gun, so you just let me handle this. First thing, let's you and me back up a few steps, and then in a minute we're goin' to follow Uncle Frank's first rule and run like hell up that little alley the other side of the saloon."

"Hell, Matt, I can't run."

Matt grinned. "Well, now, you and me may not be world beaters, but with you in your farmer shoes and me in my moccasins, we can beat those owlhoots seven ways to Sunday."

"You're crazy."

"No, I'm not. Didn't you notice? They're all wearin' pointy-toed, high-heeled ridin' boots with spurs on. They can't run a lick. Why they can't even walk too good in those." Matt bent down and picked up a couple of the loose stones and juggled them in the palm of his hand. "These'll do fine. Now, Thompson's hot tempered, ain't he, so yell somethin' good and insultin' at him."

The oncoming gunslingers were only about seventy-five yards away now, but that was still too far for accurate shooting, at least with pistols. Matlock looked at Matt and then shrugged. "Hope you know what you're doing." Then Matt's companion turned toward their persecutors and yelled, "Come on, Thompson, you lily-livered, yellow-bellied son of a bitch, let's see you do something."

At the same moment, Matt let fly with one of the stones. The range was too long for a pitcher, but he'd played the outfield, too, and had cut down many an overly ambitious runner at the plate. The first rock bounced at Thompson's feet; the second caught him in the thigh.

"God damn it, get those bastards," roared Thompson, limping and rubbing his thigh. His gun thundered, and he urged his crew forward. The whole gang started running awkwardly with delicate, mincing steps.

Matt wanted to laugh but knew he didn't have time. The man with the rifle had stopped and was trying to draw a bead. "Come on, Jack, let's get outta here."

Matt darted for the alleyway before the rifleman could bring his weapon into action. Jack followed close on his heels, and the two of them disappeared around the corner of the First and Last Chance just as the first ball from the rifle splintered a chunk of wood from the building on the far side of the alley. As they charged up the alley, Matt, in a low voice, told Matlock to keep going and head for Lanigan's Livery Stable. When he got there, he was to hide and wait for Matt.

"Lanigan's holding my belongings for me, and if I get there I got somethin' will give these rascals a real surprise. So, now get goin'!"

Matlock was already beginning to wheeze, but he knew his life depended on hotfooting it to the livery stables. He emerged from the alleyway and headed for the stables, three blocks away.

For a moment, Matt watched him go. Then, Ritter Special in hand, he threw himself flat on the ground just around the corner where they'd emerged from the alley. In a very few seconds, he heard the shouts of the enraged Thompson and his boys. From ground level, hat off, Matt peeked around the corner.

He could hardly believe his good fortune. Charging into the alley in single file like angry bulls, too furious to use good sense, came two of the gang, followed closely by Thompson himself. All three of them were blowing and puffing. The range was only ten yards. By God, Matt exulted, I've got 'em. Like ducks in a shootin' gallery.

Matt angled his gun up and fired. His first shot caught the leading rascal square in the chest. The man staggered and pitched forward. The man behind him tripped and started to fall. Matt's second shot caught that fellow in the side of the head. The thought that he'd killed a man flashed through Matt's brain. But he didn't have time to reflect on it. Thompson, brought to his senses and seeing his peril, tried to reverse direction. In so doing, he tripped and fell. The fall saved his life.

Matt's third shot, intended for Thompson, passed over him and caught the man behind him in the belly. A look of pained astonishment on his face, the man dropped his gun, doubled over, and clutched his belly. He tried to follow Thompson back out of the alley but didn't quite make it before slowly crumpling and pitching forward on his face.

"By God," muttered Matt, "three of those owlhoots down and just four to go. That evens the odds a little."

He knew he had to abandon his position, though, and head for the livery stables before he was outflanked. He grabbed his hat and leaped to his feet. Bent over, head low, he scuttled for the next cross street. Just before entering the intersection he halted. Again he flung himself flat and, sheltered by the building on the corner, cautiously peeked back toward the street where the action had started.

"By God," he breathed. In the middle of that street, feet planted, rifle ready at his shoulder, stood the rifleman, obviously just waiting for his target to appear in the intersection Matt had been about to enter. Matt braced himself on the ground and carefully took aim. Can't afford to miss this one, he told himself. Slowly, slowly he squeezed the trigger.

The gun roared.

The man, clutching his left shoulder, staggered and dropped the rifle. Obviously baffled, unable to spot the source of the shot that had wounded him, he spun on his heel and ran pell-mell for cover. Immediately Matt leaped to his feet and, putting on all the speed he could muster, headed for Lanigan's establishment, two blocks down and one over.

Astonished passersby, open-mouthed, watched him speed along, his moccasins kicking up puffs of dust. As he ran, he glanced over his shoulder. None of Thompson's gunslingers were in sight. At the very next intersection, he cut across one block and then, confident he'd lost his pursuers, slowed to a trot. At Washita Street, he made another turn and resumed his flight along the final block to his destination.

At Lanigan's he dashed into the comparative safety of the barn. Jack Matlock stood there, waving his arms, apparently arguing with Jess Lanigan.

18

"What're you two arguin' about?"

Jess Lanigan laughed. "We ain't arguin', we're augurin'. You know, talkin'. Jack was tellin' me how you two met."

"That's right," Matlock added. "Jess and I are old friends. But, come on. What happened after I ran off and left you?"

Matt described his shoot-out with Thompson and his hired guns. "I think that kind of slowed 'em down," he said, winding up his tale.

Jess cackled and slapped his thigh. "Well, now, don't that beat all?"

Matlock shook his head. "I'd like to think so, but I'm not too sure. Folks say Jim Thompson's a first cousin or something to that killer Ben Thompson. Ben and his brother Billy are a couple of ruthless sons of a bitch. They both should've been hung long ago, but juries are so scared of 'em they've gotten away with murder. Why I hear little brother Billy even shot his own best friend."

Matt nodded. "I remember now. Ben Thompson was Phil Coe's pardner in the Bull's Head up in Abilene."

"Well, he ain't in Abilene now," Jess chimed in. "I hear he's in Kansas City or Ellsworth."

"I know," said Matt. "Last October, when Wild Bill gunned down Coe, Thompson was in Kansas City. I understand he made a lot of threats against Wild Bill, but as far's I know, he never did come back to Abilene."

"Fine," said Matlock, "but the point is Jim Thompson seems to have ambitions to be the big name in the Thompson tribe. I think he believes he should be just as ruthless as his cousins, so I wouldn't count on him quitting. Not just yet, anyway."

"Well, maybe not, but he lost four men a little while ago, so now we only gotta deal with two men and Thompson himself."

Matlock slowly nodded, and then his face broke into a grin. "That's right, isn't it? And I wouldn't be surprised if those other two are having second thoughts about the whole business. Way things've been going, they probably figure they got about as much chance with you as a wax cat in hell."

"Well, right now the only thing that worries me is what they might do to you after I'm gone, what with you not even totin' a gun. I mean, I'm headin' south soon's I get Queenie saddled and my gear loaded on Horace, but you gotta stay here and face 'em."

Matlock grinned. "No I don't. I live down in Sumner County, about three miles northwest of Wellington."

"Oh. Well, what's to stop 'em comin' after you and your family down there?"

Matlock grinned again. "I guess I forgot to mention the reason I helped plow that furrow was because my first cousin is the sheriff of Sumner County. And they say Cousin Luke's cold blooded as a rattler with a chill. Even Thompson knows better than to pull any stunts down there."

"Your cousin goin' to side with a farmer in somethin' like this?"

"Oh, yes. Luke may favor the cattle people and Wellington's business crowd most of the time, but family still comes first with him. Anyway, I wouldn't worry too much once I'm down there. Come to think of it, I doubt Thompson would've pulled anything here today if Charlie Lawton hadn't been away. Charlie's a fair man, and even if he is hired by the cattle people here, he wouldn't go along with any shenanigans like today."

"Well, good. Let's get out of here then. I want to make Wellington by nightfall if I can. You got a horse?"

"I got a horse and buckboard."

"I thought we had to cross the Arkansas. How you goin' to do that?"

"Oh, we'll just drive right over Dutch Bill's bridge."

"Who's Dutch Bill?"

"Bill Greiffenstein." Matlock laughed. "He's a sly one. Built a bridge over the Arkansas and fixed it so that if people use it, they go right by his business places. Collects a toll from everybody, too. I hear he's made thousands in just tolls alone. I'll have to pay him a quarter, but it's worth it."

"Where's your buckboard?" asked Jess.

"Tied up over by the courthouse."

"All right," said Jess, "I'll send my boy over to get it, and as soon's you two have a bite to eat, you can be on your way."

"Well, that's right nice of you, Mr. Lanigan. It's just as well Jack doesn't have to show his face around town too much," said Matt. "Much obliged."

"It's my pleasure, bein' able to help out anybody who can fox that rascal Jim Thompson."

They paid their tolls and crossed the Arkansas on Dutch Bill's bridge. "I was a little worried Thompson and his gang might be waiting for us here, but I haven't seen hide nor hair of them," said Matlock, as they left the bridge behind and headed south along the Chisholm. "You must've really given those rascals something to chew on."

"Well, maybe our luck's changed." Matt looked up at the cloudless sky. "At least it looks like we'll have good weather the rest of the day."

"Well, now, it's about a dozen miles to the county line and another dozen or so from there to Wellington, so you just go on ahead. You can make better time on your horses than I can in this buckboard. No need to dawdle along with me."

Matt glanced at his companion. "Thanks, but if you don't mind, I'll just ride along with you. I wouldn't want those owlhoots to come chargin' after you and catch you all alone. After all, a man just don't abandon a friend, and Queenie and Horace don't mind takin' it easy."

Matlock nodded. "Much obliged," he said, obviously relieved by Matt's decision.

They pushed on all afternoon with only brief stops to rest the horses. They saw nothing of Thompson nor anyone else heading south; they did have to detour around one herd of about two thousand longhorns headed north. As the shadows lengthened, they picked up the pace as much as possible, but the sun had been down about an hour when they finally reached Matlock's place. Matlock had explained how he and his wife and two children had homesteaded 160 acres. "I've managed to build a barn for the animals, and now I'm hoping I can soon build a genuine house for the four of us, so's we can get out of the soddie we've been living in."

Matlock introduced his wife Sarah to Matt, and the farmer related the day's events to his spouse. She was profuse in her expressions of gratitude for Matt's intervention in Matlock's trouble. Both of the Matlocks insisted he have dinner with them and spend the night. Matt was tired and gratefully accepted their offer, but when Mrs. Matlock said he should spend the night in their sod house, that she'd have their two children give up their place to him, he declined as graciously as he could.

"Thank you, ma'am, but I couldn't let you do that. Besides, I'm used to sleepin' out, and I've got everything I need. Just gettin' a good meal's enough for me." He thought it just as well not to mention he really preferred sleeping under the stars to bunking down in a soddie.

Everybody was up at sunrise, and Matt had breakfast with the family. After another round of heartfelt thanks from the entire family, Matt hit the trail, determined to make up for lost time. He got back on the Chisholm and pressed south once again.

He stopped in Wellington just long enough to replenish his water and supplies. He was pleased to discover that, so far's he could tell, no one had heard of the events in Wichita the day before. Despite Marshal Lawton's invitation to help in ridding Wichita of baddies, Matt wasn't too sure what the marshal's reaction might've been to the shoot-out and wounding or killing of four men. In any event, eager to put distance between himself and Wichita, Matt headed south again as soon as possible. He didn't even take time to show his bedraggled picture of Bowler Bob around town. That night he camped just outside Hunnewell, just north of the Kansas-Indian Territory border.

Next morning he resumed his southward trek. It was not without some trepidation, though, that he ventured into Indian Territory. His experiences in Newton and Wichita had already convinced him his search for Bowler Bob would be far more dangerous and difficult than he'd ever imagined when, back in the safety and comfort of Abilene, he'd made his vow to seek retribution for Paw's murder.

The few Indians he'd encountered in Abilene and even in Wichita had done nothing to inspire concern in him. And from everything he'd heard, the Five Nations, especially the Cherokees, were civilized people. But what if he ran into Comanches or Kiowas? He'd heard that, along the Chisholm, the trail bosses dealt with Indians by bribing the savages with a couple of head of cattle. But he didn't have any cattle or anything else to bribe anybody with. It bore some thinking about.

By the beginning of the third day, he felt more confident. He hadn't encountered any Indians nor any of the white outlaws that were said to infest the Territory. And were perhaps more dangerous than Indians. The weather, too, had remained agreeable with only occasional white, puffy clouds marking the otherwise blue skies. Temperatures hadn't been too intense, and enough cottonwoods dotted the rolling grasslands to provide shade when he needed it. Also, his own stamina had increased. He could ride for eight or ten hours now without feeling exhausted, a big improvement over that first day out of Abilene with Oops Madigan.

In the two days that'd passed since he'd left Kansas, he'd crossed three rivers, and just as Oops had promised, Horace and Queenie had proven to be good river horses, swimming the streams with ease. Of course, so far the only river he'd encountered on the whole trip that amounted to anything had been the Arkansas, just outside Wichita, and he'd crossed that on Dutch Bill's bridge, but his confidence in his mounts had grown with each passing day.

He calculated the river he'd crossed late yesterday had been the Black Bear. He'd set up camp on its southern bank and enjoyed a good night's rest. That put him about fifty miles into Indian Territory with another 170 to go to the Red River and Texas. Maybe this wouldn't turn out to be so bad after all.

Late that afternoon, he figured it was about time to change from Horace to Queenie for the last couple of hours before making camp. At this point the trail narrowed down into a draw or ravine about a half mile wide. A little more than a quarter of a mile ahead was a fairly good sized rise, so he decided to get down and make the switch and give Horace a little rest before making the climb.

Somewhere in the distance he heard what sounded like thunder, although, looking up, the sky was as blue as ever. That's odd, he thought. He dismounted and then felt the earth trembling beneath his feet. The rumble of the thunder seemed to be getting closer, too. He stood there, debating what to do. He was just about to start unsaddling Horace when he became aware of what sounded like men yelling. He glanced up just in time to see a thundering herd of longhorns top the rise.

For a moment, he froze. The wild-eyed leaders of the herd pounded toward him. "Jesus Christ!" he exclaimed.

He leaped back on Horace, thanking his lucky stars he hadn't yet loosened the saddle cinch. Queenie's leader still in hand, he wheeled Horace to the right. The frightened animal responded with a sudden lunge, almost unseating Matt. His mount had barely taken two strides when Matt recognized his mistake. He was too close to the side of the ravine. They'd never be able to make it out of the path of the maddened steers.

He yanked back on the reins; Horace reared on his hind legs. Matt almost went backwards over the cantle but, just in time, dropped the reins and grabbed a handful of the horse's mane. As soon as Horace leveled out, Matt grabbed the reins again and swung the horse around in the opposite direction. He dug his heels in, and Horace set off directly across the path of the onrushing, strangely silent steers. Except for the shouts of the trailing cowboys, Matt heard only the sound of clashing horns and pounding hooves.

He dropped Queenie's lead, hoping the pack horse would follow him and Horace in their dash for safety. Then he yanked out his Ritter Special and began firing it into the air. A cloud of dust started to obscure his vision. Then, glancing over his shoulder, he was horrified to discover the herd leaders were following Horace and the trailing Queenie in their run for the left side of the ravine.

He almost panicked. Oh, my God, what am I going to do? Then an opening appeared between the far side of the ravine and the stampeding herd. He jerked on the right rein and headed Horace up the rise. The horse responded magnificently. Up the hill he charged, the cattle following, leaders doubling back on the rest of the herd. But now, charging up the steep rise, the herd leaders began to slow.

At this point, the hard riding cowboys who'd been chasing the herd managed to position themselves to face the oncoming longhorns. The headlong rush of the cattle slackened to a walk. Within a matter of minutes, the stampede ended, the steers merely milling in a circle, going nowhere.

Matt reined in Horace and then looked for Queenie. She was just behind Horace. Matt slid off the blowing horse and gratefully patted him on the neck. At that moment an older cowboy galloped up.

"Howdy. I'm Joe Turner, trail boss of this outfit. I want to thank you for turnin' the herd like that. That was one of the slickest jobs I've ever seen. Took real guts, too."

Matt was learning. He'd been about to apologize for causing trouble, but decided not to mention what a lucky accident his turning of the herd had been. He nodded. "Glad I could be of help, Joe. Maybe you'll do the same for me someday."

Joe Turner nodded. "Just hope I get the chance. There's plenty of water here," he went on, "so I reckon I'm goin' to bed the herd down right here. You'll be willin' to have dinner with us, won't you?"

Matt nodded. "Happy to. Much obliged."

"I reckon you'll bed down for the night, too, won't you?"

"Nothin' I'd like better. I figger you can give me news of what's up ahead on the trail."

"Glad to. Soon's Cookie gets here with the chuck wagon, you can sling your bedding down by it. And you can run your animals in with our remuda. Our wrangler'll look after 'em for you. Later, at chow time, me and the boys'll give you all the news we got."

19

"So," said Joe Turner, "you're not a cowboy."

"Nope," confessed Matt, "I'm not."

The trail boss grinned. "You mean stoppin' the stampede for us was just plain dumb luck?"

"'Fraid so," Matt admitted, feeling foolish.

"Well, boys, what do you think? Ain't that the damnedest thing you ever heard?"

"Son," said one of the hands, "with luck like that you ought to be a gambler."

This brought a burst of good-natured laughter from the cowboys. The sun was about to set, and the herd was bedded down. Except for the first shift of night guards on the herd and the nighthawk looking after the remuda, the whole outfit was gathered around the fire having their evening meal.

"Well, if you ain't a cowboy, what do you do?"

"I'm a gunsmith and a piano player."

"Can you throw a loop?"

"I did a little ropin' when I worked at a livery stable."

"You any good at it?" asked Joe Turner. "I mean can you snake a mount out of the remuda?"

Matt shrugged. "I don't know. I never tried it."

Joe Turner guffawed. "Well, by God, if that don't beat all." He wiped his eyes. "Well, I tell you, son, cutting a pony out of a remuda of a mornin' ain't nothin' like ropin' a cayuse in a livery stable corral."

"It ain't?"

"No, it ain't, but what the hell. We owe you somethin', so I'll have the wrangler cut your ponies out in the mornin'."

Matt again felt foolish but nodded. "Thank you."

"If you don't mind my askin', what in the world are you doin' ridin' through the Indian Territory all alone like this?"

"Well, sir, it's like this." Matt went on to tell the men about the murder of his father and about his search for the killer.

The men listened intently, and when Matt finished his story, Joe Turner said, "Son, I admire your spunk, but this is mighty dangerous what you're doin'. You met up with any Indians yet?"

"No sir, I ain't."

"Well, sooner or later you're goin' to, and if you do, you better just hope it's Cherokee Light Horse you meet up with."

Puzzled, Matt asked, "What're Light Horse?"

"They're the Cherokee police. They charge ten cents a head to cross their land, but sometimes they can be bought off with a head or two of cattle."

"Well, I got a little money."

Joe Turner shrugged. "Well, now, that might work, and then again it might not. At least the Cherokee are more or less civilized. We run into some of 'em a ways back, and they settled for one steer. But God help you if you run into Comanches or Kiowas. For the most part, they're west of here, but every now and then a war party comes raidin', and a while back I heard talk about that Comanche hellion Quanah bein' in the area. Anyhow, if you run into 'em, the best thing to do is skedaddle *muy pronto*."

"Why's that? What's so special about Comanches?"

Joe Turner snickered. "What's special about 'em? Well, first off, they're plumb mean. They ain't taken kindly to bein' run off their land. And they don't care much for the idea of bein' cooped up on a reservation. They want to fight, especially Quanah and his bunch. Second, they're probably the best horsemen on the prairies, bar none, white or Indian."

"That it?"

Joe Turner grinned. "And third, they're smart. That's why they're so hard to catch. An army officer told me once that the Comanches are always prepared if somethin' goes wrong. They not only turn up where you least expect 'em, but they always leave themselves a way out. For instance, they always have a temporary camp with fresh horses nearby where they're plannin' to strike. That way they can ride like hell for a hundred miles if need be and leave any pursuers behind. That is assumin' any pursuit gets organized."

"What happens to your herd if you run?"

"Well, generally the Indians don't kill animals just for the sake of killin'. They'll just take a couple of head to eat and stampede the rest. You try and round 'em up after the Comanches leave. Anyhow, if the war party's of any size, it don't pay to wait around and ask their intentions. Just assume they're hostile and act accordingly."

The next morning, good as his word, Joe Turner had the wrangler cut Horace and Queenie out of the remuda, and within an hour of sun-up, Matt said his good-byes and headed south. Another hour later, Horace and Queenie again lived up to their reputations as good river horses by easily swimming the Cimarron River. Most of the day after leaving Joe Turner's outfit, Matt reflected as he rode on the trail boss's warning about Indians, especially Comanches and Kiowas. He felt uneasy and kept a sharp eye peeled. He encountered no one, however, on the vast prairie, and late that afternoon, after the horses had repeated their swimming performance of the morning by crossing the North Canadian, Matt set up camp on the south bank of that river.

The next morning, Matt's uneasiness of the previous day had dissipated, and he'd come to believe that luck was with him. Throughout the morning, the horizon remained empty. That afternoon, though, he let the horses graze while he stood on a rise and watched a large herd make its way across the Canadian River. The weather'd continued bright and sunny—it'd been that way most of the summer—and the water level wasn't particularly high here, but it still fascinated him to see how some of the cattle seemed to enjoy swimming. Almost as though they took pride in their swimming ability.

About noon the following day, he crossed the Washita. A few miles north of the river, the monotonous rolling prairie had given way to an increasingly hilly terrain. As he pushed farther south, the hills took on more the aspect of low mountains. That night he debated whether to take a detour west into the higher elevations. He'd never been in mountains and wondered what it'd be like to gaze out over the valleys from high up on a mountain. No, Matt, he told himself, you're here for a purpose. To get Bowler Bob Bixby. You can do your sight-seein' some other time.

Next day, midway through the morning, looking at the mountains on his right, curiosity got the better of him. At this point, the Chisholm had narrowed to only about two or three hundred yards in width. Horace plodding along obediently in the rear, Matt headed Queenie across the valley and started climbing the mountain.

He hadn't really expected it to be easy, but it was worse than he'd expected. Progress was slow. With no trail to follow, Queenie had to carefully pick her way. Eventually, Matt had to dismount and lead both animals. "But, by God," he muttered, stumbling over a rock, "I ain't goin' to let this little old mountain beat me. No sir, I ain't. Not on your life!"

Slipping and sliding, he and the horses inched forward and

upward. After more than an hour's hard, tiring exertion, they reached a small grassy knoll which was more like a broad shelf. Ahead of them the mountain reared even steeper.

One lonely tree, a young hackberry about thirty feet high, standing beside a noisy stream, cast a patch of shade. The only sound was that of the narrow stream as it splashed from above and rushed across the knoll to fall precipitously into the valley below. Except for where he and the horses had gained access to the knoll, large boulders lined the edge of the shelf, partially blocking out any view of the valley floor he'd left behind.

Sweat poured off Matt and the horses. He turned and looked back the way he'd come. He judged he was half a mile or less from where he'd started the ascent on the western edge of the Chisholm and maybe four or five hundred feet up the side of the mountain. Not much to show for more'n a hard hour's effort, he thought. God a'mighty, I need a rest and so do the poor animals.

He unsaddled Queenie and removed the pack from Horace. He doubted they'd go anywhere, but just to be on the safe side, he hobbled both mounts and ran long ropes from the hackberry to each of the horses. The animals were free to graze and drink from the stream but couldn't wander far enough to fall. Then he stretched out full-length on his back in the shade of the tree and placed his hat over his eyes.

The sound of the running stream lulled him. He grew drowsy. Thoughts of Paw and Uncle Frank and Aunt Elly wandered through his mind. Memories of his night with Sally flitted through his head. His eyelids grew heavy. He just couldn't keep his eyes open. Next thing he knew, Queenie was nuzzling him. He put a hand up to push her away, then got to his feet. He jammed his hat down to shade his eyes. The sun had shifted and already started its afternoon descent. Jesus, he wondered, what time is it? He pulled out his watch. My God, I've been asleep for more'n two hours. Haven't even really done what I came up here to do.

Affectionately he patted Queenie's nose. Then he strolled over to the edge of the knoll and pushed his hat brim back. He folded his arms across his chest and leaned on his right shoulder against a large boulder, then gazed out over the valley.

"Jesus," he whispered. He'd never experienced anything like it. Almost took his breath away. Must be like a bird can see. Like an eagle or a hawk. Seemed like he could see for miles. Looking north, he thought he could almost make out the spot where he'd camped the night before along Wildhorse Creek. By God, it'd been worth the climb!

He turned to look south. Well, he thought, here comes company. A line of half-a-dozen freight wagons drawn by oxen plodded north along the Chisholm. At the head of the procession, two horse-drawn coaches crept along, obviously not wanting to get too far ahead of the freighters. Flanking the wagons and coaches on either side, rode a troop of a dozen cavalrymen.

Suddenly something seemed to alarm the whole group. Arms began to wave, and the soldiers spurred their mounts. The freight wagons began to pull into a circle that enclosed the two coaches. The blue-uniformed riders rode hell-for-leather to get inside the protective circle.

Matt, his vision obstructed by the huge boulder, couldn't make out what the trouble was. He moved back around to the other side of the huge rock. Then he saw it. Below and just to his right, a horde of at least twenty-five Indians on horseback poured out of the mouth of a canyon. Most of the warriors brandished rifles; a few seemed to be armed with only bows. Clearly they intended to assault the wagon train and were rapidly closing the gap between themselves and their target.

Matt snatched off his hat and crawled on his belly to the edge of the grassy shelf. From his vantage point, he was able to peer into the canyon, five hundred feet below.

On the floor of the canyon, a herd of horses remained, quietly grazing. Three older-looking men stood near the horses. A little farther away, closer to the mouth of the canyon, a group of Indians wearing what looked to Matt like war paint, squatted in a circle. The warriors seemed to be discussing something. Matt counted ten altogether. Must be Comanches, by God. Joe Turner said they always left a way out. These fellers must be their reserves.

He glanced up. Out on the valley floor, the battle had begun. For the moment, the wagon train defenders appeared to be holding their own against the howling savages circling the wagons. But what if the Indians reserves were to go into action? I got to do somethin', thought Matt.

Quietly he slid back from the edge of the precipice, and scuttled to where his pack lay. He slid his Sharps rifle out of its holster and dug out some ammo for it. He had started back toward the edge of the cliff when a sudden thought struck him. By God! If there was ever goin' to be a time, this was it. He laid the big Sharps down and hurried back to the pack.

He rummaged inside until he found what he wanted. He grinned. These'll give those Comanches somethin' to think about. He unscrewed the two remaining grenades Burke Harte had given him. Carefully he armed them with the percussion caps and then reassembled them. Gingerly cradling the lethal bombs, he crept up to the edge of the cliff and peered over.

The meeting looked about to break up. The warriors were just getting to their feet. Now, by God, before they separate. Carefully he took aim and then tossed the first grenade. The bomb, unobstructed, gained speed as it fell toward the circle of unsuspecting Indians. Fascinated, Matt watched. The grenade hurtled down. Within a matter of seconds it hit. The explosion reverberated within the canyon walls.

The effect was devastating. Not a single warrior escaped unscathed. Only one remained standing and blood spurted from his abdomen. Then he too doubled over and toppled to the ground. The three older Indians stood stunned, baffled as to the source of the disaster. Matt tossed the second grenade toward them. After it hit, not an Indian remained standing. All appeared to be either dead or dying.

The horses in the meanwhile had reared and begun milling about. A few of them screamed, lacerated by the flying metal from the exploding grenades. Suddenly the entire herd stampeded and headed for the canyon mouth. Matt ran back to retrieve the Sharps and his Winchester. Unimpeded by the dying or severely wounded Indians in the canyon below, Matt lay flat and pointed his weapon toward the Indians still circling the embattled wagon train.

He knew a Sharps could be lethal to a man at almost a mile, but the range was too long for accurate shooting. As a consequence, he made no attempt to hit riders but simply aimed for the Comanches' mounts. A warrior afoot would pose little threat to the soldiers barricaded behind the wagons.

Not every shot went home to the intended target, but enough did that the warriors found their horses dropping all around. They drew off out of range of the soldiers behind the wagons, but still horses continued to go down. When they tried to locate the source of the devastating rifle fire, they for the first time became aware that their reserve mounts were stampeding south across the valley floor. At this point, the Comanches broke off the disastrous engagement.

Most of them stopped to pick up their surviving, unhorsed companions and then, riding double, took off in pursuit of their herd. A few headed for what they thought would be the safety of the canyon. As the unsuspecting, fleeing horsemen came closer and closer and the range shortened, Matt shifted his aim to the riders. Only one horse and rider made it to the canyon. Now Matt brought his Winchester into action; he dispatched the last Comanche with a blast from the Yellow Boy.

Matt dropped flat to the ground. Exhausted, he could only lie there. Finally he looked up. The wagon train had formed up and was heading north as fast as it appeared able to travel. Evidently the wagon master was taking no chances on any more Indians turning up. Nor did he seem disposed to wait around to find out whom his savior had been. For his part, Matt didn't feel the least inclined to chase after them. By the time he could get down off the mountain, the wagons would be well along on their way north.

He doubted the Comanches would be back either. From what Joe Turner had said, the Comanches were probably well on their way back to the Llano Estacado, the Staked Plain where they believed themselves impregnable. Besides, dusk was approaching. It'd be too dangerous to try to make it down the mountain in the dark. Hell, it'd be tough enough in the morning.

He debated whether to take a chance on building a fire. If the Comanches did come back, they might see it and come after him. On the other hand, it was getting chilly up on the mountain, and he wanted some hot coffee and food. Then, too, maybe a fire'd scare off wild animals and snakes. He built a roaring fire.

20

Getting down from the knoll was almost as difficult as climbing up to it. Not quite, but almost. For one thing, Matt hadn't slept very well. That night after the battle, lying in his bedroll, he'd heard disturbing noises all around him. Cracklings and slitherings in the bushes that made him uneasy. On top of that, in his mind's eye, he kept seeing the effects of his grenades on the Comanches. At the time he'd dropped the bombs on the unsuspecting redskins, he'd been too busy to think much about it, but later, lying by the fire, the ghastly, gory sight of the dead and dying Indians kept recurring.

Next morning the wheeling and turning of vultures over the scene caught his attention. He took time to peer over the edge of the cliff and then wished he hadn't. Several of the huge birds were tearing at the remains of the dead Comanches, ripping flesh from the bones. Matt turned away, sickened, revolted.

Climbing the mountain had had the advantage of not looking down. Now, though, picking his way down the mountainside, he couldn't avoid it. Without a trail to follow, it was a task that'd make a mountain goat nervous. The thought of the buzzards overhead did nothing to increase his confidence. Stumbling and sliding, fearful of plunging off the mountain, he slowly, gingerly made his way down. By the time he reached the valley floor, sweat again soaked his clothes.

Down here on the valley floor, a dozen more vultures, waddling from corpse to corpse, feasted on the remains of the dead Comanche horses—and in a few cases those of their riders—that he'd gunned down the day before with his Big Fifty. The stench almost overpowered him. He immediately mounted Horace and, Queenie trailing behind, pushed off south. Hoping to leave the Indian Territory behind, he traveled as rapidly as he could, making only a few short stops, but nightfall found him short of the Red River.

All the while he rode, he mulled over in his mind the events of the last several days. The idea of killing people went against everything he'd been taught. Paw had always believed in trying to live a violence-free life, despite being a gunsmith, but even he on occasion, when sufficiently provoked, had found it necessary to resort to violence. But so far's Matt knew, Paw had never killed anyone. And even Uncle Frank had only killed by accident and then ever afterward preached brotherhood.

Now, here he, Matt, Paw's only child, had killed he didn't know how many human beings. Of course, they were only Indians, savages. Maybe they didn't count. But God Almighty, they'd had wives and children and parents, hadn't they? He wondered what Paw and Uncle Frank would've had to say about that. Or Aunt Elly for that matter. What would she think? But then, after all, he hadn't really had any choice, had he?

Yes, but what about those men he'd shot in Wichita? They

weren't Indians. Well, but he didn't know that he'd actually killed any of them. Maybe he had, but then again, maybe they were just wounded. And he wasn't planning to kill Bixby. Just haul him back to justice was all. He was no killer. He was his father's son. But he had to watch out. Seemed like once you shot people, it got easier to do. Like that feller Dingus Woodson or Jesse James or whatever his name was. He seemed to think he had the right to kill people out of revenge. Even laughed about it.

Again he slept poorly, haunted by the scenes of that morning when he'd seen the vultures at their grisly work. The next day, though, he got an early start and vowed he'd cross the Red River before the day was out. As he rode, he still debated in his mind the right and wrong of what he'd been up to and what he was planning for the future. He wished he could just forget about it. It made his head hurt. But he couldn't. At least, though, he was the only one who knew what he'd done.

He came upon the Red River before noon. When he'd started out that morning, he hadn't realized how close he was to the river. After crossing into Texas, he stopped to fix himself a bite to eat. By the middle of the afternoon, he reached Gainesville and welcomed the chance to break his journey. It gave him an opportunity to get a bath—he hadn't had one since Wichita—and a shave and a haircut. Having a fair to middling meal in a restaurant and sleeping in a real bed at the hotel that night was a treat, too. He hadn't done that since Wichita, either.

While having supper in the restaurant, he overheard a conversation that answered the question for him of who had been in the coaches with the wagon train he'd helped to rescue. Seemed the wives of some army officers were on their way from Fort Richarson to their husbands' new assignment at Fort Riley in Kansas. Matt debated saying something but then thought better of it. He didn't really want to talk about the battle, and besides, who'd believe him anyway? And, what's more, he'd heard that the citizens of Gainesville didn't take too kindly to folks from Kansas, not after the trouble they'd had with Jayhawkers during the War.

The next morning, feeling like a new man and with the horses rested, he set out for Denton, about thirty miles away. Before leaving, however, he took time to stop at the marshal's office and inquire about Bowler Bob, but nobody'd heard of the scoundrel. That night he slept in Denton; his stop there pretty much the same as his visit in Gainesville, restful but, as far as tracking down Bixby went, unhelpful.

Late the next day he rode into Fort Worth. The place appeared to bustle with building activity. That night at supper in the hotel restaurant, he overheard much loud, optimistic talk about the great future that lay ahead of the city, now that the Texas and Pacific railroad was just a few miles away. From what Matt could see, the population was growing, too. Must be three or four thousand people in this town, he thought.

That night he got a chance to play the piano again, when the piano player at one of the livelier saloons let him sit in for a spell. The man even let him keep a few dollars in tips that came his way. Playing in a saloon again brought to mind that it'd only be a few days until he reached Lampasas and Tom Adams's spread. He really looked forward to seeing the big Texan again.

The next morning, after breakfast, he stopped in at the marshal's office. A large, balding man with a star on his vest stuck out his hand. "Howdy, stranger. What can I do for you?"

Matt shook the man's hand. "My name's Matt Ritter. You the marshal?"

The man nodded and spat, narrowly missing the spittoon. He went over and rubbed the gob of tobacco juice with his boot. "That's right. Lem Johnson. I'm marshal of this here town. Now tell me what I can do for you."

Matt unrolled his bedraggled picture. "I'm lookin' for this owlhoot."

Marshal Johnson's eyebrows went up, and then he grinned. "Are you now?"

"His name's Bixby. Bowler Bob Bixby. Ever heard of him?"

Johnson winked. "Well, just let me call my Bixby expert."

He turned toward a back office and roared. "Tommy! Come on out here, will you?"

A tall, wiry, fortyish feller with a drooping handlebar mustache appeared in the doorway. "Lem, for God's sake, don't yell like that. I can hear perfectly well. Now, what's on your mind?"

Johnson nodded toward Matt. "Young feller's lookin' for Bowler Bob. I figgered you could help him out." He turned to Matt. "This is Captain Tommy Crockett. Formerly of the Texas Rangers. He's my deputy now."

Matt, elated that somebody at last seemed to know his quarry, but puzzled, studied the man. "How come you ain't with the Rangers?"

Captain Tommy snorted. "After the War, some smart Yankee closed us down. But don't you worry. I hear it won't be long before we're back in business again. Now, what's this about Bob Bixby? You a friend of his?"

"Not hardly." Matt went on to relate why he was eager to find Bowler Bob.

Captain Crockett looked at Marshal Johnson. Then he turned back to Matt. "Well, now. I'm goin' to wish you luck, but I've been tryin' to lay hands on that scoundrel for several years now. Trouble is he spends most of his time in Mexico. Of course, every now and then, he gets a hankerin' for a white woman and comes huntin' for one across the border. I just ain't been able to lay hands on him, though. He's a slippery son of a bitch."

"You know him, then?"

Captain Crockett nodded. "Oh, yes. I sure do. I've made a study of him. He's killed at least three men I know of—your Paw makes a fourth—and there's probably been others I don't know about. Been known to steal horses, too." He put a toothpick in his mouth and shook his head. "Folks seem to get more riled about that than they do the killings."

"Do you know where I can find him?"

"Most likely in the San Antone area when he's not in Mexico. Sometimes in El Paso, too, I hear." He shook his head again. "By golly, it's a shame about that feller."

Puzzled, Matt asked, "What's a shame?"

"The way he went bad. Seems like his Paw was a preacher and did a little ranchin', too. Bob's Maw died when he was born, and his daddy pretty much raised him. From what I hear, Bowler Bob worshipped his daddy. Everybody says Bob was a fine, upstandin' young feller, too, and then one night two owlhoots murdered his Paw. They say that's when he got that gray streak in his hair." Crockett turned and, toothpick still in the side of his mouth, let fly with a stream of tobacco juice. He hit the spittoon dead center.

"Well, sir, Bob swore he'd get revenge, and he did. Took him more'n two years, but he caught up with 'em in El Paso. By that time, he was real quick with a gun, and he got 'em both. Tricked 'em into firin' first and the sheriff ruled self-defense."

Matt scratched his head. "Well, then, why're you after him?"

"Oh, well, that was just the beginnin'. Seems like once he got a taste of killin', he liked it. When I said he'd killed at least three men—and your Paw—I wasn't countin' those two that murdered his daddy. Why, they surely had it comin'. But that was just the start of his career. When a man starts to kill, it can be a bad business."

Matt nodded. "I see."

Captain Crockett looked at him. "Do you? I wonder. Well, anyway, the man's a shifty one and mighty sly. If you're set on goin' after him, you better be mighty careful. You never know what he's goin' to do."

"You think I might find him somewhere near San Antone, do you?"

Crockett nodded. "Most likely. And if you do, a woman'll probably be mixed up in it somewhere."

"And what about you, Captain? You given up on huntin' him down?"

The captain's eyes narrowed. "No, I ain't. I just got business here right now, but when the Rangers start up again, he's one owlhoot that's high on my list."

Matt grinned. "What if someone else gets him first?"

Crockett scratched his behind and shrugged. "That's just fine, long's someone gets him. But, son, if you're the one thinkin' of gettin' him, I reckon when the time comes for me to go after ol' Bowler Bob, he'll still be around causin' misery for everybody."

The next day Matt debated whether to head directly for San Antonio or whether to detour west to Lampasas and keep his promise to Tom Adams. Before departing Abilene, he'd written to Adams telling him he was on his way but had no idea if his letter'd ever reached him. He decided after all this time Bowler Bob could wait a few days. The hotel clerk gave him directions.

"Well, sir, you just go pretty much due south through Alvarado and Hillsboro and then on to Waco. Should take you about three days."

"Any recommendations as to hotels?"

The clerk grinned. "Well, in Alvarado maybe you can stay at the Sprawler Hotel."

"The Sprawler?"

"I'm joshin'. Feller down there name of Bill Balch has a lot of guests, and they often times end up sleepin' out in the front yard on pallets, so they call his place the Sprawler Hotel."

Matt smiled. "I see. Any other recommendations?"

"Well, no, but at Waco you can cross the Brazos on that new suspension bridge." He grinned again. "Folks in Waco are mighty proud of that bridge. And be sure to treat yourself to a night's entertainment at the Star Variety Theater. Keep your pistol oiled, though. Waco's a mighty rough town these days."

"What do I do after I leave Waco?"

"Nothin' much excitin' from there on. You just head a little southwest and about forty miles along you'll be in Belton. At Belton you head due west and another forty miles later you'll be in Lampasas. Altogether should take you five, maybe six days, depending on how hard you ride and how long you stay in Waco."

The clerk's directions were good, and six days later Matt

rode into Lampasas. The Star Variety had been entertaining, and the suspension bridge interesting, but he didn't want to waste a lot of money in a rip-roarin' town like Waco. So, after one night he'd headed out for Belton. He'd stayed one night in Belton and the next morning departed for Lampasas.

Lampasas impressed him. The public square was large. A two-story stone courthouse dominated the business district. Riding down the main street of the town, he noted that most of the store buildings were stone also. He was eager to see Tom and meet Tom's wife, but it'd been a long ride and the shadows were lengthening. Then, too, he recalled Tom saying something about his spread being about ten miles west of town. He decided to wait until morning to push on. He got the horses settled at the local livery stable and then got himself a room at the Keystone Hotel. The hotel impressed him even more. It too was built of limestone and looked sturdy enough to last for many years. He decided to forego joining the cowhands carousing on the downtown streets and, after a good supper, turned in for the night.

Just as Tom had promised directions were easy to come by. It appeared that the Adams ranch was well-known as were the Adamses, both Tom and his wife, and the desk clerk gave Matt instructions on how to reach the place.

He headed west out of town as directed but it was almost noon before he came to the ranch gate. From there, he still had another mile to go before the main house came in view. It was a low, rambling structure but looked as though it had plenty of room. The cook was just banging a large iron triangle suspended from one of about half-a-dozen oak trees that provided shade in the vicinity of the house. The hands were heading for the cookhouse as Matt slid off Queenie and tied her and Horace to a hitching rail out back of the main house.

A tall, muscular man came out of the house. Dark-complexioned with dark brown hair, he was sharp featured, but rugged. He cradled a Winchester Yellow Boy in his arms. Expression watchful, he greeted Matt. "Howdy, stranger. What can I do for you?"

"Name's Matt Ritter. I believe Tom Adams is expectin' me."

Just then a woman stepped out of the house and came toward them. Blonde, slender, about five five, she was one of the prettiest women he'd ever seen. Or had been. The harsh Texas sun and wind as well as the years had taken their toll. Hurrying up to the two men, she held out her hand.

"I'm Patty Adams. Did I hear you say you're Matt Ritter?"

Matt nodded and took her work-roughened hand. "Sure did, ma'am."

"Well, isn't that a shame? Tom's been expectin' you ever since he got your letter a week or so ago, but he's not here right now. I expect him back tomorrow or maybe even later today. He'll be sorry he wasn't here to greet you, though." She indicated the man with the rifle. "This is Marley Savage. He's our foreman and takes care of everything for me when Tom's not around." She turned to the foreman. "This is Matt Ritter, the young feller from Abilene Tom told us about. The one who saved Tom's life. You remember, don't you?"

Savage nodded. "Sure do. How are you, young feller?"

The two men shook hands, and then Patty Adams smiled and said, "You come on right in. Don't pay any attention to Marley's rifle. These days, what with Comanches and owlhoots, it pays to be careful. But you're just in time for lunch. I'll have Maria set another place."

She turned and headed toward the house, calling for the maid. Recalling his dinner conversation with Tom Adams at the Drovers' Cottage, he realized Patty Adams must be close to forty years old. Despite her age, though, something about her excited him. But jumpin' Jehoshaphat, since that dinner with the lady's husband, Matt Ritter'd learned a thing or two. He wasn't the green kid he'd once been, although, to tell the truth, the woman's frank, inviting, sensuality stirred in him a longing that embarrassed him.

21

For all her sensuality, Patty Adams set a good table. With evident pride, she ushered Matt into a dining room that boasted finely polished wood and sparkling cutlery and dishes. He thanked his stars he'd taken the trouble to get a shave and a bath before setting out that morning from Lampasas.

That day lunch consisted of a tasty, thick, hearty vegetable soup with fresh baked bread and slathers of newly churned butter. Each of them also had a fine piece of broiled steak along with heaping servings of Matt's beloved mashed potatoes. For dessert, she had Maria bring out a delicious blackberry pie over which she poured thick cream.

Maria, the Mexican maid, served the meal. Just the three of them, Patty Adams, Marley Savage, and Matt, sat at the table in the dining room. A fourth chair, presumably Tom

Adams's, stood at the head of the table.

Patty Adams sat at the foot of the table. She urged Matt to relate what had happened to him since her husband had last seen him the year before in Abilene. Her interest seemed so genuine that Matt threw in as many details as he could. She seemed especially fascinated by his battle with the Comanches. About the only adventure he left out was his sorry performance at Madam Bam's. Patty Adams's oohs and aahs gratified him. It was the first time he'd ever felt comfortable being the center of attention.

His hostess urged him to have seconds and even thirds, and by the end of the meal, he felt stuffed. Surreptitiously he tried to ease his belt. Glancing up, he saw her smiling at him. "Had enough, or would you like some more?"

He blushed. "No, ma'am, no more. That was the best meal I've had in I don't know how long, but I couldn't possibly stuff another bite in."

Throughout the meal, Marley Savage had, for the most part, concentrated on his food. Other than to ask for a dish to be passed, he'd had little to say.

Now he sat back and winked at Matt. "Miz Adams is a fine cook, ain't she? Never known another woman who could satisfy a man's appetite like she can." He wiped the back of his hand across his lips and smiled at her. "No, sir. Not a one."

She showed her dimples and said, "Now, Marley Savage, don't you say another word. You're going to embarrass me. And Matt."

"Do I understand rightly that you did the cookin', ma'am?"

She nodded. "I usually do, but sometimes Maria fixes the supper."

"Well, I just have to tell you again that was one of the finest meals I've ever had, and eatin' at Aunt Elly's table, I've had me some fine ones."

"My, what a nice compliment. I do thank you. My Tom could learn a thing or two about pleasin' women if he'd listen to you."

Marley Savage grinned. Matt wasn't quite sure what she meant and thought it best to ignore the implied criticism of his friend. "If you don't mind my askin', where'd Mr. Adams go?"

She smiled. "I don't mind a bit. He went down to San Antone to bring my baby sister home for a visit. Amanda lives and practices down there, but she likes to come back home for a visit every now and then. The two of us were born and raised right here on this ranch."

"What's she practice? She a musician? Or a dancer?"

His hostess laughed. "No, nothing like that, although she can play the violin. She's a doctor."

The answer astounded Matt. "A doctor? You mean she takes care of sick people?"

"That's right."

He shook his head. "I never heard of a woman doctor. Or is she a nurse?"

"Well, once upon a time she did some nursing, but she's a doctor now."

"Well, jumpin' Jehoshaphat. Just think of that."

"Surprises you, doesn't it? Well, it surprises a lot of people. Surprised me, too, at first. Here I just stayed home and spent all my life on ranches, but little sister has been places and met people. And done things. And she's barely thirty years old."

"She's a pretty one," added Marley Savage. "Not as pretty as Miz Adams here, but pretty. Probably can't cook like Miz Adams either."

Patty Adams looked as though she weren't too pleased by the foreman's compliments. "Little sister does all right. After all, she was married and kept a home for goin' on ten years, in between helpin' her husband till he died."

"Oh. Sorry to hear that. What'd he die of?"

"He was a doctor, and one winter he went out in the country to a patient and got caught in a blizzard somewhere and came down with pneumonia."

Matt thought for a moment. "She have any children?"

"Mandy had a little girl, but the child caught diphtheria and died when she was only four."

"Oh. So that's why she became a doctor."

Patty Adams sighed. "Something like that. If you're really

interested, you can talk to her about it when she and Tom get here. Tom brings her here a couple of times a year. These days it's dangerous enough for a man travelin' alone, let alone a woman, so Tom brings her here and takes her back to San Antone."

He scratched his head. "By stage or buggy?"

"Neither. They both ride horses. After all, she was brought up on a ranch just like I was. She can ride and shoot if she has to."

"I see. Well, I sure will be pleased to meet the doctor." He paused and then added, "I'm hopin' to do somethin' with my life, too, soon's I find this feller Bixby and haul him back to Abilene. Maybe be a lawyer. I don't think I want to be just a piano player or a gunsmith all my life."

Late the next afternoon, two riders came up the trail. Patty Adams went flying out of the house. "They're here, they're here!" she screamed.

Matt turned from his task of tuning the piano in the parlor and followed her out of the house. He shaded his eyes against the glare of the sun. Sure enough, as the riders neared the house, he recognized Tom Adams. Tom's companion sat astride her horse, but her long, dark hair and her full, divided skirt made her easily recognizable as a woman.

Tom swung down from his mount and rushed over to greet his wife with a kiss. Matt obligingly seized the reins of Tom's mount, and when Tom's companion slid down from her horse, he gathered in the reins of her horse for her.

She turned to him and smiled. "Thank you."

Matt ducked his head. "My pleasure, ma'am."

At this point, Tom came quickly over to him and seized his hand. "By God, it's good to see you, Matt. How are you?"

Matt broke into a grin. "Fine, just fine. And how're you?"

"Couldn't be better. No sir, couldn't be better. But here now, let me introduce you to Patty's little sister."

To Matt, describing the lady as the little sister didn't seem somehow quite right. She stood at least five seven, maybe five eight, and, although not fat, he doubted anyone would call her skinny. Sturdy, maybe. And while not as beautiful as Patty Adams, Matt thought her attractive.

Tom turned to his sister-in-law. "Amanda, this here's Matt Ritter, the young feller from Abilene you've heard me talk about." He turned back to Matt. "Matt this is Patty's little sister, Doctor Amanda Klein."

Amanda Klein smiled again at Matt and slipped off one of her gloves. Then she held out the uncovered hand to him. Her voice, pleasantly modulated when she spoke, was that of an educated woman. "Tom and Patty've told me so much about you, Matt. It's a pleasure to meet you."

He took the hand she offered and they shook. Unlike Patty Adams's hand, her sister's was soft and smooth. He almost felt like he wanted to twist his toe in the dirt.

"Likewise, ma'am, I'm sure."

Then Marley Savage came up and took charge of the two horses. Tom and Patty led Matt and Amanda toward the house.

As they entered the house, Amanda Klein sighed. "It's good to be home again. That ride from San Antone is tiring. And that first day, that fifty miles to Blanco, always seems to exhaust me. It'll be good to have a nice hot bath."

"Well," said her sister, "your room's all ready so you just go lay yourself down and have a rest. I'll have Maria get a bath ready for you right pronto."

"Don't forget" chimed in Tom, "I'll want one right after Mandy has hers."

Patty smiled. "I'm not likely to forget, am I? I mean, after all, I'll be sleepin' with you tonight. Now stop worryin', and supper'll be ready in about an hour."

Matt went back to tuning the piano. The day before he'd been pleased to discover the Adamses had a piano in their parlor, but that evening when he played it for Patty Adams he thought it sounded god-awful. Apparently she didn't notice, despite the fact she was normally the only one who played it. She praised his playing, but to him the piano sounded badly in need of a tuning. Working at the Palace, he'd learned to tune pianos under the tutelage of Darcy Streeter.

"If you're going to earn your living playing the piano," Darcy'd said, "you'd better learn to tune them yourself, because out here in the West, there's not likely to be anybody to do it for you, especially in saloons. And even if the customers don't complain, you've got to listen to it, and if it's out of tune, it'll drive you crazy."

When he'd asked his hostess's permission to do the tuning, she'd been surprised but grateful. "We used to have an old German feller who came to Lampasas from San Antone about every six months who'd do it, but I understand he died about two years ago."

The instrument was in pretty bad shape, and it took quite a while. He'd started early that afternoon and had only stopped when Tom and Amanda rode up. He just hoped the constant plunking and plinking wasn't driving everybody crazy. Finally, about fifteen minutes before dinner, he finished. To try it out he sat down and ran through a chorus or two of "Beautiful Dreamer" and followed it with his own arrangement of "Rosalie, The Prairie Flower."

Just then Patty came in, carrying a steaming dish.

"Oh, that sounds much better." She sat the dish down on the sideboard. "I didn't realize how bad it had gotten. I really appreciate it."

Matt grinned. "It's the least I could do, what with all the great meals you're servin' me."

"Well, I'm goin' to tell Mandy she'll have to get her violin out, and some night soon the two of you can give us a concert."

"If she's willin', I'd be happy to, although I reckon we'd best do some practicin' together first."

Just then Amanda walked in. Matt almost goggled. That afternoon when she'd arrived, she'd worn a dusty, split-skirt riding outfit that'd obviously been subject to much hard wear and perspiration. And her hair'd hung down loose from under a black, Texas-style sombrero. Now, she wore a cool-looking, filmy white gown, and her black hair was up off her long white neck in a stylish hairdo.

She smiled. "What's this I hear about practicing?"

Matt felt the same stirrings as when he'd met her older sister but this time even stronger. She almost took his breath away. *My God, it must run in the family. How can she be a doctor?*

Aloud he explained what Patty Adams had suggested.

"Matt's a fine piano player," said Patty. She winked at her sister. "I figger the two of you can make some beautiful music together."

A slow smile spread across Mandy's face. "We might at that. How about it?" she said, turning to him. "Shall we start tomorrow?"

He took a deep breath. "Nothin' I'd like better."

Patty'd outdone herself; the meal was delicious. But once again he was the center of attention. At Patty's urging, he went through the story of his adventures since he'd last seen Tom. For Amanda's benefit, he related again the reason he hoped to track down Bowler Bob Bixby. It puzzled him, though, when she didn't seem as enthusiastic about the manhunt as did the others, but he decided not to pursue the matter.

"So, anyway," he said, winding up his story, "I'm on my way to San Antone, but of course, I figgered I just had to stop here and visit you all."

The next afternoon, Amanda got out her violin, and the two of them settled down to practice. She was an accomplished musician, he discovered, and he wasn't sure if he could keep up with her, but he sure intended to try. She told him she only expected to be at the ranch for about one week.

"That's about all I can manage, I'm sorry to say. With the three days traveling time each way, I will've been away from my patients for almost two weeks. Besides that, it'll cost Tom another six days to ride down with me and then back, and I know he's got a lot of things he has to do around here."

Matt decided to take the plunge. "Well, maybe he won't have to do that."

She smiled. "Oh. You have something in mind?"

"Well, yes, ma'am. I mean I'm goin' to San Antone and I'd sure be pleased to ride with you."

Her eyebrows went up. "Do you think you could protect a lady if the need arose?"

He grinned. "I'm pretty handy with a gun, so I think I could. And," he decided to throw caution to the winds, "I sure would love to."

She looked thoughtful. "All right, maybe we can work something out. I'll discuss it with Patty and Tom."

Tom and Patty were both enthusiastic about the idea.

"Sure would be a great help," said Tom. "I've kinda fallen behind with my work, and I got a lot of things to get done before fall roundup begins. I'd really appreciate havin' the six extra days."

"And I'd be delighted to have Tom around home," Patty said. "What's more, I don't have the least doubt Matt could handle anything that might come up on the road to San Antone."

Their confidence pleased Matt. Just to show them it was warranted, he pitched in and worked. Whatever tools weren't handy on the ranch, he managed to round up in Lampasas. With them he set to work repairing and adjusting guns for Tom and for his ranch hands. Even Marley Savage seemed impressed when Matt finished working over Marley's Yellow Boy. The foreman tried it out on some tin cans.

A broad grin spread across his face when he hit nine out of ten. "Well, sir, this weapon handles a whole lot better'n it did, I must say. I appreciate your work, son."

He didn't rest on his laurels, however. Once all the shooting irons on the ranch were in good working order, he went to work and demonstrated his blacksmithing skills. But the week wasn't completely devoted to work. Marley took time to show him some of the tricks to handling a catch rope.

"Ever do any ropin'?"

Matt shrugged. He didn't expect Marley to be any more impressed by his livery stable work than Joe Turner'd been. He was right. When he mentioned his experience at the livery back in Abilene, Marley just grinned. By this time, Matt'd learned a grin from Marley was the same's a guffaw from any other feller.

"Well, now, just any old piece of rope won't do for a catch rope. A catch rope's got to be stiff enough so that when you throw a loop, it'll sail out there nice and flat and stay open."

Matt nodded.

The foreman picked a rope off his saddle horn. "Now, this here one's a genuine lariat. Here, feel it."

Matt did as he was told.

"You see, it's made of braided rawhide. They say the Mexicans invented these. A good one's generally about sixty feet long and real easy to throw. Trouble is, they're kinda expensive and liable to break on you."

"Now," Savage went on, holding up a second rope, "this here one's made of grass."

"Grass?"

"Yep. Grass, good tough grass. You twist strands of it together, it makes a real strong rope. And it costs a whole lot less. There's one other thing, too. It's simpler to make the honda."

"What's a honda?"

"Why the honda's the little loop on the end that the main line runs through. With a rawhide lariat you gotta splice it around a piece of cowhorn, but with a grass rope all you gotta do is tie a knot, a bowline on a bight. "

The foreman worked with Matt, and gradually he learned to hold the mainline and the loop in the same hand and pay out the loop until it was about four feet wide.

"Let the honda get about a quarter of the way down the loop. Gives better balance that way."

"What'll I do with the rest of the rope?"

"Just keep it coiled up and hold it in your other hand."

"How's a man supposed to hold the pony's reins than?"

The foreman chuckled. "You use two fingers of the hand that's holding the extra coils."

Skeptical, Matt just nodded.

"When you practice a little more, you can make a bigger loop, but that'll do for now. So go ahead. Give it a try. Stand back about eight or ten feet, and when you can toss it over that snubbin' post in the corral a few times, I'll let you try it on a calf. You don't need to learn nothin' tricky. Just get so you can toss your loop over the cow's head or the cow's heels. That'll do it."

A couple days later, when Tom asked how he was doing, Matt grinned sheepishly. "Well, I practiced but never did get to the point I could regularly hang that loop over the head of a cow that was runnin' from me. And I never did rope me a cow by the heels, neither. Guess I just better stick to gunsmithin' or piano playin'."

Tom smiled and nodded. "Maybe you're right. Ropin' cows can be dangerous if you're not really good at it."

One morning he watched the contract bronc buster at work. The man's skill impressed Matt, awed him, in fact. Watching seven or eight hundred pounds of wild horse sail high in the air and come down stiff-legged with a bone-jarring impact made Matt shudder. He wondered how on earth the rider managed to stay on the horse.

"That really looks dangerous," he commented to Tom Adams, who'd come up behind where Matt was playing chute rooster, sitting on the top rail of the corral.

"Yep, it is. I guess that's why they say a rough string rider's maybe not long on brains, but he's surely not short on guts. It's rough on both the rider and the horse, though. You'll see him work the broncs over pretty good with his spurs and his quirt. Sometimes his rope end, too. He's gotta show 'em who's boss, and he ain't got a lotta time to do it. Most ranch owners just won't pay for extra time."

"How you enjoyin' your spell of ranch life?" Patty Adams asked him one morning after breakfast.

"Well, ma'am, I never had any idea how much work there was to be done on a ranch."

"What'd you think of your visit to the line shack with Tom the other day?"

"Well, the ride was pretty, but it looks to me like it'd be mighty lonesome out there."

She nodded. "It is, but it's got to be done. It's the only way to keep our cows on our range and our neighbor's on his. The line rider's got to keep an eye open for wolves and mountain lions, too, not to mention rustlers. But when a man's got to be out there for weeks at a time, it does get pretty lonely."

"Far's that goes," said Matt, "it don't look like there's much social life even back here at the ranch."

Patty grinned. "Funny you should say that. As a matter of fact, we're throwin' a wingding here this Saturday, and it'll probably go on well into Sunday. I'm surprised Mandy didn't mention it. We throw one in her honor every time she comes back for a visit. Folks come from all over, and everybody has a rip-snortin' time."

Saturday folks started to arrive by early afternoon. They came in buggies and buckboards and some in farm wagons. Most, though, were on horseback. They came from all over it seemed to Matt. One group of three cowboys rode in from a ranch fifty miles away. They'd started for the party on Friday and, thought Matt, with all the drinking there'd be, God knows when they'd get home.

And there would be drinking. Contrary to the usual rules of the ranch, Tom'd laid in a supply of beer and wine and two kegs of whisky for the fifty or so invited guests. Patty and Maria and even Amanda had slaved away preparing food, and Tom'd had four beeves butchered.

That night Matt did most of the piano playing, although Patty also took a turn or two at the keyboard. Amanda played her violin a few times, too, but women were too much in demand as dancing partners to be wasted playing in the band. In addition to Matt on piano, two fiddlers, a guitar player, and two banjo players turned up. A touch of class was added to the whole affair when a clarinet player who was passing through Lampasas on his way to San Antone happened to hear about the party and graced the dance with his horn.

Some of the folks headed for home after the midnight supper, but the dancing went on till sun-up. A good many guests stayed on and bedded down under the trees. Matt couldn't remember ever playing piano for so long a stretch as he did that night. He even played for a hymn sing in the middle of Sunday morning after Patty served a combined breakfast and lunch for the folks who remained.

About two o'clock on Sunday afternoon, the last guests departed. Matt wasn't terribly surprised to see it was the three cowhands who had fifty miles to go. He figured what with their hangovers, they'd probably put off their ride just as long's they possibly could.

22

The twenty-two miles from Lampasas south to Burnet were pleasant. The trail took them through rolling, somewhat sandy hills, and despite a bright sun in a cloudless sky, the temperature was bearable. The doctor wore her divided riding skirt and black Texas-style hat. Matt congratulated himself he'd had the forethought back in Abilene to get him a similar hat. Made him feel he fit in better down in Texas.

Doctor Amanda knew the trail, so she took the lead; Matt, on Queenie in the morning and Horace in the afternoon, brought up the rear. With the round of good-byes and all, they'd gotten a late start, and the distance to be covered was a bit longer than Matt usually made in the length of time left, but the doctor didn't set too fast a pace, and it was close to sunset when they rode into Burnet.

They left their mounts at the local livery stable, and Matt, as usual, took time to pat the horses and see to it they were well taken care of. Before leaving them, he looked them over closely and checked the condition of their hooves. Then he and the doctor each took a room in the Keystone Hotel. Fortunately, a restaurant was still open and serving; even more fortunately, fewer flies buzzed around the food than was usual in most restaurants.

They hadn't conversed much while on the trail, and Matt'd been disappointed that the doctor seemed somewhat aloof. She'd been friendly and sociable, even cordial toward him, while in the company of her family, but as they moved south, she'd seemed to withdraw into a more formal attitude. Not unfriendly, just reserved.

Over supper she seemed a bit more relaxed. As they went to work on their soup, she looked up and smiled at him.

"I like the way you handle animals. You must be a very caring person."

"Well, thank you, ma'am. It seems the thing to do."

"I understand you want to do something more than be a gunsmith or a piano player."

He nodded. "I been thinking about it."

"My sister says you're thinking of perhaps becoming a lawyer. Ever given any thought to practicing medicine?"

The question surprised him. "Be a doctor you mean? Well, no, no I ain't." He scooped up a bit more of his soup and then laid his spoon down. "But if you don't mind my askin', where'd you go to school to become a doctor?"

"I didn't."

"You didn't?"

"Out here most doctors just decide to call themselves doctor and hang out their shingle. Very few doctors in the West ever went to medical school."

"Well, then...?"

"How'd I learn the business?"

He nodded. "Well, yes, somethin' like that."

"I was married to a doctor. My husband Max was a very good doctor. I used to help him, and I read his books and watched what he did. He was always willing to answer my questions, too, and that way I learned a lot about medicine." She smiled. "Sort of on the job training."

"Well, how'd he get to be a doctor?"

She smiled again. "Max did go to medical school. A very good one, Harvard. And later, after we were married, we traveled in Europe, places like London and Paris and Vienna. Places where great discoveries are being made in medicine. So a young doctor—and his wife—could get a real education in all the latest advances."

He reflected on what she'd said, chewing on his lip for a moment. "But you never went to a medical school, huh?"

"No, there just aren't that many schools open to women, and when Max died, I decided to take over his practice. After all, you see, I knew his patients, and they knew me. Actually, I'd already taken care of a good many of them when for one reason or another Max wasn't available."

"It's kinda embarrassin' to ask, but do you…well, treat men?"

"Of course, if they're willing. Although," she frowned, "most men'll only come to me if there's no other choice. So I end up treating mostly women and children."

"Well, havin' a lady examine and treat a man does seem kinda…," Matt shrugged, "scandalous."

By this time they were eating their beef steak, and she viciously jabbed her fork into the meat. "Does it?"

Matt drew back. "Well, yes ma'am, it does. Kinda."

She slowly shook her head. "I'm sorry to hear you say that. You sound just like my male colleagues. A few of them think it's all right for me to treat women and children. But, men? Perish the thought!"

They concentrated on their food in silence for a while, then she glanced up. "Tell me. If it's all right for male doctors to treat women, why shouldn't it be all right female doctors to treat men?"

"Well…." He stopped and thought for a moment and then grinned. "I guess it don't make no sense. I guess there ain't no good reason why you shouldn't treat men."

She smiled. "Well. you are a sensible young man, after all. Maybe you would make a good lawyer."

He grinned. "Thank you. Do you mind if I ask you a question?"

She raised her eyebrows. "Depends on the question."

"Well, back at the ranch, you seemed downright friendly. I mean you laughed and talked easy like and played music with me. And it wasn't just with me. You were that way with most everybody. But then I noticed today that almost as soon's we left the ranch and headed south, you seemed to get different somehow."

She laid down her fork, put her elbows on the table, and rested her chin on her folded hands. "Different? How?"

"Well, now, don't take offense. I mean, you've been friendly again here, but on the ride today I got the feeling you didn't want to talk with me, that somehow I was like a stranger to you. Did I do somethin' to make you mad?"

She looked surprised and then laughed. "No, of course not. I guess without realizing it I must've been putting on what Patty calls my doctor face."

"Your doctor face?"

"That's right, my doctor face." For a moment, she looked as though she were turning something over in her mind. Then she leaned forward with a confidential air. "I don't know if I should tell you this, but I'm sorry to say, too often there's not an awful lot doctors can do about the sickness we see." Her face grew somber. "My husband died of pneumonia—what some people still call lung inflammation—and our dear little daughter died of diphtheria. And each time, there was nothing I could do."

Her obvious distress moved him. He nodded and softly said, "I know. Miz Adams told me."

With an effort, she smiled. "Well, things are getting a little better. We're learning, but awfully slowly. Still, people want to have confidence in their doctor, and in moments of crisis, they don't *want* the doctor to be just like everybody else. Oh, they want the doctor to be friendly and compassionate, but the doctor, whether she feels up to it or not, has to be...what?" She hesitated, then went on. "Someone special, someone they can look up to for help. Do you see?"

"Well…maybe…I guess so. But what's this doctor face got to do with it?"

"Well, if you're going to be so special, whether you feel up to it or not, you have to hold yourself apart. You have to be…reserved. You can't be on a chummy, free and easy basis."

"But you weren't that way at the ranch."

"Back at the ranch it's different. There I'm just little sister or to the neighbors, the little Carson girl who married the doctor and went off to the city. I can relax and enjoy myself, but when I head back to San Antone things are different. I guess without even thinking about it, I start to slip back into my professional role."

He resumed eating for a few moments and then looked up again. "Must get kinda lonely, being special like that."

Her countenance turned gloomy. "It does. Especially when your husband and your child are gone." Then she shrugged. "At the ranch, I feel relaxed, freer of responsibility, but of course, when I get back to San Antone, I have to take over again and be the doctor. And in time of trouble, there's no one else folks can look to for help—except maybe the preacher and God."

The next morning they left early, headed for Marble Falls, a little over thirty-five miles to the south. Again the doctor led the way, but this time the journey was much more companionable. Even though he could see she had to set her mind to it, it pleased him that she smiled and chatted with him as she had back at the ranch.

A few miles south of Burnet, she pointed off to the east. "Over in that valley is Mormon Mill. A fellow by the name of Lyman Wight who apparently didn't agree with Brigham Young led a bunch of Mormons here back 1851. They were the only Mormons to come to Texas. The rest of them all went to Utah. The mill's still there, I believe, but I doubt any Mormons are. They were doing well I understand, but for some reason, in 1853 the old man sold the place and moved the whole colony elsewhere."

The route continued through rolling hills, and they spent another pleasant day on the trail. Early that evening, they reached Marble Falls, a small town in a valley, surrounded by cedar-covered hills. As in Lampasas and Burnet, many of the buildings were made of granite. They again each took a room for the night in the local hotel, and the next morning left for Blanco, another thirty-five miles to the south.

Just south of Marble Falls, they crossed the Colorado River. Looking upstream about a quarter of a mile, they saw the falls that gave the town its name. That day the trail wound up through slopes covered by oak and cedar, and by the time they reached Blanco that evening, Matt figured they'd climbed more than five hundred feet. Again many of the buildings were constructed of stone.

With no hotel available, they pushed on another six miles to Twin Sisters and camped on the south bank of the Little Blanco River.

"It's just as well," said Doctor Amanda. "Going the extra six miles leaves us with only about forty miles to go tomorrow and pretty much all of it downhill. My place is on the northern edge of town, not far from the Ursuline Convent. The sisters there run an academy for girls, and I provide most of the medical care for the girls."

"Are you far from the center of San Antone?"

"Oh, no," she said, shaking her head. "My place is just a bit north of the river. Perhaps a little more than half a mile from the center of town. In fact, I also provide a great deal of the medical care for the students at the German-English School down on South Alamo."

By afternoon of the next day, Queenie just ambled along and Horace plodded behind. Sweat soaked through Matt's shirt, and dust caked on him. Well, after all, he reminded himself, it was late summer, and they were much farther south and getting down out of the hills; temperatures were bound to be a lot hotter. As the afternoon shadows lengthened, he was glad the route'd been downhill, because the ride had seemed much longer than forty miles.

Matt knew he was tired, and he could see Doctor Amanda slumping, too, seeming to droop in the saddle. He wondered if she were dozing? He also got to wondering how fast he still was on the draw. Maybe he couldn't even hit a target beyond twenty feet anymore. He hadn't done much practicing since leaving Abilene. And Abilene was a long way away. He'd mailed a letter in Lamapasas to Uncle Frank and Aunt Elly, but God only knew when they'd get it.

Just then he heard a familiar warning buzz. He jerked upright. A rattler coiled just off the trail, tongue darting in and out, ready to strike. The gun in Matt's hand exploded before he even realized he'd drawn it. The ball caught the diamondback dead on, flinging the snake high in the air and back off the trail into a mesquite bush.

The dozing Amanda's spooked mustang reared. Its rider, suddenly jarred awake, reached for the pony's neck, but missed. She made one more frantic grab, missed again, and began to slide back over the cantle, finally bouncing off the horse and landing with a thump on her back in the dust. Fortunately, she'd hung on to the reins, keeping the startled horse from bolting.

Suddenly a chattering sound erupted in the underbrush; out of it burst six, stubby, snorting, dark gray beasts. To Matt they looked like some strange kind of hog. The six charged straight at Amanda. She struggled to her feet, screaming, "Javelinas! Shoot them, shoot them!"

His Ritter Special roared. Each shot went home, and the wild pigs in their death throes turned away from the terrified woman. Just then a seventh beast, the biggest of the lot, charged out of the brush. Matt's last shot blasted out. The wild hog went down a dozen feet short of Amanda.

Matt slid off Queenie, dropping the reins to the ground in front of her, and rushed over to Amanda. He threw his arms around the sobbing woman. "It's all right, Amanda. It's all right. They're all dead."

He held her close, trying to comfort her. Gradually her sobs subsided. At last she drew a deep breath. "Those wild pigs are vicious. Look at the tusks on them."

She freed herself from his arms and, reins still in her hand, her horse following her, walked over to view the dead beasts. Then, a puzzled look on her face, she began counting the bodies. She shook her head and turned to him. "How in God's name did you do it? With these seven wild pigs and the rattler, that took…eight shots. What's the trick? You've only got a six-shooter."

He looked at his gun. "Well, no, ma'am, this is what you might call an eight-shooter." He went on to explain the history of his unusual weapon. "First time I ever used all eight shots, though. Good thing I don't have to keep the hammer on an empty chamber, so it don't fire accidental. Ain't necessary with this. I can keep all eight chambers loaded at once." He scratched his head with the end of the barrel and grinned at her. "Paw fixed it so I can't shoot myself accidental like."

She laughed shakily. "Well, I'm certainly glad your Paw was so clever." She reached up and pulled his head down to her and planted a kiss on his cheek. "Thank you, sweet boy. I hate to think what would've happened if you hadn't acted so quickly."

His heart beating wildly, he took a deep breath. "Yes, ma'am. Glad I could be of service. You all right now?"

She smiled and nodded.

"Good. I'll load this thing, and then we better be on our way. It's gettin' kinda late."

There was still some daylight when Amanda Klein turned off what was no longer a trail but for the last mile had been a broad road and directed her mount up a curving driveway, lined on either side by tall overhanging trees. The doctor turned and smiled at Matt.

"We're here."

He'd thought Madam Bam's place in Wichita was something, but this house was a mansion. In the deepening twilight, the gleaming white of the main part of the house rose two stories. A broad veranda ran along the front and disappeared around the right side.

On the left, a single story wing, also gleaming white, extended about forty feet from the main portion of the house. At the main entrance, a roof, supported by two huge white columns, projected out over the veranda.

"This is where you live?"

She smiled and nodded. "That's right. The stables are around back."

"Well, Doctor, it's gettin' late. I wonder if you can recommend a hotel in town."

"There's the Menger, but you're not going to stay there."

"I'm not? Why's that, ma'am? Too expensive?"

"It is a bit expensive, but that's not the point. I've got plenty of room right here, and I insist you stay with me tonight."

"Is there anyone else here?"

"No, not right now."

"Well, ma'am, I'm not sure it'd be right for me to stay here."

"After you saved my life today? Don't be silly. As for the future, we can discuss that tomorrow." She slid down from her horse and handed the reins to Matt. "Now, I'm dreadfully tired, so you take the horses to the stables and get them watered and bedded down, and I'll open up the house and see what I can find for us to eat."

He grinned and nodded. "Yes, ma'am!"

They were both tired and dined on a simple meal that she managed to rustle up. Gazing at Amanda across the table, Matt marveled at his good fortune. Supper over, she showed him to his room and retired to her own. Within minutes, he drifted off.

He awoke to find her shaking his shoulder. "Matt, Matt! wake up!"

He couldn't believe it was morning. Looking out the window, he saw it was still pitch dark. He tried to shake her off, so he could roll over and go back to sleep. "Go away," he mumbled.

She shook him even harder. "Matt! Wake up. Come on. I need your help."

Groggy, he sat up, yawned, and looked around. "What's the matter?"

"Get up and get dressed." She sounded excited. Fully dressed, she lit a lamp from the candle she carried. "Meet me downstairs. And don't waste any time. You've got to help me."

23

Yawning and rubbing his eyes, still half asleep, Matt stumbled downstairs. He couldn't imagine why the doctor was up at this ungodly hour of the night.

"Oughtta be gettin' her rest," he mumbled to himself. For that matter, so should he.

At the foot of the stairs, he peered around. Off to the right, he could see a glow of light. It seemed to come from a doorway that opened into the single story wing of the house he'd noticed upon their arrival earlier that night.

"Where are you, Doctor?" he called out.

"I'm in here." Her voice reached him through the doorway from which the light emanated. "Hurry up. Get in here."

He hurried through the doorway and found himself in a long, whitewashed corridor from which several doors opened.

Light spilled out of the first one on his right. At first he didn't see her. Then suddenly she appeared in the lighted doorway and urgently beckoned to him.

"Come on, Matt. We don't have much time."

She retreated into the room, and he followed her. Warm, steamy air assailed him as soon as he stepped across the threshold. He knew this wasn't the kitchen, but Amanda stood at a large, black cook stove that had pots and pans sitting on it.

"Come over here," she commanded. "These containers of water are just starting to boil, and I want you to keep the fire going good and hot."

Had she gone crazy? "But why, ma'am? It's the middle of August. I mean we sure don't need all this heat. And you can't be goin' to do some cannin' in the middle of the night."

"Don't argue! I'll explain it later and—" She stopped dead. "Haven't you got any cleaner clothes?"

He looked down. He'd thrown on the same shirt and pants he'd been wearing since leaving the Adamses' ranch, and she'd never complained about them before.

"Well, I don't know, ma'am. Are we fixin' to go visit somebody?"

She put her hands on her hips and surveyed him. "Never mind. The moccasins are fine, but take off that filthy shirt and throw it into the hallway. It's warm enough you won't need it."

He nodded and stripped off the shirt. "That's a fact."

She shook her head in exasperation. "I suppose you'll have to keep those pants on, though."

He felt himself blushing. "Well…uh, yes ma'am. I'd sure be obliged if I could."

He didn't like to admit it, even to himself, but the idea of stripping in front of her excited him as well as embarrassed him. What did the woman have in mind?

She took his shirt and hurried out the door, leaving him to tend the stove. Five minutes later, she reappeared. This time she smiled at him and laid her soft, white hand on his back. A shiver ran through him.

"You wondering what's going on?"

"Well, yes ma'am, I am."

"I'm about to perform an appendectomy."

"What's...uh...an appendectomy?"

"An operation. A surgical operation."

"Oh."

"There's a young woman in the room next door and she's very sick. She suffers from what in Europe or maybe even back East, they'd call appendicitis."

He wrinkled his forehead. "What's that?"

She sniffed. "Out here my colleagues might say it's a knotted bowel or inflammation of the bowel, but actually, it's a just little piece of bowel about as big as this," she held up her left hand, little finger extended, "that's inflamed and infected. If it ruptures before we can remove it, all her insides will be infected, and she'll almost surely die."

"Yes, ma'am, but what're we goin' to do with all this boilin' water?"

"We're going to put my instruments, knives and such, into the flat pan to boil—that gets rid of the germs on them—and in another flat pan I'm going to boil these little packages of thread. Then we'll put the instruments in some pans filled with alcohol and take them into the surgery."

"What're the big kettles for?"

"To get them as clean as we can, we'll boil some sheets and towels in the big kettles. When they've boiled for about twenty minutes, you and I are going to scrub our hands in soap and water and then bathe them in alcohol. When our hands are good and clean, we'll use these tongs I've already boiled and left soaking in alcohol—"

"Excuse me, ma'am, but what's the alcohol for?"

"Alcohol kills germs. Anyway, we'll use the tongs to lift the sheets and towels out, and then we'll wring them as dry as we can. We'll cover the operating table and the patient with the towels and sheets, and then we'll be ready to begin."

"Begin what?"

"I'm going to cut the woman's abdomen open, lift her

bowel out, and remove the appendix. Then I'll slip the bowel back in her belly and sew her up. Any questions?"

The doctor's description of the proposed surgery left Matt a bit queasy. "You goin' to do all this alone?"

"I hope not. There's no time to summon the nurse who usually helps me, so I'm hoping you'll help me."

He swallowed. "Me?"

"Yes, you. I've watched you in action for several days now, and it looked to me like you're cool under pressure. Whether performing on the piano or shooting snakes and javelinas." Her voice softened and took on a pleading tone. "I need your help, Matt, and so does that young woman in the next room."

"Ain't she got no friends or kin?"

"Her husband's out on the range somewhere. Her ten-year-old daughter drove the wagon here. So, what about it?"

He took a deep breath. "All right. What do I do?"

"You'll handle the chloroform." She reached into a cabinet and took out what looked like a wire tea strainer. "We'll just put a couple of pieces of lint cloth over this and you'll hold it just above her nose and mouth. Then you'll let chloroform drip on it drop by drop, and she'll inhale the fumes." She allowed a few drops of chloroform to drip out of the bottle onto the mask to demonstrate. Then she let him try it.

"What's this do?"

Her words chilled him. "It'll put her to sleep, so she won't feel any pain. But you've got to be careful you don't give too much, because that could kill her."

"You sure we should do this? I don't want to kill anybody, especially somebody I've never even seen before."

"Don't worry. If we're careful, she'll come through just fine. And if we don't operate, she'll almost surely die."

He scratched his head. "You ever done this before?"

She nodded. "Oh, yes. Twice. This'll be my third appendectomy. So there's nothing to worry about."

"This all I have to do?"

"Mostly. You'll stay by her head, and I'll tell you when to

pour the chloroform. When we start, I'll have you drape the towels and sheets over the patient. Of course, I might have to have you come down to where I'm working and lend a hand now and then. And, Matt."

"What?"

"Keep your own head away from the chloroform mask." She smiled. "We wouldn't want you to inhale the fumes and pass out. Oh, and one other thing."

He looked at her.

"When we go in there, try to look confident." She winked. "We don't want the patient any more worried than she already is."

They scrubbed their hands and transferred the instruments from the boiling water to the pans containing the alcohol. Then they wrung out the towels and sheets, and Matt followed the doctor into the next room, each of them carrying a bundle of towels and sheets.

In the middle of the room sat a sturdy table. Hanging from the ceiling above the table were several oil lamps. Lamps also were mounted on the walls all about the room. They draped the table with the clean sheets and placed the flat pans with the instruments on a small table beside the operating table. Near the head of the operating table, stood another small table. On it, the doctor placed the mask and the bottle of chloroform, then Doctor Klein looked at him. "All ready?"

He nodded.

The doctor disappeared into the patient's room. He could hear her murmuring reassuring words for the benefit of the patient and the patient's young daughter. In a few minutes, the doctor reappeared, leading a thin, pale young woman who walked hunched over, grimacing with pain. Her blonde hair was tucked up under a towel wrapped tightly about her head. To Matt, she looked no more than twenty-five. And frightened. For her benefit, he tried to assume an air of calm confidence.

But inside his stomach churned.

The doctor helped the patient climb on the table and lie flat on her back. Next Amanda scrubbed her hands one more time and then, holding the hands in the air, shoulder high, stood at her station beside the table and explained to the terrified woman what was about to take place. That done, she nodded to Matt, and following her instructions, he draped a sheet over the patient from the waist down. Next he drew the woman's nightdress up, baring her abdomen.

The patient started to protest, but the doctor soothed her with a few calm words, pointing out that her lower body was hidden under the first sheet Matt'd draped over her. Finally, he draped a second sheet over her upper body, covering her from chin to just below the ribs. As he worked, he could feel the quivering of the woman's body.

The drapes arranged, at the doctor's bidding, he scrubbed his own hands again. Then he returned to his place at the head of the table. He saw the question in the doctor's eyes and responded with a slight nod.

"All right, Mr. Ritter. You may begin."

He picked up the mask and held it in one hand, a few inches above the patient's mouth and nose. Then, with the other hand, he let a few drops of chloroform fall on the lint covering the mask. As the fumes began to form, the patient attempted to turn her head. He tried to reassure her, at the same time clamping her head between his elbows. "It's all right," he murmured in what he hoped was a soothing voice. "Just breathe deep. Soon you'll be asleep."

He glanced up to see Amanda smiling approvingly at him. Reassured, he resumed comforting the patient. Gradually the woman relaxed; her breathing slowed, became more regular. Relief flooded him. He was doing it, by God. He was putting the poor woman to sleep, helping save her life. Suddenly she began moaning, twisting and turning, seemingly attempting to rise from the table. Her shoulders hunched, and he had to hold her down. Frightened, he stared at the doctor.

"Don't panic. Just give her a little more. They do this sometimes. It seems to be a stage they have to go through before they're really asleep."

He turned the dropper bottle up until chloroform ran almost in a stream.

"No, no, Matt. Not too much."

Good God! Now the doctor sounded worried, almost scared. Christ! What'd he done? He stopped pouring. He felt a little light-headed. Suddenly the patient went limp. Jesus! Had he killed her? He looked up.

Amanda smiled and nodded at him. "Good job. Everything's fine now. I'm going to start. If she begins to stir, pour a few more drops. But gently, gently. I'm starting now."

Matt watched, fascinated, as the doctor tipped the pan containing alcohol and let it run onto the patient's abdomen. She swabbed it around with a piece of lint they had boiled. Then she coated the woman's lower abdomen with some brown fluid.

"What's that?"

Amanda glanced up. "Tincture of iodine. It'll help kill any germs on the skin. I'll use some carbolic acid, too."

She draped more towels over the woman's abdomen, leaving only a small area of skin about six or eight inches square exposed. Now, knife in her right hand, a piece of lint in the other, she drew the knife slowly but firmly across the skin. A thin red line sprang into view. Matt caought his breath and turned his head away.

He occupied his mind by gazing around the room. Then the patient stirred and immediately he poured a few more drops of chloroform.

"Matt! I need you! Come here! Quick!"

Amanda's tone was peremptory. He didn't hesitate. He set the mask and the chloroform on the side table and, shaking inside, hurried to place himself across from where Amanda, shoulders hunched, sweat glistening on her brow, worked.

He looked down. Projecting from the woman's belly, a gray, glistening tube with fine red lines running through it rested on the abdomen. Amanda held the tube with one hand. In her other, she grasped a swollen, inflamed-looking tube, smaller than her little finger. The bloated little tube appeared to be attached to the larger tube.

"I've got her bowel in one hand, and the appendix in the other, but I need some help in order to work."

He looked into her eyes. "What do you want me to do?"

"First of all, rinse your hands with some alcohol and then that carbolic acid there."

He did as he was told.

"Now take hold of her bowel with both hands and, for God's sake, don't let it slip away from you."

Gorge rising, stomach churning, he did as she directed.

"Good! Now just hold on while I tie off the appendix."

He wanted to turn away but couldn't. His eyes remained riveted on her hands. She worked her needle, catgut attached, in and out through the base of the appendix. Then she drew the catgut tight and knotted it, sealing the wormlike structure off from the bowel from which it sprang. Next she took her knife in hand and sliced through the base of the small appendage, severing it cleanly from the large grayish tube. She laid it aside and then pushed the stump of the appendix back into the bowel; a few stitches sealed the stump over.

Amanda glanced up. "Almost done. You're doing just fine. I'll wipe it with some of this carbolic acid, and we can slip the bowel back into the abdomen."

She suited action to words, and he was relieved to see it all slide easily back into the dark cavity.

"Now. Just help hold the sides of this incision together, and I'll sew her up."

She set to work, taking neat stitches, tying them off, and snipping away the loose ends. Layer by layer she closed the abdominal wall. Finally, with nothing more than a layer of yellow fat projecting through the incised skin, she told Matt he could return to the head of the table. Gratefully he resumed his original post.

"There," said the doctor. "I'll just put this drain in place...anchor it with a stitch...and close the skin."

She wiped her brow with the sleeve of her gown and straightened up. For a few moments, she gently massaged her lower back. Then she smiled at him. "Matt, you were wonderful. I don't know what I'd've done without you."

Bursting with pride, he grinned. "What now?"

"We'll get her to bed, and I'll watch her until she comes around. I've got a bed ready for her, and once she wakes up, her daughter can watch over her. If you'll get that stretcher in the next room, we can get her to bed and you can go back to sleep."

He laughed out loud. "To tell the truth, I don't feel like goin' to sleep. I just feel too good right now. I'll clean the place up and fix some coffee."

She smiled and shook her head. "Coffee sounds like a good idea, but never mind the cleaning. Phoebe'll be here in the morning—she's one of my two nurses—and she knows where everything goes."

An hour later, Amanda joined Matt in the kitchen. A lightening of the sky presaged the coming dawn. He poured a cup of coffee for her. She looked tired but triumphant.

He smiled. "You look pretty tired, ma'am."

She nodded and brushed her hair back. "I am."

"How's the lady doin'?"

"Well, she's awake and talking. Having some pain, too, I suppose. Her daughter's with her, but the little girl knows where I am. Any problems, she'll come running."

"The patient goin' to be all right?"

Amanda shrugged. "Too soon to tell. But at least we got that appendix out before it burst. That gives her a pretty good chance I'd say."

"Will she be able to eat?"

"I hope so. Eventually. For now we'll stick to clear fluids and hope for the best. The main thing we have to worry about is infection. If she gets by for a few days without infection showing up, then I believe she'll do just fine."

"You goin' to have to look after her all by yourself."

The doctor laughed. "Oh, no. No, I've got a couple of ladies who are pretty good nurses, and when I have a patient here in the house they come in and help out. They'll be here later this morning, and so will Lettie Sawyer. Lettie comes in days and handles the cooking for me. In fact, when she gets here, she'll fix us a good breakfast. She's a very good cook."

Matt took a sip of coffee and thought for a minute.

"That wing of the house is kind of like a hospital, isn't it?"

"Well, yes, but I don't call it a hospital. Most people don't trust hospitals. They say a person only goes to a hospital to die. Most people prefer to be at home when they're sick, so I have a patient here only now and then. If, for example, they don't have a home or maybe don't have anyone at home to care for them. Then there's those who're too sick and need special care."

"Your ladies handle the special care, then?"

"That's right. They each have their own home, but if need be, they stay here and trade off days and nights. I can't pay them much, but they're both widows and every little bit helps. Then too, I think nursing gives them something to do. Without it, I suspect they'd be pretty lonesome. Being a widow myself, I know all about that, being lonesome, I mean."

"Well, ma'am, this certainly has been an excitin' night for me." He grinned. "Who'd ever've thought I'd end up helpin' out with surgery?"

Her smile was warm. "I'm so glad you were here. Like I said, I don't know what I'd've done without you."

He nodded. "Thank you, but I was happy to do it." He yawned. "But I sure wouldn't want to have to be up in the middle of the night like that very often."

She laughed again. "Well, it doesn't happen every night, although sometimes, if babies decide to come three nights in a row, I don't get much sleep."

"I don't suppose that's much fun. But speakin' of not havin' fun, I got to get down to business and find that owlhoot Bixby. I've heard tell he's often right around here in San Antone. So, I reckon I better find me a place to stay and get on with it."

"What's wrong with staying right here?"

The question surprised him. "Here? Well, but ma'am. I couldn't afford a place like this."

She sat silent a moment, tracing a design on the table in some spilled coffee with her finger. Then she looked up.

"Matt, I wish you'd stay here. It wouldn't cost you anything. I need your help."

He rubbed his chin and thought a moment. "How so, ma'am?"

"Well, last night was a good example. And I've been hoping you'd be willing to ride out and find the lady's husband for me. She'll be wanting to go home soon, and she'll need him. And there's times I have to go out of the city to see patients, and I'd certainly feel much safer if I had you along with me. I'd be awfully grateful if you'd stay."

"But what're folks goin' to say? What with you bein' a widow and all alone here at night with a young feller like me. I wouldn't want to harm your reputation."

Her eyes flashed. "Don't concern yourself about it. If I worried about what all the nasty little Mrs. Grundys said, I wouldn't even be able to practice medicine. I'm used to outraging those narrow-minded creatures." She grinned. "In fact, I kind of enjoy it."

He smiled. "Well, ma'am, if you put it that way, I guess there's nothing else I can do." He nodded. "Of course, I'll stay, and I'm much obliged."

24

Despite the stimulation of the coffee and the exhilaration of helping the doctor save a life—at least temporarily—Matt, after a filling breakfast prepared by Mrs. Sawyer, grew sleepy. He went back to his room, hoping to revive with a few hours sleep. He slipped out of his clothes and, nude, covered only by a sheet, fell asleep almost immediately. He awoke in less than an hour, bathed in perspiration.

San Antone in August was hot. Hot and humid. Not a breath of air stirred. The curtains at his window hung limp. He looked to where he'd discarded his shirt and pants. After the surgery, he'd slipped back into his shirt to have coffee, and later breakfast, with the doctor. But he saw no shirt. And, even more alarming, no pants. His moccasins were all that remained. No, not quite. His gun belt with the Ritter Special in the holster hung over the back of a chair. But right now the gun was no help.

Good God, what was he going to do? Here he was the only male in a house with at least three females—four and a half, if you counted the patient and her little girl—and not a stitch to cover his nakedness. Jesus! Who'd taken his britches? He recalled the doctor's remark the previous night about it being too bad they couldn't get rid of his pants. Was she the thief?

Up here on the second floor it was getting to be too hot to stay very long, but what was he going to wear? Finally, sweat rolling off his body, he slipped into his moccasins and wrapped himself in the only thing available, the sheet, and ventured out into the hall.

He wondered which room belonged to the doctor. Maybe she was asleep. He tiptoed along the hall trying doors and peeping into rooms. The first three he peeked into were obviously bedrooms, but nobody occupied them. Must be this one, he thought, starting to turn the handle on the door of the last one.

"Can I help you?" The female voice startled him.

He jumped and whirled, almost losing his sheet. Standing behind him, a bundle of clothes in her arms, was a slender, dark haired, creamy-complected woman. She appeared to be a few years older than the doctor.

He gulped. "Who...who're you?"

She stared at him for a moment, then smiled. "I'm Lorena Akins. I work for the doctor. I'm her housekeeper."

"Oh." He indicated the bundle of clothes. "Those mine?"

"No, these belonged to her husband, Doctor Max Klein. But Doctor Amanda wants you to try them on. After your bath."

"My bath?"

The woman, still smiling, nodded. "That's right. Your bath. The doctor had me fix one for you. It's waiting downstairs. In the meantime, I'm washing your clothes for you. So come along. The doctor wants to see you at lunch."

Warily Matt followed the woman. As they passed through the kitchen, he nodded to Lettie Sawyer. She was busy preparing lunch but took time to smile at him. In a small room, just off the kitchen, sat a large wooden tub, filled with

steaming water. Matt dipped his toe in. The water felt good.
"Satisfactory?"
He nodded.
She showed him the soap and indicated a large towel draped over a chair. She set the bundle of clothes on the chair. "If you need anything else, just give a shout." She smiled. "If you'd like, I can come in and scrub your back for you."
"Ah...no, no. I can handle it. Thank you."
"Whatever you say. Lunch'll be ready in just minutes."
He dropped the sheet on the floor and climbed into the tub. For a minute, he leaned back against the side of the tub, luxuriating in the cooling of the water. Then he set to work soaping himself all over, including his head. To rinse the soap from his hair, he climbed out of the tub and knelt beside it. Next he stuck his head in the water and washed his hair free of soap. When he looked down at the tub, it was filled with suds. Damn! How was he going to rinse himself? "Miz Akins," he called, "is there any more warm water?"
Before he knew what was happening, the door to the kitchen flew open, and the woman appeared in the doorway, a bucket in each hand.
"Oh, hey!" he yelped. He did the only thing that occurred to him. Quickly he hopped back in the tub and squatted beneath the soap suds, hoping to preserve his modesty. Shoulders hunched, hands crossed in front of him, he looked at her in mute appeal.
"Well, now, young man, if you'll just stand up, I'll pour this water over you, and then you can dry off."
Horror-struck, he stared at her. "Stand up?"
"Well, no, first just sit up straight, and I'll slosh one bucket over the top half of you. Ready?"
Unbelieving, he reluctantly straightened up.
She poured a bucket of water over his head. It ran down over his shoulders and chest rinsing him free of soap on his upper half. "Now, stand up."
"Are you...are you serious?"
Her eyes sparkled. "Of course I'm serious. Stand up!"

Still unable to believe what was happening, he slowly rose from the tub and stood there dripping, hands crossed in front of him. The housekeeper sloshed half a bucket over his back and buttocks, the water running down his thighs and into the tub. "Now," she said sternly, "turn around and, for God's sake, put your hands down."

Hoping his incipient excitement didn't show, he closed his eyes and did as she'd ordered. By now the water had cooled noticeably. When she sloshed the last of it over his front, he gasped.

"There, now," she said, "doesn't that feel better? Here, open your eyes." She handed him the towel. "As soon as you're dressed, come on out. Food's on the table."

Bemused but clean and dry, he slowly struggled into the lightweight, white trousers she'd left him. They fit a bit snugly in the thighs, and rode about an inch above his ankle bone but, wearing moccasins, the latter was of no consequence. The extra-thin white fabric of the shirt pulled a bit snug across his chest, but on the whole, the garments were cool and comfortable.

Finally, he dried his hair. Then he looked around and spotted a coarse-toothed comb sitting on a small table. He picked it up and ran it through his hair. Now, dressed in fresh clothes, he felt almost up to facing the stern Miz Akins. Hesitantly he opened the door and sidled into the kitchen. Lettie Sawyer was just carrying a steaming bowl into the dining room. Inclining her head, she indicated he should precede her through the doorway.

Seated at the head of the dining room table, her housekeeper on her right, Amanda Klein appeared to be giving the older woman some instructions. Lorena Akins listened intently while slurping up a bowl of soup. Upon Matt's entrance, the doctor glanced up and smiled at him. She gestured for him to take the chair on her left.

"Feeling better?"

"Yes, ma'am. How're you? And how's the lady you operated on?"

Doctor Amanda smiled. "I'm fine. A bit tired but otherwise

well, thank you. And our patient, Mrs. Schmidt, is doing about as well as can be expected. Mrs. Todd is looking after her."

"Miz Todd? She one of your nurses?"

Doctor Amanda nodded. "That's right. She's looking after the little Schmidt girl, also. Poor child's sleeping in the room next to her mother's."

Matt spooned up some soup and then, curious about the mansion, asked, "How many rooms are there in that wing of the house."

"Besides the room where we operate and the one where we prepare the instruments and linens, there's four for patients. I can't recall ever using more than three of them at one time, though."

"This is a pretty big house. I never been in one like it, not even my Uncle Claude's place in Kansas City. This soup's mighty tasty," he added as he resumed spooning it up.

Doctor Amanda smiled. "I'm glad you like it. Lettie'll be pleased to hear it. As for the house, it belonged to my husband's parents. They were originally from Castroville, just west of here, but when the drought hit their town, they came to San Antone and went into business. Ran a grocery and later did some banking. Became quite prosperous, too. Even during the War. Before the War, they were able to send Max off to Harvard, and he stayed and went to medical school there. That's where I met him."

"But I thought you said you didn't go to medical school."

"I didn't, but I was a student at Mount Holyoke Female Seminary, and at Christmas one year, I spent a week at a friend's home in Boston, and that's when I met Max. He was a student in Harvard's medical school at the time."

Matt reflected on this information while Lettie Sawyer served the salad. After chewing a bite or two of the lettuce and cabbage, he put down his fork. "Seems like a terrible long way to go for schoolin', specially for a lady. Why didn't you just go to a school in Texas?"

Doctor Amanda looked vexed. "Because when I finished my studies at the Ursuline Academy—"

"The one right here in town you're the doctor for now?"

"That's right. I was the lucky one." Her face took on a troubled air. "I still feel a little guilty my sister didn't get to go to school, but she's nine years older than I am. And the Ursuline Academy didn't exist when she was a child. In fact, it'd only been open a year when I started there. I was only ten at the time."

"Your folks must've had money too, then. How long'd you go to the academy?"

"I finished my studies there when I was sixteen, and you see, at that time there weren't any colleges in Texas open to women. That was way back in 1858, but even now there's nothing much available to women, at least not in Texas. Anyway, my folks sent me off to Mount Holyoke."

He thought for a moment and then grinned. "Kinda funny, ain't it? You go all that way and end up meetin' someone from right around the corner, so to speak."

She nodded and smiled. "I've thought about that. Maybe there's something to these ideas about Fate and Destiny. Anyway, after Max graduated—that was the year before the War broke out and he was twenty-four—we came home and were married right here in this house. My folks had wanted to have the wedding at the ranch, but they finally agreed it'd be easier for the guests to come to San Antone."

"Well, that must've been excitin'. I recall your sister sayin' you'd met people and been places and done things. After all that travelin', it must've seemed a little dull to just settle down in San Antone."

"Oh, we didn't settle down. To get a really good medical education a doctor has to go to Europe and study, and since Max's parents could afford it, we went to New Orleans and sailed for Europe."

This revelation impressed Matt. "You've been to Europe?"

"That's right. We went to all the places where medicine was advancing. London, Paris, Vienna, Berlin, even Budapest. In London we heard about a doctor named Lister, Joseph Lister, and we even went up to Glasgow in Scotland to meet him. Max and I learned a lot from him."

"How long'd you stay in Europe?"

"The War broke out while we were there, and we stayed until it ended. While Max studied, he also arranged for supplies for the Confederacy to be shipped by way of Mexico to his folks here in San Antone. That way, even though we opposed slavery, we saw to it his parents did well, and we got to stay in Europe."

"Kinda killin' two birds with one stone, huh?" He thought for a moment, toying with his food. "Feelin' the way you did about slaves, didn't it bother you, helpin' the Rebels that way?"

Lorena Akins had been quietly eating her lunch throughout the conversation. At Matt's implied criticism of Doctor Amanda's ethics, she frowned. "Young man,—"

With a quick shake of her head, the doctor silenced the housekeeper. Then she sighed. "Matt, you can't always be an idealist. Sometimes a person has to be practical."

Matt kept his eyes on his plate and said nothing.

The doctor waited for him to speak, but when he continued to concentrate on his food, she broke the silence. "Well, all right!" she cried out. "Sometimes I wonder if what happened to Gretchen was God's way of punishing Max and me for ignoring our own principles and helping the Rebels."

The sadness in her voice caught his attention. He looked up. He saw a tear rolling down each of her cheeks. "What do you mean?"

"Gretchen was our little daughter. Max and I both adored her so. She died of diphtheria while we were in Paris in January of 1865. She was only four. I've never gotten over it. I keep wondering why? Why?"

Matt didn't know what to say. He glanced over at the housekeeper. She sat stone-faced. Doctor Amanda took out a handkerchief and wiped away the tears. "I don't know why I'm running on like this, telling you my sad story." She essayed a tremulous smile. "But you remind me a bit of Max, you know. He was blond and blue-eyed, too. Of course, he was thirty-four when he died, and you're a little taller and a little more muscular, but you do remind me of him. Maybe it's because of those clothes you're wearing. They were his."

"Well, ma'am, as soon's mine are dry, I'll be glad to change."

"Oh, no! I like you in those. I want you to wear them." She tucked her hanky away and smiled. "I hope you weren't too offended when I complained about your shirt and pants last night."

He shrugged. "That's all right, ma'am."

"Well, you see it's so important that everything be clean. It makes such a difference. I learned that from Doctor Semmelweis."

"Doctor who?"

"Semmelweis, Ignaz Semmelweis. He insisted that his students wash their hands before attending the women in labor at his clinic. And, would you believe it? As soon as they started doing a simple thing like that, the death rate from childbed fever dropped way down."

Again her enthusiasm impressed Matt.

"Where'd you meet him?"

"As a matter of fact, we went to Budapest where he was practicing at the time, just so I could have him for my doctor when Gretchen was born. Max and I managed to talk to him quite a bit, and we became believers."

"That important, huh?"

Her eyes flashed. "I find it incredible that some doctors still don't wash their hands before doing surgery and even stick their needles in the lapels of their dirty old frock coats during surgery." Then she laughed. "Anyway, that's why perhaps I'm a bit tetched about cleanliness. I think your own clothes will be ready for you soon, and I suppose they're useful when you're in the saddle. I do hope you'll wear some of Max's things, though, when you're helping me around here."

"Well, thank you, ma'am. I'll be happy to. I got to admit in this heat, they're a whole lot more comfortable than mine. Now, is there anything you'd like me to do, or can I go downtown and see what the sheriff knows about Bob Bixby?"

"Well, I would like you to ride out and see whether you can find Mr. Schmidt. If the poor man's come home to find his wife and daughter gone, he must be going crazy with worry. And it'd do her a world of good if she could see him."

"Well, sure. Whatever you say. No rush about seein' the sheriff. I figger Bixby'll keep. But where is the Schmidt place?"

"They're about eight or ten miles to the northwest of here. If Mrs. Schmidt isn't up to giving directions, I'm sure her little girl can."

An hour later, Matt saddled up Horace and, shoving his Yellow Boy into its sheath, set off. Mrs. Schmidt hadn't been up to giving directions, but for a ten-year-old, her daughter had proved to be a levelheaded child and had provided him with what seemed to be pretty clear instructions. Horace stepped right along, and at times, for short distances, with no pack horse to lead, Matt urged the pony up to a gallop.

By mid afternoon, Matt almost regretted he hadn't worn the clothes he'd been wearing that morning. They certainly would've been cooler and a whole lot more comfortable than what he was wearing, even though his own things were at least clean.

In the late afternoon, the temperature began to drop and the sky darkened. Huge black thunderheads boiled up. In the distance, thunder rumbled and lightning flashed. If there was one thing that scared Matt, it was being out in lightning when it was striking anywhere near. He estimated he had to be near the Schmidt place, but it was still at least a mile or two ahead and he'd have to ride straight into the approaching storm.

He debated whether to turn around, but the thought of Doctor Amanda's confidence in him wouldn't let him. He pressed on into the ever darkening gloom. Then he saw the place about half a mile ahead. But Horace was showing signs of not wanting to proceed. He kept trying to turn back and at times put his head down between his knees and moaned. Somehow Matt managed to keep the horse headed for the buildings ahead.

Then the hail hit. Stones the size of baseballs pelted down from the sky, raising welts and bruising both horse and rider. After one particularly bruising encounter with a hailstone, fearful of the consequences if one struck him in the head, Matt dismounted and, holding onto the reins in one hand, managed to get the saddle off.

He crouched on the ground with the saddle covering his head. Huge hailstones bombed the saddle and ricocheted off into the darkness. He tried to think if Uncle Frank'd ever taught him a prayer for such situations. He finally settled for the Lord's prayer which he kept repeating over and over, all the while hoping a stone wouldn't catch his poor horse in the head.

In a matter of minutes, the hailstorm passed. He leaped to his feet and, working faster than he could ever recall, got the saddle back on Horace and remounted the reluctant animal. Forked lightning was now striking off the side of a low hill only a few hundred yards away. The bolts gouged out great chunks of earth as though a bomb had struck.

Suddenly the lightning turned blue and balls of it rolled along the ground. A sulfurous odor assailed Matt's nostrils, and a blue light lit up his hat brim and the tips of his horse's ears. Horace reared and plunged, and Matt barely managed to stay in the saddle. Straining, urging, he headed the horse for the buildings now only a hundred yards ahead.

Fifty yards from a low-lying barn, huge raindrops splatted on them. Just as they reached the barn, the heavens opened. Rain came down in sheets. At least, he thought, the lightning's passed and thank God, we lived through it. He and Horace, chilled by the rain, huddled in the shelter of the barn. Peering out the door, in the direction from which the storm had come, he could see, off in the distance, bright blue sky and a rainbow. Where he was, dark and gloom still prevailed.

Then he noticed a light in the house. Schmidt must be home. At least he wouldn't have to go off searching for the feller. In a few minutes, the rain slackened. Matt tied Horace in the barn and then dashed through the little bit of rain still falling and up onto the back porch of the house where he pounded on the door.

Suddenly the door flew open. A thirtyish, disheveled, wild-eyed, black bearded man, at least two inches taller and twenty pounds heavier than Matt, shoved a Winchester into his face. Knowing he was on a mission of mercy, it'd never occurred to Matt he'd meet with a hostile reception.

Startled, he fell back a step or two, and the angry man followed him out the door, still brandishing the rifle.

"Where are they?" the man roared. "What'd you do with 'em. By God, if you hurt them, I'll carve you into little pieces and leave you for the buzzards."

Matt threw up his hands. "No! Wait! They're fine. Your wife and daughter are fine. They're at Doctor Klein's place in San Antone. Put the gun down and let me explain."

Suspicious, finger on the trigger, the man stared at Matt. Finally, Matt's words seemed to get through. Slowly the distraught man lowered the weapon and stepped back.

"You sure they're all right? What happened to 'em?"

"Let's go inside, and I'll tell you about it," said Matt, in as soothing a voice as he could muster.

In the kitchen, over a cup of coffee, Matt explained the situation. "So when I left, your little girl was up and having some lunch, and Mrs. Schmidt was taking water and some broth. Doctor Klein's got great hopes your wife'll be fine in a few days and able to come home."

The man put his head down on his arms and broke into tears. "Oh, Jesus," he said through his sobs, "I was so worried. I didn't know what'd happened to 'em." He sat back, tears streaming down his face, and then leaned forward and stuck out his hand. "I want to thank you, mister, for all you've done. Now, let's get goin'. I want to see them."

Matt tried to persuade him to wait until the following day. "My horse is pretty tired, and we're liable to run into that storm if we head back to San Antone now. We'd do better to wait till mornin'."

Schmidt shook his head. "I can't wait," he growled. "I want to go now." He glowered and began fingering his rifle.

Tired as he was and longing for a good night's sleep, Matt decided he'd do better to take his chances with the storm rather than with this upset, anxious husband and father.

"Well, let me feed and water my horse, and we better have something to eat, too. Be ready in about an hour."

He and Schmidt rode up to Doctor Klein's place well after midnight. An exhausted Matt, after rousing the doctor and introducing Schmidt, at last bedded down the horses.

25

Five more days were to go by before Matt got to see downtown San Antone. After bringing Schmidt in, Matt got a chance for some sleep, but in the morning, when he came down for breakfast, Doctor Amanda had another task for him.

He took his place at the table. She sat in her usual place at the head of the table, sipping a cup of coffee. She smiled at him. "Sleep well?"

"Yes, ma'am. Sure did."

"Good." Her expression turned serious, "Now, I hate to have to ask you to do this, but you're the only one I can turn to for help. At least for something like this."

Remembering his night in the surgery, Matt felt elated. Maybe they were going to do some more surgery. Nothing he'd like better than to assist Doctor Amanda again.

"Ma'am, you just tell me what you need done, and I'll be happy to help you."

"Well," she said, laying a soft, cool hand on his forearm, "it's this way. Mr. Schmidt naturally wants to stay with his wife, until I can be sure she's out of danger. You can understand that, can't you?"

Puzzled, wondering what she was getting at, he nodded. "I reckon so."

She gently squeezed his arm. "Good. I knew I could count on you."

He screwed up his face. "For what, ma'am?"

"Well, someone has to look after the Schmidt place. Mostly care for the animals. Poor things can't be left without food and water, can they?"

He shrugged. "No, I suppose not."

She patted his arm. "So, knowing how caring you are about animals, I was hoping you'd ride out there and look after things for a day or two. Could you do that?"

He hesitated. This wasn't what he'd envisioned at all. He wanted to help her with her doctoring.

As though reading his mind, she added. "Practicing medicine involves a lot more than passing out pills or cutting on people. More often than not, a doctor has to try to help with the problems that illness brings to people."

He nodded. "Yes, ma'am."

"Mr. Schmidt'll come out in a day or two and either stay himself or make some arrangement with his neighbors. And, Matt." She smiled. "I'd be ever so grateful."

Her smile did it. The whole idea didn't particularly appeal to him, but he'd smiled back and put as good a face on it as he could.

This time he rode Queenie. At least the weather remained pleasant, even cooling down a bit, and that afternoon found him hard at work watering and feeding Schmidt's horses and milking Mrs. Schmidt's cow. Upon his arrival, he'd fed the two dogs and looked after the little Schmidt girl's cat.

A doctor's life is sure different than I thought, he mused, as he lugged water for the horse trough. Might's well be back on the farm with Uncle Frank.

Schmidt turned up about noon on the fourth day. He reported his wife was doing well, and Doctor Amanda thought she was out of danger.

"Says Florence'll be able to come home soon. Says I should come back in another three days and drive her home in the wagon." He grasped Matt's hand. "I want to thank you again, friend, for all you've done. The place looks in real fine shape. I figger when I come in to get her, I can get Emil Carlson—he's my neighbor—to look after things for a day or so. He's only about three miles away over that hill yonder."

The next morning Matt finally got to ride into downtown San Antone. The place was bigger than Abilene, but a good deal quieter. He headed directly for the Bexar County sheriff's office. The sheriff wasn't in, but one of his deputies lounged in a tilted back chair on the ramada in front of the adobe building whittling.

The man was lean and wiry. His Texas hat rode on the back of his head. He looked like he might be in his thirties and sported a long handlebar mustache. When Matt rode up and dismounted, the deputy let his chair come down flat and cut loose with a stream of tobacco juice that sent a puff of dust swirling up from the road. The man shoved his Bowie knife back in its sheath and nodded.

"Mornin'. Can I hep you?"

Matt explained about his mission and Bowler Bob Bixby.

The deputy, looking thoughtful, chewed for a few moments and then raised another puff of dust. "Bowler Bob, huh? You say you got a picture?" He stood up. "Well, let's go in the office."

Matt followed the man in and spread out the now faded and tattered drawing on a table. The deputy studied the likeness for a few moments. "Well, I reckon it does look a little like Bowler Bob, but I can't be absolutely sure."

The deputy's skepticism shook Matt. "Captain Crockett didn't have any doubts when he looked at it up in Fort Worth."

"That where old Captain Tommy's got himself to? Well, he should know. As I understand it, Tommy's made quite a study of Bob Bixby, but sometimes I think he gets a bit carried away on the subject. Claims Bowler Bob's killed three or four men." Another stream of tobacco juice hit the spittoon a bit off-center. "The fact is, though, two of 'em were the rascals that murdered his father, and from the way I hear it, two others certainly deserved killin'."

Matt flared up. "My Paw didn't deserve killin'."

"Whoa, now. I didn't say he did." The deputy scratched his head. "When and where'd you say it happened?"

"In Abilene in June of '71."

"Well, now that presents us with a problem. Seems to me, I heard something about Bowler Bob almost bein' guest of honor at a rope stretchin' last year in El Paso. I just can't recall whether he was in the El Paso hoosegow in June or July. If it was June, he could've been rustlin' cattle around El Paso, but I don't see how he could've been shootin' anybody that same month in Abilene, Kansas."

"It wasn't June. He was in Abilene, shootin' my Paw, I tell you."

"Well, now, maybe you're right, but if I was you, I'd sure want to be certain of my facts. Maybe it was some other owlhoot. You wouldn't want to get the wrong man, would you?"

Matt thought for a moment. "How can I make sure?"

The deputy shrugged. "Well, you could ride to El Paso, but that's a pretty fur piece. Or, if the Comanches or the Apaches ain't cut the wires, maybe the sheriff'll wire to the sheriff in El Paso to find out for you. Stop by tomorrow. Maybe then we can do somethin' for you."

At the noon meal, Doctor Amanda asked Matt what the trouble was. "You look like something had upset you."

He nodded. "It has." He went on to tell her about his interview with the deputy and about the man's doubts regarding Bowler Bob being the culprit in his Paw's murder.

She was a silent for a moment. Then she laid her hand on

Matt's. "Matt, remember back at the ranch when you told me about your crusade to get Bob Bixby?"

"Yes, ma'am. What about it?"

"Well, I found it hard to believe then, and I still do. I just can't imagine Bob Bixby killing anybody for no good reason."

Surprised, he stared at her. "What do you mean? What do you know about that scoundrel?"

"He saved my life. And Max's."

Astonished, Matt laid down his fork and drew back in his chair. "He what?"

"Saved my life. And Max's."

Matt wrinkled his brow. "When was all this?"

"In October of '69. Max and I had loaded up our saddle bags and gone up to the J.C. Schultz place, just this side of Boerne, about 20 miles from here, to deliver a baby."

"Seems like a long way to go just to deliver a baby. Wasn't there a doctor in Boerne?"

She smiled. "Yes, there was, and you're right. It was a long way. We didn't really like to go so far, but Max was in great demand. Not only was he kindhearted, but he was very skillful at delivering babies. And poor Max just couldn't resist. If a woman wanted him, he went."

"Did you always go with him?"

She nodded. "In those days, I often went on calls with Max, especially on obstetrical cases. I'm sure one reason women wanted him was the fact he had me to assist him. I know the women appreciated someone like me being around to help out. So did Max."

"So where does Bixby come into the picture?"

"Well, the delivery went just fine, so next day, late in the morning, we headed back. We were about halfway home when, just as we came over a rise, three men waylaid us. I guess they were what you call owlhoots, outlaws."

Amanda didn't know when she'd seen such a filthy-looking lot. Unshaven, they looked as though they hadn't had a bath in weeks. Dirt caked their clothes, and their hair, what she could see of it, was matted and greasy. The middle one of the three grinned at her. The other two sat staring solemnly at her. Each of those two held a six-shooter in his hand; the grinning one cradled a Winchester in his arms.

She glanced at Max. He gave a barely perceptible shake of his head and sat back, apparently calm. She'd known him too many years, though, to be fooled. A slight twitching of the corner of her husband's mouth betrayed his concern.

"Well, now," said the fellow in the center of the three, "ain't this a pleasant surprise." A large man, he must've been over six feet tall. He was brawny, but starting to run to fat. His belly bulged noticeably over his belt.

He gestured toward the man on his left, a short, squat, walleyed, older man. "That's Lunk. Say howdy, Lunk."

Lunk spat tobacco juice through a missing incisor. It almost hit her horse's foreleg. "Howdy."

The one in the middle, evidently the leader, then gestured toward the remaining member of the trio. "That's Javelina. Nice feller most of the time, but he can get nasty. Likes the ladies, too. Sometimes he acts like a Mexican and sometimes like a Comanche. That's because he's half and half. Say howdy, Jav."

The halfbreed, fondling his pistol, leaned forward in his saddle and suddenly showed his white teeth in a feral grin. "*Sí. Bueños días, señor.*" He ran his tongue along his lower lip and narrowed his eyes. "*Y señora.*"

Amanda tried, but couldn't suppress a shudder. Max nodded. "Afternoon."

The brawny one giggled. "And I'm Mackenzie Wright. You can call me Mackie. And who might you be?"

"I'm Doctor Max Klein, and this is my wife, Mrs. Klein."

"A doctor, are you?" Mackie turned to his companions. "Well, what do you think of that, me boyos."

The two said nothing.

Suddenly the grin disappeared from Mackie's face. "You got a Christian name, Mrs. Klein?"

Amanda glanced at Max. He shrugged. She turned back to

the outlaw. "I'm Amanda Klein."

The man nodded. "That's better. I always like to know who I'm dealing with. More congenial like. Don't you think?"

She didn't know what to say. The man was repulsive. She was downwind of him and, even though ten yards from him, she could detect an unpleasant body odor. She merely gave a slight shrug, and without thinking, sniffed and gave a quick, disdainful jerk of her head.

Mackie grimaced. "What's the matter?" he growled. "You too good to talk to me? You a high and mighty princess?"

His sudden ferocity frightened her. She swallowed.

"No, of course not."

Mackie grinned. "That's better. I don't much care for bitches who think they're too good. They have to be taught a lesson."

"Mackie's a good teacher, too," interrupted Lunk. "He used to teach school."

Amanda could see Max was seething inside. He looked at the outlaw. "Mr. Wright, we have patients to see, and it's still a long ride to San Antone. So, if you and your friends will excuse us, we'll be moving along."

The thug smiled. "Not yet, Doctor. We have business to attend to."

Suddenly he raised his rifle and pointed it at Max's chest. Amanda stifled a scream.

"Now, you two sit nice and still and hold out your hands. Lunk here's going to tie your wife's, and Jav'll take care of yours, Doctor."

"And if we don't sit still? I mean, you're going to shoot us anyway, aren't you?"

Mackie grinned again. "Look at it this way, Doctor. Right now you and your missus are still alive, and while there's life there's hope. But if you don't do what you're told, you'll be dead real pronto."

"Max," she screeched, "do what he says."

Mackie turned to her. "Good thinking, Amanda. Now hold out your hands."

The two outlaws tied their hands securely. Then Lunk

grasped the reins of her horse and Javelina the reins of Max's pony. They set off toward a thick stand of cottonwoods about a mile away. As they approached the wooded area, it appeared, even from a short distance, to be an unremarkable growth of trees and dense foliage. But as they penetrated deeper into the forest, Amanda realized it was more extensive than she'd first thought.

Eventually they came upon a small stream running through a good sized clearing. In the clearing, along one bank of the stream, cooking utensils and food supplies along with four bedrolls and a lean-to gave evidence that someone had camped there for quite some time. Amanda wondered to whom the fourth bedroll belonged.

Mackie gestured with his rifle. "All right, you two, get down."

Amanda, despite her bound wrists, managed to dismount without falling by grabbing the saddle horn and sliding to the ground. Max did the same. Lunk and Javelina dismounted and tied all four horses to trees and then turned back to their captives.

Without saying a word, as though this were something they'd done before, the two tied Max to a tree, facing him outward so he could see what was happening. Then they slipped a lariat over Amanda's head and let it slide down around her waist. Mackie, still mounted, reached down and grabbed hold of the end of the rope and drew up the slack; she found herself hauled around like a dog on a leash.

Then Mackie jerked his head at his confederates. They quickly searched the medical saddle bags, but evidently found nothing that interested them. Next they went through Max's pockets, turning up only a few dollars.

"That all you got?" snarled Mackie, disgusted. "What kind of sawbones are you, anyway? Well, I suppose the horses and the saddle bags'll be worth something. And the drugs'll be useful."

Then he grinned and turned to Javelina and Lunk. "Well, let's see what the high and mighty princess has to offer."

"Somethin' better'n money, I reckon," said a grinning Lunk.

A slow grin spread across the halfbreed's face. he winked and nodded his head. "Oh, *sí*."

Mackie dismounted and handed the end of the catch rope

to Lunk. "Here hold this and don't let go of it."

Then Mackie started to haul on the rope, drawing the terrified Amanda ever closer to him. "Now, your highness, we can do this the easy way or the hard way. And," he winked, "remember. While there's life there's hope. So you see, as long as you do what you're told, you might live a little longer. Understand?"

Shivering, she nodded.

"All right. I reckon that outfit you're wearing ought to be worth something, so take it off. Every stitch."

"Oh, no," she moaned, trying to pull away.

"We going to have to do it the hard way? I can cut 'em off, you know. Or," he drew his pistol and thrust it against her temple, "I can shoot you in the head and not even put a little hole in the garments."

She began to stammer. "Oh, no. Don't…please…don't. I'll do it."

He narrowed his eyes. "All right. I'm going to untie your hands, and you shed those clothes." He turned to Lunk. "Let a little slack in the rope so she can slide out of that stuff."

He untied her hands, and she felt the pull on the rope around her waist slacken. Behind her she could hear Max yelling, "Leave her alone, goddamn you, leave her alone!"

The outlaws ignored Max. Mackie made a sudden gesture with his pistol. "Come on! Stop wasting time."

Amanda bit her lip and then reluctantly began to shed her clothing. When she stood naked, Mackie stared at her and nodded.

"Very nice, your highness." He turned to Lunk. "All right, Lunk. Tie her hands again." He turned back to Amanda who, shoulders hunched, hands crossed before her, attempted to maintain some degree of modesty. "Like Lunk told you, I was a school teacher, and I learned early on how to deal with unruly pupils."

He drew his knife from its sheath and walked over to a tree. He reached up and cut a thin switch. Then he came back to her.

"Now, your highness, before Jav and Lunk have their turn with you, I'm going to teach you a few manners. Turn around."

She couldn't believe it. Surely he wasn't going to whip her like a schoolgirl. She began to tremble and tried to pull away. "What are you going to do?" she moaned.

Mackie grinned and turned to the halfbreed. "Jav, turn her around."

The halfbreed grabbed her and twisted until her back was to Mackie. Mackie raised the switch. Then it sang through the air and cut down hard across her naked buttocks. Pain and fear overwhelmed the surge of rage that had flooded her. In spite of her resolution to maintain her dignity and silently, stoically bear the chastisement, the searing pain of the switch across her bottom defeated her. She leaped and twisted, letting out a yell, "Ahhh! Please, my God, no more, no more."

Mackie laughed. "Say, please, sir."

Rage and defiance welled in her. But only for a moment. The pain of the switch still fresh, tears ran down her face.

"Please, sir, no more," she sobbed. "I...I apologize for hurting your feelings."

"Well, Miz High-and-Mighty, that's more like it. But we've only just begun. You're good for at least another six or seven."

"Oh, no!" she screamed. "Oh, please, don't. I apologized."

"What're you doin', Mackie?"

Mackie, switch raised to deal a second cut to her bottom, halted the switch in mid air and looked over his shoulder.

"What's it look like I'm doing, Bowler? I'm teaching this slut some manners."

She managed to turn her tear-streaked face enough to get a view of the newcomer. He sat astride a large black horse, a bowler hat tilted slightly forward. He had long, black hair and his face, tanned and clean shaven except for a couple of days stubble, would've have been handsome if it weren't for his nose. His nose, large and Roman, caught the eye.

Suddenly Mackie brought the switch down once again across her tender, bare buttocks. Again, despite herself, she yelled and leaped convulsively. Humiliated, enraged, she nonetheless begged. Tears welling in her eyes, she couldn't help herself. "Please, no more, no more."

"All right, Mackie, stop it."

She turned her head while at the same time trying to twist her body so her bottom would no longer be exposed to the merciless switch. Javelina, still holding on to her arm, stepped back a pace. The stranger had dismounted and now advanced toward the former schoolmaster.

Mackie saw him coming. "Now you just stay out of this, Bob. It's none of your business. She had it coming, the snotty bitch. She's too goddamn high and mighty. One thing I can't stand's a high and mighty bitch."

Arms fold across his chest, Bob came to a halt a few feet from her tormentor. "I know how you feel, Mackie. You've told me often enough, but this is no way to deal with her. You don't want to mark up that beautiful bottom. What she needs is proper lovin'."

Mackie gave vent to an ugly laugh. "I'm going to leave that to Lunk and Javelina. They like that sort of thing. Now just stand back and let me finish, so they can have their fun."

Bob dropped his arms to his sides. "Sorry, boys, I can't let you do it."

Javelina released her arms and took a step toward Bob.

"*Amigo*, do not *impedir*...interfere." He leered. "I am planning to make love, *muy emociante amor*, with this lovely *señora*. I will demonstrate to her *marido* how he should've made love to her when he had the chance." He shrugged. "*Por supuesto*, it is too late now. They will both soon be dead, but perhaps in the next life?" He smiled. "Perhaps that is why they call it Paradise."

Amanda edged away from the halfbreed but couldn't get far. Mackie still held the end of the lariat.

Just then Lunk, who stood about twenty feet away, spoke up. "Aw, now, Bob. Why do you want to spoil our fun? You can have a turn. I'll even let you go before me. You can have her right after Javelina." He bared his snaggled teeth in a lecherous grin. "I don't mind waitin' for somethin' nice like this. Just makes it better."

Bob shook his head. "Nope. Can't let you do it. Robbin'

and maybe rustlin' a few head of cattle or a horse or two's one thing, but abusin' the ladies? Uh, uh. So let her put her clothes on, Mackie. I don't doubt you've taught her a lesson. She apologized to you."

Mackie looked uncertain. "Mind your own business," he growled but didn't raise the switch.

Bowler Bob's voice took on a hard edge. "I'm makin' it my business. I've tried to be fair with you owlhoots, but I'm tellin' you. Leave her alone."

Suddenly he whirled, a gun in his hand. Two shots roared out. An invisible hand plucked Bob's bowler, a hole through the brim, from his head. Ten feet to Amanda's right, Lunk knelt, as though in prayer, a smoking revolver held in front of him. He loosed a wild shot and tumbled forward on his face.

Bob flung himself to the ground, and his gun roared again, a fraction of a second before Javelina's pistol exploded. The halfbreed whirled as though performing some sort of Mexican jig, staggered, seemed to bow, as though acknowledging an unseen partner, and crumbled to the ground. He managed to raise himself just long enough to get off one more shot and then collapsed.

In the few seconds consumed by the deadly fusillades, Mackie had dropped the switch and mounted his pony. He fired once with his six-gun and spurred the horse. His shot caught Bowler Bob, who'd just been getting to his feet, in the right thigh. The wounded man fired once at Mackie as the schoolmaster disappeared through the trees. The sounds of the galloping horse crashing through underbrush faded in the distance.

Amanda, bound hands before her mouth, paralyzed by fear, gazed about her. Two men lay dead. Bowler Bob, clutching his thigh, struggled to get to his feet but fell back. Max, cursing in German, struggled with his bonds.

Bowler Bob yelled at her. "Come here, lady. Let me untie your hands. Then you can get the doc loose."

At his command, she regained the ability to act. Rushing to the side of the wounded man, completely oblivious now of her nudity, she knelt before him. Mouth slightly open, a slow smile spreading across his face, he stared at her nakedness. After several seconds of unabashedly gazing at her, he reached out to struggle with the thongs binding her wrists. Finally the knots unraveled, freeing her hands.

Without a second thought, she threw her arms around her savior and kissed him hard on the lips. "Thank you," she murmured.

His eyes opened wide. Still clutching his bleeding thigh, he laughed. "I can see why Javalina had it in mind to make love to you."

Suddenly embarrassed, she jumped up and hurried over to free Max.

26

Amanda Klein interrupted her story to take a sip of tea and then a bite of food. Slowly, reflectively she chewed. She and Matt were alone at the table. Apparently Lorena Akins had eaten her noon meal and gone about her business before Matt had returned from his visit to the sheriff's office. Lettie Sawyer, after placing Matt's food before him when he'd taken his place at the table, had retired to the kitchen.

After a few moments, the doctor placed her elbows on the table and folded her hands together, fingers interlaced. She nestled her chin on her joined hands and stared into Matt's eyes.

"I don't think I'll ever forget that whole horrible episode with Mackie Wright. Not as long as I live." She slowly shook her head. "I can still recall how humiliated I was. And how embarrassed I felt when Bob Bixby just sat there and stared at me before untying my hands. He didn't even seem aware of the blood oozing from his thigh." She gave a harsh little laugh. "There I knelt, absolutely naked, holding out my hands, and he took his own sweet time, carefully looking me over, a little smile on his face."

Eyes half closed as though trying to more accurately recall the details, she ran her tongue along her upper lip. Then she gave a little shake of her head and resumed.

"That appraisal of Bob's angered me, but do you know, oddly enough, it excited me, too."

She stopped, apparently lost in thought. As he waited for her to go on, Matt found himself going over in his mind's eye the scene she'd recounted, trying to visualize it in detail. Erotic fantasies sprang to mind. He felt himself growing excited. Then a wave of guilt washed over him. He ought to be ashamed of himself. How could he allow himself to have such notions about a nice woman like Doctor Amanda? But try as he might to suppress the thoughts, he couldn't help wondering what she'd look like naked.

Finally, she seemed to come back to the present and Matt. She gave a little shrug and sat up straight, hands resting palms down on the table. "Anyway, as soon as Bob untied my hands, I rushed over and untied Max. Then I grabbed up my clothes and got dressed. The medical saddle bags were still there, and Max dressed poor Bob's wound and bound it tightly enough to pretty much control the bleeding, at least for a while. Then we headed home."

Matt thought for a moment. "What about the bodies?"

Her face hardened. "We left them for the buzzards and any varmints that wanted them. We took their horses and guns though." She grimaced. "That ride home was terrible. Bob's wound began oozing blood again, but he managed to hold himself in the saddle despite the blood loss."

For a moment she hesitated, as though uncertain whether to go on. Face flushed, she looked a little embarrassed. Finally, though, she resumed. "For me, it was painful and humiliating. Thank God, Mackie only had time to give me two welts across my bottom, but those two were awfully tender and located right where they made it difficult for me to sit in the saddle. At times I couldn't stand it and had to get off and walk beside my horse." She wiggled slightly, as though again feeling the smart of Mackie's switch. Then she sighed and shook her head. "That ride seemed to last forever. I recall thinking if there were nothing else but that ride home, I'd never forgive that beast Mackie Wright!"

"But the owlhoot got clean away, huh?"

She nodded. "That's right. Clean away. On that trip home, I thought a lot about him, though. In fact, I thought about him for a long while. Thoughts of revenge filled my mind. For a good many months those thoughts so preoccupied me I wasn't much use to myself or anyone else. The hate in me ate at my soul like acid."

Thinking about her story, Matt gazed off into space for a moment. He wondered what had brought her to tell him the whole humiliating episode in such detail. Finally he turned back to her. "Well, it wasn't like with Bixby and my Paw. At least Mackie didn't kill anyone."

She gave Matt a fierce look. "No, but he would've if he'd gotten the chance. If it hadn't been for Bob coming along when he did, Mackie and his friends would've murdered both Max and me. At least they would've after they got tired of abusing me. I don't have the slightest doubt about that."

"So, then you still hate him, huh?"

"I don't know, Matt. Maybe, but I don't think about it much anymore. I've learned to put it out of my mind. I've got better things to occupy me."

Surprised by her conciliatory response, he thought about his own vow to find justice for his father. He recalled his feelings of bitterness and hatred when he'd heard how his father'd been murdered. Was it any different than her hatred of Mackie? Hatred that seemed to have faded with time. Of course it was. Mackie hadn't killed anyone. Maybe he'd meant to, but he hadn't. But he, Matt, was sure goin' to hunt down Bixby for killin' Paw. By God, he was. It was plain and simple justice, that's all there was to it.

Suddenly she broke into his thoughts. "You still set on hunting down Bob?"

He started. She must be able to read his mind. "Yep. I sure am."

She laid her soft, cool hand on his. "I'm sorry to hear that, Matt. There are better things you could do with your life you know."

"You think so?" He drew his hand back. "So what changed things for you?"

"Well, after Max died, I was devastated. I felt terribly unhappy and alone. And guilty—?

Surprised, he asked, "Guilty? Why should you feel guilty?"

"I felt I'd let Max down. I was so wrapped up in my planning and plotting about revenge I had no time for the poor man. After he died, I realized how hard those last few months must've been for him. He'd had to carry on the practice alone without any real help from me. Not even any emotional support. I barely found time to keep the house and do the cooking."

Her last statement surprised him. "I thought you had help to take care of those chores."

"I do now, but back then I only had a woman who came in a couple of days a week to help out. Otherwise I handled it myself. I enjoyed cooking and still do, but I don't have time for it now."

"But I don't understand. Why should you feel guilty?"

She sighed. "Max and I always shared our life, but after that run-in with Mackie and his thugs, I just withdrew, all wrapped up in my bitterness and hate. I practically shut Max out. I could see he was hurt, and yet he tried so hard to be patient with me. I just didn't seem to care, though. But then when he died, it hit me what I'd lost."

"But you didn't have anything to do with his dyin'."

She shrugged. "I suppose not, but sometimes I wonder. You see, after that Mackie thing in October, I was afraid to go out of town, so Max made his calls by himself. Even the deliveries. Then that next February, he made a call about five or six miles out of town and on his way home was caught in a norther. The temperature fell twenty degrees in about two hours. It was a terrible blizzard and a miracle Max even made it home."

Matt hesitated. He wanted to put his hand on her arm but was afraid she'd think he was being fresh. Finally he settled for saying in a sympathetic tone, "Probably a good thing you weren't with him, or the two of you would've been caught. And neither of you gotten home. Probably both of you'd've frozen to death."

She sighed again. "Max did freeze three toes, but worse than that, he came down with pneumonia." Matt must've looked puzzled. "Some doctors call it lung fever." She bit her lip, and tears welled in her eyes. "I nursed him, but there was really nothing I could do except try to make him comfortable. He died in less than a week."

Seeing the doctor's tears made Matt uneasy.

"Couldn't...couldn't your husband tell you what to do?"

"Oh, Matt, even the best of doctors can't do anything against pneumonia. Not even Max. Not even with all his up-to-date European knowledge."

She dabbed at her eyes, and he finally found the nerve to reach over and pat her hand. She smiled tremulously.

"So many times that's what's hard about being a doctor. You may know the correct diagnosis and exactly what ails the patient, but you're helpless. You can only sit by and watch the patient die. At times like that, about all you can do is try to maybe comfort the family."

He scratched his head. "If you can't do anything, why do folks keep comin' back to you?"

"Hope, Matt. They need hope and someone to turn to. If you weren't drunk and the family feels you did your very best, they don't hold it against you. At least not most of the time."

"What do you mean not most of the time?"

She smiled wryly. "Well, more than one doctor's been

killed by an angry, grief-stricken father or husband. But most of the time, people know what to expect. And they don't expect miracles. After all, just cholera alone has killed more people out here than all the Indian arrows or bullets ever fired. And a lot of doctors have died when they caught the diseases they were trying to treat."

He frowned. "I never thought of it that way, but it sounds like doctorin's more dangerous than gun fightin'."

She nodded. "Now that you mention it, it probably is."

He studied her for a moment. "You ever feel like quittin'?"

She sighed. "More than once, Matt. More than once, but never seriously. People need you, and besides, sometimes you do some real good. And that keeps you going. Just consider what we accomplished with Mrs. Schmidt and her appendix. She's doing extremely well and'll probably go home in a few days. Doesn't that make you feel worthwhile?"

He grinned. "Sure does. I figger it's the most worthwhile thing I ever did. Better even than helpin' to fight off those Indians from the wagon train. And surely better'n any piano playin' or gunsmithin'. Yep, makes me feel real good."

She smiled. "I still say you ought to give medicine some thought as a career. And each year we learn a little more, you know, so someday I'm sure we'll be able to do something about most of these diseases that make us feel so helpless now." Her smile broadened. "Why, one of these days, I might even go back to school and get a genuine M.D. degree."

"Really? I thought you said there wasn't much chance for women in medical schools."

She shrugged. "Did I say that? Well, things are getting better. Back East there's a couple of schools for just women, and now the University of Michigan's started to accept women into its medical school."

He chewed on his lip for a moment. "But what would folks around here do while you're off studyin' back East?"

She nodded. "I know. That is a problem, and I don't know the answer. Anyway, I'm not going anywhere soon."

He mulled over what she'd just said. He was surprised how

relieved he felt that she wasn't about to leave anytime soon. He was getting to feel attached to her and didn't want to lose her. He almost wished he didn't have to keep chasing Bowler Bob. Thank God, San Antone was the best place to be looking for the owlhoot. He glanced up at her.

"Whatever happened to Bixby after that dustup you had with Mackie?"

"I wish you could get Bob off your mind." She stared into his eyes. "No, I see you can't. Well, by the time we got here, he was pretty weak. Max and I helped him down from his horse and managed to get him into a bed in the hospital wing. There's no decent hospitals here in San Antone, you know, and, thank Heaven, when we took over the house, Max added it. He figured we'd need it for his patients and he was right."

"Bixby was all right, then?"

"Oh, no. Not by a long sight. When Max unwrapped the bandage, the wound was still oozing at a pretty good clip. Max knew he had to go in and try to find the source of the bleeding and tie it off. We got Bob into the operating room, and while I administered the chloroform—like you did the other night—Max explored the wound. And just as he'd thought, not one but two pretty good sized vessels were pumping away. So he went to work and tied them off."

Matt frowned. "And that saved Bixby, huh?"

She shook her head. "No, there was more to it than that. Tying off the bleeders was the simple part. The ball from Mackie's gun had glanced off the femur—"

Puzzled, Matt wrinkled his brow. "What's a...a femur?"

"The thigh bone." She seemed surprised he didn't know the word. "Luckily," she went on, "the bone wasn't broken, but the ball was still in Bob's thigh. On top of that, the ball had carried bits of pant leg deep into the wound."

By that time, Matt had resumed eating. "That's bad, huh?" he said, shoveling a forkful of beef into his mouth.

"Very bad. Those bits of dirty pant leg were sure to cause infection. So Max opened the wound wider so he could see what he was doing and fished out the ball and the bits of pant leg and any other foreign bodies he came across."

Again puzzled, Matt said, "And by foreign body you mean...what?"

She smiled. "Well, you might say that anything that's where it shouldn't be is a foreign body. Like a speck of grit in the eye, or a bean up a kid's nose, or as in this case, bits of pant leg deep in his thigh."

"So that did it, I suppose. Max sewed him up and he was on his way."

She chuckled. "Wrong again. After Max tied off the bleeders and picked all the little bits and pieces out of the wound, he lavaged it." Before Matt could interrupt, she raised her hand and went on. "That means he rinsed it out thoroughly with water that'd been boiled and allowed to cool."

Matt grinned. He couldn't be wrong again. This time he had to be right. "*Then* he sewed it up."

She shook her head. "No. He packed the wound open with pieces of lint cloth smeared with carbolic acid paste."

Perplexed, Matt stared at her for a moment, then said, "Why'd he do that? Why didn't he just sew it up? Didn't he want Bixby's leg to heal?"

"Of course he wanted it to heal. After all, Bob had saved both our lives. Max did everything he possibly could for him. So did I for that matter."

"Well, I don't understand. Why didn't he sew him up?"

"Max wanted it to heal from the inside out. So an abscess wouldn't form, and so there'd be drainage. Then too, he hoped the carbolic acid paste would prevent infection. And it did," she said triumphantly. "The wound healed nicely. But slowly. It took almost six weeks."

"Pretty long time, wasn't it?"

"Well, but if Max had sewed the wound, infection and mortification of the tissues would almost certainly have set in, and Bob probably would've died."

"But," said Matt bitterly, "if you hadn't saved Bixby's life, my Paw'd still be alive."

She looked stricken. "Oh, Matt, I wish you wouldn't say

things like that."

He looked at her challengingly. "Well, it's a fact, ain't it?"

She sat up straight. "No, Matt, it's not a fact. You don't know that Bob shot your father. I thought you just told me the sheriff said Bob Bixby was maybe in jail in El Paso when your father was shot. So you can't *know* any such thing, now can you?"

He put his fork down and stared sullenly at the table.

"No, I guess not," he admitted grudgingly.

"What's more," she went on softly, "even if Bob weren't in jail, I just cannot believe he'd shoot anybody for no good reason at all. I spent a lot of time with him, and I can assure you he's a decent man."

"What about what Captain Crockett told me?"

"Oh, I know Bob's killed some men, but never without good reason. Like when he killed the two that murdered his father and then when he shot those two thugs who intended to kill Max and me. Oh, no, Matt. Bob Bixby's a good man."

Matt took a swallow of coffee and thought over what she'd said. Then he leaned forward and waved his fork at her for emphasis. "How'd you come to talk with him so much? I thought you said you were too busy plottin' revenge to do much of anything. Even for Max."

She looked slightly taken aback by Matt's suddenly aggressive attitude. It was the first time she'd seen such a display from him.

"I owed Bob Bixby my life," she stated unequivocally. "So," she went on in a more conciliatory manner, "I nursed him. At first, when he ran a high fever, I spent a lot of time bathing him all over with cool cloths and giving him alcohol rubs to bring that fever down. I changed his bed and helped him answer nature's calls. I saw to his food and, later, helped him get up and down. And, besides, he was the only person I knew who was acquainted with Mackie Wright and could advise me. So, over that six weeks or so span of time, I came to know him quite well. Certainly better than Captain Crockett knows him."

Matt put his fork down and sat back. "Ma'am, I'm sorry if I was rude, but when'd he finally leave your place?"

She smiled as though to indicate acceptance of his apology, then said. "About ten days before Christmas."

Matt mulled over her answer. "And you never saw him nor heard from him again?"

"No."

They resumed eating. Neither said a word. Matt scarcely noticed what he was eating. The discussion had left him confused. He didn't know what to think. The picture Doctor Amanda had painted of Bob Bixby was completely different from what he'd heard from others. Yet how could that be?

Doctor Amanda wasn't just a beautiful woman, she was a smart one, too. And she was a doctor. Not only that!, she obviously knew Bob Bixby better than anyone else Matt'd met. So how could she possibly be wrong? The answer was simple. She couldn't be. He'd been searchin' for the wrong man. Maybe he *was* on a wild goose chase. Maybe he should just forget the whole thing and settle down right here and learn about doctorin'. He'd surely be a lucky feller to have someone like Doctor Amanda as his instructor. But it was truly a mystery to him what she saw in him to treat him as nice as she did.

He took his last bite of apple pie and wiped his lips with his napkin. As he got to his feet, he glanced at Doctor Amanda. Then he looked more closely. She seemed troubled. Jumpin' Jehoshaphat, had he vexed her? That was the last thing he wanted to do. Maybe he should apologize again.

He opened his mouth, but before he could utter a word, she spoke. "That wasn't true about Bob Bixby," she mumbled.

"What wasn't true, ma'am?"

She bit her lip and looked down at her plate. Her face flushed. She grimaced as though in pain. Finally she spoke. "I saw him again."

Matt slowly resumed his seat. "When was that, ma'am?"

At first it seemed she wasn't going to answer. Then she took a deep breath and responded in a low voice. "He turned up here late one night in the middle of the summer after Max died. He'd been hiding out in Mexico, but somehow he'd heard about Max's death. He said ever since he'd left here, he'd thought about me. Said he didn't see how he could get along without seeing me again." The corners of her mouth turned up in a slight smile. Her face took on a dreamy expression. "Bob said Captain Crockett was after him, but he'd decided to risk it. He said even if it cost him his life, it'd be worth it just to see me again."

Matt placed his arms on the table and leaned forward.

"So what'd he want?"

She hesitated and glanced away. Then she moistened her lips with her tongue and stared down at the table for a moment. Finally she slowly raised her head and looked Matt's eyes. She drew a quick little breath and then, face flushed, eyes wide, almost in a whisper, slowly said, "He wanted to make love."

27

"He what?" Matt roared. He couldn't believe what he'd just heard. He sprang to his feet, his chair toppling over with a crash. Then, chin thrust out, he leaned across the table. "What did you just say?"

Obviously alarmed by Matt's outburst, Amanda drew back. Clearly she hadn't expected such a violent reaction from her normally polite young admirer. "He...he said he wanted to make love."

Matt straightened up and, shaking himself like a spaniel coming out of a creek, turned away and began pacing about the room. Lettlie Sawyer's frightened face peeked through the kitchen door. Amanda waved her away, and the bewildered cook hurriedly withdrew back to the safety of her pots and pans.

Unaware of the effect he'd had on Amanda, Matt, pounding

his fist into his palm, prowled the room. "Why that dirty scoundrel!" He whirled and, face contorted, eyes flashing, not realizing the threatening appearance he presented, addressed the doctor, "How could that scalawag say such a filthy thing to a fine woman like you? How could he even think it?"

Amanda finally seemed to realize Matt's anger wasn't directed at her. She took a deep breath and then got up and went over to where he, still glaring, stood. She laid a hand on his arm. "Matt, Matt, for Heaven's sake. Try to calm down."

He frowned and looked around as though bewildered to find himself on his feet. Then he focused his attention on her and nodded, as though to acknowledge he'd heard her plea for calm. "I'm sorry." He raised his fists to shoulder level and stared at them, then slowly allowed them to fall to his sides. "I don't know what came over me."

"You aren't angry at me, are you?"

His eyes widened. "Angry at you? Oh, my God, no! How could…oh, God, did you think…?"

She laughed a little shakily and leaned her head on his chest. Then she looked up at him and smiled. "Thank God for that." She reached up and ran her soft hand caressingly along the back of his neck. "With that six foot frame of yours and," the caressing hand ran along his bicep, "those incredible muscles, you could break me in half anytime you were of a mind to."

Matt shivered. He couldn't help it. Her hand on his neck and chest aroused feelings in him reminiscent of his adventure with Sally at Madam Bam's. Jesus, he thought, how could he blame Bob Bixby for thinking those things when here he was doing the very same thing? He put his hands up and grasped hers. Gently he forced her arms down to her sides before releasing her hands.

He looked into her eyes. Without thinking, for the first time since the attack by the wild boars, he used her Christian name. "Oh, Amanda, I'd never hurt you. Or let anyone else hurt you. I admire you so. You're…you're the finest woman I ever met."

Lips slightly parted, she gazed up at him. "Oh, Matt, Matt. You just don't understand much about women, do you?"

He could feel himself blushing and shuffled his feet. "Well, no, I reckon I don't."

She reached up and patted his shoulder, then went over and resumed her seat at the table. She indicated his chair. "Sit down, Matt. I want to talk to you."

He hesitated, but then went over and resumed his seat. Before she could say anything, he spoke. "What happened that night? Did you send for the sheriff?"

Smiling slightly, she shook her head. "No, Matt, not that night nor the next."

Shocked, Matt felt his mouth hang open. "You mean you let that owlhoot stay for two nights?"

"That's all he wanted to stay. He was afraid Crockett would hear he was in town and come for him. He didn't want to cause trouble for me."

Perplexed, Matt said, "You mean you'd've let him stay longer if he'd been of a mind to?"

She nodded. "That's right."

Matt thought for a few moments, then shook his head. "I don't understand it. I surely don't."

She stared at him for several moments, all the while chewing on her lip. Finally, she heaved a sigh and spoke.

"Matt, you say you admire me. Do you like me? Are you glad to know me? Do you enjoy sitting here and talking with me?"

With her fragrance still in his nostrils, he found it hard to concentrate on what she was saying. But, he wondered, where was all this leading? "Well, yes, ma'am. All of those things."

She leaned towards him. "Well, then, hasn't it occurred to you that if it weren't for Bob Bixby, I wouldn't be here? That I wouldn't be a live woman for you to look at and admire? That I'd be just a pile of bones, picked clean by the buzzards and left moldering somewhere out on the plains?"

Abruptly he grimaced and sat back in his chair. "Good God, don't talk like that."

But sweet Jesus, what she said was true. Maybe he owed

Bowler Bob Bixby a debt. And an apology. If it wasn't for Bowler Bob, he'd probably never've come to San Antone. And even if he had, there'd've been no Amanda Klein for him to meet and admire. Besides, he really didn't know that Bowler Bob'd killed Paw. Damn! Why'd life have to be so blamed complicated?

He looked up. Doctor Amanda was studying him.

"It's not simple black and white, is it?"

He sighed. "No, ma'am, I guess it ain't."

"Now, for a few minutes can we forget about your vow to get Bob?"

He nodded.

"Good. Now you say you admire me, but hasn't it ever occurred to you that I admire you, too?"

His eyes opened wide in astonishment. What was she talking about? "No, ma'am, it hasn't. What could you possibly see in me?"

She shook her head in mock exasperation. "Matt, Matt, what am I going to do with you? I admit your lack of worldliness is a refreshing change from the lechers I constantly seem to meet up with, but sometimes I wonder if you can be as naïve as you seem."

She sighed and shook her head again. "Anyway, if you're going to get along in this modern world, I think I'm going to have to introduce a little sophistication into your life."

Pleased by the thought she found him admirable, but utterly confused, he could only stare at her for a moment. Then he scratched his head and said, "Ma'am, I love the way you talk, but I don't really understand what you mean."

She sighed again, but then smiled and spoke seriously.

"Never mind. But, Matt, it's obvious to me you're a resourceful, intelligent, caring person who at heart is a gentle sort, like you tell me your Paw was. On top of that, you're ambitious and want to make something worthwhile of yourself, but thank God, you're not burdened with unwarranted conceit."

He squinted. "Really? You mean all that? You're not joshin' me?"

"I'm not joshing you." She chuckled. "It's probably just as

well you've never realized how attractive you are to women with that curly blonde hair and those incredibly blue eyes. Not to mention that beautifully proportioned body. And on top of everything else, you don't have the stench of alcohol or tobacco on your breath or clothes."

Matt felt himself blushing again and squirmed in his chair. "Aw, ma'am."

She smiled again. "I'm sorry if I'm making you uncomfortable, but I believe in speaking the truth. And just because I'm a widow and a doctor and ten years older than you is no reason I can't see what's plain before my nose. In fact, those may be reasons I see things plainer than other women."

He heaved a sigh. "Why're you tellin' me all this?"

She laid her hand on top of his. "Many reasons, some of which I prefer not to get into right now, but for one thing, I want you to appreciate yourself. And I think you should become a doctor."

Astonished, he shrugged and sat back in his chair.

"How in the world could I ever do that? I ain't even had much of a proper education."

"Don't worry about it. With a little hard work, you and I together can remedy that. Now," she went on earnestly, "I know you set great store by what your father thought, so do you think he'd like it if you became a doctor and fixed up people instead of guns?"

Matt stared down at the floor and slowly ran his palm along his cheek. He thought about Paw and how gentle Paw was. Only time he ever knowed him to get really riled was if somebody treated animals bad, specially dogs. And he knew Paw wanted the best for his only child, not just for his own sake but for Maw's sake, too. He began to slowly nod.

"Yes, I reckon Paw would've liked to see me become somethin' like a doctor. But I doubt it ever entered his head I could do somethin' like that. No more'n it has mine."

"Well, you can. To get into a good medical school like the University of Michigan, for example, all you have to have is a proper knowledge of English composition and an acquaintance with literature and some mathematics, including algebra and geometry. Oh, and you have to know a little Latin and something about chemistry and biology."

Matt snorted. "That's all?"

"No, you have to exhibit evidence of good moral and intellectual character, but" she grinned, "I don't expect there'll be any trouble about that."

"But, I don't know any of that stuff."

"No, but if you're willing to work, I can teach you."

Matt looked skeptical. "What about the money? What's it cost?"

"Don't worry about it. There's a one time admission fee of twenty-five dollars for nonresidents of Michigan and then a ten dollar fee each year of school."

In spite of himself, Matt was growing interested. "How many years do you have to go?"

"Two. From October through March."

"That's it?"

She smiled. "Not quite. In addition to the two years at school, you have to show evidence of having pursued the study of medicine and surgery for three years with, to use the words of the school's own rule book, 'some respectable practitioner of medicine.'"

He squinted and rubbed his chin. "What's that mean?"

"It means you have to serve as an apprentice to a doctor, like you did when you helped me with Mrs. Schmidt's appendix."

His face broke into a slow smile. "You mean I just help you like that for three years, and that would do it?"

She nodded. "That's right. Even though presently I don't have an M.D. degree, I do qualify as a 'respectable practitioner of medicine.'"

He grinned. "Well, don't that beat all?" Then he grew serious. "But why do you want to do all this? It's wonderful for me, but what do you get out of it?"

"I get your help for three years, and Matt, I do need your help. And it solves a big problem for me."

He wrinkled his brow. "What problem?"

"The problem of who'll take care of my patients. After you get your M.D., you could take care of the patients while I go to school and get my M.D."

He thought about it for a few moments. To get to spend three years with her, he was more than willing to work and study. "It'll take an awfully long time, won't it?"

She shrugged. "What difference does that make? You're young, and," she smiled, "I'm not really all that old. Anyway, think it over. And, Matt," she laid her hand on his arm, "I do need you."

The next day Matt returned to the sheriff's office. Horace ambled along at a leisurely pace through the streets of San Antone while Matt continued to mull over the things Doctor Amanda had said the day before.

Actually, he'd thought about nothing else ever since that astonishing lunchtime conversation. At supper even Lorena Akins seemed to have a different attitude toward him, no doubt influenced by Doctor Amanda's out-and-out approval. Throughout his daydreaming, his thoughts kept returning to what she'd said about her not being around if it hadn't been for Bowler Bob. By the time he arrived at the sheriff's office, he was hoping the sheriff could take Bowler Bob off the hook. But no such luck.

"No, sir," said Sheriff Lonnie Winston, "Bob Bixby wasn't in the calaboose in El Paso last year. Jodie, here," he nodded toward his deputy, "had it all wrong. The owlhoot they hung was a feller by the name of Billie Biddlebee. I got no idea where Bob Bixby was."

Matt held out his hand. "Well, thank you, Sheriff. Much obliged to you for lookin' into it for me."

Lonnie Winston nodded and took Matt's hand. "Think nothin' of it. But, son, if you hear anything of Bowler Bob's whereabouts, let me know, will you? I believe his reputation for killin's a mite exaggerated, but I got no doubt he's a thoroughly no-good horse thief and cattle rustler."

When Matt arrived back at the house, he found Doctor

Klein about to start seeing patients in her consulting rooms in the hospital wing of the house. Earlier that morning, before he'd set off for the sheriff's office, he, at the doctor's request, had accompanied her on her visit to Mrs. Schmidt's sickroom.

After greeting the patient and reminding her that Matt had assisted at the lifesaving operation, she'd ascertained the woman was feeling well that morning.

Doctor Amanda smiled and reassured the patient. "I'm delighted to hear you're feeling well, Mrs. Schmidt, and I'm very pleased with your progress. We'll have you up and on your feet in a day or two, and before you know it, you'll be home with your family."

Then, with Matt watching intently, the doctor, without violating the woman's modesty, changed the dressing covering the surgical incision.

After they left Mrs. Schmidt's room, the doctor pointed out that she didn't believe in addressing patients by their first name. "Not unless they invite me to do so. Remember, Matt, always treat your patients with dignity and respect."

She'd then gone on to explain that, unlike some doctors, she preferred to use one room for patients to wait in and another separate room in which to interview them so they could describe their complaints in privacy.

"It seems to me patients deserve a little privacy, no matter whether they're telling me about themselves or whether I'm examining them. Too many of my colleagues ignore this simple courtesy. Besides, patients are much more likely to speak freely in private. And, of course, it's much easier to persuade them to allow me to examine them."

The doctor said that she generally saw patients in her consulting rooms between ten in the morning and noon and then again after lunch from about 1:30 until 3:00.

"After that, if there are any home visits to be made, I handle them before supper time. A couple of evenings a week, I see patients who can't come in during the day."

Matt looked dubiously at her. "That sounds like you're awfully busy, ma'am. I don't see how we're goin' to find time for all that teachin' you were talkin' about?"

She smiled. "Oh, don't worry. We will. Most mornings I'll be able to work with you on your lessons right after breakfast for at least an hour. And Lorena Akins is going to help out. She's very skilled in English composition and literature as well as Latin. In fact, when she was younger, she taught English and Latin in a girls' academy. But, Matt, I have a favor to ask of you."

"What's that, ma'am?"

She laid her hand on his. "When we're with patients or strangers, address me as Doctor Klein, and I'll refer to you as Mr. Ritter, but when we're alone, please call me Amanda." She smiled. "It's friendlier."

He nodded. "Yes, ma'..." He caught himself and grinned. "I mean Amanda."

Now, this morning, he'd hurried back and, without even taking time to unsaddle Horace, rushed in hoping to catch her before she started seeing her morning patients. He'd found her seated at her desk alone, clad in one of her cool-looking white gowns, hair drawn back and fastened by a scarlet ribbon. She looked up, a quizzical smile lighting her face. She nodded toward a chair, and he sat down.

Quickly he related what the sheriff had told him.

"You know," he continued, "I've been thinkin' about what you said about Bixby savin' your life, and I admit what the sheriff had to say was kinda disappointin'. I'd been hopin' he could clear Bixby of anything to do with Paw's death."

She leaned back in her chair and gazed thoughtfully up at the ceiling for a few moments. Then she focused back on him. "It doesn't really change anything, does it? You're still going to stay here and help me, aren't you?"

He shifted his toothpick from one side of his mouth to the other, then glanced out the window.

"Ride with me and be my bodyguard if I have to go out into the country? Assist me in surgery? Help me prepare bandages and surgical equipment? Mix medicines? Sometimes see patients with me? Help me do whatever it takes to run a modern medical practice? And live here and prepare yourself for medical school?"

He grinned. "Sounds good, ma...I mean, Amanda."

"And most of all, stop dwelling on Bob Bixby and revenge?"

Scratching his head and looking thoughtful, he got out of his chair and went over to stare out the window. "I don't know's I can promise that."

"Matt, remember what your uncle said about Sir Francis Bacon? How revenge is a kind of wild justice that the law should weed out."

Still staring out the window, he nodded. "I remember him sayin' somethin' like that."

"Well," she went on, "Sir Francis had a couple of other things to say, too. He said if a man concentrates on revenge, he just keeps his own wounds open. Doesn't let them heal."

She got up and came over to stand behind him. "Bacon was a very wise man. He also said what's past is gone. Irrevocable. That wise men have enough to do dealing with the present." She reached up and laid her hand lightly on his shoulder. "Matt, you can't keep grieving for your father. Let your wounds heal. Move on to other things."

He turned and faced her. Sorrow and pain lined his face. He nodded. "I reckon you're right, Amanda." He heaved a sigh. "Maybe you can help me to move on. I mean, if anybody can, surely you can. After all, you lost your husband and your little girl, didn't you?"

28

At first, wanting to please Amanda Klein, Matt entered on his studies with enthusiasm. Then he went through a period when he wondered what he'd gotten himself into. Lorena Akins was a demanding instructress with, it seemed to Matt, an unreasonable attachment to people like that fellow William Shakespeare.

"Ma'am, I just don't see why I have to read this feller's stuff. He's got such a funny way of puttin' things I have all kinds of trouble makin' out what he's tryin' to say."

Lorena Akins shook her head and sighed. "Matt, I don't know where you learned to read, but I find it hard to believe you never before made the acquaintance of the Bard of Avon."

Matt shrugged. He didn't like to oppose Miz Akins, but then he didn't care for her implied criticism of Miz Gregory.

He'd admired Miz Gregory and worked hard for her back there in that one room school in Abilene. She'd used the same McGuffey readers he'd first learned on when he started school in Cincinnati, and she'd made Paw happy when she told him, Matt was a good student. But she'd never mentioned this Shakespeare fellow.

Lorena Akins pursed her lips. "I can see you don't approve of what I just said, but that just shows me how much you have to learn. If you expect to gain entrance to any good university, you'll certainly have to demonstrate a knowledge of Shakespeare. What's more, you'll be surprised at how many things we say today came from his works."

Matt nodded. "Yes, ma'am." His reply lacked enthusiasm.

"And, Matt. It's about time you started to speak less colloquially. In addition to your reading, we'll try to improve your diction. Henceforth, please address me as Mrs. Akins, not Miz Akins. The same applies when you address or speak of any other married woman or widow. Strike 'miz' from your vocabulary. And please cease to use 'ma'am.' The word is 'madam.'"

Weeks slipped by. In November word came that President Grant had been elected to a second term. A week later, Grant's principal opponent, Horace Greeley, died. By that time, Lorena Akins's incessant reminders had started to take effect. Only occasionally did Matt slip and use ma'am, and most of the time, he now said fellow instead of feller.

At their Thanksgiving celebration, Amanda Klein found occasion to comment on his progress. Lettie Sawyer had prepared most of the dinner and, for this special day, took her place at the table. Doctor Amanda had, however, assisted Lettie in the kitchen, and when they sat down to dinner, she indicated that Matt should carve the turkey.

"If you're going to become a surgeon," she said with a smile, "you should at least do the honors with that bird."

He grinned. "Yes, ma'am—I mean madam."

Lorena Akins looked up and smiled, a rare event with her, as far as Matt could recall. "Matt's really working at improving his diction you'll be pleased to know, Doctor. Once in a while he slips, but by and large, the colloquialisms are disappearing. And he's even learning to attach final g's to his words."

"Oh, how nice." The doctor turned to Matt. "Are you enjoying Shakespeare?"

"Well, I'm not sure enjoy is the right word. But I'm beginning to get the hang of what he's driving at, and I've got to admit some of the things he says do make a lot of sense."

"We're also working on some of Shakespeare's contemporaries, including Sir Francis Bacon," added Matt's instructress. "I was surprised to find Matt was already acquainted with him."

Matt grinned and winked at Amanda.

"I think in a month or two," Lorena Akins continued, "we'll take up some American writers such as Poe and Emerson. Maybe even that eccentric fellow Thoreau, although I'm not sure about him. And I certainly don't intend to subject Matt to that radical Walt Whitman. Besides, I doubt Whitman's work will ever amount to anything."

"What about some of the newer writers?"

"Oh, yes. I'm sure he'll enjoy Mark Twain. Maybe even Bret Harte. And, of course, we'll soon have Matt writing some essays of his own. Nothing like composition to sharpen one's grammar and spelling, you know."

Amanda turned to Matt. "Sounds like you're going to be very busy. I only hope you have time for your studies and duties with me, although I must say, so far, you seem to have a talent for mathematics, both geometry and algebra."

Matt, who throughout this analysis of his educational progress had been studiously carving the huge turkey, handed the plate of carved meat to the doctor. "Thank you," he said, acknowledging her complimentary remark on his mathematical talents.

"Well," said Lettie Sawyer, smiling fondly at Matt, "I do hope our Matt has time to continue playing the piano in the evening. I do so enjoy that. Especially when you join him with your violin, Doctor."

Doctor Amanda smiled and reached over to pat the cook's hand. "That's very kind of you to say, and I'm sure Matt and I will play whenever the opportunity offers. And I know Matt enjoys playing even when I'm not available."

Matt glanced up but said nothing. He did enjoy playing and at one time had even thought of getting a job in a local saloon to make a few dollars, but it had soon become evident he wouldn't have time for any such extra activities. And Lorena Akins hadn't even started him on Latin yet—she'd said she planned to start that after the New Year—and at some point, he and Amanda were going to have to start on the natural sciences. Whatever that meant.

Studying literature and mathematics wasn't all that kept him busy, either. Not by a long shot. He really was working. Ever since agreeing to become Amanda's apprentice, he'd been so busy he hadn't had time to think about much else.

Just as Amanda had promised, Mrs. Schmidt had made a fine recovery after the operation to remove her diseased appendix. Two weeks after surgery, Amanda had sent Matt out to the Schmidt home to report that the patient was ready to travel. Overjoyed, her husband had hitched up his buckboard and, with his daughter beside him, had returned with Matt to take the wife and mother home.

A month after the operation, Matt and Amanda had ridden out on another call just a few miles from the Schmidt place and on the way home had stopped by to see Mrs. Schmidt. According to her husband, the lady was back to her old self, and the husband was loud in his praise of Doctor Amanda. Mrs. Schmidt's gratitude, although a bit quieter, was just as heartfelt. She realized her life had been spared by the surgical intervention and was especially fervent in her appreciation of the fact that her daughter hadn't been left motherless.

The doctor had smilingly acknowledged the couple's gratitude but, at the same time, had generously pointed out Matt's role in saving the woman's life. Matt still felt a warm glow of satisfaction and pride every time he recalled the scene and how pleased the Schmidts were. Even two months later he'd think of those moments and savor them. It wasn't something he was likely to forget. And he had to admit it sure beat fretting about Bob Bixby.

But the success of the Schmidt operation had another, more practical effect. Even though the Schmidts lived in a somewhat isolated spot, somehow word of the seemingly miraculous cure seemed to spread. More and more patients turned up at Amanda Klein's door, not all of them women or children, either. Apparently some men had come to the conclusion that her knowledge and skill outweighed the problem of her sex. And more and more, messengers turned up asking that she attend patients unable to come to her. All of which meant Matt was increasingly busy in a variety of ways, some of which he wouldn't previously have thought of as a doctor's duties.

One morning in late September, a fifteen-year-old girl had ridden in to summon Doctor Klein to attend her father. The father's normally gentle horse had shied and thrown the man, resulting in what from the girl's description sounded like a compound fracture of the leg. After listening to the young woman's story, Amanda had directed Matt to hitch up the buckboard and, after loading what supplies she thought they'd need, they set off on the five mile journey to the site of the man's accident.

By the time they arrived at their destination, a light rain had started to fall. They found the man still lying on the ground where the horse had pitched him, in great pain and with the bone protruding from a bloody wound in his right leg. His wife stood by him, trying without much success to comfort him. Both of them knew, as did Matt, that a fracture of this nature was a serious matter and that, more often than not, the victim eventually died of sepsis or at the very least was severely crippled.

After examining the leg, Amanda turned to Matt. "Mr. Ritter, we have to get Mr. Watson into the house out of this rain and mud and onto the kitchen table where we can work. But I don't want to disturb the wound if we can possibly avoid it. Any ideas?"

Matt looked around. They were about fifty yards from the house. "I think so. I can bring that kitchen door over here, and we can carry Mr. Watson on it, and at the same time, it'll be out of the way and not interfere with getting him through the doorway. We can kill two birds with one stone, so to speak."

He noticed Amanda's pained expression and realized his figure of speech had, in the circumstances, been unfortunate. Ignoring his gaffe, though, and using the victim's own tools, Matt proceeded to take the kitchen door off its hinges and lugged it over to the prostrate patient. Gently as possible, with Amanda supporting the damaged leg, they slid the victim onto the door. Then with Matt at the head of the improvised litter bearing most of the weight and Amanda at the foot and the man's wife and daughter each lending a hand at the sides, they slowly bore the man into his house.

Once in the kitchen, the doctor directed them to set the litter down to one side of the kitchen. "Now, Mrs. Watson, I want you to scrub this table as clean as you possibly can with hot, soapy water. And have your daughter boil up a gallon or two of water as soon as she can. I'll need it."

She turned to Matt. "Mr. Ritter, bring our supplies in here, and then before we put him on the table, I want you to get all the patient's clothes off of him. We can't have those filthy garments contaminating the table. So that you don't disturb his leg, cut his pants off and his right boot. The left one too, if need be."

In a weak voice, the patient started to protest. Amanda Klein simply shook her head gently and laid her hand on the man's sweating forehead. "Then cover him with a blanket down to about the middle of his thighs." She looked down into the man's face. "Oh, and place something under the end of the door so that his feet are elevated."

Once preparations were complete, they moved the patient onto the newly scrubbed table. The doctor explained that she'd need Matt to administer chloroform again so that the patient wouldn't thrash about under her painful, but necessary ministrations to his leg.

With the patient anesthetized, the doctor set to work employing her version of Joseph Lister's technique. Having scrubbed her hands with soap and water followed by a thorough dousing in alcohol—she had Matt do the same in case she were to need his assistance—she cleaned the skin in the area of the wound with carbolic and tincture of iodine.

Once satisfied the skin was clean, she cleaned out all the clotted blood and dirt she could from the wound and then lavaged the wound with the boiled water. Then she swabbed out the wound with carbolic and cleaned the surfaces of the protruding bone with alcohol, followed by another thorough cleansing of the bone with carbolic. She closely inspected the wound and then, convinced it was as clean as possible, she gently but firmly manipulated the leg until the bone settled back into the leg in satisfactory alignment.

Next, she placed a dressing of lint cloth soaked in carbolic directly over the wound and then, faithfully following Lister's recommendations, she placed a piece of malleable tin over the dressing. She glanced up at Matt.

"The reason for the piece of tin is to have easy access to the wound and the dressings. When the time comes for changing dressings, just lift up the tin, pour some more carbolic on, put the tin back in place, and you're all set till next time. First, though, be sure to wash your hands thoroughly. That's absolutely essential. Never forget it!"

Then she resumed her work. Absorbent wool was packed around the wound and splints applied. While the patient was still anesthetized, they carefully moved him into bed.

"Now, Mr. Ritter, while I talk with Mrs. Watson, could you go out and look after Mr. Watson's horse and then chop enough wood to last a day. You can chop some more when we ride out tomorrow to check Mr. Watson's condition."

A bit miffed to be relegated to such a mundane task after participating in surgery, Matt shrugged and nodded. The following day, after he and Amanda inspected the wound and Amanda pronounced it satisfactory, he found himself chopping more wood. After that first follow-up visit, Amanda sent Matt out every couple of days to check on the patient's condition, and while he was there, he ended up doing chores and chopping more wood. Might's well be back on Uncle Frank's farm, he thought. Wouldn't be doing any more chores than I am now. One evening at dinner he voiced his complaint.

Amanda put down her fork and looked at him in apparent surprise. "I thought I'd made it clear there's a lot of things to be done for patients and their families besides giving medicines and doing surgery. God knows, too often there's nothing much we can do about their illnesses, but even when we can do something about the disease, doing things like chopping wood and other chores is important."

Matt regarded her with skepticism. "Well, I don't see how doing chores has anything to do with folks getting well."

She reached out and patted his hand. "Things like that serve to put the patient's mind at ease. If they're in a good frame of mind, they're more likely to recover. And much quicker, too. So please keep right on doing what you're doing. You'll help the patients, and you'll help our practice grow. And you'll be taking a burden off my shoulders."

"You really mean it?"

"I do indeed, Matt. I do indeed."

Fortified by the discussion, Matt continued his efforts at the Watson place with vigor and enthusiasm. A week after the surgery, Amanda came out with him to check the patient's wound. "Looks good, Mr. Watson. I believe it's going to heal nicely. Of course, the bone'll take a few weeks to knit, but it doesn't look like there'll be any problem with sepsis or mortification."

"Thank God for that," said her patient. "And you, too, Doctor."

"And thank you, Mr. Ritter," interjected Mrs. Watson. "I don't know what we'd've done without your help. It's meant an awful lot to Ezekial. I just hope you can keep on for another week. My brother'll be here by then to help out."

Matt nodded and smiled. "I'll be happy to help out for another week."

One week later, Amanda again accompanied him to the Watson's home. This time she pronounced the wound healed. The dressings were removed and she demonstrated to Matt how to apply a quick-setting plaster cast that would remain in place for several weeks.

"Max and I came across this stuff in Paris, and it works wonderfully for holding fractures in place until they heal. I understand it was invented by a fellow named Mathijesen back in the 1850s. A Dutchman, I think, although I'm not absolutely sure of that."

By this time, Mrs. Watson's brother was on hand to take over the chores, but Amanda and Matt returned two days later to check the cast. "You always want to make sure the cast isn't too tight or causing any sores," she explained. "This one looks good, though, so you'll only have to come out every three or four days for a week or so and then weekly will do. If the cast shows any signs of cracking you can reinforce it."

One day not long after Matt began his apprenticeship, Amanda took time to show him some more of the instruments she used. She took a few from a cabinet and laid them out.

"This," she said, picking up a slender glass tube, "is a thermometer. I place it in the patient's mouth and it tells me whether the patient has a fever and if so, how much. In Europe, thermometers are used routinely, but I find that my colleagues here in the Wild West tend to disdain them. They claim they can tell all they need to know by simply touching the patient. I disagree. I prefer the scientific method."

Next she showed him her stethoscope. "This makes it possible to readily hear sounds inside the body. Especially the heart and lungs. Not just chest sounds either, but also abdominal sounds."

Then she showed him her ophthalmoscope. "For all I know, this may be the only such instrument in Texas, maybe the only one west of the Mississippi. Science hasn't made much headway out here yet."

She called Lettie Sawyer in and had the cook stand straight

and stare fixedly at a previously marked spot on the wall. Next Amanda drew the drapes enough to slightly darken the room. After a moment she placed the instrument close to Lettie's face and directed a beam of light from the instrument at Lettie's eye.

"Now," she said, "I'm looking right inside Lettie's eye. I can even see the blood vessels on her retina. It's the only place you can actually see a person's blood vessels without cutting on them. You can see the optic nerve, also." She straightened up and turned to Matt. "Here, you try it."

She handed him the instrument.

At first he was clumsy, but after several trys and with a little coaching from Amanda he began to get the hang of it. Finally he glimpsed what he was looking for. The thought that he was peering into the eye of another living human being filled him with a combination of awe and delight.

Amanda took the ophthalmoscope from him. "We're running out of time, and I've got some more things to show you before office hours start. You'll get lots of practice with that later. Right now, let me show you the laryngoscope."

She put the ophthalmoscope back in the cabinet and picked up a tubular instrument. She had Lettie lie flat on a table with her head hanging over the edge. She told Matt to stand behind her and look over her shoulder. Then she directed Lettie to open wide. Next she inserted the tube into the cook's mouth and seemed to slide it down the woman's throat. With a mirror she angled a beam of light into the tube.

"Lettie, say aaah." She turned to Matt. "Now, look down the tube."

"Well, now, if that ain't just the slickest! But what am I seeing?"

"Those are Lettie's vocal cords, the things that make it possible for her to talk. All right, Lettie you can stop now," she said, withdrawing the tube from the cook's throat. "You can go back to the kitchen. Thank you."

The cook sat up and, with a shy smile, climbed off the table and scurried back into the kitchen.

"Max got those things just before we left Europe," said Amanda, putting the laryngoscope back in the cabinet, "and sometimes they come in very handy."

"I can see where they would, but what's this?" He picked up a T-shaped instrument that had a wooden handle.

"That's a turnbuckle for pulling teeth. There aren't too many dentists around, so as a doctor, you may end up pulling teeth. You put the clamp on the tooth and then twist the handle and, if all goes well, the tooth comes out. It helps, though, if you have nitrous oxide, what's called laughing gas, to give the patient."

Matt thoughtfully rubbed his jaw. "I would surely think so, but what do you use to bleed people?"

She shook her head impatiently. "I don't. There's still some misguided physicians who do it, but thank God, it's losing its popularity. After all, the last thing you want to do to sick, weakened patients is to bleed them and make them even weaker. I'm sorry to say doctors have probably killed more people with that foolishness than I care to think about."

"Oh."

"And that brings me to another bit of foolishness, giving patients purgatives such as antimony. If the poor patient has cholera, for example, and is dying from fluid loss, it makes no sense to give them a cathartic. And I can't see how it helps to poison people with calomel, either."

"What do you mean, poison them?"

"Just that," she said impatiently. "Calomel is mercurous chloride, and I don't see how mercury poison can help anything."

Matt nodded. "I suppose not. So, what medicines do you give people?"

She glanced at the grandfather clock standing in the corner. "Well, I guess we still have a few minutes." She went to another cabinet and opened it. Its shelves were laden with small boxes, bottles of varying sizes, and several large jars. "I won't try to explain everything right now. In the next few weeks, though, I'll go over everything." She smiled. "Eventually you'll be in charge of this room, Matt, and the responsibility for mixing and preparing medicines will be yours."

He frowned. He wasn't sure he liked the idea of so much responsibility. "Really?"

She seemed to read his mind. "Well, no, not entirely. As the physician, I'm like the captain of a ship. The ultimate responsibility's mine, so I'll keep an eye on things and guide you. Now, let me just go over a few of these things with you."

She showed him her supply of laudanum and paregoric.

"These are both tinctures of opium, that is, alcoholic solutions, but the paregoric is camphorated. Both of these are good for relieving pain, but the paregoric works well against diarrhea, also. The best thing for pain, though, is this morphine," she added, indicating another small bottle. "It calms people, too, so it's useful in a lot of situations. You have to be careful with it, though. Some people get to liking it too much."

She showed him the quinine she used to relieve fever and to treat malaria. "What most people out here in the West call the ague or the shaking ague. Quinine doesn't cure ague, but it does relieve it. You might say that along with morphine and digitalis, it's a doctor's best friend because those three things can be very effective and make a physician feel useful."

"What's this digitalis stuff?"

"Digitalis is made from a plant called foxglove and is very effective for treating heart ailments, especially heart failure. It seems to stimulate the heart."

Quickly she ran through several more medicines, including belladonna, ergot, jalap, nux vomica, ipecac, arnica, Dover's Powder, Bland's pills, and Seidlitz Powder. The flood of information poured over Matt until he felt as though he were drowning in it. Finally, in desperation, he held up his hand. "Whoa, Amanda, I don't think I can remember even half of what you've said so far."

She looked at him and then laughed. "I don't expect you to remember all this right now, but eventually you'll have to know it and a whole lot more."

"There's more?"

"Oh, yes. And we mustn't forget the Indian remedies, either. Some of them really seem to work. Things like powdered roots of skunk cabbage for asthma and boiled wild mint for nausea."

Matt just rolled his eyes.

"And then," she added with a smile, "there's everybody's favorite remedy, whiskey. Or at least, considering how it's ladled out, it seems that way."

Christmas came and went. The information continued to flow over Matt in ever increasing quantities. He learned about treating scurvy with its telltale bleeding gums and swollen, painful joints. "These people need a better diet," Amanda told him. "They've got to start eating vegetables instead of so much meat. Things like tomatoes and cabbage or even potatoes. Better yet, limes and lemons, if they can get them."

At a ranch ten miles northwest of San Antone, he watched while Amanda extracted arrowheads from the flesh of two men who'd been victims of marauding Indians in an attack on a line shack another ten miles west of the ranch. With Matt's assistance she'd used her Listerian technique to treat the wounds and prevent sepsis and putrefaction. A month later the ranch owner visited San Antone and reported the two men had some scarring but were otherwise well and back at work.

Matt listened while Amanda railed against the general filth and unsanitary conditions that existed everywhere.

"I can't prove it," she said, stamping her foot, "but I'm sure germs and infected water have something to do with things like cholera and typhoid. Flies swarming everywhere and all this spitting that goes on can't be good for anyone's health. And, my God, it just stands to reason that letting urine and feces get onto food and into drinking water can't be healthy."

Matt almost got into fisticuffs with another physician, a tall, burly fellow who seemed about to attack Amanda when she confronted the man about emptying waste into the ditch that ran along the street in front his house. The fellow just didn't believe in what he called the germ theory.

At times, Matt's duties included hauling home things such

as cows, chickens, canned goods, cabbages, cord wood, almost anything, items people had used to pay for Amanda's medical services. Some days the weather around San Antone was remarkably warm, on others bitterly cold. In January Matt, for the first time but not the last, encountered for himself the phenomenon known as a Texas norther. Following that storm, he helped Amanda amputate frozen, blackened fingers and toes.

In late January, Amanda, with Matt's assistance, performed another appendectomy, this time on a young man but again with gratifying results. Her success impressed Matt, but she was less sanguine. "Matt, we've been lucky so far. One of these days a patient's sure to die, but there's no other choice. We've just got to keep trying and hope we have more successes than failures. That's about all we can do, I'm afraid."

Then one cold afternoon in late February, a man arrived at the house and begged Amanda to come attend his desperately ill four-year-old daughter. When the man described the child's condition, Amanda's face turn somber, but she told Matt to hitch up the buckboard while she prepared the medical supplies and changed into traveling clothes.

With a sense of foreboding, Matt donned his riding outfit. By now, the clothes he'd worn on his trek from Abilene had long since worn out, but at Amanda's urging, he wore her dead husband's clothes. The clothes, both summer and winter things, were of a much finer quality than Matt would ever've dreamed of buying for himself and, except for a little tightness across the chest, fit him well.

"I'm glad I saved those things. They look so good on you," she'd said, gazing admiringly at him. "And it's amazing how much you remind me of Max, especially wearing his things."

Attired in Max's warm winter coat and a pair of Max's almost new woolen trousers, Matt swiftly hitched a team to the buckboard. Accompanied by the worried father, he and Amanda, a buffalo robe tucked around them, set out for the man's home.

29

As they traveled the three miles to the patient's home, the day's gloomy overcast deepened Matt's foreboding. Amanda huddled under the buffalo robe, somber and preoccupied. When he tried to engage her in conversation, she had little to say and answered only in monosyllables. Their destination, when finally they arrived, proved to be a small house, originally constructed of logs, to which a kitchen fabricated of wooden planks had been added.

Jake Regan, the anxious father, volunteered to look after the buckboard and team, while Amanda hurried into the house, followed by Matt lugging the chest containing medical supplies. Once inside, Amanda gestured to Matt to set the medical chest down in the kitchen. That done, she beckoned him to rejoin her in the main part of the house. At the same time she shrugged out of her coat and let it fall to the floor. Seeing this, Matt did the same with his greatcoat.

A thin, wooden partition separated the log portion of the dwelling into two rooms. The larger, the one they were in, seemed to be the main living area. He saw no bed in the living room, so Matt assumed the smaller room, hidden from view by the wooden partition, was the sleeping quarters of the parents. One corner of the living area was curtained off, and when he and Amanda approached it, Matt became aware of a peculiar, shrill, strident whistle emanating from behind the curtain.

Amanda yanked the curtain aside. Behind it, a scrawny, angular woman, face contorted by fear, hovered over a narrow bed in which lay a small girl. The child's chest heaved and strained as she labored to breathe. A thin, bloody, foul smelling discharge trickled from her nose. Sweat bathed her body; her eyes mirrored the terror in the woman's face. Veins and cords stood out in the little one's neck. Each time she fought to get air into her lungs, hollows indented the base of her throat. With each agonizing effort, she produced the terrifying, high-pitched sound that had mystified Matt.

"Quick, Matt!" screamed Amanda. "She's choking to death. Get her in on the kitchen table!"

Galvanized by the urgency in Amanda's voice, Matt shoved the tearful mother aside and snatched up the child. He hurried into the kitchen with his burden and stretched her flat on her back on the table. Close up, he saw that the child's lips had a bluish cast.

On her knees, frantically rummaging through the medical chest, Amanda muttered over and over, "Jesus, Jesus! Where is it? Where is that goddamned tube?"

Finally she found what she was searching for and clambered to her feet. Tucked in the breast pocket of her dress was a wad of lint cloth. In one hand she held a gleaming knife and, in the other, a polished silver tube, its diameter about twice that of a goose quill. She transferred the silver tube to her mouth, clamping it between her teeth. Then, leaning her body firmly across the child's body, she subdued the little one's struggles.

"Matt," she grated between gritted teeth, "stretch her neck out over the edge of the table and, for God's sake, hold her head still. I've got to do a tracheotomy."

He did as Amanda ordered, tightly clamping the little girl's head between his elbows. Frightened, yet fascinated, he watched as Amanda, sweat beading her brow, ran the fingers of her free hand along the girl's throat. In the background, the tearful mother, her hands to the sides of her head, sobbed and whimpered.

Then once again Amanda seemed to find what she was searching for. Her fingers drew the skin taut over the child's throat. Quickly, but carefully, she drew the point or the knife half an inch down the midline of the throat. A red line appeared. She eased the point of the scalpel deeper into the flesh. Bright red blood oozed. A twist of the knife enlarged the opening. Instantly she snatched the silver tube from between her teeth and deftly slipped it into the opening, at the same time withdrawing the knife.

Immediately, a sibilant whisper replaced the harsh, high-pitched whistle. Air rushed into the child's throat and out again through the silver tube. Her convulsive, thrashing efforts ceased, and she lay quietly.

Amanda, still carefully holding the tube in place, straightened up and arched her back. "Matt," she said peremptorily, "hold on to this tube and don't let it slip."

"Yes, ma'am—I mean, Doctor Klein." Chewing on his lower lip, he seized the tube between the forefinger and thumb of his right hand and held on tightly. He glanced down at the child. The bluish tinge had disappeared from her lips. Her eyes no longer held the terrified expression that only a few moments before had chilled Matt's blood.

Amanda pressed the lint cloth tightly against the incision, stanching the bleeding. "Here," she ordered, "hold this tight, too."

He did as she said, while she took a needle and thread from the medical chest and quickly sutured the small incision. At the same time she ran a length of thread through a small ring on the silver tube and then looped it around the little girl's neck. "So the tube can't accidentally slip down into her throat," Amanda said over her shoulder.

Next she swabbed the skin with iodine and carbolic and then placed a pressure dressing on the wound. She put a hand to the small of her back and straightened up again, at the same time mopping the sweat from her brow with the sleeve of her gown. After taking a deep breath and letting it out, she told Matt he could relax for a moment. "I wish we could've used Lister's aseptic technique," she added, "but there just wasn't time."

Then she turned to the mother, who, by this time was weeping quietly as she gazed lovingly at her now pink-cheeked daughter. "I think the crisis is over for now, Mother, but we still have work to do, and we'll have to watch the little one carefully for at least a week for complications. How long has she been sick?"

The mother, after clutching Amanda's hands and repeatedly expressing her gratitude for the doctor's lifesaving intervention, turned to her husband who had, by this time, come in and been hovering in the background. "It's only been three or four days, hasn't it, Jake?"

He nodded. "That's right, Lizzie. Just three or four days. She got feverish and sick to her stomach, but we didn't think much of it," he added, directing his words to Amanda. "Next day she had a bit of sore throat, but then earlier today, she was much worse, so that's when I came to fetch you."

"What ails her, anyway, Doctor?" asked the mother.

"I'm afraid your daughter's afflicted by diphtheria. It can cause swelling in the throat and, more often than not, forms a thick, tough membrane on the tonsils that can spread down into the throat and obstruct breathing. That's why we had to operate on your little girl like that. It's a good thing your husband got us here in time. She was so obstructed she only had a few minutes left to live."

"Oh, my God," whispered the mother, putting her hand to her mouth.

"And," Amanda continued, "we've all got to wash our hands well, so we don't catch it." She turned to the father. "Do you have any whiskey around? Some strong stuff."

The man, relieved by the passing of the immediate danger, grinned. "Sure do, Doctor. A whole barrelfull of real fine stuff. And you're welcome to as much as you can hold."

Amanda smiled wearily. "We're not going to drink it. We're going to wash in it. Soon's we get done using soap and water."

She turned to Matt. "First, though, I want to get that membrane out of the child's throat. I saw an Indian medicine man do it once by slipping a sinew string with sandburs and tallow on it down a child's throat to hook the membrane. I remember he brought it up like a fish on a line, so I reckon I can manage it with a laryngoscope and a forceps. And, even if it does cause a little bleeding, it's better than leaving it in there."

"Can I help?" asked Matt.

Amanda smiled. "I certainly can't do it alone. We'll trade places. I'll work from her head, and you lay across her body like I did. I'll have to work quickly. And thank God you're so strong, because you'll have to hold her still. And, Matt, whatever you do, be sure the breathing tube doesn't get dislodged."

Amanda got her tools from the medical chest, and the two of them traded places. Amanda told him to wrap the child in a blanket, pinioning her arms to her side. Then he leaned across the child as Amanda had done earlier while at the same time reaching up to hold the little head steady.

Matt braced himself. Quickly Amanda, a mirror with a hole in its center mounted by a band around her head, inserted the laryngoscope. Utilizing light reflected from the mirror, she sighted through the instrument and slipped a long, slender pair of forceps down the scope. In a matter of seconds, Matt heard her satisfied grunt. Then, a triumphant, "Got it!" She withdrew the laryngoscope and the forceps. Trailing behind, firmly locked in the forceps, came a bloody, creamy-colored, raggedy thing that looked to Matt like a piece of leather for making a lady's glove.

A smiling Amanda told Matt he could relax but should still watch the child. The change in the doctor struck Matt as near miraculous. Saving the little girl had worked wonders. The gloomy preoccupation that had gripped Amanda during their ride out to the Regan's place was gone, replaced by a buoyant exhilaration. Firmly holding the deadly membrane in her forceps, she beckoned for the child's father to follow her outdoors. "I'm going to have Jake dig a hole, and we'll bury this where it can't do any more harm."

When she reappeared, Amanda washed her hands and arms thoroughly in soapy hot water and then directed Jake Regan to splash copious quantities of his prized whiskey over the newly washed hands and arms. With a look of pained regret, he did as he was bid. Next a jovial Amanda oversaw the two parents and Matt as they carried out the same procedure. When they were done, she laid out her agenda for Matt and herself.

"Matt, I'm going to stay here at least for tonight to watch over little Melanie. I want you to go home and tell Lorena what's happening so she can let tomorrow's patients know to come back later, probably the next day. Then you come back early tomorrow afternoon with the buckboard to pick up me and the medical chest."

Matt wasn't too pleased at the idea of leaving Amanda on her own, but by this time, he was accustomed to obeying her orders. He simply shrugged. "All right, Doctor."

Jake Regan helped him hitch up the buckboard, and Matt set out in the early evening darkness for San Antone and home.

The next day, the weather took a turn for the better. During the night, the wind had died down and the gloomy overcast had dissipated. The day dawned bright and clear. By the time Matt had the buckboard hitched and was on his way to pick up Amanda, the air felt almost balmy. The early afternoon sun beat down on his back, creating a pleasant warmth. Rolling along, he whistled sprightly choruses of "The Day of Jubilo."

Yesterday's gloom was gone, and he looked forward to a cheerful ride home with a happy Amanda. A smile stole across his face. Her moods, he realized, tended to rub off on him. Maybe her jubilation at yesterday's success in saving the Regan child had rubbed off on the weather. At such a fanciful idea, he laughed out loud.

As the Regan dwelling came in view, Matt pulled out his watch. Only a few minutes after two o'clock. He'd made good time. As far as he could see, everything appeared quiet. Maybe he and Amanda could make an early start for home.

Then, as he neared the house, he heard across the hundred yards or so separating him from the place heartrending screams and sobs. Suddenly, the angular figure of Mrs. Regan burst from the front door. Arms flailing, tearing at her hair, she ran in circles. Scream after piercing scream poured from her throat. Then Jake Regan charged from the house in hot pursuit of his distraught spouse. Within seconds he caught up with her and gathered her into his arms, trying all the while to calm her. As far as Matt could see, the weeping man met with little success.

Baffled by the scene being played out before him but thoroughly alarmed, Matt urged the team on. As soon as they reached the house, Matt sprang down and, pausing only long enough to anchor the reins, rushed into the house.

Inside, he found Amanda, arms hanging limply at her sides, slumped in a chair, staring at the floor. She seemed unaware of his presence. He hurried to her side. She continued to stare at the floor. Placing his hand under her chin, he gently elevated her head and searched her face. Except for tears trickling slowly down her cheeks, her countenance was wooden, devoid of expression.

"Amanda, what is it? What's happened?"

Slowly she seemed to focus on him. "She's dead. The little one's dead."

"Dead! But what happened?"

Amanda struggled to her feet. Then she took him by the sleeve and led him to the bed behind the curtain. He gazed down at the small body. No longer was there the sibilant whisper of air passing in and out. The child lay unmoving.

"Oh, Jesus." He turned to Amanda. "But I thought she was all right, that the operation saved her."

Amanda closed her eyes. She seemed to waver as though

assailed by an attack of vertigo. He put his arms around her and held her. Finally she opened her eyes and took a deep breath. Gently she pushed him aside and went back to slump in her chair. Then she looked up at him. "This happens sometimes with diphtheria. The heart just stops beating. Nobody knows why. Usually though it doesn't happen so soon. With my little Gretchen, it didn't happen until three weeks later, just when we thought she was getting well."

Suddenly she lowered her face into her hands and burst into tears. At a loss as to what he should do, Matt could only stand there, stroking her hair. In the distance, the sound of the grieving mother's keening could still be heard. After a few moments that, to Matt, seemed like hours, Amanda's sobbing ceased. She sat back and wiped her sleeve across her tear-streaked face. "I feel so sorry for that poor woman. And her poor husband, too. I know he wants to comfort her, but there's so little anyone can do."

Feeling on the verge of tears himself, Matt asked, "Can't you give her some medicine? Something to help calm her?"

Amanda sighed. "I'll try. I'll give her some morphine. Maybe that'll help." She stood up and clutched his arm. "Oh, Matt, I'm so glad you're here. I don't know what I'd do if you weren't." Again she took him by his sleeve and this time led him to the window. "You see that hill over there about half a mile away?"

He nodded.

"There's a middle-aged couple lives about a mile the other side of it who don't have any children to catch anything. Take the buckboard and fetch the neighbor woman, will you? Mr. Regan says they've been good neighbors, and he thinks she'll be willing to come help out."

Darkness was about to fall when Matt and Amanda set out for home. Melancholy enveloped the trip. Amanda, remote and lost in her own thoughts, had even less to say than on the way out. Occasionally she brushed a tear from her eye, but for the most part, simply stared stonily out at some distant point on the prairie.

Matt made a few halfhearted attempts at conversation, but when his efforts met only silence, he retreated into his own thoughts. Mrs. Sills, the neighbor lady, had come willingly with him. Her husband had said he'd do his best to round up other friends to help out as soon as he could.

When Matt and Mrs. Sills reached the Regan place, they discovered a calmer, almost lethargic, Mrs. Regan. Amanda told him she'd given the anguished mother a potent dose of morphine, and it seemed to be helping the poor woman. Mrs. Sills had immediately started preparing a meal, and both Matt and Amanda had forced themselves to eat something before setting out on their journey home.

Because of the highly contagious nature of the child's disease, Amanda had urged that burial take place as soon as possible, certainly no later than the next day. Matt offered to help by digging the grave, but the distressed father, tears standing in his eyes, insisted that he'd do it himself. "It's the last thing I can do for my little darlin'," he said, his face contorted by grief.

A bright full moon lit their way home. As soon as Matt brought the buckboard to a halt, Amanda climbed down from the wagon and, without a word, disappeared into the house. Matt, concerned about her but not wanting to intrude on her mood, merely slowly shook his head in sympathy as he watched her go. Then he unhitched the team and saw to it the horses were fed, watered, and bedded down.

That accomplished, he lugged the medical chest into the supply room. He didn't bother to unpack anything but headed for the kitchen to find something to snack on. He was rummaging in the pantry when a worried Lorena Akins found him. Apparently Amanda had been no more forthcoming with the housekeeper than she had with Matt. While Lorena fixed him a sandwich and a cup of coffee, he filled her in on the day's tragic events. To his surprise, she accepted without comment his suggestion that Amanda be left to herself for the night. Then, having prepared the food, the housekeeper retreated to her own room.

His appetite stayed, Matt checked all the doors and locks and then headed up to his room and bed. He stripped off his clothes and, as was his custom, slipped nude into bed. In the beginning, after that first embarrassing encounter with Lorena Akins, he'd been wary of going nude. Once he'd settled into his apprenticeship, though, the women tacitly recognized the room as his domain, and no one, not even Amanda, invaded his sanctuary. Eventually, he felt secure in the room and began sleeping in the nude to help alleviate the discomfort of the hot southern Texas summer. He discovered, too, that he took pleasure in the sensual feel of the soft, clean sheets, supplied by Lorena twice a week, so that, even after winter chilled the air, he continued to sleep soundly in the nude, buried under two blankets and a thick quilt.

But tonight, tired though he was, sleep shunned him. He tossed and turned, vivid memories of the past two days tumbling through his mind. He wondered how Amanda felt. Her emotional distress had shocked him. He'd never seen her so upset before. He wished that somehow he could comfort her and ease her distress. Finally, he lay on his back, hands clasped behind his head, and studied the shadowy patterns formed on the ceiling by the bright moonlight flooding through the window. Gradually he grew drowsy. Sleep stole over him.

Suddenly he pushed himself to a half sitting position, supported by his elbows. He hadn't heard the door open, but someone was in the room. A fragrance floated on the air. Amanda's scent. Was he dreaming?

"Matt, can I get in with you? I need you," a voice whispered. Amanda's voice.

Hair released and flowing over her shoulders, one hand clasping her robe about her, her face hovered above him. In the moonlight, anguish lined her features. He sat up and quickly turned back the covers. Silently she shrugged out of her robe and slid into bed beside him, lying on her back. Then she rolled on her side. Her back brushed against his belly, her soft buttocks pressed against his upper thighs.

"Cuddle me, Matt, cuddle me."

He slipped his arms about her and snuggled her close. Her hands grasped his. She pressed his lower hand into her soft belly and drew his upper hand to her breast and held it tightly against her. "There," she whispered, "that feels just right."

They lay quietly for several minutes, neither moving. Finally, she spoke in a soft, low tone. "Oh, Matt, I hope you don't mind my coming to you like this. Today has been so hard. That little girl's death brought back so many memories of my little girl. I just couldn't bear to be alone. I tried, but I couldn't. And I miss my poor dead Max so."

He nuzzled his face into her hair, then gently kissed her neck. "I've been hoping I could do something to help you. And I've dreamt of holding you like this, but never thought I would."

She turned in his arms and stared into his eyes. Then she smiled an sat up. Pulling her nightgown off over her head, she dropped it on the floor and once again lay back. She turned and drew him to her. "Oh Matt, I need you."

Her breasts pressed against his chest. Excitement engulfed him, followed by panic. Memoried of his fiasco with Sally at Madam Bam's flooded him. He feared that any moment he'd lose control and disgrace himself. Just when she needed him. Sinuosly she wriggled her hips.

"Don't do that," he whispered.

She seemed to sense what was happening "Don't move," she breathed. "Just lie still."

He bit his lip and froze in place. For a moment, he thought it would work. But urgency mounted. Suddenly, he could no longer restrain himself. He surged convulsively and collapsed against her. "Oh, no!" he groaned.

She drew his face to her and kissed him on the lips.

"Don't worry about it," she whispered. "It happens to most men. Let's just cuddle for a while."

"Ah, what good's that?"

"It's what we both need. Loving. Then we'll try again."

"You're just trying to be nice."

She smiled. "Of course, I am. But look at it this way. Making love's kind of like practicing medicine. They both require learning the art of postponing the inevitable." Then she drew him close and whispered in his ear. "I love you, Matt."

Again they lay quietly. In his mind, doubt alternated with hope. A great feeling of tenderness stole over him. After a few minutes, she again began caressing him. Soft hands slid back into the hair at the base of his skull. Lips brushed his chest. Once more passion surged. Then she stopped and held him quietly. Again the excitement abated.

After another few minutes, she reached down and caressed him. Carefully she positioned herself above him. "Just lie still on your back," she cautioned. "Let me do all the work."

Gently she guided him into her. He held his breath.

"No, no, breathe deeply," she whispered, "and lie still."

He tried to obey. Gradually the urgency eased. They lay quietly in each other's embrace, she on top, her mouth on his. Then gently she once again began to move, easing him in and out. Tension rose, but he lay still, looking up at her.

Excitement began to play across her face. Eyes half closed, lips slightly parted, her tongue peeked from the corner of her mouth and ran excitedly along her upper lip. Then her lips drew back; sounds issued from deep in her throat. Her breathing grew rapid.

Fascinated by the changes in his normally reserved partner, paying little heed to himself, Matt, without thinking, began to initiate movement of his own. His hips rose to meet hers. "Oh, Max, MAX," she suddenly cried out, then gave a shuddering gasp and collapsed limply on Matt.

"Oh, my God, I love you," he whispered, aware but not caring that she'd called out the name of her dead husband.

30

"Good morning, Matt."

At the sound of Amanda's voice, he glanced up. She looked tired. As tired as he felt. Yesterday had been an exhausting day for both of them, emotionally if not physically. And last night's lovemaking hadn't left much time for sleep. Although, when they'd finally settled down in each other's arms, he hadn't had any trouble falling asleep. He didn't know about her.

He'd barely awakened when, just as the sky had begun to lighten, she'd quietly gathered up her gown and robe and slipped out of his room. Before leaving him, though, she'd kissed him lightly on the lips, thoroughly destroying any possibility of further sleep. He had lain there, drowsy, half aroused again, trying to decide whether he should be angry with her for crying out her dead husband's name at her first climatic moment. But he couldn't summon up any anger. He felt too good. Their lovemaking had been too successful and too exciting for him to feel any animosity. She may've called out Max's name, but it'd been he, Matt, who'd aroused her passion and received the benefit of it.

A little later, with him still marveling at that first tremendous success, they'd made love again, this time in a more leisurely, less urgent, fashion. And, by God, he'd enjoyed it even more. And this time she hadn't dragged Max's name into it. She'd clearly pronounced his name, Matt, even at the height of her passion. So don't be a damned fool, he told himself. Don't complain. Be grateful. After all, she'd handled his problem just right, and now he could look back on that fiasco with Sally at Madam Bam's and smile.

After lying there and reflecting on the situation, he'd come to the conclusion he was a lucky young fellow. He'd never felt more like a man. The future looked good. Humming to himself, he'd gotten dressed and come down to the dining room where Lettie Sawyer had breakfast waiting for him. Lorena Akins had already breakfasted and gone about her business.

He smiled. "Morning, Amanda."

She nodded and gave a quick, fleeting smile and then focused her full attention on the breakfast that Lettie set before her. Once again she appeared somber and preoccupied. Probably still brooding over the death of that little girl yesterday and memories of her own dead child, he told himself. Actually, when he let himself think about yesterday's tragic events, he felt a sense of oppression himself. Think how much harder it must be for her. Probably best to remain silent. Not intrude on her thoughts.

Eventually she set her coffee cup down and looked up.

"Matt, I'm afraid there won't be time for lessons today. We've got yesterday's patients to see as well as today's, and I'll need your help, so you won't be able to work with Lorena, either."

He nodded. "All right. I understand."

He wanted to say more, wanted to pour out how good he

was feeling about himself and how grateful he felt toward her and how sorry he felt about yesterday's tragedy, but it seemed best to say nothing. As it was, they got a bit of a late start, and on top of everything else, it was a Wednesday, the day Amanda customarily visited the Ursuline Academy. They barely had time to grab a bite of lunch.

Matt usually went with Amanda when she made her weekly visit to the German-English School on South Alamo down in San Antone but did not accompany Amanda on her visits to the girls' academy. She felt that assisting on her visits at the one school provided him with sufficient opportunity to see a variety of children, both ill and well. She'd pointed out to him the importance of seeing children when they weren't ill, so he'd recognize the difference when they were ill. But she knew the Ursuline Sisters wouldn't approve of Matt coming to the Academy and preferred not to push the issue.

This day was no exception. While Amanda went off to the Academy, Matt stayed behind and caught up on the ravaged supplies from the morning's rush and readied the office for the afternoon's business. When the patients began to trickle in, to save time, he took them aside and gathered as much routine information as he could so that he could brief Amanda upon her return. By this time, many of the people were familiar with Matt and his place in the scheme of things and were willing to cooperate.

"Anything to help Doctor Amanda," as one woman put it.

They finished well past the usual dinner hour, but before departing for home, Lettie'd set out a light meal for them. Lorena Akins had eaten at the usual time, so Matt and Amanda dined alone. Not surprisingly, Amanda looked even more fatigued than she had at breakfast. She had a number of comments to offer about the day's events, though, and didn't seem as preoccupied. It looked to Matt as though the day's successes had taken the edge off her melancholy of the previous day. He had a few questions, and she even went into her answers at some length. But, even though they were alone, nothing was said about the previous night.

A few minutes after finishing the meal, Amanda yawned and stretched and bade Matt good night and then retired upstairs to her room. Tired himself, Matt cleared the table and then, as usual, checked all the doors and windows. He had long since attended to the animals and was happy to head upstairs.

Less than an hour later, he awoke to discover Amanda, without a word, slipping into his bed and snuggling against him. Within minutes, they were both asleep. Again, at the first sign of dawn, Amanda rose, kissed him on the lips, and slipped out the door.

Three weeks after the first night they'd slept together, Amanda gave up all pretense. She maintained her own room but each night came directly to bed in Matt's room. It was only a matter of a few more days before she ceased rising at the crack of dawn to slip off to her own room. They didn't make love every night, but not many nights went by without it. After that first night, Amanda never again called out her dead husband's name. And less and less did she speak of how much Matt reminded her of the dead Max.

At first, Matt wondered what Lorena Akins thought of all this, but the housekeeper said nothing, so he assumed she approved of the arrangement as long as the doctor seemed happy. The practice was so busy now that a visit to the ranch was out of the question. However, when Tom Adams or other visitors from Lampasas turned up to occupy a guest bedroom, Amanda bowed to convention and slept in her own room. But she no longer urged visitors to stay on.

By March, winter had completely disappeared. Matt had never in his life been so busy. In addition to his studies and his work with Amanda, he had complete responsibility for maintaining the house and the barn as well as the animals. Anything requiring manual labor was his to manage. Once in a great while, he got to play a little baseball, but he no longer dreamed of being a professional baseball player. He was committed to becoming a doctor. He practiced with his guns as often as he could, but only sentiment, the fact it'd been a present from Uncle Frank, kept him from selling his Sharps "Big Fifty." Occasionally, he and Amanda went to the theater or out to dinner, and now and then, he'd sit in on piano at one of the local saloons. But most of the time, he was too busy for much in the way of recreation. Chopping wood and lugging the medical chest helped to maintain his physical condition.

And helping to dig graves.

Sad as it was, Amanda had only spoken the truth when she'd bemoaned the fact that all too often doctors could do little for their patients and could only try to bring some comfort to the families. But, when Matt grew discouraged, she reminded him of the tremendous progress medicine had made in the nineteenth century and predicted even greater progress in the years to come.

"Why, Matt, who knows? With the education we're going to have, maybe one of us will make some great discovery."

With the coming of warm weather to southern Texas, the spring roundup occupied everybody's attention. By late April, drovers had organized cattle drives and headed north. Most of them went by way of San Antone and the town's population burgeoned. The place filled with cowboys, gunmen, gamblers, whores, and all the other hangers-on that a cattle boom was sure to attract.

The number of gunshot wounds and broken bones increased in San Antone and the surrounding countryside. The warm weather also brought rattlesnakes and bears out of hibernation. And even though she was a woman, Amanda's reputation as a doctor who could do marvelous things spread, not only in San Antone but in other towns and places for miles around. She and Matt found themselves treating more and more men as well as women and children.

Because of the lack of sanitation and the congregating of increasing numbers of people, the burgeoning of the population also brought disease. Amanda constantly complained to Matt of her fear that there'd be another outbreak of cholera or typhoid. She tried to combat smallpox by, free of charge, vaccinating everyone who'd accept it. Malaria was rife, and she prescribed and dispensed great quantities of quinine. And she delivered more and more babies.

Through all this, Matt worked at her side, observing and learning. When he wasn't actually at her side, he labored at his studies, supervised by Amanda and Lorena Akins. Lorena confessed that, in the beginning, she'd been skeptical of the whole business, but now she had to admit Matt had turned out to be an excellent student, one of the better ones she'd ever encountered.

She gave this as the reason why, when Matt had been working hard at his studies, she took the liberty of trying to relax him by having him strip to the waist while she massaged his back and shoulders. Matt allowed as how he did find these efforts of hers soothing and told her he appreciated all her help. Amanda was inclined to regard these attentions to the young man by the forty-year-old housekeeper with a sardonic smile but said nothing, apparently secure in her knowledge that Matt was hers.

Letters had been exchanged with the administration at the University of Michigan, and the faculty had agreed that, when he'd completed his three year apprenticeship with Amanda, Matt could present himself for examination. If he passed, he could begin his formal medical studies. At times, Matt marveled at the way his life had changed since leaving Abilene. He wrote to Uncle Frank and Aunt Elly, and they in turn wrote to him. But his past life seemed almost a mirage, something that had never existed, that had been only a dream.

He still thought about Paw, but the pain was no longer as sharp. And as for Bob Bixby, the man rarely came to mind. But, even when he did, Matt could only feel grateful to the owlhoot for having saved Amanda for him. Amanda was right about that Bacon fellow. The man'd had the right idea, all right. It didn't pay to brood and go looking for revenge.

May came and went. In June, the ladies celebrated Matt's twentieth birthday. Lettie Sawyer prepared an especially appetizing meal, the highlight of which was Matt's favorite, roast beef, and she outdid herself with the cake she baked for him. That evening, to Matt's complete surprise—but not Amanda's—Lorena Akins kissed him. First, though, as dinner neared its conclusion, she'd offered a toast.

Getting to her feet and raising her tulip glass—it was his birthday but inasmuch as, living in a household that stocked an excellent wine cellar, he'd acquired a taste for wine, they were honoring him with champagne—she smiled and bowed to him. Surprised, he wondered how many glasses of champagne she'd already consumed. Maybe she started early, he thought.

Then she turned and addressed the other two women.

"In recent months I've had occasion to confess to the fact that I was wrong. That, contrary to my original expectations, Matt has proven to be a fine and apt pupil. Now tonight I think it time to acknowledge that, whereas when Matt first arrived here, it was evident he was a diamond in the rough, now it's clear he's rapidly evolving into a gentleman of sophistication and refined speech." Then the normally reserved Lorena winked and smiled at him over the edge of her glass. "Your health, Matt."

Overwhelmed, not knowing what to reply to Lorena's totally unexpected speech, feeling slightly ridiculous, he glanced around. Amanda and Lettie were both smiling and raising their glasses to him. Finally he turned to Lorena and managed to stammer, "Thank you."

But she wasn't finished. "And, I think, notice should be taken of Amanda's extraordinary reversal of Ovid's myth of Pygmalion."

The reference puzzled Matt, but he noticed that Amanda's smile became a bit strained.

Lorena sailed blithely on. "You look a bit perplexed, Matt, but have no fear. I'll introduce you to that Roman poet's works in your Latin class. And I like to think I may've played a small part in the transformation, maybe the role of Ovid's Venus. Anyway, sir, drink up!"

With that, she tossed back her champagne and then, to his utter astonishment, came around to where he was seated and kissed him full on the mouth.

Dinner over, he and Amanda went off to Dawson's Sanctuary, a downtown saloon where, when he had the time, he occasionally filled in on piano and where he'd committed himself to making an appearance on his birthday. He wasn't sure how Amanda would fit into such a place, but he needn't have worried. She adapted well, joining in the laughter at the well-intentioned, but sometimes crude jokes and downing her share of beer. She even managed to smile tolerantly when the working girls present at the party, laughingly offering licentious invitations, put their arms around Matt and kissed him warmly.

When they finally returned home, despite all the champagne and beer they'd consumed, they made satisfying love. Later that night, lying naked beside her, Matt again reflected on what a change a year had wrought in his life and what a happy man he was.

And how lucky he was.

In July, they celebrated Amanda's birthday. Lettie baked a cake, but Matt had let it be known beforehand that he had reservations for dinner for two in the Menger Hotel's dining room. In class, Lorena had enlightened him on the meaning of Ovid's Pygmalion myth, and this had encouraged him. Tactfully he made it clear to Lorena and Lettie that he had something special in mind and that he and Amanda would be dining alone. The two tried to wheedle his secret from him, but finally settled for cake and coffee in the parlor.

When finally seated by the maitre d' at a secluded table in the Menger dining room, Matt, after examining the menu and consulting Amanda, ordered dinner and wine for both of them.

Then, when the waiter had disappeared into the kitchen, Matt sprang his second surprise. The first had been when he'd appeared in the parlor wearing a new suit of clothes, a suit that would have done Max proud if he'd been alive to wear it but which had been made for Matt and was Matt's very own.

Now he smiled across the table at Amanda. "I've got a surprise for you for your birthday. Well, actually two surprises. I know you'll love the first one, and I hope you'll love the second even more."

Amanda smiled a quizzical smile. "What on earth is going

on? Matt, have you been nipping at the bottle early."

He grinned. "No such thing."

"Well, then, what are you trying to say?"

"Amanda, I know you love the violin, but did you know the Joachim Quartet is playing a special concert here in San Antone tonight?"

Her eyes opened wide. "No, I didn't. Oh, I wish I'd known. I've always wanted to hear Joseph Joachim play."

Matt grinned. "Well, tonight's the night." He reached in his pocket and held up two tickets. "Your birthday present."

"Oh, my God!" squealed Amanda. "You darling, you."

"I knew you'd love it."

"Oh, I do. I do."

His face grew serious. "Well, now for the second thing. I hope you love it as well."

He reached in his pocket again and drew out a small black velvet sack. Slowly, almost holding his breath, he opened it and drew out whatever was in it. Then he reached across the table and took her left hand in his. He turned her hand over and placed in the palm of it the object he'd extracted from the velvet sack.

She looked down and gasped. Lying in her hand was a sparkling diamond ring. Slowly she looked up at him.

"Amanda..." He moistened his lips and then took a deep breath. "Amanda, will you do me the honor of becoming my wife?"

She opened her mouth, started to speak, and then closed it again. She shook her head and then clasped her hands together and began wringing them. She bit her lip and stared into his eyes. "Matt, I...I don't know what to say."

Deflated, he shrugged. "Never mind. You don't have to say anything. It's just that I thought the ways things were going, we...we—"

"—ought to get married?"

"Well, no. I *want* you to be my wife. I love you, that's all there is to it. But I was afraid you'd say no. You are saying no, aren't you?"

"No! I mean, no, I'm not saying no. I'm just not saying yes, at least not right now. I...I want a chance to think. You took me by surprise. I mean, I had no idea."

Matt looked closely at her. He'd never seen her so flustered. Maybe he did have a chance. After all, she wasn't actually turning him down. Not yet, anyway. He became aware she was asking something.

"...I mean, where'd you get the money for all this? This dinner and...and the concert, let alone a diamond ring."

He shrugged. "Well, I save my tips when I play at the Sanctuary, and I got a pretty fair price for my Big Fifty."

"Oh, Matt. That's the gun your uncle gave you."

"I know. But it was worth it, just to be able to ask you." He grinned. "Besides, you haven't actually turned me down yet, have you?"

She smiled and reached out to lay her hand on his.

"No, I haven't. Just give me a few days to think."

By the time they arrived home, it was almost midnight, and he was feeling optimistic again, having managed, in his enjoyment of the evening, to shove the disappointment of her hesitation to the back of his mind. The dinner had been excellent, and her appreciation of the concert everything he'd hoped. And, once they were in bed, their lovemaking was more passionate than usual. He'd just have to allow her a little time was all.

Sometime after he'd drifted off to sleep, his arms wrapped about her, he awoke to the sound of a tapping at the door. Instantly, she was up, grabbing her robe as she went to answer the summons. The room was dark, and he could barely make her out. Then he heard the rain thrumming on the roof and against the windows. By God, he thought, the night's so black outside I'll bet even the bats stayed home.

Amanda slipped out into the hallway where Lorena Akins waited for her. He could hear the murmur of voices but couldn't make out what was being said. Being awakened like this wasn't all that unusual. The housekeeper's room was on the first floor, and when some emergency turned up, Lorena would hear the knocking and answer the door. Then she'd come up and report to Amanda. What was unusual was that, this time rather than coming back into the room to awaken Matt to come assist her, she quietly slipped downstairs.

For a few minutes he lay there wondering what was happening downstairs. Then curiosity got the better of him. He lit a lamp and checked his watch. Two thirty in the morning, by God. What was going on down there? Why hadn't Amanda summoned him? He slipped into his pants and shirt and padded downstairs in his bare feet. Much as the first time he'd come down in the middle of the night, almost a year ago, he saw light spilling from the doorway into the medical corridor. Then he heard Amanda speaking, her voice soft and urgent, followed by the lower pitched rumble of a male voice, apparently answering her.

His curiosity increasing, Matt padded quietly toward the examining room where the voices were coming from. Now he could distinguish the words.

"Aw, Mandy, I couldn't stay away. Christ knows, I tried, but I couldn't. I been hiding out down in those godforsaken little Mexican towns for two years now and every night thinkin' of you."

Matt heard Amanda laugh bitterly. "And I suppose you never had a woman in all that time. Really, Bob! What do you take me for? Now, hold still. I've got to stop this bleeding."

The man grunted. "All right, so I did have a few women, greasers all of them. What'd ya expect? But it ain't the same. Hell, it wouldn't be the same if it were the Queen of England, for Christ's sake. Once a man's made love with you, gal, no other woman will ever do. Not ever. You ought to know that. How often do I have to say it?"

"For God's sake," Matt heard Amanda plead, "will you keep your voice down? And don't talk that way."

Enraged, Matt burst into the examining room. Half reclining in a chair, supported on his right side by a scared looking Lorena Akins, a large man turned his head to stare at Matt. The fellow's clothes were dirty and sodden, his shirt stained by a mixture of dried and fresh blood. What looked like at least a three day growth of beard covered his face. His huge nose and black hair, the latter plastered to his scalp by rain, a wide gray streak running through the middle of it, instantly identified the wounded man.

Amanda, still clad only in her robe, the tie working loose, one thigh exposed, ministered to the man. Feverishly she attempted to dam the flow of blood that still oozed from the wound in his left shoulder.

Matt thrust his face close to Amanda's. "What's going on here? What're you doing with this owlhoot?"

"God damn it, Mandy," growled the wounded man, "who in hell's this young bastard?"

"Shut up, Bob!" She straightened up, holding a pressure dressing against the wounded man's shoulder, and turned to Matt. "Matt, I'm sorry. I'll explain later, but right now we've got work to do. Help me get him into the operating room."

"Explain later be damned! I want to know right now!"

"Later!" Her voice cracked like a whip. "Now help me, before he bleeds to death."

Matt hesitated.

"Matt, please. Help me."

Matt stared into her eyes.

"Please, Matt?" Her voice was soft, pleading.

"Aw, hell."

He waved Lorena Akins out of the way. The housekeeper scurried from the room. Matt got his shoulder into Bixby's armpit on the unwounded side, draped Bixby's arm across his own shoulders, and hoisted the man to his feet. "Come on, you murdering son of a bitch. Amanda wants you on the operating table."

"Supposin' I don't want to go?"

"Who cares what you want, Bixby?"

With one hand, Matt grabbed the outlaw's belt at the rear and, with the other, anchored the arm lying across his own neck and shoulders. Amanda, her robe gaping open, kept the pressure dressing tight against the wound. Matt half lifted and half dragged the man into the operating room and there grunted and strained until he managed to heave him into position on the operating table. Immediately, with one hand, he began ripping away Bixby's blood-soaked shirt, while, with the other, he applied pressure to the dressing Amanda'd been holding in place.

Meanwhile, she slipped an apron over her head and knotted the ties behind her, effectively closing her gaping robe. Next she fashioned a head dressing from a towel to keep her hair back and out of the way. Quickly she set to work scrubbing her hands and arms. Then she hauled out a set of emergency instruments and placed them in position on a side stand next to the operating table. Ready at last, she looked up at Matt, standing at the head of the table.

"Who is this young pup, Amanda?" demanded Bixby.

Before she could answer, Matt cut in. "I'm the young pup who's going to give you chloroform and the son of the gunsmith you murdered in Abilene two years ago."

Bixby laughed. "Boy, you don't know dung from wild honey. I never been in Abilene."

"Why you lying bastard, you were seen. I got witnesses. And a picture of you. You stick out like a new saloon in a church district."

"You got the wrong man, son." He grinned. "Maybe it was my twin brother."

Matt turned to Amanda. "Has he got a twin brother?"

She shrugged. "Not that I know of, but—"

"Besides," said Bixby, still grinning, "two years ago, I couldn't of been in Abilene. I was right here with Amanda. Wasn't I, Mandy?"

Her face set, she said, "That was three years ago."

"Well, whatever. I still ain't no killer. And I don't want this young hellion givin' me no chloroform. Way he's runnin' on, he just might overdo it. No way of tellin' which way a dill pickle'll squirt, you know."

Amanda positioned herself, ready to go to work. She looked down at Bixby. "Stop running on yourself and let me get to work."

"Well," he grumbled, "with this angry young whelp helpin' you, I figure I got about as much chance as a snowball in hell."

"You'll have to trust me, Bob. Just lie still. I know Matt. He won't hurt you." She looked at Matt. "You won't hurt him, will you?"

Matt, stony-faced, clamped the mask over Bixby's mouth and nose and began to pour the chloroform.

31

As he began losing consciousness, Bixby started to struggle. Matt, prepared for this phenomenon, having seen other patients do the same thing when chloroform began to take effect, merely held the mask tighter and poured the liquid so that it ran from the dropper bottle a bit faster. At the same time, Amanda lay her weight across Bixby's chest, and helped by securing the weakened man's arms. In less than a minute, Bixby's struggles ceased and he lay quiet.

Amanda, a worried expression on her face, straightened up and looked at Matt. "You will be careful, won't you?"

Matt said nothing.

"I mean it now. You will, won't you?"

"Of course, I will," he replied, a bit testily. "I never meant to kill the bastard. All I ever intended was to haul him back to

Abilene to stand trial."

She smiled and set to work. First, she swabbed the area around the wound with carbolic and followed that with tincture of iodine. Then, working quickly, she enlarged the wound opening with a scalpel. Spotting a pumping artery, she clamped it and tied it off. With the main source of bleeding controlled, she proceeded at a more leisurely pace, clamping and tying smaller vessels. Next she probed until her instrument struck an object that gave off a metallic clink. Deftly she seized the foreign body with a pair of forceps, worked it free, and drew out a mashed, misshapen chunk of lead. Triumphantly, she held it up for Matt to view.

"There it is. What do you think?"

Matt took the forceps from her and inspected the chunk of metal closely. "Pretty good size. Probably came from a rifle, a Winchester maybe." He looked at Amanda. "How'd Bixby get here? And how'd he get shot?"

She evaded his question. "Matt, his horse is probably still tied up out back. Lorena says Bob woke her up pounding on the back door. Why don't you go out and take care of the poor animal? I'll finish up here while you do that, and then we can get Bob to bed in one of the rooms." She reached for the forceps.

"I'll take care of the horse, but don't try to put me off. What's Bixby doing here?"

She broke eye contact and resumed working on the wound.

"Amanda."

She continued to concentrate on her work but replied softly. "He said he came to see me. Said it was my birthday, and he had to see me. Said he had to chance it. So he sneaked into town from Mexico two days ago?"

"Where's he been since then?"

"Hiding out down in the Mexican quarter. Says he saw us tonight in town. That's how he knew I was here and not visiting Patty and Tom at the ranch. He wondered who you were, too. Didn't realize you lived here."

"How'd he get shot?"

Head down, she continued to work. "Just bad luck. Seems

Captain Crockett's back in town, and Bob ran into him. They had quite a scrap, but Bob got away. He was almost free when one of Crockett's cronies got off a lucky shot. Bob dropped his gun but still managed to dodge Crockett and his men. Being wounded, though, he knew he had to get to me. He figured nobody knew of his connection here." She looked up. "I'm the only one he could trust."

She refocused her attention on the wound. "I believe this is fresh enough and clean enough I can just put a drain in it and close it up." She resumed working.

"Fine. And then what?"

She looked up, surprise written on her face. "And then what? Why we get him to bed and look after him till he's fit to travel."

"I see."

"Well, I am a doctor, Matt. And you soon will be. We owe it to a patient."

"Even though he killed my Paw?"

"You don't know that," she snapped. "Not for certain."

"Well, no, I guess I don't. Not for certain. But I'm more than 98% sure. Still, if what you told me is true, I owe him for saving you, don't I?"

Her face hardened. "What do you mean, if it's true? Do you think I lied to you about it?"

"No, no, I guess not." He heaved a sigh. "Well, if you'll excuse me, soon's I can get my boots on, I'll go look after his horse."

She nodded curtly, dismissing him.

When he came back in, Amanda was just washing up. The wound was bandaged, and she was placing the instruments in the sink to await cleaning in the morning. She slipped her apron off and removed the towel from her head, shaking out her hair as she did so. She tied her robe securely and glanced down at the patient who was beginning to stir. Then she shifted her gaze to Matt and smiled. "I'm sorry I snapped at you. Did you take care of the horse?"

He nodded.

She put her hand on his arm. "Bob'll be awake soon. Why don't you see if you can find Lorena, and the three of us can get him into bed in one of the rooms. All right?"

He nodded. "All right."

He didn't have far to go to find Lorena. She was talking to a man at the front door. Then she stepped back and the man came in, followed by two others. Matt recognized Sheriff Lonnie Winston and his deputy Jodie. The third man was Captain Crockett. Through the open doorway, Matt could make out several other men on horseback, their shoulders hunched. The heavy rain had dwindled to a drizzle, and the clouds had broken enough so that the night was no longer as dark as it had been.

Lorena started to speak. "Matt, the—"

The sheriff interrupted. "Never mind, ma'am. We'll find him."

The three men brushed by her and advanced on Matt, Captain Crockett in the lead. "All right, young feller, where is he?"

To his own surprise, Matt planted himself defiantly in the doorway of the medical wing. "Where's who?"

"That owlhoot, Bixby," growled the sheriff, stepping in front of the other two lawmen.

Matt spread his arms and grasped the door frame, barring his advance. "You can't come in here. Doctor Klein's treating a patient. And she'd not dressed to receive strangers."

The sheriff grinned. "Treating a patient, is she? Glad to hear it. Jodie thought he'd winged him."

Matt was almost nose to nose with the lawman but didn't budge. "What'd Bixby do?"

The sheriff snorted. "What didn't he do? Why, hell, just tonight he stole three horses and wounded one of my men. So step aside, Ritter. We're coming in."

Matt, chewing on his lip, hesitated for a couple of seconds. What the hell are you doing, you idiot? he asked himself. Then aloud he said, "All right, Sheriff, I guess I can't argue with that. Come on in, but let me lead the way."

When they reached the operating room, Bixby was mumbling and trying to sit up. Amanda was pressing him down on the table. She looked up and started to say something to Matt. Then she spotted the lawmen crowding in behind him. She clutched her robe more tightly about her. "What's the meaning of this?"

"Sorry, ma'am," said Captain Crockett, "but we're here to take that owlhoot off your hands."

Amanda looked at Matt. He repeated what the sheriff had told him. "I don't think there's much you can do. One way or another they're going to take him."

She looked horrified. "But the poor man's wounded. And he needs time to heal. If he doesn't stay here, the wound might get infected. It could kill him."

"Well," said Captain Crockett, "I suppose it would be a shame if all your hard work went for nothing. But, don't worry, I reckon there won't be time for infection to set in. He'll be dead before then."

Shocked, Amanda could only repeat, "Dead! What do you mean, dead?"

"The man's a horse thief! We found his horse out in your barn. The brand says it belongs to the Milligan outfit, and unless you or Ritter here stole the animal, I reckon Bixby stole it."

"But it's only a horse!"

"Ma'am," said the sheriff, "I'm surprised at you. It ain't like you're new to these parts. Why you've lived here nigh on most of your life, and you know how folks feel about horse thieves. I might overlook him wounding my deputy, but horse thievin' is somethin' else."

"But he hasn't been tried in a court of law."

The sheriff grinned. "Oh, don't worry, ma'am. He'll get a nice fair trial tomorrow. Just so happens Judge Walcott's holdin' court. We won't hang the owlhoot till the next day."

Amanda bit her lip. Then she thrust out her chin defiantly and jammed her fists akimbo on her hips.

"No, I won't let you do it!" But her challenge lost its authoritative tone when her robe started to gap open and she had to hastily clutch at it to save her modesty.

By then the sheriff was growing a trifle irritable.

"Ma'am, I don't like to have to say this, but folks are goin' to start wonderin' why you're so anxious to harbor a criminal. Now, kindly step aside and let us get on with our business."

Matt took her arm and gently tugged on it. Reluctantly she allowed him to lead her to one side of the room. Bowler Bob sat up and looked blearily around. When he saw the three lawmen, he shrugged and slipped down from the table. "All right, boys. I'm comin'. If I got to be hung, though, just let me do one thing."

The sheriff stepped back, and Bixby grinned. Then he quickly lurched over to where Amanda stood and, before a surprised Matt could interfere and using his uninjured arm, swept her to him and planted a moist kiss flush on her mouth.

When he finally released her, he winked and smacked her smartly on the bottom. "If you ever run into Mackie Wright again, tell him if he doesn't leave you alone, Bowler Bob's ghost'll get him." Then he looked at Crockett. "All right, Captain, let's go."

Two hours later, the first streaks of dawn began to lighten the sky. The lawmen had departed with their prisoner. As soon as they'd left, Lorena had retired to her bedroom. Amanda had changed her mind and decided that, never knowing when an emergency might turn up, she and Matt should clean the instruments and set the operating room to rights. Now they sat at the dining room table, drinking coffee and eating eggs and bacon that Amanda had prepared.

"What a night! What a birthday. Thanks to you, it all started off so nicely and then ended up so horribly." She slowly shook her head. "Poor Bob. I still think down deep he's a good man but somehow things went wrong for him." She looked across the table at Matt. "You don't mind if I visit him in jail, do you?"

He scratched his chin, then sighed. "I guess not."

She stared off into space, apparently lost in thought. Or

fantasies. Finally Matt reached across and took her hand in his. "You lied to me, didn't you?"

She focused on him. "About what, sweetheart?"

"About making love with Bixby."

She sighed. "Matt, I never actually lied to you that day we talked about it. You became so violently angry I just thought it best not to say anything more. So I just changed the subject. That's all."

He nodded. "I guess you're right. Come to think of it, I guess I never out-and-out asked you, did I?"

She looked at him warily. "No, you didn't."

He looked squarely into her eyes. "Well, now I am asking. Did you make love with Bixby when he asked you that summer after Max died?"

"Oh, Matt, do we have to keep on talking about that?"

He squeezed her hand. "Yes, we do."

"But, why? It's not important."

"It is to me."

"But that was so long ago."

"Only three years. Besides, maybe you saw him again after that time."

"I didn't, Matt. I didn't. I swear it."

"Well, I'm glad to hear that. But, now tell me, did you make love with him?"

She jerked her hand away. "All right! Yes, I did make love with him. Both nights. And yes, I enjoyed it. I enjoyed it tremendously. Both nights." She broke into tears. "Jesus! You just can't understand how I felt. Max and I had a good sex life, and I missed it. Terribly. I felt lonely and desperate. And when Bob turned up that summer, I was attracted to him. Hell, I was attracted and thought about him even when Max was still alive. Christ! The man had saved my life, and I liked his devil-may-care approach to life. But that's all water over the dam."

Matt sat back in his chair. "I see."

"No, you don't see. I enjoyed sex with him, but with you it's even better."

He challenged her. "Oh? Well, why's it better?"

"Because, you damned fool, I love you!"

"Oh, you love me. Is that why you don't want to marry me? Don't want to be my wife?"

"I didn't say I don't want to marry you. I said I need to think. I don't take marriage lightly. And please get this through your head. What happened between me and Bob Bixby on two summer nights three years ago has nothing to do with now. Absolutely nothing." She stood up. "I'm going upstairs to my room and try to get an hour's sleep. We have a busy day ahead." Then she came around the table and bent to kiss him. "Matt, I love you. We can talk about this some other time. Right now, I'm exhausted."

Judge Walcott had a large number of cases on his calendar to dispose of so that, contrary to the sheriff's prediction, Bowler Bob Bixby's trial didn't actually take place until three days later. On a Saturday at that. Matt and Amanda took seats in the back of the courtroom, Matt not wanting to appear conspicuous. He'd debated with himself whether to even attend the trial or not. Conflicting emotions still troubled him. The night before the trial, he'd tried to explain his feelings to Amanda.

"If I was absolutely sure he killed Paw, I wouldn't have any problem." He paused a moment. "Well, yes I would, too. Because if I was positive he killed Paw, then I'd want the owlhoot tried and hung back in Abilene for Paw's murder. Then Paw could rest in peace."

"Oh, Matt, do you really think your Paw was a vengeful sort of man? I mean, you always talk of what a kindly, peaceable fellow he was. Surely he can rest with God without his killer being caught and strung up."

Matt shrugged. "I don't know. Maybe you're right. I just don't know. I wish life wasn't so complicated, though. Sometimes it's hard to know what's right and what's wrong. Anyway, I'm almost positive Bixby did it. Almost. But what if he didn't?"

"He didn't, Matt. I'm sure of it. I've visited him every day in jail, sometimes twice. And I've asked him about it, your Paw's death, I mean. But he denies it. And if he did do it, what would he have to lose by admitting it to me now? He knows his chances at this trial are slim and none."

"He wouldn't admit it to you, for God's sake. He doesn't want to lose your good opinion of him. That's about all the bastard's got left, isn't it? And he would lose it, wouldn't he, if he admitted to the cold-blooded murder of a peaceable man like Paw?"

It was her turn to look troubled. "But I'm sure he didn't. You know, Matt, I wanted to appear as a character witness, but Bob refused to let his lawyer call me. He told me to forget it, that it wouldn't do him any good and would only harm my reputation."

"Well, that was decent of the man, and I can't forget that he saved you. I keep thinking I owe him for that. But if he didn't kill Paw, then some other son of a bitch is still out there somewhere, thinking he got away with murder. And I don't want to have to start looking all over again."

She looked at him sympathetically. "You wouldn't have to, would you?"

"Well...no...I suppose not. I know I don't want to. I just want to stay here with you and become a doctor."

Amanda smiled. "Well, then, it's settled. Right?"

He nodded. "Right. At least I guess so." He paused for a moment, then burst out. "But, damn, I wish I was sure."

The trial was short. The judge allowed the prosecutor to bring in witnesses to other episodes of horse stealing and cattle rustling dating back a good many years. The most damaging witness was Captain Crockett. He recited his stories about Bowler Bob being not only a rustler and a horse thief but a killer in the bargain.

The defense lawyer objected to this testimony as being irrelevant to the charge at hand, but the judge told him to forget it. "No pettifogging's going to turn this rascal loose on the good folks of San Antone, and if I hear much more from you, counselor, you can join your client in his cell."

In less than ninety minutes, Bowler Bob was convicted and sentenced to hang. Bixby's lawyer wanted to appeal, but when he mentioned it, the judge glowered at him, and he withdrew the motion. Although Mr. Hartwell, the hangman, was on hand, Judge Walcott, being a religious man, postponed the hanging until Monday. He said he didn't want to disturb the Sabbath.

The following Wednesday, with Bob Bixby by that time having rested forty-eight hours in his grave, Amanda paid her customary weekly morning visit to the girls' academy at the Ursuline Convent. Matt, as usual, remained at home to get the office ready for the afternoon's schedule of patients. Lorena Akins assisted him. As they worked, he caught her studying him.

"Why're you staring at me like that, Lorena?"

"Well, Matt, to tell the truth, I'm wondering what's come over you. You're usually such a cheerful sort, but ever since Amanda's birthday, you've been moping around. Surely it's not all due to the trouble over that Bob Bixby."

Silently he continued with his task at hand. Finally he looked up. "You're right. It's not."

She took a seat. "What's troubling you?"

He hesitated. "I don't know if I should tell you. No reason to bother you with my troubles. And I'm not sure Amanda'd like it."

"Matt, Matt, please. I promise not to say anything to Amanda. And haven't you guessed by now that I care about you?"

"You do?"

She nodded. "I do. Now, pull up a chair and tell me about it."

With a sigh, he slumped into a chair across from her. Haltingly he told her of his proposal of marriage to Amanda and of her ambivalent response. "I thought she loved me, but now I don't know. You know, don't you, that we've been sleeping together most nights?"

It was the housekeeper's turn to sigh. "Of course, I know.

How could I not know?"

"So why doesn't she want to marry me? Am I just a body to sleep with? And someone to do the hard physical work around here?"

Lorena laughed out loud. "Oh, good heavens, no! Where'd you ever get such an idea?"

Matt smiled sheepishly. "Well...but I thought she'd say yes right away, but instead she said something about wanting to think it over."

"And why wouldn't she? No matter how much I thought I loved a man, I'd want to think it over, especially if he were ten or eleven years younger than I."

He shrugged. "I don't see why that should make such a difference. Not if you love each other."

"But, Matt, what about ten or twenty years from now. When you're only forty and she's fifty-one? What then?"

"Wouldn't make a bit of difference."

"Well, maybe not, but a woman has to think of those things. So don't rush her. Frankly, I suspect she does love you." She grinned. "I wish she didn't, because then I might have a chance myself." She noted his startled look at this admission and almost laughed. "Oh, yes. If I didn't think Amanda cared about you, I'd try to seduce you myself. But as it is, I'm sure she'll come around in time."

After his conversation with Lorena, Matt felt a bit more optimistic. Pay attention to what Lorena said, he told himself. Just give Amanda time. But it was difficult to do.

Two nights later in bed he asked, "Amanda, what happens if you get pregnant? Would you marry me then?"

She smiled. "Uhmm, probably. But I won't. Get pregnant that is."

He rolled on one elbow and stared at her. "How do you know you won't? Other women do." Then it hit him. "You mean there's something wrong, that you can't have children?"

She shook her head. "No, nothing's wrong, not that I know of, anyway. But I take precautions."

He wrinkled his brow. "What do you mean, precautions?"

She sighed. "Oh, well, I guess if you're going to be a doctor I'd better explain about birth control, and now's as good a time as any."

Matt listened fascinated as she described "safe periods" and withdrawal. "It's called coitus interruptus, but it's not much fun for either party involved, and it's certainly not reliable. Neither are so-called 'safe periods.'"

Then she went on to describe pessaries and collar buttons. "Those are more modern. They've only been used here in the nineteenth century, but I have my doubts about them. Then there's condoms." She described how condoms were worn by men and had been around since the sixteenth century. "They say Casanova used condoms. Until just lately condoms were made out of all kinds of things, including—can you believe it?—linen, fish membranes, and animal gut. Now, though, they're made out of vulcanized rubber."

Matt was astounded. The whole business was completely new to him. "But I haven't been using any such thing."

"I know, but I wouldn't rely on them in any case. I use a cervical cap."

Matt stared at her. "What in hell's that?"

"It's just like it sounds. A little cap made of rubber that fits right over the opening of the cervix so that the sperm are blocked and can't get into the uterus."

"Well, I'll be damned! Where do you get such a thing?"

"The doctor—that's you someday—takes a wax impression of the woman's cervix and uses that to mold the cap. Then he fits it in place. Every month or so, he checks it and from time to time puts in a new one. That's why I make those trips to Austin every month. Doctor Gralnich up there takes care of it for me."

"He does! Jesus God! Well...well, do you fit other women with these contraptions?"

"Of course, and I think pretty soon you'll have to start learning to do it. I doubt they'll teach you the technique at medical school. They tend to be kind of prudish in medical schools, at least here in the U.S. And besides," she grinned, "then I can stop making those damned trips up to Austin."

"Well, God Almighty, what'll they think of next?"

"A pill that works, I hope. Drinking gunpowder potions and water that's been used to wash a dead person certainly hasn't done anything useful. Nor has water that a blacksmith used to quench his tongs. But for now, I'll stick to my little rubber caps."

"So that's why you're so sure you can't get pregnant."

She smiled and nodded. "That's why."

The day was blistering hot, August in San Antone at its worst. He wiped his brow and the back of his neck. Only nine o'clock in the morning and not the slightest hint of a breeze. He wiped the inside of his straw hat with his bandanna. Jesus! Must be ninety already. Sure was glad to be wearing the lightweight stuff that poor Max had left. Amanda had told him to get the buckboard ready and to be sure and put plenty of water jugs aboard. They were going to make a call about five miles out, and it was going to be one hot ride. Thank God he'd fitted out the wagon with an awning. Without it, that sun'd fry them both before they'd gone a mile.

He'd been patient with her, tried not to badger her, but, by God, it seemed to him he deserved some kind of answer soon. Maybe he could get her to talk on the way out to the Martin place.

She came and climbed aboard the carriage. "My God, but it's hot! Do you have plenty of ice packed around the chloroform?"

He nodded.

"All right, let's go and get this over with then."

Matt climbed in and headed the horses out. Amanda tried to stir a bit of breeze with her palm fan, but perspiration beaded her face anyway. Glancing at her, Matt decided she looked too hot and uncomfortable to try and question her about something important. Then, after they'd been rolling along for about a mile, a cooling breeze sprang up.

Immediately her good humor returned. "Oh, my! That's much better."

After another quarter of a mile, he decided to risk it.

"It's been almost a month now. So what about it?"

She glanced at him. "What about what?"

"Marrying me. You said you wanted time to think. Well, that was almost a month ago. Surely by now you can give me an answer. Or didn't you think about it?"

She pulled a bandanna out of her pocket and mopped her brow. Then she turned to him. "Yes, I've thought about it. I've thought about it a lot."

He looked straight ahead, out to the horizon. "Well?"

"I'm not sure. Oh, not that I don't love you. But I don't want to marry you and then lose you. I just couldn't stand it."

He looked at her. "Well, now, I know you lost one husband, and having lost my Maw and then my Paw, I can understand at least a little how you feel. But, damn it! I'm in good health and I ain't—I mean, I don't plan to die anytime soon. Now that the Bixby business has been settled, I'm not planning to get mixed up with any owlhoots or gunslingers. I just plan to settle down and be a good, worthwhile doctor."

"I know, but that's part of the problem. A big part."

He turned to squint at her again. "I don't follow you."

"You're young and handsome, and in another year or maybe two, you'll be going off to medical school. We'll be separated for ten months."

"I thought it was nine months."

"The school year is, but you have to allow a month for travel. Anyway, you may change your mind. You may meet someone else back there in the East. You may not want to come back to me."

Shocked, for a moment Matt could only stare. "Oh, no. No, you're wrong. There'll never be anyone else. There's just no way anyone else would do."

Amanda smiled, a sad smile. "I hope not. But I don't want to take the chance. And then, too, I can't forget that when you're only forty, I'll be fifty-one. That's worrisome to a woman. There'll be enough women trying to steal you when I'm still young enough to fight them off let alone when I'm getting old and wrinkled."

He pushed his hat up off his forehead. "Lorena said something about that, but I told her it wouldn't matter. And it wouldn't."

Her eyebrows went up. "You talked about us to Lorena?"

"Well, I had to talk to someone, and you didn't want to talk."

Silently they rode another mile. Then she put her hand on his arm. "Matt, suppose we do this. For now let's keep on the same as we have. Then, after you get back from your first year at medical school, if you still want me, I'll take that engagement ring."

He thought for a moment. "And then?"

"When you finish your second year, we'll get married."

The carriage bumped along for a few more minutes, and then he turned to her and smiled. "Well, if that's the best you can do, I'll settle for it. It's not what I want, but I'll settle for it. Maybe you'll change your mind and marry me sooner. Or, who knows? Maybe you'll get pregnant and we'll have to get married."

"I won't and I won't. I won't change my mind, and I won't get pregnant. But Mrs. Martin's pregnant, and I was expecting to deliver her baby sometime today or tonight." She grinned at him. "But Mrs. Martin likes you, so maybe it's time for you to try your hand at it. I've been showing you how to fix women so's to prevent babies. Now maybe it's time to start a new life by delivering one. After all, I'll be there to help out and do the chloroform."

Grinning from ear to ear, he turned and put his arm around her. "By God, you're on!"

Medicines
Chapt. 23
p. 214